THRILL OF FEAR

THE HARPIES
BOOK ONE

DINA HAWTHORN

For M.A.A.

FOREWORD

The story about the Harpies isn't suitable for those who don't enjoy dark romance.

It's dark.

It's gritty.

It's steamy.

Not all answers will be given, there are characters who like to play games, and characters whose motivations aren't revealed until later.

Triggers include:

Kidnapping, graphic violence, sexual scenes, slavery, and flashbacks to traumatic childhood memories. For a complete list of triggers, please see my website.

Reader discretion is advised. This book is *not* intended to be read as a standalone.

CHAPTER ONE

KATE

I'D ALWAYS WONDERED if I was a closet masochist. It would explain why I had agreed to go speed dating with Petra at the Inspiration club in Kittington.

Despite its ceiling height and black walls reminiscent of a tomb, there was nothing wrong with the club. As always, the atmosphere buzzed. Expectations were clear on every inch of exposed skin, with every whiff of sweet perfume.

Eager partygoers huddled over dark wooden tables littered with glasses, their eyes glistening with excitement, lips never resting as they exchanged pleasantries before the event. If pheromones were visible, they would've hovered in the air like ominous shadows.

The true test of my masochistic tendencies had to be the peroxide blonde on the makeshift stage at the back of the room, who was cooing into the microphone about undying love and betrayal.

Heart-tugging notes streamed in smooth harmony from the sleek, black piano, moulding couples on the dance floor in heated embraces. All this perfection soon culminated in a whistled cele-bration and enthusiastic clapping.

'Caitlin.' Petra's voice brought me back to our small table in the corner by the windows. 'I don't know what sort of man you're trying to attract with that face, but how about less Miss Moody and more Miss Booty?'

'I'm not moody.' I sipped on my second glass of white wine spritzer. The cheap, fruity concoction did nothing to quench my thirst or dull my senses. 'I'm people-watching.'

'You're moody, grumpy, gloomy—'

'Hey.' I waved my glass in her direction, spilling wine. 'Stop naming dwarfs. You're the one who had this grand idea of speed dating. I wanted to stay at home, eat a tub of ice cream, and pretend men don't exist.'

I'd wanted to drink, but that excuse hadn't worked on Petra earlier. She had an annoying habit of talking me into doing things I shouldn't do – like picking up men at clubs.

'Fine, Miss Not-Moody-At-All. God, we need to get you laid before you tear someone's head off.' She eyed a group of men walking past, like a magpie looking for something shiny to steal. 'How about that guy?'

I didn't even bother looking. 'No.'

If only I could separate sex from love as Petra did. It would've been easy to find someone to screw me into oblivion weeks ago.

The sliver of hope of finding someone special while speed dating was how she'd got me here, but the type of man I was looking for wouldn't wander into an ordinary club in Kittington. They had their own type of club – the kinky kind not even a bottle of wine would give me the courage to seek.

'See anyone you like?' I asked.

'No. I told you we should've tried to get in at The Yard.' Petra pushed her blonde curls away from her face. Unlike me, she'd had time to prepare, and the delicate corkscrews in her bob-cut hair should've alerted me to her intentions when she'd turned up at my front door.

'You know I'm not allowed.'

'All the better reason to go,' she countered with a smirk.

The Yard was an exclusive club only a few streets over with a reputation for wild parties, exotic dancers, and invite-only events. The kind of establishment that would've made my mother faint if I even thought about attending. Good girls didn't go to clubs like The Yard.

Because karma truly was after me, my ex-boyfriend now worked at The Yard. Petra thought he'd taken the bartending job because he knew I'd never dare approach him at a club like that. It was the kind of thing Tom would do to get away from me.

'Perhaps you'll find someone else tonight?' Petra tilted her head, watching me through her thick, fake eyelashes. 'Someone kinkier than Tom?'

'Maybe we'll see flying pigs on the way home.' I gestured towards the crowd still pouring in through the doors. 'Look at these people. We both know this is a waste of my time.'

'Are you claiming it's possible to spot kinksters by how they look? Like a dress code? Or a secret sign?'

'Secret greeting,' I deadpanned. 'If you bend over, I'll show you.'

'Hilarious, Kate.' Petra nudged her empty glass of G&T out of the way to lean closer. 'Be as grumpy as you want, but I got a written complaint from your vibrator that it's about to keel over from overexertion—'

'Petra!'

'So put on a happy face and take that built-up frustration out on a warm body for once.'

'I don't have a vibrator,' I lied, checking no one had heard me.

She laughed. 'You're such a rubbish liar. Your vanilla days are over. I know what kind of freak you really are.'

'No, you don't.' I rose, brushing down the tight red dress she'd tossed in my face an hour earlier when this madness had started. 'And if this is another play-therapy session with in-depth analysis of all my mistakes, I'm getting another drink.'

'Aww, Kate, come on. I was only joking.'

No, she wasn't. Maybe I was a freak, only too sober to admit it, and too afraid to figure out what to do about it.

I pushed my way through the crowd towards the bar. My whole life, I'd been fighting a war between being a good girl and giving in to my darker desires. Unlike me, Petra had grown up in a household where sex was not considered a mortal sin.

My family expected me to be a sweet girl, and I'd tried to be – even qualified as a nurse, much to my mum and stepdad's approval. I'd found an ordinary boy who wanted kids, a house with a white picket fence and a Labrador named Marley. But nothing good ever lasted because I couldn't hide that inner freak for too long.

Two years into our relationship, Tom had said we should be more adventurous, and I'd wanted to try new things, but that exploration of boundaries had turned into the worst humiliation of my life when I'd got carried away. It had shattered all hopes of salvaging our relationship and forever labelled me as a reincarnation of Edward Scissorhands.

'Stupid arsehole,' I muttered, edging an elbow up at the end of the bar, hoping the barman would take pity on me before I slammed my head against the woodwork. 'Bloody stupid arsewipe of a man.'

'Pardon?'

I cursed under my breath and turned to face a man two seats over. 'Sorry, I was... Never mind.'

With dark, gel-spiked hair and deep blue eyes glittering with humour, he wasn't hard to look at. Tall, well-dressed in a grey jumper and black jeans. He looked fit. Strong arms and a slim waist. Interesting.

'Are you all right?' His full lips stretched into a grin when my gaze snapped from his body to his face.

He was gorgeous, but despite his charming smile and good

looks, there was no connection, no spark, when I looked into his eyes. What a shame. He looked familiar, though. Why was that?

'Sorry, I don't know what's wrong with me tonight.' I pushed my hair behind my ear. 'A little nervous about speed dating, I guess. Are you here for that as well?'

'No, I have a girlfriend.'

Of course he did. 'That's nice.'

'But my brother is.'

'Oh?'

'He's already upstairs. I think it started five minutes ago.'

'Shit.' I glanced at my wristwatch and scanned the room for Petra, finding our table empty. 'I have to go. It was nice meeting you.'

'You too,' he called after me as I raced towards the staircase as fast as my high heels would allow.

The vast space in the function room upstairs abolished all my visions of a cramped, disorganised doctor's waiting room. Round tables stood in long rows along the walls on either side of a bar, with candles flickering over the crisp white linen. The tables stood out against the deep red walls like small islands of intimacy. Over the speaker system, Nelly Furtado declared herself as a maneater.

Petra's green, all-too-tight dress made her easy to find despite the crowd. 'Thanks for waiting for me,' I said to her, wiping sweaty palms on my hips.

She linked our arms and moved us forward in line, her hips swaying to the music. 'You're the one who stomped off like a stroppy teenager. I actually want to meet someone. If you'd rather sit at the bar and mope about the incident with Tom, be my guest.'

'I'm sorry. That wasn't... I didn't mean to be moody.'

'Call Kamron if you're only interested in hooking up with someone for the night.'

I shuddered. 'Please don't. Just the name dries me up like a desert.'

'Sorry.' She giggled. 'I didn't realise it was that bad.'

It was worse. Kamron was the reason I'd never do one-night stands again. Learning that he knew Tom had only made it worse. The only reason Petra and I had made the trip out to Kittington was to avoid anyone local. Between us, we had seen all that Ladeworth offered, and none of it impressed. If this trend continued, we would have to branch out of Suffolk.

Another reason we needed a new playground was my step-dad. He was an MP, and thanks to his conservative view of women and sexuality, we never got along. When the organiser handed me the clipboard to sign my name, I glanced at Petra, then wrote my middle name, Peterson.

Petra smirked. 'Forgoing the Howard name tonight?'

According to Mum, my birth father hadn't been involved in my life since I was conceived, and the Peterson name was the only thing he'd left me. Mentioning him or his name was another thing forbidden in my family.

I hadn't even learnt his surname until a few years previously when I'd overheard Paul, my stepdad, talking to my mother. When I'd legally changed my name to include it, Paul had been oddly delighted, but Mum had seemed worried.

'You told me to accept who I am.' I handed her the clipboard. 'If it's one thing the past couple of months have taught me, it's that I'm no Howard.'

'Best of luck, Miss Peterson.' She pushed me towards a table with a gentle nudge. 'Be brave, Kate.'

Brave? I snorted. The last time I'd been brave, I'd ended up naked and homeless. But I sat down, fingers linked over the stiff tablecloth as sweat trickled down my back. On the other side of the room, a horde of men waited. Could there be someone here for me? Someone with similar interests? My shoulders crept up at the sound of the first bell.

'I'm Chris.' A booming voice made me jump. The blond man standing at my table flashed a charming smile and extended his arm. 'Nice to meet you...'

'Kate,' I croaked and cleared my throat. His grip could crush rocks. As soon as he released my hand to sit, I hid it in my lap, rubbing it. 'I'm not sure how this works... Do we ask each other questions?'

'That's right. Anything you'd want to know.' Chris's eyes settled on my cleavage. 'Tell me about yourself, Kate. What does a beautiful woman like you do for a living?'

'I'm a nurse.'

'That's interesting. How do you like it?'

I pulled at the tight dress Petra had forced me to wear. 'It's rewarding, but also difficult—' I caught Petra's gaze across the room. She glanced at Chris and gave me an encouraging nod. 'What I meant is that most of my patients are critically ill. Or drunk. How about you?'

'I'm a refuse technician.' Chris was still lost in my cleavage and only lifted his gaze when I coughed. 'I work for the council.'

'Like a binman?' I scratched behind my ear. 'That's nice. You must get a lot of... fresh air.'

'Yes, I do.' His smile deepened faint lines around his eyes, but when he started sharing details of his working day, I was grateful his focus was on my chest, so I only had to fake interest with the occasional nod.

When the bell rang, Chris rose, handing me his card. I flicked it across the tablecloth as soon as he'd moved on.

Absolute waste of my time. I could have eaten half a tub of ice cream by now.

A tall man with a potbelly and bright ginger hair took his place within seconds. 'David,' he said, shoving a beast of a hand in my face.

I flinched. 'Kate.'

'I'm a lorry driver.' He pushed his chair back to make more

room before intertwining his fingers over his stomach. 'I drive cross-country, mostly deliveries for supermarkets and department stores. How about you?'

'I'm a nurse. I work in A&E and do some shifts at a hospice across—'

'You should've put on that nice uniform before you came here,' he said with a croaky laugh. 'I bet you'd walk out of here with a hundred phone numbers.'

It took everything I had not to roll my eyes. 'I doubt that. Our uniform is both shapeless and ugly. It wouldn't attract anyone.'

'A pretty little thing like you – I'm surprised you don't have a line for your table. How long have you been single?'

'A little over two months.'

I nibbled on a nail as he told me about his last girlfriend and his interest in fly fishing, and sighed with relief when the bell rang. David moved on, leaving his card behind.

What had I been thinking, coming here? I dropped my head in my hands.

The next half-hour wasn't much of an improvement. I met John, a high school teacher who collected tropical fish, followed by Sam, who enjoyed long walks, sandy beaches, and dressing up in women's clothing.

When he asked if he could borrow my nurse's uniform, I shot Petra a murderous glare across the room. She tapped her finger on her wristwatch, indicating a break was coming soon. I couldn't have been happier. The bottles behind the bar in the centre of the room called to me, and I planned to dull my senses before the next round of torture.

As soon as the bell rang twice, I abandoned my last date at the table. 'Bloody Mary,' I snapped at the barman, drumming my nails on the counter until he put the drink down.

Petra came up next to me and gushed about every potential match she'd met. In her world, all men were perfect for about a week. 'So, how was it?' Petra fanned herself with her stack of cards. 'You looked a little flustered.'

I took a long sip and patted my lips. 'How was it? Let's see.' I slid onto a bar stool. 'Two guys wouldn't stop staring at my tits, one thought I should've worn my work outfit, and one wanted to wear it himself—'

Petra burst out laughing. 'To be fair, your tits look great in that dress.'

'The last one was a wannabe musician who I'm hoping only had a persistent itch on his inner thigh.' I pulled out my phone to call an Uber. 'I'm done, Petra. This is not for me.'

She snatched the mobile from my hands. 'It's a slow start, I promise.'

'Slow start? What's next, a convicted rapist? And thanks to your mission to cheer me up, I've missed a whole evening with Dylan.'

'Who's Dylan?'

'My vibrator,' I muttered behind the glass.

Petra roared with laughter, sputtering something about vibrators and musicians, which I ignored. All I wanted to do was drink, go home and wallow in self-pity, but she wasn't giving up.

'No, sweetie, listen now—'

'I don't want to. You're pure evil.'

A sensation spread across my nape, like soft fingertips caressing fine hairs. I flicked around, expecting to find some creep feeling me up, but there was only a woman with her back to me.

Strange.

The guy I'd spoken to downstairs stood at the end of the bar, deep in conversation with someone hidden from my sight. His brother? I wondered what he looked like.

Petra caught my attention again with a hand on my elbow. 'You want to meet someone different from Tom, am I right?'

'Cross-dressing was not what I had in mind,' I said, my moth-

9

er's attitude spilling out of my mouth. She found all kinks abhorrent. If she hadn't given birth to three children, I would have thought she'd always been celibate.

'Maybe not. But remember what you told me? You wanted to leave good Kate behind and explore other...' Petra pouted. 'Fantasies? Kinks?'

Damn my drunken confession and her excellent memory. Cross-dressing was harmless compared to what I'd done to Tom. It was nothing compared to what happened in my dreams. Dreams of men coming to our house when I was little that seemed like memories, but that my mother claimed were only my imagination and refused to discuss.

'I do, but I won't find someone like that here.'

Would I find them anywhere? Ever since the incident that had ended my relationship with Tom, everything and everyone reminded me I wasn't like them.

Something had happened that night; a switch in my brain had flicked on. I didn't know how to turn it off or if I wanted to.

'I'm sure there's someone here for you,' Petra said. 'And since you got yourself banned from every dungeon in a hundred-mile radius—'

'I did not!'

'So why's your name on their list?'

'Must be Paul.'

'Right.' She rolled her eyes. 'Well, treat this like it's a dating app. Forget about what they do for a living, and focus on what you want to know.'

'What do you mean?'

'Ask them if they're into kinks.'

'Are you insane? Do I need to have you sectioned?'

'You're the one who's into restraints.' She winked, unaffected by my scowl. 'If you don't ask these questions, how can you ever find what you're looking for?'

I blew out a breath of air. How was I supposed to know how

to ask such questions? I didn't even know what I was looking for, what I was, or where I fit in. I was having a midlife crisis in my twenties, and she acted as if I only needed to say 'please' to the right man.

'You know I'm right. When you refuse to do online dating—'

'I can't take any more exposure to strangers' genitals. I see enough of that at work.'

'Well, then.'

I held up my hands. 'Fine, I'll ask more direct questions, but if I'm kidnapped by some foot-fetish pervert who's into tickling and I kick him in the face, I'm holding you responsible for that incident.'

As Petra laughed, I dragged my feet towards the ladies' room to freshen up before the next round of torture, but something brought me to a halt.

The temperature in the room shifted. The fine hairs on my nape rose again.

Someone was watching me; I was sure of it.

I looked around, and for a moment, I thought I saw someone I briefly remembered seeing over twenty years ago, but it was impossible. My mother claimed my dreams were not memories.

CHAPTER TWO

JACK

LEANING against the end of the bar, I tapped my cards against my chin, curious how I got to this point where I would hand my phone number out to strange women. From a speaker somewhere, a breathy female singer asked if we were having fun yet.

Soon, I hoped.

Despite the crowd, Freddy found me minutes after the first break started. It was no surprise because my brother was always nearby.

'This has got to be the stupidest idea you've ever had, Jack.' Freddy slid onto the bar stool next to me. 'Why couldn't you have pulled a woman at work?'

I rolled my eyes. 'Maybe I grew tired of fishing in the same pond.'

'Maybe you shouldn't be fishing at all.'

'True. Fisting is always better than fishing,' I joked, failing to contain my chuckle. Christ, even my sense of humour didn't fit with this crowd. Especially not my brother, who didn't understand that it kept me from falling apart.

His snort deepened my laugh. I would do anything for him, but his insistence on checking on me every five minutes was grinding on my nerves. Freddy was only following Dad's instructions, but now, wherever I turned, my brother was always there.

Speed dating had been my idea because I loathed his background checking. It was worse than when we were kids and he'd unwrapped my Christmas presents only to claim he had no idea what our parents had bought me.

At twenty-eight, I shouldn't need anyone to oversee every aspect of my life, especially not my sex life. But Dad thought my ADHD made me reckless.

I looked around at all the unvetted women in the room. Maybe he was right.

'Just so I'm prepared...' I shifted my glass of water around on the bar. 'Are you planning on watching me all evening?'

'What do you mean?'

I tilted my head. Honestly, sometimes my brother was painfully slow.

Freddy rolled his eyes. 'For Christ's sake, Jack. I'm not some pervert.'

'Could've fooled me.' I took a small sip and patted my lips. 'You seem to have perfected your orgasm denial skills. I only wish you'd practise them on someone else for a change.'

His withering stare amused me, and my laugh further soured his expression.

It was a twin thing; I joked about sex and pain, and Freddy reacted with obvious disgust. My brother was the most vanilla person I knew, and it was always comical how easily I could embarrass him.

Our family had been in the scene for generations, so he was nowhere near as innocent as he pretended to be. Dad was also well aware of how submissive Freddy was, and he should've known better than to think my brother could control me.

As Freddy looked around, I entertained the idea of running away. It had become a recurring fantasy after Dad turned my life into a goldfish bowl over a year ago and banned me from every dungeon in the country.

I was a Marquis, for god's sake – a trained sexual sadist belonging to the Harpyiai – but Dad expected me only to pursue vetted vanilla women and refused to tell me why.

Always tuned in to my moods, Freddy's narrowed gaze soon found mine. I smiled innocently before focusing on the crowd. The room was full of possibilities, but none of the women I'd met interested me, not even for one night.

I wanted what I couldn't have: a normal life.

The branded *H* on my back should've made it clear that any chance of normality had ended the night I'd met Marquess Juliet Stepanova. Whenever I thought about Juliet now, it made me rub my temples.

'Headache?' The flicker of concern in my brother's eyes irritated me as always. He worried too much about me having a flashback, even if they rarely happened anymore.

'Yes, I'm talking to it right now. You really need to get laid, Freddy. Maybe that'd get you off my back for even a minute.'

And fuck those pills he was trying to hand me. What was it this time? Valium? Ritalin? Some tranquilliser Dad hoped would make me forget about my years at the Harpyiai castle?

'Don't think I can't tell you didn't take your Ritalin again.' Freddy grabbed my hand and pressed the pills into my palm. 'And yes, I plan to see Lily as soon as you're done with this tantrum.'

Tantrum? I clenched my jaw, hating my father and the Harpyiai more than ever.

'What's the point of this, Jack? You know that as soon as they figure out who you are – what you're like – they'll leave.'

What I was like?

'Jesus. Don't hold back.'

He raised his hands. 'I'm preparing you, that's all.'

'For what? More vanilla? I thought I was supposed to be the sadist, but you sure like to torture people.'

He looked around, always worried someone would overhear me talking. 'Take your damn Ritalin. I'm trying to help.'

'Like how you won't even let me date anymore? How you helped Dad send Larissa running?' I signalled for a refill from the barman. 'I get it. Nobody's happy that I'm trying to have a life.'

'That's not—'

'You and Dad would love it if I spent the rest of my days on a leash.'

'Given what a pain in the arse you are to deal with, that'd be brilliant. We both know you're into that, anyway.'

My brother, the comedian.

I grabbed the new glass, tossed back the pills meant to keep me compliant and content to forgo everything I craved, and swallowed them with a mouthful of water.

'Are you happy? I'm taking the bloody pills. Can you leave me the hell alone now?'

Hostility never worked on my brother. The only reaction I ever got was a roll of his eyes.

As always, when we were out in public, I looked around. Dad's guards looked conspicuously like the security staff at most clubs, and I eyed the one in the corner. His beady stare found mine, but he made no attempt to retrieve me.

He wasn't one of Dad's.

'This isn't how I wanted to spend my free Friday night, you know.' Frustration leaked into Freddy's voice as he made the same sweep of the room. 'I'm doing you a favour.'

Oh, please, a favour? He was my ball and chain.

Dad had set up a club – The Yard – and instructed Freddy to ensure none of the women who walked through its doors had ties to the Harpyiai.

It was Dad's way of making sure I never accidentally broke the Harpyiai's cardinal rule by sleeping with an illegitimate – a child of a Marquis and a woman born outside the approved Harpyiai bloodlines.

'It'd be nice if you appreciated that I'm putting my arse on the line here as well.' Freddy frowned at something behind me. 'Dad would lose his shit if he knew you're out prowling again.'

He would, and Dad was the kind of sadist no one wanted to piss off. Sometimes I admired my brother's courage. Unlike me, he was terrified of Dad.

Most people were.

I turned to see who had caught his attention, expecting to see my father standing there. It wouldn't be the first time, and I mentally prepared myself for his deep sigh and pointed look, but he was nowhere in sight.

Strange.

'The petite brunette at the bar,' Freddy said. 'Red dress. Great tits. I spoke to her briefly downstairs. She seems nice.'

Nice?

I turned back with a low growl. 'You had to use that word, didn't you?'

All these women were nice, but I was done with that. Nice didn't work for me. I could no longer pretend to be vanilla or that I was happy being alone for the rest of my life. I wanted what Freddy had; a life worth living.

'If you're going to be that picky, I'm giving you one more round of this nonsense. No more.'

'Else you'll tell Daddy I'm out past my bedtime?'

His scowl was hilarious, as always.

Dad lived in London, far away. If he hadn't realised I was at speed dating by now, it could only mean he was preoccupied with something else related to the Harpyiai. Some Head Marquis business I couldn't care less about.

'You're not even supposed to be in the scene anymore.' Freddy pulled out his phone and smiled as he read a message. 'Find a nice woman, let off some steam, get to work tomorrow, and take your goddamn pills.'

'Sometimes I wonder if we're even related,' I said, trying to ignore his grin as he texted his girlfriend.

'If we weren't, you think I'd be doing this?' He looked up from his mobile. 'I have a life, you know.'

His words stung more than they should have. There was so much he didn't know about the years I'd spent at the castle. I kept it from him because he was sensitive. Fragile. My brother would never have survived their training. Without my brother, I wouldn't have wanted to live.

'You know something, don't you?' I asked.

Dad's restrictions made no sense. Determined to make me his successor, he'd had me trained as a Marquis at the castle, then as a Dom, and allowed me unrestricted access to all our clubs for years, only to take it away overnight. He was keeping something from me.

'Of course not,' my brother tried, but he couldn't fool me. Whenever Freddy refused to look at me, he was lying; only I couldn't figure out why. We'd always been close, and neither of us liked Dad's restrictions on our lives.

'You do.' I stepped closer to him. 'Is it about Juliet? Is she after you?' My words rushed out as I assessed the danger my brother might be in.

He put his mobile away and raised his hands. 'I don't know what Dad's up to, but none of us wants to be in this situation, and you know you shouldn't take risks.' He lowered his voice to a whisper. 'If you fuck an illegitimate, we're both in trouble, and I don't just mean with Dad because he's Head Marquis. Do you want to end up in The Hunt again?'

No, I didn't. And I would never put Freddy at risk.

I dragged a hand through my hair. What on earth could my father be up to, trying to control my sex life like this?

'Will it make you feel any better if I let you vet her first? If I can even find anyone interesting in this place.'

Whenever my brother narrowed his eyes, it was hard not to laugh. He reminded me of Mum when she'd suspected me of doing something I shouldn't have.

'You'll wait for me to vet her?'

I smiled. 'Sure, if it makes you feel any better.'

'You know that'll take days.'

'I'm not a wild animal, you know.' I dipped my head, peering back at him. 'You do your checks, and I get to take someone on an actual date. Deal? Dad never has to know.'

Freddy leaned in, scrutinising every inch of my face as if he could read my thoughts. 'You're up to something again.'

It took everything I had not to laugh. 'You're as paranoid as Dad.'

With one last sweep of my placid expression, Freddy pulled back. 'And you have the same annoying ability to conceal your emotions. Let's go back to The Yard. I've had enough of this.'

I rolled my eyes. 'I'm not hiding anything, but as always, you can't understand that I don't want another one-night stand with some nice woman.'

'Dad said—'

'Fuck Dad.'

'Jack.' Freddy pinched the bridge of his nose. 'Apart from what Dad thinks, you know this'll only end in disaster. You get your hopes up, and they run away as soon as—'

'They realise I'm in a fucking cult?' I gritted out. 'That my only purpose in life is to breed with a Marquess so we can add another generation of inbred freaks to stick in a castle somewhere in Scotland?'

His eyes widened. 'Keep your voice down! And it's not a cult.'

How many times had I heard that before?

It was not a cult. It was an *order*.

Cults recruited their members; we were born into the Harpyiai order.

As if labelling it an order somehow made it any easier to know none of us could live in the real world.

The Harpyiai existed because four men had challenged each other to take sadism to the extreme. The crimes implicated all of them, and a secret was formed and carried on for generations. We kept it hidden because we had no other choice – to protect ourselves and our families. Theo had once said that if one of us went down, all of us did.

'It's a century of nonsense rituals, protocol, and stupid fucking bullshit about honour. I'm done with it. I want a normal life.'

He gave me a pointed look. Yeah, it was wishful thinking. No one could walk away from the Harpyiai. Our father had tried.

Before Freddy could dig out his phone to call Dad and tell him I was spinning out of control again, I walked away, dragging a hand through my hair.

With no access to the clubs, I'd leapt at a chance of finding someone at speed dating, but who was I kidding? My brother was right; I might as well go back to The Yard and continue to live this non-existent life in my father's shadow.

Halfway across the room, a scent drew my attention. It smelt like summer, roses, and sex. Freddy thought my synaesthesia was nothing but an excuse to make fun of his cologne. I liked to tease him, but now remnants of someone arose like faint smoke in blue and purple hues.

It seeped into my pores, flooded my senses, and vibrated in my chest, soul, and, most of all, groin. Entranced, I looked for the source, and the moment I found her, I almost tripped over my feet.

Fucking Freddy.

It was the woman in the red dress.

CHAPTER THREE

KATE

Next up was Adam, a solicitor passionate about modern art. I tried to focus on his wavy brown hair and take an interest in his non-stop ramble, but all my attention was on the questions that sat at the tip of my tongue.

Are you into pain?

Will you let me hurt you?

My foot bounced as nerves played havoc with my body. This was a terrible idea. I'd ruin my family's reputation. Ha, I wanted to laugh. What was left to ruin?

My nape still tingled. What was that? Who was watching me?

'Tell me, Kate, what are you looking for?' Adam asked.

'Something adventurous, I suppose.' I grasped my glass.

'What kind of adventure? I'd like to travel to Australia one day, maybe—'

'No,' I said, swallowing another mouthful I hoped would quiet my mind. 'I mean a different type.'

Adam's bushy brows knitted. 'Aren't you after a relationship?'

'Yes, I am.' I fiddled with a crease in the tablecloth. God, why was this so hard? 'Just one that's different.'

He leaned forward. 'What—'

'I want someone who will push – and let me push – boundaries.' I let the alcohol take over and leaned in. 'How are you with pain?'

The bell rang. Adam was out of his seat before the ringing had ceased.

Great.

I blew my hair out of my face, resisting the urge to bang my head against the table again. This was stupid. I wasn't crazy. Maybe on some level, but I didn't live in the 18th century, and no one would lock me up for devious urges.

I snorted. Maybe I was devious? My family sure thought so. Last month, Petra and I tried to get into a club called The Aurora for an introductory evening, only to find that I was banned. She had thought it was hilarious, that I must've been there before and got my name added to the list, but I'd never been to a dungeon.

The only rational conclusion was that my stepdad had used his connections to blacklist me, so I couldn't do anything else to embarrass him.

We'd tried two more clubs in the region and even drove three hours to Kent, but it seemed Paul knew how to pull strings and close every curtain I wanted to peek behind.

'Well, if it isn't my new favourite Kate.'

Oh, crap. I squeezed my eyes shut at the sound of his voice. When I opened them again, Kamron – my last one-night stand – was sitting across from me. Was this who had been watching me?

'What are the odds of running into you twice in one month?' he asked.

'Pretty good if you follow me around, I guess.'

'You'd like that, wouldn't you?'

No, I would not.

I wasn't nearly drunk enough to deal with this. Hoping he would go away, I shifted my glass around, took a long sip, staring into the room. Had he left? Nope. He was like a mozzie on a hot summer evening, desperate for another bite.

'That depends on what you want from me.' I ran the tip of my tongue over the sharp peaks of my teeth, wishing I could sink them into someone.

'A date, obviously. Isn't this why we're all here?' Kamron reached for my hand. 'I think I could make you a very happy woman tonight.'

'Why?' I wrapped my fingers around the hot candle holder. 'Are you leaving?'

Kamron chuckled. Though he was hot in a rugged way with his short, sandy-blond hair and stubble – and might have shifted my focus for the full twenty minutes I'd spend with him – I wasn't interested. Yet I smiled. Maybe it was the heat burning my fingertips. The warm pain distracted from his stare.

'Damn, woman, has the sun come out or did you just smile?'

What?

I barked a laugh. 'You think a line like that'll work on me?'

'It did once.'

It had. What could I say? I had been lonely, with an itch not even Dylan the vibrator could scratch, and Kamron kept refilling my drink until the alcohol impeded common sense. Thankfully, I remembered little about it. I was two drinks away from making the same mistake.

'Yeah, keep talking. Who knows, maybe one day something intelligent will come out of your mouth?' I crossed my arms. 'Stranger things have happened.'

His gaze dropped to my breasts. 'So, what are your plans for this evening? Weekend. Whatever.'

I snapped my fingers in the air. 'Eyes up here. Let me tell you a story, Kam, about this one time I let this guy fuck me…'

'Yeah?' He flashed me a grin.

Sipping my drink, I took my time, knowing he was waiting for the hook, the move he could use to get me on my back – or front. 'Actually, I let him fuck me twice. I'm still not sure how that happened. Clearly, I was drunk, but do you know what I got from it?'

My glass wobbled as I put it down. I edged my elbow up, fully aware that the angle gave him a perfect view of my cleavage. As expected, Kamron was lost in my tits.

'Nothing, Kam. No big O. No little o either. No aftershock. No god-I-almost-died. Nada. Not even as much as a slight toe-curl.'

Someone choked on their drink behind me.

'That's not what I remember.' Kamron's voice dropped to a sharp whisper as heat rushed to his cheeks. 'You left marks on my shoulders, arms… It took weeks to heal. Weeks. I'd say—'

I smirked. 'Well, if I'd had my way, you would've been tied up and gagged. Maybe that would've let me reach that peak instead of having the rug pulled out from under me. Repeatedly.'

His eyes widened. 'You're sick.'

'I know,' I said, dipping my finger into the candle's hot wax.

Those were the words Tom had spat in my face the night he kicked me out of our flat, with no money, no mobile, and only a loose sheet wrapped around my naked body. Paul came to the same conclusion when Tom's solicitor called. His stepdaughter was sick. Perverted. No good for the Howard family name.

'Send my best to Tom, will you?' I peeled the wax off my finger. 'Tell him that next time he sends someone to embarrass me, at least let it be someone who doesn't need a map to find a clitoris.'

Kamron's chair scraped as he shot up. Hands clenched by his side, he glared at me before storming off.

I exhaled. What was the matter with me? Paul had wondered the same. So had the rest of my family once the news about Tom filtered through to them, with every glorious detail of my one dip into those fantasies I'd never dared to explore before.

My cheeks burned from the memory of Paul agreeing to write

a cheque to keep Tom from going to the press or, worse, the police.

I'd had to promise I would never explore that part of my sexuality again, else I would have to pay Tom myself and find a new place to live. Not to mention putting up with my mother and her hysterics every time I even thought about doing something that wasn't vanilla.

'You seem as fed up with this as I am.' A deep voice drew my attention to a man standing by my table.

I craned my neck and lifted my gaze further before finding his face. Once I did, it was hard to look away. The tingling from before rushed over my skin in waves as the man looked down at me.

Dressed in a pale blue shirt with a thread count higher than the balance in my new bank account, he looked too sophisticated for his own good. The soft lighting glistened in his dark hair, casting greedy shadows over his full lips, feeling up the sculpted planes of his face. Coupled with his smile, it teased out thin lines that framed the most startling blue eyes I'd ever seen.

He was at least a foot taller than me, burly and beautiful to look at, but that wasn't what made it hard to speak. The power and dominance he exuded were unassailable and curiously hot. He was temptation and danger wrapped into one, but with a hint of something softer teasing at the core for those who dared step closer.

His smile was slow and confident, almost arrogant. Amusement flared in his eyes as he watched me struggle to find my words. 'May I sit down?'

No.

He looked like trouble. The kind my family would not approve of.

'Haven't we already met?' Instead of doing the sensible thing and sending him on his way, I gestured to the chair opposite me.

'I don't believe so. I would've remembered meeting you.'

He sat and propped his elbows on the table, bringing with him a masculine, alluring scent. Sandalwood and musk mixed with the smell of autumn leaves. I wanted to smell it on my sheets, on my skin.

God, I'd had too much to drink, hadn't I? It was the only explanation for the heat rushing to my core. I pressed my thighs together to assuage the ache.

Tapping a finger to my lips, I tried to place him – and buy myself a minute to clear my head. It was the guy from the bar downstairs. Only it wasn't.

'Yes, we have. I spoke to you earlier, but you wore different clothes and had a girlfriend.'

'Ah.' He rolled his eyes. 'That would be my brother. Ignore him. I'm the better twin.'

'Is that so?'

His laugh was low, dark, and full of forbidden promises. 'I can guarantee it.'

I bet he could.

He obviously came from money, same as me, but with a difference. I'd been pushed out of my nest, but his gold cufflinks and attitude suggested he hadn't. I'd met men like him before – young, from a prominent family, out on the town with Daddy's credit card. They were nothing but trouble.

This one looked like a new breed. It intrigued me when it shouldn't have.

'It must be interesting, being an identical twin.'

I scanned his face for any difference between him and the man from the bar downstairs. Nothing obvious stood out, yet every time this one looked at me, I felt it in every inch of my body.

Something else about him was familiar – beyond similarity to his brother – but I couldn't put my finger on what or where I would've met him before.

'Interesting is not the word I'd use, but it has its perks,' he said with a wry smile.

'I'm not sure if I want to know what that means.' He didn't need to tell me. There was nothing wrong with my imagination.

His smile widened. At least he had a sense of humour. It put him ahead of most guys I'd met that evening.

'I couldn't help but overhear what you said to that guy.' His eyes glittered with amusement. 'I was sitting behind you.'

'Eavesdropping is rude.'

He lifted one shoulder in a shrug. 'Wish I could say I'm sorry, but I'm not. I liked your honesty. It's only fair you get the same from me.'

He wrapped his fingers around the candle. The sight of his large hands, and the allure of what they could no doubt do, did me no favours. Maybe Petra was right; I needed to get laid before I started humping a table leg, or worse, Kamron.

'We're old friends. It's nothing to worry about.' I peered into my empty glass, hoping he didn't notice how my nipples had puckered. What the hell was in that drink?

'I'm not easily scared.' He waited until I lifted my gaze. Once he caught it again, the corner of his mouth twitched. His voice dipped lower, taking on a more sensual edge. 'I was curious what kind of bondage you would've used on him.'

'You're curious what…' I lost the words.

'I want to know what bondage you would've used.'

I pushed my hair behind my ear. 'W-what sort of question is that?'

Was this a trick? Another one meant to shame me?

'Call it morbid curiosity.' He waved his hand. 'After an hour of meaningless chitchat about my job, family, hobbies, and favourite movies, an intimate exploration of your choice of bondage could not have come at a better time, don't you think?'

I tried to focus on the flame struggling against the sea of melted wax – on anything but him, the question he'd asked, how low his voice dipped, and how hard it was to break away from his steady gaze. This guy had to leave. He was dangerous to my senses.

'You don't want to hear about my family, job, or hobbies?'

'I do. Something tells me I want to know everything about you. Your hopes and dreams, your every wish and desire.'

The calmness – and seriousness – of his voice stole my breath. It wasn't just the deep notes that played a hard game of attraction, but the velvet they were coated in. Like sleek chocolate smoothed over a crunchy nut, his outer elegance seemed to harbour the hardness within.

His captivating gaze only confirmed my theory – those deep blues were forgoing their innocence for a darker, far more alluring and, no doubt, forbidden shade.

It should have scared me. He did frighten me, but the response he provoked in my body was unfamiliar, so taboo it should have been a stark warning to walk away. But he enthralled me.

He raised a brow, challenging me with a soft curl of his full lips. 'Do you not want to talk about it?'

'My job?'

'No, what bondage you would've used,' he said with a soft chuckle. 'We can talk about your job if it makes you more comfortable.'

'Why would you want to know about that?' I looked around, lowering my voice. 'About bondage?'

'For the reasons I just stated. It's not often you overhear a conversation like that in a club. At least not this kind of club.'

I watched his lips as he spoke. His damn alluring mouth was nothing compared to his deep voice, though. I wanted to bottle it and listen to it in a dark room alone with my vibrator.

Hell, I wanted to bottle the whole man and lap up every drop. Heat crept to my cheeks, and I stared at the tablecloth.

'Eyes on me.' His deep command lifted my gaze. 'That's better.'

27

His smile suggested he could make me do more than simply look at him. I wasn't sure how I felt about that. My body, that damn traitor, enjoyed it far too much.

'I'd love to know,' he said, softer.

I scowled. What had just happened? 'Why?'

'Because this is the most intriguing conversation I've had for some time.'

Conversation? It felt like foreplay. Something told me he had a different definition of foreplay than everyone else. He was the kind of man I'd expected to find in any of those clubs they'd banned me from. Only I hadn't wanted to find a Dominant. That was a role I'd wanted to play.

'No offence, but maybe you need to get out more.' Even I was aware of the dip in my voice. I sounded breathy and submissive. It took everything I had not to squirm in my seat.

'Yes, maybe I do. But now I'm here, with you, hoping for an answer to my question.' He tilted his head. 'Humour me? It would be the highlight of my evening.'

'Who are you?'

'I'll tell you once you've answered my question.'

'Bossy, aren't you?'

His grin was halfway between mischievous and lethal. 'I can be.'

I sat back in my seat. Yes, he was definitely a Dom, so why did he seem so familiar? As far as I knew, I'd never met anyone from the scene, except for those men from the dreams of my child-hood. That couldn't be why it felt like I knew him; he was my age.

'I don't like bossy men.'

'Don't you?' He laughed softly. 'All I've asked of you is to answer a simple question.'

His smile was as disarming as his steady gaze. Was he toying with me? I didn't think so. His eyes rested on me as if he was studying a piece of modern art and needed to understand its meaning. The lift of his dark brow made it clear he wanted a reply, and I drew an unsteady breath.

'I would...' I dragged my teeth over my bottom lip. 'I'd use a rope.'

He scrubbed the faint coating of stubble on his chin. It was impossible to tell what he was thinking. Was he curious? Surprised? Horrified? I'd never met anyone who could hide their emotions that well.

'What kind of rope?' he asked.

'What do you mean?'

'What type of material?' He counted on his fingers. 'Manila, synthetic, jute, sisal, cotton, coir... Which one appeals to you more?'

Feeling out of my depth, I stumbled through the words. 'Something thin, harsh... Sisal, perhaps.'

'Sisal can leave marks on your skin. It can burn if not applied right.' His voice was dangerously, deliciously low. 'Your choice of bondage could cause discomfort, pain even.'

'I know,' I whispered. Though I had limited knowledge of what it felt like against bare skin, it still heated my whole body. 'That's the point.'

Now he would run. I had told him my secret, and he would get up and leave. Only he didn't. A dark glint of glee teased in his eyes as he offered me his hand.

'I'm Jack.'

My body, the traitor, responded by lifting my hand to meet his. 'I'm—'

'Mate, your turn's up,' a man standing beside me interrupted. 'Didn't you hear the bell?'

Jack looked up at him, then back at me, his raised brow a silent challenge – an invitation perhaps, but to what?

My mouth opened. Words bubbled at the back of my throat but never tumbled out. The darkness and all its hidden promises engulfed Jack's eyes again, and desire rushed through me, right down to my toes. I sucked in a breath, giving myself away, and his mouth twitched in amusement.

The urge to devour him thickened with each steady throb of my pulse. But it was wrong. So wrong. Lust was more dangerous than any love. This kind of lust would burn me for sure.

Before either of them decided for me – or worse, questioned why I sat there looking like I'd been caught with my whole head in the cookie jar – I leapt out of my seat and made my escape.

CHAPTER FOUR

JACK

OF COURSE SHE RAN.

Every look from her dark, hooded eyes – her nipples showing through that red dress – and how she writhed in her seat had revealed her struggle. She wanted to play, but something spooked her.

I tutted. It shouldn't have amused me as much as it did. She had still run away, and there was nothing funny about that, but I hadn't expected to stumble upon a sexual sadist at speed dating.

Every once in a while, I came across a woman with a kinky fantasy she wanted to explore. Only some could handle a Marquis. None, if you asked my brother.

There was nothing innocent or weak about this one – only unexplored new darkness. It called to me like a lighthouse in a storm. I wasn't supposed to step into the murky waters anymore, but dammit, who could resist the forbidden when it found you?

She'd run at the worst time; I didn't even have a name for this new temptation. All I had was a restless, euphoric feeling rushing through my body, and the faint scent of her perfume.

Failing to hide my grin, I tilted my head at the next guy in line. 'She's an interesting one.' Even my raspy voice revealed the effect of those few minutes with her.

He huffed and walked to the bar. Fuck him. His loss.

Was I supposed to run after her? I'd never chased a submissive. It had never been necessary. Feeling out of my depth, I laughed, tunnelling a hand through my hair. Something told me it wouldn't be the only thing she'd make me change in my life.

Freddy came up to me. 'What's that look on your face? What did you do?'

'I didn't do anything.' I cleared my throat to regain normal volume. 'For once, I was well-behaved. Polite, even. You'd be proud.'

His snort revealed the depth of my brother's distrust in me. Despite what he thought, I didn't need him with me to avoid getting into trouble. But fuck did I want to do something with her even if it caused problems.

Her body, those curves, and her eyes blazing with lust. I hadn't evoked a response like that in a woman for... I couldn't even remember. But it intrigued me.

She intrigued me.

Her long dark hair, silky and perfect for twisting around my fingers. Her delicate neck and creamy skin made for sinking teeth into. I blew out an unsteady breath. Even her voice almost destroyed me. Soft, dreamy, like a whisper in a dark room.

I could've come just looking at her.

The funny thing was that I seemed to have the same effect on her.

She'd responded to me like a natural submissive; only I was willing to bet she knew nothing about any of this and had never been to a club. The thought of training her sent a rush of excitement down my body.

'Come on.' Freddy tugged on my arm as if he intended to drag me out of there like I was some disobedient child. 'We're leaving.'

Leave? Had he lost his mind?

'The fuck we are.' I pulled my arm out of his grip.

'I don't like this, Jack. Don't like the look on your face, either. This has got trouble written all over it.'

I chuckled. 'Oh hell, yes. That's why I can't leave.'

'Did you get her name?'

'Not yet.'

'So we don't know who she is.' He looked around in case anyone was close enough to hear him worry about the impossible. Dad would've known about her if an illegitimate had lived this close to me. She would've been taken years ago to be trained as a slave.

Why the Harpyiai was so obsessed with honour was beyond me, but if a Marquis had a child with a woman who wasn't from one of the four families wrapped up in this damn order, that child was an illegitimate.

Unclean.

Half-bloods.

Sinful mistakes.

That was the cardinal sin my father had committed when he had us. Mum was an outsider, making Freddy and me illegitimates.

Male illegitimates ended up as prey in The Hunt, and the females became slaves at the castle; that had been the Harpyiai tradition for generations – until my father had me trained as a Marquis.

'So what?' I shrugged. 'Isn't that part of the fun?'

He pulled me to a corner, lowering his voice to a whisper. 'You know I need her name to vet her.'

'Come on, Freddy. Live a little.'

'But Dad—'

'Fuck Dad.'

'You know we have to be careful.' Freddy scowled.

I rolled my eyes. 'She's not linked to them. Nobody our age could stay hidden this long.'

'Oh really?' he countered. 'I'm an illegitimate.'

Sometimes I truly wanted to smack some sense into my brother.

'You were never taken because Dad sacrificed *me*. Come on, Freddy. Juliet would've turned you into prey years ago if he hadn't become Head Marquis when I graduated. It doesn't mean there are hundreds of other illegitimates roaming the streets.'

'I can't risk you breaking protocol just to get laid. This is exactly why I said this was a terrible idea.'

Sleeping with an illegitimate dishonoured a Marquis and forced us to sacrifice an illegitimate to The Hunt. If I refused, Freddy was at risk of being taken.

It was the one rule I couldn't break, a condition my father had set so I could live with Freddy rather than be stuck in the Harpyiai castle in Scotland.

The odds of running into an illegitimate in a club in Kittington were still slim to fucking nothing. Dad would've known. He had gone to so much trouble turning his illegitimate son into a Marquis, defying the Harpyiai traditions, and would never put me at risk of breaching protocol.

Without me, he had no successor.

'Freddy.' I lowered my voice. 'It's been almost a decade since I left the castle. Nobody has contacted me. Nobody you've vetted has had any links. We've found no illegitimates and—'

'You're not supposed to play.'

'At clubs, yes.'

'He also said not to date anyone in the scene, and you wouldn't be this interested in her if she wasn't like you.'

'You can't even let me have *one* date with a woman who might actually be into what I like?'

Blowing out a breath, he ran a hand through his hair. 'What the hell did you say to her? Why did she leave?'

'I'm not sure,' I said, already crossing the room. Christ, I really was about to chase a woman, wasn't I? Theo and Mark Williams would've paid money to see this. For the first time, I was grateful my father had forbidden me from speaking to other Marquises.

Freddy – my identical, annoying shadow – followed me to the staircase. 'You probably scared her away, as you always do. I told you, didn't I?'

Ah, but fear was such a powerful aphrodisiac. I needed to see if it had the same effect on her. Something told me it did; if that were the case, I'd chase her for as long as it took.

In all those years as a Dom, I'd never come across someone who responded to me like this. Finding someone who became aroused by fear was too tempting to walk away from when I'd spent my whole adult life being told I only scare women away.

'I'll back off if she tells me to, but I don't think that's why she ran.'

His feet pounded on the staircase behind me. 'You know I need her name.'

'Relax. I'll get you her name, so you can do your little checks and leave me alone.'

'Jack, think about it. Make smart choices.'

I couldn't help but laugh. He was waiting for the Ritalin to kick in, but no amount of Ritalin in the world would stop me from chasing someone like her.

Freddy pulled on my arm again. 'Jack.'

I swung around. 'For Christ's sake, will you calm down? Go home and see Lily, blow off some steam, take your multivitamin and get to work tomorrow.'

His glare made me laugh. 'Sorry, but you asked for that one. Seriously, mate. I've dated before. The world didn't end, did it?'

Concern marred my brother's features, tangling itself up with his frustration with being the one who had to intervene. 'If Dad gets pissed off and…' He looked away, his lips thinning.

Oh, that's what this was about.

35

'Freddy.' I put my hands around his face and rested my forehead against his. 'You're the most annoying person I know, but I'd never let Dad or anyone else hurt you. You know that.'

He sighed. His dark lashes lifted, and the conflicted emotions in his eyes confused me. This was about more than Harpyiai protocol and the risk of sleeping with an illegitimate, wasn't it? My brother knew something that I didn't – something about our father.

'What is it, Freddy?'

'I'm supposed to watch you, keep you out of trouble…'

'You suggested her, remember?' I smiled to reassure him. 'You wouldn't have done that if you didn't think she'd fit me.'

He pulled back, frowning. Sometimes, when he couldn't understand me or my struggles, I wanted to tell him about the worst moments of my years as a slave, how hard I had resisted my training, and about the night of my branding, but Freddy didn't need to know. His guilt was already bottomless.

No one had told him that the Harpyiai gave me a choice to swap places with him. If he had known, he would've offered. But my brother wasn't strong enough, and it was my job to protect him.

I only wished he could understand that I wanted more from life than this, even if Dad said relationships were too much of a risk. I wanted someone like her – if only for a little while.

Taking the steps two at a time, I scanned the room below. Where the hell did she go? The space was still packed with people, too dark to make out faces, too many colours to find hers. My heart thudded in time with the beat of the music.

'Jack,' my persistent brother growled in my ear. 'Walk away. It's not worth it.'

He was right; my family wanted me to be good, restrained, and content with the occasional quickie up against the wall somewhere, fleeting moments of this new normality before returning to the rough existence of my life – forever tailed by my brother and guarded by my father.

But goddammit, none of it stopped me from wanting more from life.

CHAPTER FIVE

KATE

THE MUSIC PUMPED through the crowd downstairs. Bodies swung and jerked under the flickering lights. The room was sticky with heat, and people bumped into me everywhere I turned.

For months, all my thoughts and dreams had focused on finding just one person who understood. It never occurred to me what it would mean – or how frightening it would be – when I did.

A fantasy was fine as long as it was confined to my mind, but when it walked up to my table, it overwhelmed me.

It took me back to Tom and that last night we'd spent together.

Tom handcuffed to the bed had been arousing. New. Exciting. But the thrill hadn't come until later. I hadn't meant to scratch Tom, not to that degree anyway, but there was no way to undo my actions when I did.

Perhaps I shouldn't have touched the dribble of blood, tried to catch it as it slid along his warm skin, and maybe I shouldn't have smeared it over his chest or leaned forward to taste it, but it had fascinated me.

Like an addict, I was hooked after that, always seeking a rush, losing myself in fantasies of the forbidden, whilst drowning in the shame my family handed out. I never thought I would find someone who might understand.

The DJ switched to a slow song. I stopped in the middle of the dance floor, halted in my pathetic escape from my darkest fantasy as the crowd formed into pairs.

At times like this, I even missed Tom. By twenty-seven, my life should've been mapped out already. I should've settled down like my brother and sister, but I was here alone.

'I thought you were leaving,' a deep voice rumbled in my ear, 'but I guess you were just running from me.'

As Jack circled me, his eyes found mine, and there it was again, that need to jump him. Christ, what was it about him? One look and I wanted to rub against him just to get some friction.

The soothing tunes wrapped us in a cocoon, and each word of longing hit me harder than ever.

I moistened my lips, preparing my lie. 'I wasn't running away from you.'

Having no desire to be lured by his deep blues, I looked up, down, to the DJ and over to the bar, but he reined me in again. Those damn eyes. They hooked, charmed, and stole my mind.

'That's a shame, as I was hoping for a bit of a chase.' Jack moved closer, towering over me as his broad shoulders enveloped me in darkness.

'A chase?'

He was so close that his cologne made me dizzy, an intoxicating scent I wanted to bathe in and sniff when no one was looking. Why did he smell of autumn leaves? I'd never met anyone who smelt like a season before, but his scent reminded me of long walks in the countryside, hot chocolate and open fires. Warmth and comfort, with an undertone of raw, sexual energy. So profoundly male and dominant.

His size and intensity were enough to warn me that this man was capable of things that should have made me run away, only I didn't want to. That tease of danger had the opposite effect on me.

'A chase would've been fun,' he said, coming closer. 'Or you can just let me take you home so I can fuck you.'

My mouth dropped open. Heat erupted in my core, but waves of outrage at this man and his obvious bad manners flooded all other emotions. 'You're an arse,' I hissed.

Jack tipped back his head and laughed; his dark hair lit up under the flashing lights above.

'It's not funny. Who says that?' I propped my hands on my hips. 'Tell me, Jack, how often does that actually work?'

'More often than you'd probably think.' Humour glittered in his eyes. 'Is that a no then?'

My mouth wanted to send him away, but my body struggled to resist his invitation.

He reached out his hand. 'Can I at least have this dance?'

'Depends... Are you going to behave?'

'Probably not.' His hands found my hips, and he directed me back into the soothing beat of the distant music. 'You're not afraid to bite back, are you? I like that.'

Oh, I would bite back. At that moment, nothing excited me more than the thought of sinking my teeth into his flesh. I didn't care if it was deviant, not after a line like that.

I put my hands on his shoulders, feeling the hardness of his muscles and the heat of his body. 'If you try a bullshit line like that again, I promise you won't like what I do next.'

Jack took my hand, spun me around, and caught me again when I made a full circle, pressing me close to him as if we were one. 'You'd be surprised by the things that I like.' He leaned in to whisper, 'And the things I can do.'

'You're arrogant. Has anyone ever told you that?'

'No, you're the first.' His smile told me I wasn't. He tightened his grip on my hips. 'Tell me your name.'

But I shook my head, keeping the tiny bit of control I had left as he took over everything else.

'Why not? Are you sure you're not running away from me?'

'Would you chase me if I did?'

'Do you want me to?' The corner of his mouth tipped up, and again something about his demeanour and steady gaze irked me.

We swayed together as I tried to grasp why he seemed so familiar. His knee worked its way further between my legs, and my body betrayed me again as I pressed my groin against his thigh.

His hand on my back didn't help either, as he held me closer. It only made my breaths fast and shallow, and the throbbing in my core increased, deepening, desperate for a release. His deep chuckle against my neck did me no favours.

He caught my earlobe between his teeth, one sharp tug soothed by a soft kiss, sending a bolt of electricity down my body. 'Do you want me to take care of this for you?' he asked, angling his knee between my legs.

'No,' I lied, hating how my ragged breathing gave me away. 'You should run from me. I'll ruin you.'

His eyes widened, but the storm beneath lingered. 'Will you now? Tell me how.'

'That's what I do.' I leaned forward, my lips barely grazing his ear. 'Ruin people. You'll wish you'd never met me, Jack.'

I wasn't even sure why I wanted to warn him. Because he tempted me? Because he seemed to promise me something I'd wanted for so long, and he deserved to know?

'You couldn't ruin me.' He lifted my chin as though observing something new and exciting. The feel of his firm hands and the angle with which he tilted my neck brought me under a spell I wasn't sure if I wanted to break free from. 'And you're definitely worth the risk.'

The dangerous spark in his gaze called to me, and I sucked in a breath as it took effect on my treacherous body. He was playing a game, a slow seduction, as he felt around the edges of my limits, and it was working.

'What's your name?' he asked, spinning me slowly again before catching me, moving our bodies together.

'None of your business.'

'I feel it's important to know the name of someone you're chasing.'

'You don't strike me as someone who bothers with names.'

He laughed softly. 'I always do, yet you won't tell me yours. I guess I'll just call you *ropes* for now.'

'What? Oh, you're unbelievable.'

'Most women call me memorable, but we'll get to that stage later.' His laugh deepened despite my scowl. Maybe because of it. 'If sex is off the table, for now, have dinner with me? I promise I'll be on my best behaviour.'

'I don't think you even know what that means.'

Was it wrong that I wanted to see what he was capable of doing?

'I can be well-behaved. I can be anything you want…' He moved us to the beat in slow, agonising movements. His breath was warm on my lips when he leaned down. 'If you tell me your name.'

'Ropes,' I whispered, too aware of how much alcohol I'd had. Its effect was creeping up on me, making me weaker.

'Your real name.'

I shifted up on my toes and kissed him softly, hesitantly, afraid to unleash those dark longings. It was more of a peck, too weak to show him who was in charge, too soft to quench that thirst.

Jack moved his fingertips slowly over my cheek until he cupped my face. 'Your name,' he said, firmer, 'or I won't kiss you back. Properly.'

'You're so arrogant. You can't give me what I want, can you?'

'It depends on what you want. Right now, I want to take you

home. I can take care of that ache you've been struggling with since I sat down at your table.'

'I know your type, Jack.' I pushed him back. 'Just a player looking for a bit of fun. Shame about that, as you're not a half-bad kisser.'

In the end, I walked away from him, from my urges, towards the exit as I implored myself not to look at him. He was dangerous. Arrogant. Just that was reason enough to run. It would end badly, in either tears or blood, and neither terrified me as much as it should have.

Darkness had embraced the street outside, with only a few people staggering around, trying to wave down a cab. Leaning against the corner of the building, under the orange glow of the street lamp, I watched them get into one and drive off.

As I closed my eyes, I cursed myself for being so foolish, so easily affected by someone. Obviously, it had been too long since I got laid. One whiff of cologne and I was on my back. The chilled May air rolled over my bare arms, and I soothed the goosebumps.

'There you are.' Petra's voice startled me. 'I've been looking everywhere for you. Who were you dancing with earlier? He looked hot.'

'It's complicated. He's...' I blew out a breath. Hot. Frustrating. Dominant. Familiar? 'Complicated. Can we leave?'

'Are you okay? You look flushed.'

'Too much excitement for one night,' I muttered, glancing at the door in case he came out, and I was too weak to resist. The doorman stared at me, and I edged further away, around the corner of the building. 'And too much alcohol.'

'Come on, let's grab our coats and go home.'

'No,' I mumbled, leaning my head back. 'You get them. I need the fresh air.'

'Are you sure?' She twisted her hands, but I waved her off,

wanting to be alone with my thoughts and regrets, and closed my eyes.

He'd overwhelmed me again, or maybe the alcohol was finally kicking in. The whole situation reminded me of when I was five and had stared transfixed at a frosted lamppost. I'd told myself not to lick it. *Don't lick it, Kate. Don't lick it.* I'd licked it and probably still had a scar on my tongue to prove it.

'For someone who's not scared, you seem to run away a lot.'

'Jesus.' I put a hand on my chest, falling back against the wall. 'Jack, are you trying to give me a heart attack?'

'I'm sorry.' His smile suggested he was anything but sorry he'd found me again. 'We were just leaving, and I thought I'd say bye…' Frowning, he came closer. 'Are you drunk, ropes? Should you be out here on your own?'

'Only a little squiffy.' I pushed away from the wall, steadying myself with a firm grip on his shirt. 'All those drinks caught up with me, so if you still wanted to fuck me, this would be—'

'The absolute wrong time to do that.' He steadied me with a hand on my elbow. 'But if I may, I'd like to correct a misconception you have of me.'

'And what misconception would that be?' I crossed my arms. So now he didn't want me? 'That you're an arse?'

He laughed, holding up a hand to someone exiting the club. 'No, I'll give you that one. Few people have the balls to say it to my face, though.'

As Jack talked, a man rounded him, a mere blurry blob at the edge of my peripheral vision, until he came into view. I blinked, trying to focus. Why were there two of him? God, I'd had too much alcohol.

'But I'm talking about a completely different misconception,' Jack said. 'One I cannot let slide.'

'What?' My eyes flitted between them.

'Focus on me, ropes. Ignore my brother,' Jack said, commanding my attention again with his deep voice.

His brother walked a few steps away, his back to us as he raked a hand through his hair.

Jack ran his fingertips over my cheek. 'You said I wasn't a half-bad kisser, and I'd like to set that straight. If given a chance, I can easily top that last kiss.'

'Is that so?' I swallowed hard, trying to keep my voice steady. 'Caught you at a weak moment, did I?'

He'd found a weakness in me; I wasn't sure how I felt about that. I wanted to be stronger than this. He continued fighting me for control, and I kept losing.

Jack smiled, his gaze fixed on my mouth as he ran his thumb slowly over my bottom lip. 'I guess you can say that.'

'Okay.' I tipped my chin up, determined to win this surreal battle between us. 'I'll give you one more—'

I lost the rest of my sentence as Jack gripped my hips and pushed me against the wall. There was no time to prepare or resist before he kissed me. Desire exploded within me, with each touch of his lips on mine, with each flick of his tongue. It was no soft or gentle kiss. He devoured my mouth until I whimpered and pressed my hands against his back, wanting him closer, needing more.

The thought of him taking me with the same intensity, fucking me as hard, as skilfully, and mercilessly as his tongue moved against mine – did something to me. I forgot where I was, who I was, and everything I wasn't supposed to explore. All that mattered was Jack and his body against mine. His kiss lured out that dark longing, and I gripped his hair and tugged, craving that response from him.

His deep groan shattered my reluctance and fear of embracing those forbidden urges. It rumbled in his chest, vibrating through me. He pressed so hard against me I felt his cock hardening between us, and my sex clenched. It wasn't enough. I needed more of him, to feel more and explore more. I forced my hand between us, cupped his groin and squeezed, hard, not releasing until Jack hissed out a breath.

'Ropes,' he whispered, his mouth still touching mine. 'Only grip me this hard if you don't care who's near us.' He took hold of my hands and pressed them against the wall beside my head. 'Don't do it unless you want me to tear these clothes off.' Jack trailed his fingertips slowly down my bare arms, leaving goose-bumps behind.

'Maybe I do,' I breathed.

'Not tonight.'

'Why not?' I put my hands on his shoulders, sliding them down his arms as I dragged my bottom lip between my teeth, but the move that would've convinced men like Kamron to take full advantage of my weakened defences didn't work on Jack. He wrapped his fingers around my wrists, shaking his head with a slow, deliciously arrogant smile.

'I want to see you again when you're not squiffy. Tell me what I have to do for that to happen.'

'Just fuck me now.'

'No.'

I scowled. 'I told you I don't like bossy men.'

Amusement flickered in his eyes. 'Yes, you do.'

'No. No, I don't.'

'Tell me your name.'

I lifted my chin. He was not getting what he wanted. I would win this battle. But then his gaze darkened as he dipped his head, peering back at me, and the danger and dark urges beneath that innocent blue surface made my breath catch.

'Kate?'

I was so caught up in the moment that Petra's voice sounded like a dream. A remnant of a life left behind, of life before Jack.

'Kate? Where did you go?'

'I think she might be over there,' his brother answered. 'Jack. We should go.'

'In a minute, Freddy,' Jack said.

My brain screamed at me to get rid of him, but my body wanted him close like this, looking at me like he would tear my clothes off any minute – like he could give me everything I'd ever wanted. But he couldn't, could he? Someone like him would never want to be hurt.

Petra's heels clicked on the pavement nearby. 'Oh. Let me guess,' she said, giggling. 'This is Mr Complicated?'

Oh, god. I draped a hand over my face, pushing him back. Damn my drunken brain.

Jack chuckled. 'I've been called worse tonight.'

'Petra,' I muttered, 'meet Jack. He's—'

'Complicated.' Jack smiled as he tilted his head, observing me like he'd caught sight of a flickering flame and couldn't wait to stick his hand into it no matter the burn. 'And you're Kate.'

He offered me a card, holding it between us as a silent challenge. I'd left behind all the other cards men had given me, but I took this one and held it close to my chest.

'Call me.' He kissed me again, softer, before joining his brother down the street.

As soon as they disappeared from view, I leaned against the wall, closing my eyes. My whole body was on fire, knees threatening to give in. Petra's laugh didn't help as I fought the urge to run after him.

CHAPTER SIX

KATE

* * *

I COULDN'T FIND my mother again. She was not in her bed, the bathroom, or even my little brother's bedroom. I didn't like the dark and hugged my favourite doll as I padded the long corridor looking for her. Paul went to the city yesterday, so she had to be home.

That noise came again, the one that woke me – someone was crying downstairs.

As I started down the staircase, it came again but low and deep, like a sob, so unlike Mum's normal voice.

'Good girl,' a man said, his deep rumbling voice stilling my movements.

A sharp whistling noise tore through the air, then a crack followed, like wood splitting apart, and a piercing scream sent me running up the stairs, around the corner, crashing into a dark-clad man so tall I couldn't see his face.

'Where are you going, little one?'

* * *

'KATIE.' My shoulder shook under a firm grip. 'Hey, you're having another nightmare.'

My half-brother's voice sank in, and it was clear my attempts at resistance would be futile. I pulled a cushion over my head. 'Sod off, Owen.'

He exhaled. 'That's something, I guess. How long have you been on the sofa?' He shook my shoulder again. 'Kate? Do I have to get a bucket of water or something? Don't think I won't.'

Oh, I believed he would. With a strained groan, I flopped onto my back and flinched from the bright sunlight.

So this was what it was like to be run over by a thirty-foot lorry.

Repeatedly.

'Jesus Christ,' Owen whined.

My eyes cracked open for a nanosecond – barely enough to glimpse him sitting on the edge of my coffee table.

Why was he in my flat?

Nose scrunched up, Owen stared at me as if I was some disembowelled mouse a cat had left on the doormat.

My lips were dry and cracked, and I darted my tongue out to moisten them. 'You're very loud,' I whispered.

His laughter made my head pulsate. 'It's past one o'clock, Kate. Time to get up.'

I wanted to bite back, make fun of his auburn hair that never behaved or how that too-tight grey jumper made him look like a twat, but his expression confused me.

'Katie, sweetheart.' He shielded his eyes with a crooked smile. 'You're sort of half-naked.'

'What?' I gasped when I saw I wore nothing but a pair of red lace knickers. 'What the—? Where the hell are my clothes?'

Christ, I couldn't remember what I'd worn the night before. I'd had that dream again. One of the many dreams I couldn't be sure was a memory or something my imagination made up. Mum claimed it was only in my head, further proof of my deviant urges.

'At least you're alone this time.' With a laugh, Owen walked into the kitchen area. 'Nothing worse than coming to see your big sister and finding her… otherwise engaged.'

I grabbed a fleece off the back of the sofa to wrap around myself. Thankfully, there was no one else in the room. But disappointment hit me when I remembered Jack. Why was I alone?

'Do you want water or juice?' Owen called from the kitchen, his voice muffled by whatever he had found to shove into his mouth. He poked his head around the fridge door when I didn't answer. 'What can I get you?'

I brought my hand up to my nose, still smelling Jack on me. It didn't ease my regrets.

'Water, I guess.' I tried to stand up. The room spun, swirling the TV unit in one corner with the bookcase on the opposite side. Jesus, I had to curb my drinking.

Owen pulled a bottle of water from the fridge door and tossed it. I yelped and flung my arms up, losing grip on the fleece. The bottle hit the sofa behind me.

'For fuck's sake, Owen. Have you lost your mind?'

Sometimes I could kill him. Four years younger than me, he'd taken his role as my little brother only too willingly. Our childhood was a string of ponytails being pulled, whoopee cushions, and sugar swapped for salt.

Owen had always been the family's troublemaker, but now I rivalled him, and he loved it. It didn't matter what trouble he or our sister Hannah got into; what I'd done to Tom would always top it.

'When you first hit the bottle, you sink to the bottom, don't you? Your vibrator is on the floor, by the way. Looks like one hell of an after-party.'

'Oh, shut up.' I kicked it under the coffee table and picked up the fleece again. 'Why are you even here? I want my spare key back.'

'Mum sent me to make sure you don't forget about lunch today.' He took in my panicked look and laughed. 'This'll be so much fun. Don't worry. You've got thirty minutes to look human again.'

I rushed to my bedroom. 'If I know you right, you're here to ask me to be the demon child again so you can be let off the hook for whatever you've done this time.'

'There was one little thing...'

Owen rested against the door frame, surveying my bedroom. It was large enough for a double bed in white cast iron and two bedside tables. The back wall had built-in wardrobes filled to the brim with clothes, most never worn.

The remaining floor space was a dumping ground for clothes, books, DVDs, and everything else I'd never had time to put away since Tom kicked me out of our flat.

My stepdad paid for this; on my salary, I could never afford a flat in this part of town, and my mother insisted I lived somewhere safe, somewhere she could still have a key to so she could stop by and check I wasn't up to anything she would disapprove of.

'Jesus, do you ever tidy in here?'

I moved effortlessly between the piles. 'Don't judge. There's a system.'

'If you say so.' He picked up a bra from the floor and tossed it to me. 'Mum will rip into you if you turn up without one again.'

Dodging the bra, I pulled a pair of black leggings from a drawer. 'At least I'll know Paul won't be asking me too many questions.'

'Why don't you want to talk to Dad? Did you and Petra go to The Yard?'

I snorted. 'I'm not that careless. Paul would've killed me. I can't wait for him to give up on this dream of shutting down every exclusive club in the county. If it weren't for you and Hannah, I would've been surprised if he'd ever been laid.'

'Katie...' Owen averted his gaze as I hopped into my leggings. 'I need to tell you something.'

'Whatever you did, just tell me how much I need to distract them, okay?' I pulled a grey singlet over my head and rushed to the mirror to fix my hair. 'I'm sure I've fucked up enough to cover murder if that's necessary.'

Like that kiss last night. Damn. My mother would've fainted.

I gave up on my hair and gathered it in a high ponytail. How could I have forgotten about lunch? My mum gathered us around a table every month to catch up on our lives. Confession time, as I called it. Unfortunately for me, there was no reward for wickedness. Not even a lolly.

Owen cleared his throat. 'I'm leaving Em.'

I snapped around so fast that I had to steady myself on the wardrobe. 'You're what?'

Owen and Emily had married only a year before. A massive wedding with the reception in my mum and stepdad's back garden, all their snobby friends invited and shown around the grand property. No wonder he needed my help to deflect them.

He nodded, looking at the floor. 'I was hoping I could stay with you for a few weeks. Just until I find somewhere of my own.'

'What did you do?' The way he avoided my scrutinising gaze was admirable, but he didn't fool me. I could smell the guilt on him and grabbed my hairbrush, waiting for that confirmation.

'There's this woman I like, but I swear it's not – ow!' The hairbrush bounced off his head and landed on the floor behind him. 'What the hell, Kate?'

'Shame on you!'

'Yeah, I know.' He rubbed his head, 'But if you can just do this—'

'No fucking way.' I stomped towards the bathroom. 'I'm not covering for you this time.'

'I didn't cheat on Em,' he said, daring to look innocent with his pale blue eyes. 'But I wanted to, and no matter what I do, I can't stop thinking about her. I thought you'd understand.'

I did. Before Tom, I'd had the unfortunate experience of being cheated on repeatedly by a twat called George. Owen knew my philosophy: leave the moment you feel the temptation. That was when the relationship ended.

'I'll owe you, okay? I'll do whatever you want.' He stopped in the doorway, his conflicted expression reflected in the bathroom mirror. 'Please?'

I grabbed a face wipe. 'You'll do whatever I want? Are you sure you want to offer me that?'

'I'll talk Mum into letting you speak to your dad. She'll listen to me.'

'Where have you been for the past twenty-odd years?' I scrubbed off the remnants of mascara and rinsed my toothbrush. 'Whatever my dad did, she's still not forgiven him.'

'I'll get you in at The Yard?'

I barked a laugh. 'Now I know you're just trying to get me into trouble.'

But Owen didn't let up. He followed me around my flat and insisted on driving me to the pub. By the time we ran through the door to The Raven to escape the rain, he'd worn me down. I promised to bring up the subject of my birth father before he told them about his marriage.

Nothing riled my stepdad up more than the mention of my birth father. Whatever Owen said after that would be a welcome change of subject.

The quaint country pub by the riverside was warm and inviting. White walls, dark wooden beams, and surreal framed paintings of cows set the theme. But the cosy atmosphere soon lost its power in the chill of my mother's gaze from across the worn wooden table. I still preferred her icy nature to my stepfather's dismissal.

Like every time we met for lunch, Paul had hired the big room at the back of the pub. My stepdad enjoyed flaunting his wealth, pretending he was from an upper-class family when he actually came from a working-class one in London.

He'd once told me his money was from investments, but although he'd left that behind to pursue politics, the money never seemed to run out. If he weren't so damn unattractive and thought sex was a mortal sin, it wouldn't have surprised me if he had a rich sugar mama.

As a server filled our water glasses, Mum lined up the cutlery on the pale-yellow napkin. The frown between her pencil-thin fake brows deepened. 'You don't look well, Caitlin. Are you under the weather?'

Was I ill? Badly hungover and frustrated. I shouldn't have drunk so much. It had made me miss the opportunity to go home with Jack.

'Just a little bug, Mum. I'll be fine in a few days.'

Her gaze dropped to my chest, and her lips thinned. 'Caitlin—'

'If my tits offend you, feel free to stop staring at them.'

She looked away; her thin lips flattened to an almost invisible line.

My mother and stepdad had certain expectations, and I'd never lived up to them. I didn't dress like Hannah – black silk blouse, red pencil skirt – nor did I behave like her. She laid the napkin on her lap and straightened in her chair, always the dutiful daughter.

My mother wore another stiff blue dress, and Paul was in his usual dark suit. Only Owen and I dressed casually – always the outcasts.

I downed another mouthful of water, praying the headache would go away. A twelve-hour shift at the emergency room waited, and it was stressful enough without the pounding behind my eyes. It had been Petra's idea to take extra shifts at A&E.

She thought it would add excitement to our lives. Patching up stupid people wasn't the excitement I wanted in my life. I could only imagine what my drunken brain had told her about Jack on our cab ride back to Ladeworth, and hoped she wouldn't be on the rota.

'Jessica said she saw you out in Kittington last night, Kate,' Hannah said. 'Dancing with this hot guy—'

'Kittington?' Mum put her menu down. 'Where did you go? What club?'

I rolled my eyes. 'Calm down, Mum. We were at the Inspiration club, not The Yard.'

'Oh, Caitlin. You're not dating again, are you? Who is he? I want his name.'

I slid a fork into my lap and clenched it in a sweaty palm. 'No, Mum,' I muttered, dragging my thumb over the sharp tines. 'I'm not dating anyone.'

'I think it's best for everyone if you focused on' – Mum cleared her throat – 'your career at the moment until everything with Tom settles down. No more dating.'

If my mother had her way, I would have been married off to one of her friends' sons years ago. Those stuttering, stumbling boys had pounced on me the last time she'd dragged me along to the social club under the pretence of wanting to show off my chess talent.

But that was before I had crossed the line with Tom, and now my mother preferred it if I was celibate.

She wanted me to go back to being a good girl, but I craved a man who could astound me, accept me as I am, and challenge me on every level. Someone like Jack? I couldn't hide the grin stretching across my face.

Shit. Where had I put his card? I checked my bag, dumping tampons, loose change, and lip balm onto the table.

'Caitlin, honestly.' Mum placed her menu over the tampons. 'Can't you do that in private?'

It wasn't in the bag. Where the hell had I put it? I shoved everything back in and slumped in my chair. The bounce of my breasts caught Paul's attention, but I ignored him, running my fingers over the sharp tines of the fork. The card was probably at home. Owen had promised to drop me off at work after lunch, so I wouldn't find it before my shift.

'Are you sure you're all right?' My mother's brown eyes studied me. It was the only feature we shared. She had once said my dark hair came from my father, the man nobody wanted to discuss. 'You look flushed.'

I nodded, even if the heat rising to my cheeks had nothing to do with a bug but memories. Nor did it explain why my nipples had hardened. My mother noticed, but she said nothing.

I was glad. I wanted to dig out those memories and savour them for a moment. My back against the wall, Jack's hands on me. His mouth, his tongue. God, I wanted to feel that again.

'Caitlin?'

I blinked at my mother. 'Pardon?'

'Perhaps you should call in sick today?' She patted that ridiculous hairstyle she'd insisted on since I was five. There was so much hairspray in her dark blonde curls that my fingers felt sticky.

'No, I'm fine, really.' I suppressed those forbidden thoughts and tried to focus on something else. 'Paul,' I said, catching my stepfather's stern green-eyed gaze. 'Did you find Dad's phone number?'

When Tom and I'd moved in together, my mother had hoped for a wedding. It was the only way I got her to agree to contact my birth father again. Paul was supposed to have made contact months ago but kept making excuses. I had so many unanswered questions about my childhood, things my mother was unwilling to discuss.

'Are you ready to order?' A petite woman approached our

table, pen and paper pad ready to jot down five different meals, but there was no need.

'We will all have fish and chips. No mushy peas,' Paul said, dismissing her with a wave.

'I'm waiting,' I said when he ignored me. He never let me order my own food, but he was not getting away with this again. 'And I wanted soup.'

Paul wrinkled his dark moustache, looking away again. 'No, I don't think it's wise for you to speak to your father.'

'What?' I gripped the fork harder. 'Who the hell gave you the right to make that decision?'

Mum put a hand on her chest. 'Caitlin.'

Paul's narrowed eyes found mine, but the shine on his bald head from the ceiling lights distracted too much for the sternness to take effect. 'The effort didn't seem warranted now that there's no potential wedding to prepare for.' He looked away again. 'And I don't appreciate your tone, young lady.'

'I don't appreciate your meddling. He's my father.' The uncomfortable look exchanged between my mum and my stepdad unsettled me. 'What are you not telling me? Has he passed away?'

'Sweetheart.' Mum put her chilled, slim hand over mine, patting it. 'If there's ever a chance of a wedding, we can look into finding your father again.'

I pulled my hand back. 'What's wrong with now? Surely it can't be that hard to find him? You know his first name, don't you?'

It wasn't on my birth certificate. That would've been too easy, but I even had doubts about my date of birth. All I had was the Peterson name she had reluctantly allowed me to add as a middle name. But there were too many Petersons in Britain, far too many men with dark hair, and I needed more information.

'You're not getting married now, are you?' Hannah glanced at me over her phone. 'So what difference does it make?'

'Easy for you to say. You have a father.'

She picked at the invisible fluff on her shirt to avoid my hard stare. 'I'm sure he's moved on, and Dad will walk you down the aisle, won't you, Dad?'

'Of course,' Paul muttered.

I glared at him. There was no chance of that toad doing it, but this wasn't about a potential future wedding, and they knew it.

Mum patted my hand again. 'We need to focus on getting you better first, sweetheart. Paul and I wouldn't want anything to upset your nerves, not when you're making good progress.'

'My nerves?' I hissed. 'Will you stop talking about me like I'm some raving lunatic?'

'Well,' Hannah said, a smile curving her thin lips. 'You did nearly slash Tom to death.' She yelped when I poked her thigh with the fork. 'Bloody hell!'

'Hannah.' Mum looked around, lowering her voice. 'We do not use that kind of language. You know this.'

'Sorry, Mum,' Hannah mumbled.

I gritted my teeth. Damn Hannah. She was the one I'd turned to when Tom had kicked me out, and she'd called Mum. The day after, the search for my father was called off. My mother wanted me to dress like a nun and never speak of sex again. If I even looked at a man twice now, she wanted his name, address, and complete family history.

I swivelled around in my seat and gave Hannah my full attention. Pale green eyes set under dark blonde hair widened, expecting the worst from me as always.

'I did not nearly slash him to death. Excuse me for wanting something other than missionary for the rest of my life. I know you and Greg are so fond of the good old vanilla, but I'm not.'

Hannah's face pinked up. 'I don't understand how you can talk about it like it's—'

'Perfectly normal?' I rested an elbow on the table. 'Guess what, Hannah? Everybody fucks.'

'Caitlin,' my mother protested.

'That's enough,' Paul said. 'We're in public.'

'So what? I'm only naming the elephant in the room. Everybody's so interested in my sex life but refuses to talk about their own. So what if I scratched Tom? He suggested the handcuffs, or have you forgotten about that?'

My mother's lips thinned. 'Are you quite done?'

'Depends... Are you going to tell me where my father is? His full name? Date of birth? Anything other than that he's short with dark hair?'

Her dismissive stare into the room told me every effort would be futile, but I wasn't ready to give up.

'For god's sake. You act like he's a hardened criminal, or worse' – I laughed – 'a sex-crazed maniac like your daughter.'

My mother deflated as if someone had popped her like a balloon. Paul glared at me.

'Oh my god! I'm right, aren't I? That's why I remember seeing—'

'Caitlin.' Paul stood up. 'One more word out of you and—'

I sprung off my chair as well. 'And you'll do what? Bend me over your knee? Are you into that as well, or is it just Mum?'

My mother's face turned a deep scarlet, and I laughed. Her obvious embarrassment shouldn't have thrilled me, but this new information was like catnip, and I was a tiger with sharp claws. Paul continued to glare at me; my mother looked like she wanted to sink through the floor.

Two female servers entered the room to serve our meals, obviously pretending not to feel the suffocating tension between my stepfather and me. Before they could ask if we wanted any condiments, Paul dismissed them with another wave.

'This conversation is over,' he said when they were out of earshot. 'We will not speak of this again. If you mention your father again, I won't transfer the funds to Tom. You can foot your own bill for the assault.'

I gaped. 'You know that would financially ruin me. And it was not assault. Tom wants money for emotional damage, like the wuss he is.'

'Since you can't afford it, I suggest you stay away from the clubs, Tom, and all these men you've been chasing all over town. And curb your urges,' he added in a sharp whisper as if he couldn't wait to get rid of the words – and me.

'Don't talk about my father, don't talk about sex, don't go to dungeons or The Yard.' Shame crept over me as my mother looked away, refusing to acknowledge my existence. 'Is there anything else I mustn't do to derail your political career?'

'Don't upset your mother,' he said, sitting back down. 'You've caused her enough embarrassment. Are you incapable of controlling yourself, young lady?'

'Young lady?'

Oh, fuck him. A lump formed in my throat, but I refused to cower under his glare.

'I cannot have a stepdaughter who runs around—' Paul's lips thinned. 'We've raised you better than this.'

'Maybe my life would've been better if my birth father had raised me.'

Mum's gasp warned me I'd gone too far. What the hell had happened between her and my father? Who was he?

Owen tugged on my arm. 'If we're done with Kate's sex life, there was something I wanted to tell you all.'

I ignored his grateful smile and dropped back into my chair as Owen told everyone about himself and Emily.

Maybe I was a raving lunatic. Time spent with my family sure emphasised how different we were. As much as I wanted to squash that thought, a small part of me hoped my birth father wasn't so different from me. There were things I had seen as a child – things my mother tried to explain away – that I was sure weren't mere figments of my imagination.

Mum claimed I'd never met him, that she hadn't seen him

since she got pregnant with me, but it was impossible. I remembered a man coming to our house when Paul was out of town on business.

I couldn't remember the man's face, only his voice, and sometimes I thought there had been more than one man. They had argued, and Mum had been upset. Those memories scared me, and they were harder to make sense of, but it had happened.

As my mother spoke softly to my brother, giving him the comfort he didn't deserve for cheating on his wife, I wondered if Paul knew she'd cheated on him. If he knew about the things I thought I'd witnessed her letting those men do to her.

CHAPTER SEVEN

JACK

Saturday afternoons at The Yard were a chance to clean up, restock the bar, and prepare for another busy night. On paper, Freddy ran the club, and I was behind the bar.

Dad focused on our clubs and his restaurants in London, the franchise he'd set up soon after leaving the Harpyiai when Mum got pregnant with us, and The Yard was supposed to keep me happy and safe – hidden away.

Our strict admissions policy was ridiculous. We missed out on so much revenue even though we'd been running the club for years with no problems, but Dad insisted.

I thought he secretly liked to gather information on people and tuck it away in his files. It was what my father had done all his life – collect information on people he could call in favours to.

Unlike the other Marquises trained by the Harpyiai, my family had the right to use our title. My great-grandfather, the Duke of Bridlype, had been a founding member of the order, and he'd allowed the others to use one of his titles as a sign of indoctrination – as if a fancy title made any of us less of a monster.

Because the order wanted to distinguish between the genders, male members were given the title of Marquis upon graduation – pronounced '*Maa-kwhus*' – and the females got the title Marquess at birth – pronounced '*Mar-kess*'. Regardless of the minor differences in spelling and pronunciation, we were supposed to be equal in rank, but as Theo used to say, the Harpyiai protocol was so riddled with sexism that the Marquesses couldn't achieve any sense of equality.

To give the women a voice, my grandfather convinced the others to allow the eldest female to gain the title of Head Marquess. Of course, the Russians also ruined this when they allowed Juliet to become Head Marquess, despite her young age.

Five Marquises now lived outside the castle thanks to her – Dad and I, Mark, Theo and Nathan Williams – everyone who was tied up in this battle between my father and the damn Head Marquess.

My brother sat nose-deep in paperwork at one of the dark brown tables by the staircase. Cooking was my passion – Mum had been a chef, and we'd always spent time together in the kitchen – but Freddy only cared about the club and didn't want us to work in one of Dad's restaurants. Freddy enjoyed dealing with drunken customers and shifting numbers around on a spreadsheet that made no bloody difference because Dad paid for everything we needed.

As a Scottish aristocrat, my father had better connections and more money than anyone at the Harpyiai castle – than most people in Scotland. Not that I ever saw any of it. Our family funded the Harpyiai and the clubs my half-uncle, Nathan, managed under Dad's orders, but it wasn't the only thing that gave the Harpyiai power.

Exclusive clubs, like The Aurora, attracted wealthy, influential individuals. Those willing to pay large sums of money to satisfy their needs in exchange for discretion. Only, that discretion came at a further price – favours and information that Dad used to keep us hidden.

If only he would use our family's money to get these damn Russians off my back for good. Maybe then I could sleep through the night.

Before Freddy got up that morning, I'd taken a little bike ride to burn off some energy. When I came home, my brother had been pacing the kitchen, prepared to call Dad to report me as missing. My argument had been that Dad already knew I had taken my bike out. He always knew. The cameras outside my house made sure of it. And his guards, who followed me everywhere I went.

My narrowed eyes remained on Freddy as I wiped down more glasses behind the bar. No doubt aware of my stare, he still ignored me.

The deep blue feature wall behind him contrasted with the glossy black staircase. Worn wooden tables and chairs stood haphazardly throughout the vast space. Those creepy, framed fairy-tale caricatures on the walls made me shudder. He was nagging me to do a makeover before the club's anniversary the following Friday. A bulldozer would have been better, but then where would I work?

As my brother prepared numbers, I thought about when Juliet had talked to me about Dad for the first time. We had been in her chamber on the upper level of the castle. Peter, Theo's dad, had taken me to her. He was head of the Williams family branch and responsible for training the illegitimates. Used to females, he rarely knew what to do with me – or my behaviour.

My father had forbidden the trainers from leaving permanent marks on me, so Peter often handed me to other high-ranking members when he struggled to control his temper around me. That morning, he had taken his Marquis ring off to clean his hands, and the opportunity had been too good to resist.

'You are a *parshivets*!' Juliet's black silk robe swished against her bare ankles as she paced the floor in front of her four-poster bed. 'Only you would even consider stealing Marquis Peter's ring.'

'Thanks, *Gospozha*.' I watched her bare feet as she crossed the red Persian rug. It had been strange to see Juliet out of her knee-high leather boots; she almost seemed normal without the outfit she wore downstairs. That she called me a brat happened every time I saw her.

'It is no compliment. Your insubordination disappoints me. Where is the ring?'

Juliet's voice had been calm, though how she'd ordered me to kneel when Peter brought me inside left no doubt that she was displeased with me. She always was. Her trainers couldn't handle me, couldn't curb my mind to their will, and Juliet was growing frustrated with me and my resistance to train as a Marquis.

'You sound like Dad, *Gospozha*,' I said, moving my jaw around to stretch out sore muscles. 'And I don't know what ring you're talking about.'

My face still hurt from the gag Andrei had claimed was invented for people like me. Maybe it was. It was in Juliet's hand now, swinging back and forth as she considered what punishment would be appropriate for my insubordination.

Andrei Popov was the trainer in charge of the Marquises, and like the other Russians in the castle, his solution was to gag the slaves he couldn't shut up in other ways. When they put me with him, I simply asked for the gag, so I wasn't tempted to talk to him and risk his punishments. He was almost half the size of Peter, but when he smiled, even Juliet took a step back.

As always, any mention of Dad brought Juliet to a halt. The gag dropped to the floor with a thud. She picked up a glass of vodka from the wooden chest at the end of her bed and gulped down a mouthful before answering.

'Your father disappoints me as well. Your bratty behaviour is no surprise, given how he prefers his women. If only he had used his fine skills on his son rather than allowed him to become a common thief.'

I waited until I heard her swallow another mouthful. 'Can I ask a question, *Gospozha?*'

She sighed. 'Go on.'

'What happened between you and Dad?'

Though I didn't dare look, I could feel her glare. Some days she'd answer my questions about the Harpyiai under the pretence of teaching me things she believed my father had neglected to share. On other days, I might as well not have existed. When Andrei was alone with me, I wished I didn't.

'Your father took something that belonged to me.'

'Is that why you took me, *Gospozha?* To make a trade? Maybe if he knew where I—'

'You cannot look me in the eye and still want to know our story, *detka?* I think not.'

I couldn't do that. Looking Juliet in the eye was like offering bare skin to Andrei. Even I had learnt that lesson.

'Your father will not come for you. He dares not.'

'That's a lie. If he knew where—'

'He knows, *detka*,' she purred. 'He has always known where you are.'

Her words stung. I stared at the pattern in the carpet and bit back the tears. Andrei had laughed in my face a week earlier when he told me they had declared me dead. Had it been true?

'Then why am I still here? Why keep me as a slave when it's him you clearly want?'

'Because he gave you to me.'

My jaw slacked. 'I'm a human being. Not a piece of property!'

Juliet's sharp giggle rang out. 'You are an illegitimate, and you belong to the Harpyiai. Your father gave you to me to do with as I please.'

'What the hell do you want with me?' The question tumbled out no matter how foolish it was to ask.

'To train, of course.' Her voice dropped to its usual seductive bite. 'Your father breached protocol when he bred with an outsider. Since the Lawrence family branch is the cleanest, we agreed you would become a Marquis. Our child cannot be unclean, or it will be useless to me.'

'*Our* child?' I looked into her steely gaze for the first time in a year, seeking confirmation that she had said those words.

'*Da*. You are the Lawrence heir, *detka*. Too valuable to turn into prey for The Hunt.'

Dad had never told us about the Harpyiai, how it worked, or that there was a castle somewhere in Scotland where I would be taken to restore his honour. If he had, he would have warned me that he had made a deal with Juliet and the current Head Marquis, Ivan Popov, to spare my brother and mother.

But whatever arrangement he'd made, I wanted nothing to do with them.

'I will never breed with you or anyone else in this damn cult!'

Her footfalls came hard and fast against the floor; I shrank into myself. 'We are not a cult. We are a family and the most powerful order in the underworld! It is a true honour to breed with a Marquess.'

Underworld was a fitting word for the delusional reality Juliet had to be living in to imagine I would ever agree to this.

'I'm not related to you,' I spat out. 'And I never will be. I don't care what my father promised you. We will never have a child, and you're insane to think I would go anywhere near you.'

She grabbed her cane off the bed and raised it. I flung my arms up to shield myself.

Juliet tutted. 'I have told you before to control your fear. Fear is rooted in the unknown. Marquis Andrei should have taught you that irrational fears are unexplored experiences.'

I resisted the urge to glare at her. All my fears were rational, and most of them involved Andrei.

For those years I was a slave, I had learnt to face all my

fears, rational or not, but the trainers somehow pushed my limits whenever I thought there was nothing new to be afraid of.

I rubbed my temples, wishing I had no memories of Juliet and my time at the castle. She would never give up on getting that heir. All I wanted was a normal life, a relationship with someone who wasn't pursuing me because of my bloodline, wealth, or title. Not that I knew what normal actually meant.

'Jack.' Freddy's deep voice was thick with concern. 'Are you all right?'

I wiped sweat off my forehead. 'Yeah, fine. Stop worrying.'

He glanced at Tom, that arsehole Dad had hired to work alongside me in case I had another episode. Insulting. As much as I hated it, I'd never had a problem doing my job, and Tom was incompetent in every aspect except for flirting with customers and staff.

The powdered sugar on Tom's T-shirt irritated me. He always brought in doughnuts, claiming they were for everyone, even if he ate them all himself. Tom's tendency to wear only black clothes – like the jeans and T-shirt he had on that day – didn't help my feelings about him.

All-black clothes reminded me of the Marquis uniform. My leather trousers and black dress shirt were still in the wardrobe at home, packed with the rest of my kit in case I broke their rule about illegitimates, or if Juliet took Freddy and I had to get him back.

'Tom,' Freddy said. 'Do you mind grabbing another crate of cider from the back?'

Tom saluted him, put down a half-eaten doughnut, and disappeared through the door to the storeroom.

'Did you take your meds this morning?' Freddy challenged as soon as we were alone.

'Yes, Dad.'

'Don't.'

I held up my hands. 'Sorry, but you have to stop. If it makes you any happier, I'll take another Ritalin.'

'You know better than that.'

Freddy failed to realise I liked skipping my meds. My thoughts bounced around so much with my ADHD that it was easier to cope with my memories. It irritated my brother, though, and when I started drumming my fingers on the bar, his gaze fell on me again.

I smiled innocently before engaging in idle conversation with Tracey, one of our servers. I skipped from one topic to another, keeping my voice down so Freddy wouldn't overhear us.

When Tracey went to grab more bin bags, I took the steps two at a time to find something to do upstairs. I had to. My mind refused to settle. Riding that euphoria, I hummed as I swept up broken glass from the floor, whistled as I wiped down the tables and thought about Kate as I refilled the ice buckets behind the bar. I stopped to check my phone every few minutes in case she had messaged me.

'What's up with you?' Freddy's voice startled me. He was on the top step, arms folded.

'Nothing?'

'You've been humming Meatloaf songs all day.'

I laughed. 'What's wrong with that?'

He came towards me, and as always, his scowl amused me. 'What have you done?'

'Done?' I flung the dishtowel onto my shoulder. 'I did the bar downstairs, the floor, the tables, the—'

'Cut the shit, Jack.' He leaned over the bar. 'Look at me.'

Grinning, I stared into my little brother's eyes. What was going on with him? He had been acting odd for weeks now. 'Did you break up with Lily? Is that why you're riding me so hard? You can talk to me, you know.'

Dad used to put the same restrictions on Freddy's dating life until my brother met Lily when her car broke down close to The

Yard. Of course, Lily had no links to the Harpyiai, so Dad ran out of excuses for why my brother couldn't date her, but it still irritated me. The only relationship I'd had was with Larissa, but despite how vanilla she was, Dad had put his foot down as soon as he realised.

'We're fine.' He pushed back. 'Did you take something? I swear to god, if you're on—'

'Jesus fucking Christ, man.' I threw the towel in his face. 'Can't I be happy for one minute without you crawling up my arse?'

He threw it back. 'You're acting... strange. Fucked off on an eighteen-mile ride. Almost burnt down the kitchen. Messed up my car. It's not even three o'clock... Did you take your meds? Have you even slept?'

Strange? Maybe he was right. I felt different. Lighter. Determined. Buzzing. But it wasn't what he thought. Why he would suspect such a thing was an insult. I didn't even touch alcohol and never anything else. The only thing I took was the medication he shoved down my throat every day, except for that morning. He forgot to ask before we drove to the club.

I rolled my eyes, moving past him. 'You're so dramatic, mate.'

Freddy came after me downstairs, always on my tail. 'No, you're up to something.'

'Who, me?' I ducked behind the bar. 'I'm having a good day. Do I need written permission to be happy?'

He looked like he considered saying *yes*. It made me laugh. His hand moved around the outline of his phone, always tucked in his pocket, ready to call Dad. I challenged him with a raised brow. Neither of us wanted Dad to visit. It never went well.

'Lighten up, Freddy. Your face is ruining those nice pink hues you've got today.'

'Stop.'

What was the point of having synaesthesia if it couldn't be used to tease my brother?

I clapped my hands, startling him. 'I know what we should do!'

'What?'

'Add a small stage upstairs. Fuck, I should've done that years ago.'

'You didn't take your meds, did you?'

It was pointless trying to deny it; he knew me too well, so I raised my hands. 'Don't shoot. I'm unarmed.'

He handed me one. 'Nightmare?'

I shrugged. Always.

'Or is this about her?'

I couldn't hide my smile. Kate. As if on cue, my cock throbbed. Fuck's sake. She hadn't texted yet, but she would. I was sure of it. No one would walk away from chemistry like that. But it wasn't only chemistry; she intrigued me in ways no woman had before. Like she was made for someone like me, a match I had believed was as much of a fantasy as ever escaping the Harpyiai.

Sighing, Freddy massaged his temples. 'Jack, you know you can't.'

Can't?

I knew that. Can't date, can't have a relationship, can't take any risks. But I would. He simply had to realise that this would happen whether he liked it or not.

'I can date and fuck whoever I want as long as they're not an illegitimate,' I countered. 'Why else would the Harpyiai spend so much time training us if we weren't supposed to show off our skills? That's why we have so many clubs.'

'Dad's Head Marquis. Protocol also says you cannot defy his orders.'

Protocol.

Like my father, it was the bane of my existence.

No one had ever told me who had come up with the name Harpyiai, but nothing fitted the order better than the Latin word for Harpies.

We were people-snatchers.

The four founding fathers – Aleksei Stepanov, Douglas Lawrence, Stephanos Popov and John Williams – had stolen women from all over the country for decades to use as prey in the annual hunt or to keep as slaves at the castle. Then someone decided it would be good to keep our rituals a *family matter*.

Our bloodlines had to be kept pure.

Of course, like all dumb ideas, the order ran into trouble after a few generations of breeding between the families. Few of us could have *clean* children.

That was why Juliet was after me. But no matter what my father wanted, I would be the last Lawrence ever to train as a Marquis, and I would never have children.

Giving Freddy my most innocent smile, I picked up a glass and swallowed my pill. He glared at me as I washed the glass. Freddy clenched his jaw, and I suppressed a laugh.

Tom gave up on flirting with Tracey. 'What are you guys doing?'

'Ignore them,' Tracey said, rolling her eyes. 'It's a twin thing. Jack will win. He always does.'

She was right. I folded my arms, and my brother copied my move.

'Come on, mate,' I teased Freddy.

My brother said nothing. Maybe he was waiting for the Ritalin to kick in, but he would give up before that. He always did. Dad was the only one who wouldn't, and he'd left Freddy in charge of me. His mistake.

As expected, Freddy raked a hand through his hair. 'One,' he said, holding up a finger.

One date was better than no date. If Freddy thought he could stop me from seeing her again, he was the one who needed medication. There was no way I'd let her slip away. All I had to do now was get her full name.

I bowed my head. 'Meatloaf and I thank you.'

'Stop bloody singing that song. It's driving me mad. And leave my car alone. I don't know what the fuck you were trying to fix, but—'

'We should paint that wall,' I said, nudging my head. 'Red. Fuck, red is a brilliant colour.'

Sighing, Freddy went back to his table and paperwork.

'Not red?' I called after him. 'Could do green, I suppose. It's my favourite colour, you know. We could make it part of a theme. It's been far too long since we've had a theme party.'

'Oh, I love the theme parties,' Tracey said, brushing her long blonde hair over her shoulder.

'No theme parties,' Freddy grumbled. 'And no strippers. Don't think I don't know what you're planning, Jack.'

'Your brother's no fun,' Tracey whispered to me. 'You should do it, anyway.'

Maybe I would. 'You can go home now. We're all set here.'

'You're sure?' she asked, already grabbing her coat and purse from under the bar.

I shooed her. 'Quick, before Freddy finds you something to do. I'll see you later tonight.'

I wished I could go home before we opened, but Freddy was still working on the accounts. How much trouble would I get into if I played music upstairs? As if on cue, Freddy's gaze found mine.

'Don't.'

'Hey, Jack, check this out.' Tom tossed a bottle in the air and caught it just before it hit the edge. He filled up a glass over his elbow. 'Not bad, huh?'

'I bet you can't manage two at once.' Tom was always trying to impress me. It was amusing how much he wanted my approval since I couldn't stand him.

'Jack,' Freddy warned. 'Don't encourage him.'

'Learning tricks is an important part of the job.' I pulled up a tumbler, the glass squeaking under the pressure as I rubbed. 'I'm showing him the ropes, as you told me to.'

'No, you're stirring shit as usual, and this is a place of business, in case you've forgotten.'

'You should really get laid,' I bit back. 'Maybe that'd snap you out of this shitty mood.'

Freddy chuckled. 'I got laid this morning, Jack. How about you?'

Arsehole.

He knew how long it had been and the reason behind it. I would've taken her home if it wasn't for how drunk she was. Despite what Freddy thought, I learnt from my mistakes.

'Clearly, you're having the wrong kind of sex. Want some tips? Or a whip?'

'Fuck off, Jack.'

I shrugged. 'Your loss.'

Tom flicked another bottle into the air again but missed, and it crashed to the floor. I jolted. The tumbler slipped from my hand and bounced along the floor tiles. The outline of my vision crackled, and I pressed my thumbs into my eyes.

'Jack?' Freddy's chair scraped against the floor. 'You all right?'

'Fine,' I grunted.

'Migraines suck,' Tom said, clicking his tongue.

'Tom, get out.' Freddy's footfall came across the floor.

I slammed my hand against the bar, but the sting eluded me as the memory robbed me of everything. The glasses behind me rattled as my mind slipped into the past, and my heart hammered. A piercing scream echoed in my head, and my pulse spiralled out of control.

I was back at the castle.

Juliet's sharp giggle consumed me.

Shoving a shaky hand into my pocket, I tried to grasp a pill, but they avoided me. My vision tipped and turned, morphing colours into a nauseating whirlpool. Freddy's voice intruded into my space, slipping under my skin, but the words didn't register.

The memory of the pain took hold of me, wave after wave of heat scratching at my skull. It shot across my scalp as I reached for something to steady myself on, but the world tipped again. I lost my balance and fell.

CHAPTER EIGHT

JACK

'STOP BLOODY STARING AT ME.' My head was in my hands, throbbing, but Freddy's eyes still burnt my skin.

We'd been in A&E for five hours, surrounded by mechanical beeps, the stench of disinfectant and rowdy patients – five hours of Freddy's trainers slamming against the linoleum.

How he was still alive was a miracle. Another hour of this, and he'd be in the morgue – or I'd be in the psychiatric unit. A nice government-funded break from my brother had never appealed more.

Sometimes I wished I was insane. Dad would've given me better drugs that would block out all my memories rather than pills that were only a temporary plaster.

'You split your head open.' Each footfall was like a sledge-hammer to my head as Freddy stomped around. 'What were you thinking?'

Thinking? What the hell? There was no thinking involved – only memories of all those things he never had to experience.

'For the last time, I don't remember asking for your opinion – or help.'

'Dad will lose his tits if he finds out you've had another episode.'

Honestly, who cared? I sure didn't. This was all Dad's fault; if my problems bothered him, he should have thought about that fourteen years ago. His solution was to shove pills down my throat and hope the problem went away, but it didn't.

'If he finds out, you're explaining it.'

I shrugged. 'Happy to.'

Dad only spoke to me if he had to, and I'd never talked to anyone about the night of my branding. Not even Freddy knew the story behind my scars. Like Dad, I had run away from the Harpyiai, but I never left. I had the Marquis brand, and there was a ticking time bomb in my brain.

Everything would've been fine if I'd been prepared for the glass bottle to smash. Instead, it had taken me back to moments of my life that I never wanted to remember.

Freddy checked outside the curtain again for Dad's guards. 'I'm sure there's one of them out there,' he whispered.

'Of course there is. I can't even go to the post office alone.'

Freddy swallowed noisily. He'd always feared our father, but the Harpyiai had introduced me to worse sadists, like Andrei. Just thinking about the trainer made me nauseous, and miss Theo more than ever.

The first time I'd spoken to Theo Williams, Andrei had dragged me into the red drawing room at the front of the castle and barked at me to kneel next to a skinny boy my age with a mop of dark copper hair. Theo looked so much like Peter that I didn't need to ask what family he belonged to. Peter Williams was the only Marquis with a collared submissive, and their three children had the same copper hair and grey eyes.

Like other legitimate children, Theo had spent his whole life at the castle. Bred, born, and expected to live there. As an illegitimate, I wasn't allowed to talk to any of them, but following rules didn't come easy for me.

Theo was sitting cross-legged on the floor with his hands casually resting on his jeans-clad thighs. My hands were behind my head, assuming the slave position, the chill of the room raising goosebumps on my bare skin. As soon as Andrei's heavy bulk stomped up the stairs to get Juliet, Theo flashed me a crooked smile, revealing deep dimples.

'Nice to have some company in the naughty corner for a change.' Like the others at the castle, he spoke with a peculiar accent – a strange mix between Russian and Scottish. 'You come here often?' he added with a throaty chuckle.

'What did you do? I've never seen a legitimate get in trouble before.'

'I didn't address Dad as Marquis,' Theo said with a roll of his eyes. 'Stupid fucking rule.'

'He wants you to call him Marquis Peter?'

'When we're around other Marquises, yes. Isn't it fun having a high-ranking Marquis as a father?'

I snorted. The trainers put protocol over heritage. No matter their father, every child of the Harpyiai had to start at the bottom and climb up from the darkest pits of the stone castle. No one stumbled more than me. Maybe it was because I was the only one there who didn't see it as a privilege or an honour to train under the best.

How hard I'd resisted my father's wishes was clear by Theo's expression when he noticed the scabs on my bare chest. '*Blyad*. You don't bend easily, do you?'

'Haven't you heard? I'm their biggest *parshivets*.'

He chuckled. Those grey eyes swept my face, but given who his father was, it surprised me how warm and friendly his gaze was. 'I've only seen pictures of Marquis Hugh, but damn, there's no doubt you're his son. To see the Lawrence heir as a slave, though...' His lips flattened. 'Lower your arms. No one should have to sit like that all day.'

'I can't. The trainers love sneaking up on me.'

He glanced at the open door. 'I'll tell you if anyone's coming. I know Dad gets pissy about the smallest of things.' He shuddered when he spoke about his dad, and who could blame him? Peter loved nothing more than to make my life miserable. I couldn't even imagine what it was like to have him as a father.

'He's put me with Marquis Andrei again,' I said, rolling my sore shoulders. 'But at least he's not as bad as Marquis Ivan.'

The eldest male in each family was supposed to become a trainer, but protocol prohibited my father from training me – not that he'd been at the castle since before I had been born. It left me with no choice but to put up with Peter and Andrei because the Stepanov family had no males left.

The oldest of all Marquises became Head Marquis, but Arthur Williams hadn't been well since his castration over a decade ago, Dad was dishonoured because of Freddy and me, leaving Ivan Popov in charge. That damn Russian broke all slaves he was allowed near. They had taken me years before I was supposed to be handed over, a move that no doubt had left my father infuriated with Juliet and Ivan. Only days after I'd arrived at the castle, my father had threatened to pull all funding unless the Popov family picked another trainer.

'I heard Marquis Ivan's sick again,' Theo whispered. 'If he dies, things might get easier for you.'

I shook my head. Nothing would be better for me if Andrei took over the role from Ivan as head trainer, and if Ivan died, Peter would become Head Marquis, a scenario not worth thinking about, but Theo didn't comment on my dilemma. He did glance at the peeling wallpaper, though. Withholding funds from the Harpyiai was one of the few tricks my father had left, but it would take more than disarray for the order to give up on training me.

'How old are you?' Theo asked.

'Seventeen, I think.' It was hard to keep track of time in the castle. There were no calendars or clocks in the lower levels where I normally was. With so little daylight, I couldn't even be sure what time of the day it was. It was almost worth getting in trouble to see the sun streaming through the windows and kneel on something other than cold stone.

'Same as me, then. We will train together soon.'

'I don't want to become a Marquis.'

'Me neither, but it will get me out of this damn place.' He gave me a soft smile. 'I've never left the castle, but it will be the first thing I do after my branding. Dad will get pissy again but screw him. He can sit in the basement with his bugs for all I care.'

I smothered a laugh. 'He loves his bugs.'

'Loves them more than his kids, that's for sure. I swear he wishes he hadn't collared my mother, and he takes his frustration out on everyone because he can't go to any of our clubs or play with the slaves. Not you, of course,' he quickly added with a wary look. 'I meant the female slaves. Dad's not gay. Even if he were, he wouldn't dare touch Marquis Hugh's son.'

'It's never stopped Marquis Ivan,' I muttered, but when Theo blanched, I wished I'd kept my mouth shut. Not knowing what to say, I stared at the floor.

After Dad had banned Ivan from coming near me, the Russian began terrorising the clubs my father had set up with Nathan Williams. A month ago, Juliet had thrown a bottle of vodka at me when she learnt all Russian members of the order were now forbidden from entering any of our clubs. The growing conflict between the families threatened to tear the order in half, and it was clear protocol was the only thing that kept it from escalating into a war.

Though I hadn't had any contact with Dad since I was taken, Juliet often told me about his disappointment with my defiance. It was becoming increasingly difficult for him to influence any decisions made by the Harpyiai – including what happened to me at the castle. So far, he had managed to keep me out of the grand hall, the largest room at the castle where the Marquises played with the trained female slaves, but if I didn't start my training at eighteen like the others, who knew what she would do?

If she hadn't needed me, she would've been pleased with the trouble I was causing my father.

'Who are they to say you're less *clean* than us just because your mother isn't a Marquess?' Theo muttered. 'Stupid fucking rules. Everyone knows we're screwed. If we don't change protocol soon, there'll be nothing left of the order.'

'Maybe Dad should've collared Mum. If she'd become a Marquess, it would've protected us all.'

Theo's brows knitted in confusion. 'Even if a Marquis collars an outsider, their children will become illegitimates, but you know what the Lawrences are like,' he added with a roll of his eyes.

'Actually, I don't. No one told me about the Harpyiai until I woke up in a cell downstairs three years ago.'

'Oh.' He scratched his head. 'You didn't know your dad was a sadist? He's one of the most respected Marquises in the country.'

Heat crept to my cheeks, and I had to look away. 'I did know he was a Dom.' Freddy and I knew about the clubs and that our parents were in a non-monogamous D/s relationship. It was everything else he had neglected to tell me – like this damn order.

'Marquis Hugh is also far more dangerous than anyone in this damn place,' he said, his thin lips curled in amusement. 'Even Marquis Andrei is terrified of him.'

'He is?'

Theo laughed. 'Hell, yes.'

'But he's nothing like any of the sadists I've seen here. He's never hurt my brother or me, nor treated my mother like she's a... I mean, she holds all the power in their relationship.'

I cast him a wary gaze, remembering Theo's mother was a collared sub. The Harpyiai-collared subs lived in a monogamous

Master/slave relationship, and I could only imagine what it was like for Marquess Nikita to be fully under Peter's command.

'Oh,' Theo said again. He appeared puzzled by the idea of a submissive being treated as anything but a slave. 'What's your mother's name?'

'Alexandra Grant.'

'What's she like?'

I smiled. 'Dad used to say I inherited his looks, but my mother's ability to push his buttons.'

'She's a brat?'

'Oh, definitely.'

His eyes widened. 'And he doesn't mind?'

'No,' I scoffed. 'Mum's tiny, but Dad says what she lacks in size, she more than makes up for in attitude and spirit. He once told me he couldn't imagine having a submissive that didn't challenge you.'

He tipped his head back with a laugh. 'Now I see why he hasn't collared her. She'd never pass The Culling.'

'There's nothing he wouldn't do for my mother,' I said, more defensively than intended. 'Just because she's a brat, it doesn't mean she's not good enough for a Marquis. You know they only call us brats because we don't fold easily. It's not a crime to voice an opinion.'

Theo ruffled my hair. 'I meant no offence. You Lawrences are a special breed.'

I snorted.

'I don't know how he kept the Harpyiai a secret from you for so long. Learning about it like that must've been—'

'A shock? Yeah, Marquis Andrei thought it was hilarious.'

'I bet he did,' he said with a knowing chuckle. The little Russian loved nothing more than family drama and secrets. 'Well, the Lawrences have always resisted our rule about clean bloodlines. Dad says if your family didn't own the castle, they would've eradicated the lot of you generations ago.'

'The lot of us? There's three of us left, and Dad's the only full member.'

'Exactly,' he said with a smirk. 'Marquis Arthur promised your father to Marquess Juliet, but…' He paused as if listening in case someone was nearby. My gaze swept the long, darkened corridor outside the room, not seeing anyone. 'Marquis Hugh refused to breed with her. He wouldn't breed with my mother either because she's from the Popov family. The Lawrences have always refused to have anything to do with the Russians.'

'But if you're a Williams and your mother is a Popov, why isn't Marquess Juliet after you? Why go to so much trouble with me?'

'Dad and Marquess Juliet are half-siblings.'

I grimaced. 'She's your aunt?'

'Half-aunt,' he corrected with a steady gaze, as if that made all the difference. 'I can't breed with anyone from the Stepanov or Popov family, and you have no females left in yours.'

'My deepest apologies,' I said, failing to hide my sarcasm.

Theo chuckled. 'Marquises Mark and Noah Williams have the same father as Marquess Juliet, so I'm not the only one with this problem.'

It all made my head spin. But that was the point of the Harpyiai; it was supposed to be confusing. If you couldn't understand their complicated rules and intermingled family trees, you were less likely to step out of line in fear of breaching protocol.

'You don't know protocol well, do you? They've made you a slave to trick you into thinking you're powerless, but when you become a Marquis, you have to consent to the breeding ritual.'

'She has never struck me as someone who cares about consent,' I said drily.

'Doesn't matter. Protocol requires explicit consent for a breeding ritual. If she tried anything, your father could use the pear of anguish on her.' Theo's throaty laugh shook his chest. 'Nothing would please him more than to dust off that old tool.'

'What's… umm, what's the pear of anguish?'

Maybe it was foolish to ask. The basement was full of disturbing toys. Andrei often made me clean them, and took immense pleasure in telling me about the torment each instrument could cause. He'd once said that if it weren't for my father, he would've used the tongue tearer to shut me up for good.

'It looks like a closed, metallic flower,' he said, cupping his hands. 'You insert it into someone's mouth – or another orifice – and expand its petals until it… well, it tears people apart. It's the punishment we use when someone tells an outsider about the Harpyiai. It's also used for rape of a full member.'

'How…' I swallowed hard. 'How do you know these things?'

'Dad loves two things: bugs and medieval torture instruments.' He clicked his tongue. 'They shouldn't keep these things from you. Protocol makes you an illegitimate, but it doesn't mean they can do whatever they want with you. Don't trust anything the high-ranking members tell you. They love playing with people's fear.'

'My father is a high-ranking member,' I said with a deep sigh.

Theo squeezed my shoulder. 'Marquis Hugh will be back for you. If not, I'll burn this castle to the ground to get you and the other slaves out.'

'I bet trainers squeak and pop when you roast them, like your dad's cockroaches.'

Theo's wide eyes found mine. For a moment, I feared I'd gone too far, and he would tell his father, but then he snorted a croaky laugh that set me off, and by the time Juliet came downstairs, we were in even more trouble, but it didn't matter. I'd finally found a friend at the castle, someone who didn't treat me like I was worthless because my mother was an outsider, and during those last few months before our Marquis training started, Theo and I often met in the drawing room.

Fuck, I missed Theo and his laugh. Everything we went through at the castle had bonded us in ways my brother could never understand. Theo wouldn't stomp around or blame me for how my brain could blow up, but like everything else in my life, contact with him was now forbidden.

Freddy continued pacing the floor. 'I knew something was up with you today. Should've fucking known this would happen.'

'There was nothing up with me,' I muttered, rubbing my temples. 'I was having a good day and got fucked over again.'

'Good day?' His bark of a laugh was pure torture. 'No, you were fucking around with your meds again. Jack always does whatever he wants, and I have to clean up the mess.'

My fingers itched to wrap around his neck and squeeze. I'd do it – if he didn't shut up, I'd strangle him.

I was two minutes older than him. Two minutes. That was all it took for our lives to take completely different paths. The Harpyiai didn't take Freddy because of those precious minutes. He grew up in comfort and wealth, and I was now so co-dependent that I couldn't even go to the hospital without him. How could I? I didn't even exist.

That's what happened to every illegitimate the Harpyiai took. They were declared dead. Erased from society. It meant the trainers could do whatever they wanted to them at the castle. Illegitimates weren't supposed to be trained as a Marquis, so no one had restored my identity. Dad said it wasn't necessary when I had an identical twin. My father failed to realise that I was more than his heir. I was a person, goddammit, not just an asset to him and the Harpyiai.

Someone ripped the blue paper curtain back to enter our cubicle, rushing metal along the steel bar. I gripped my head. Bloody hell. Why did everyone have to make so much noise?

'Sorry for the wait, Mr Lawrence,' an achingly familiar voice said. 'I'm Kate, one of the…'

I gaped.

No fucking way.

Ropes stared at me, plump lips parted. Her long, dark brown hair sat high in a ponytail, emphasising her delectable yet deceptively innocent features. A blue uniform failed to hide those curves I hadn't been able to forget.

A nurse? Oh, fuck me.

'Well, hello there,' I drawled, finally finding my voice.

Kate visibly swallowed, her hands tightening around a plastic tray. 'Jack…'

My name on those lips was music to my fucking ears. I hadn't even considered this possibility. This almost made up for all that time spent with Andrei.

'Is something wrong, Kate?' I asked, loving how her dark eyes struggled to find somewhere to rest. 'I hope I haven't left you speechless again?'

'No, but I thought they said… and you're not…' She looked at Freddy, then at my forehead.

Shit. She knew.

Would she ask why we'd swapped names? Freddy looked worried she might. The narrowing of my eyes warned him to let me have this moment with her, however short it might be. I needed something positive in my life, and if that was time spent with a woman like her, even better.

To my surprise, she said nothing. She wasn't happy; that much was clear, and she moved to walk away. 'I'll get someone else to do your stitches. It will only be a—'

'Stay.' The deep, low tone slipped out as if I'd never stopped using it.

Kate froze. A host of emotions played on her face – fear chased by lust, then defiance – but her eyes found mine, waiting. Her struggle amused me. She was so responsive, yet had that flare of defiance it was impossible to resist.

'Please,' I added, softer.

'I'm at work, Jack,' she whispered. 'You can't—'

'Stay. I won't do anything weird.'

I was a selfish bastard, but it wasn't so bad when she looked at me. Even the edges of my vision had stopped shaking, and the pain was changing into something warm and comfortable, throbbing in just the right way.

The tip of her tongue darted out, moistening her lips. 'Says the guy covered in blood.'

'Does the sight of blood bother you?'

She scoffed but stared, transfixed, at the smear on the left side of my face, following the trail down to my white shirt. Like yesterday, she wore no bra, and the puckering of her nipples was hard to miss. Biting back a smile, I tilted my head, even more intrigued by this woman who had stumbled into my life completely by accident.

'Of course not. I don't have an issue with blood.' She rushed through the words, revealing herself further. 'I'm a nurse.'

'Yes, you are.' I bit my lip to keep my face neutral. 'It would be odd if blood affected you in any way.'

'Do you have an issue with it?'

Were we talking about the cut to my head or blood play? It had been years since I'd done edge play, but her reaction piqued my interest. Even Freddy looked at her as if he didn't understand what was happening. He still suspected it was something I'd done and glared at me.

'No,' I said to Kate, struggling to contain my smile. 'As I told you yesterday, the things I like might surprise you.' Her eyes widened in a curious mix of intrigue and shame. 'But my brother doesn't like blood,' I added, offering her a way out of this, 'so maybe you can patch me up?'

'Patch you up?' she repeated slowly as if the words meant nothing to her, and I smothered a laugh. I'd wondered when karma would reward me for all those years at the castle, and here it was, a small nurse drawn to the dark and dangerous.

I cleared my throat. 'You came to do my stitches?'

'Oh, yes, of course.' Her cheeks flushed as she snapped out of whatever dark fantasy her mind had slipped into. She flicked that ponytail out of the way and put the tray next to me. 'Sit up properly. I need to clean you up.'

'Bossy thing, aren't you?'

Her snort amused me, but she fumbled with the gloves, getting her fingers stuck. Did I make her nervous? I wanted to tell her there was no need to be nervous around me. All I wanted was to get to know her, to see what else she was hiding and if I could help her explore these things.

'So, Kate...' I turned over the hospital ID dangling from her neck. 'Caitlin, actually. Cute. Caitlin P. Howard. What does the *P* stand for?'

She ripped the badge back and tucked it inside her uniform. 'None of your business.'

Defiant Kate won the battle, it seemed. Never mind. Freddy would find out everything about her. But the shape protruded from the fabric, drawing my attention to her tits.

I sighed. 'Now you're just tempting me.'

'Jack...' My name slipped from her mouth like a plea coated as a growl, just as I wanted it.

'Sorry.' I straightened. 'I'll sit here nicely, well-behaved.'

Freddy rolled his eyes. He always expected the worst, as if I were a wild animal with no self-control. He couldn't be more wrong.

'I don't think you know what that means,' Kate countered like she had the night before.

'For you, I'll be good.' I wouldn't even question why she looked so conflicted – like she wanted to run away not just from me but from herself.

'I will clean you up, okay?' she said, bringing a sponge to my face.

'Don't mind me.' I let her get on with it, loving her obvious torment as she focused on every part of my face but my eyes.

It wasn't a deep cut, but even Freddy had freaked out from the amount of blood. All that drama faded near this woman, her hand nudging my head back or to the side. Those dark brows furrowed as she concentrated. Freddy lost interest in us and dug out his phone.

'I didn't know you were a nurse,' I said, trying to catch her gaze, but she still refused to look at me.

'You never asked what I did for a living,' she snapped.

I deserved that. Her fascination with ropes had derailed my attention.

'I'd like to know more about you.'

'I'm not very interesting.'

'No, I don't think that's true at all. You're the most intriguing person I've met for some time.' If not ever. I'd never met anyone who responded so well and seemed to struggle so much with her desires. Who had shamed her?

She didn't answer, just gripped my chin to turn my head, digging her fingers into my skin harder than necessary. The sharp jolt of pain left my face tingling. Heat spread to my toes, making them curl. Damn.

'Have you worked here long?' I asked, grasping for any kind of distraction before my body responded.

'A few years.'

'What made you want to become a nurse?'

'Stop talking.' She gripped my chin harder. 'And stop moving.'

I chuckled. 'Do you treat all your patients like this, or is it something I bring out in you?'

What else could I bring out?

A low growl played on her exhale. Defiant Kate was back.

She was a little *parshivitsa* – what a treat. Most Doms wouldn't deal with brats, but Kate reminded me of myself. I could only imagine what it would be like to take her to bed. She would no doubt fight me for control there as well, but it thrilled me how easily she responded to me, even in public.

Dad had once said that kinksters could smell it on each other, like kindred spirits, but Kate hid her desires. Maybe that was why she'd run away from me. Only when she'd been under the influence did the truth come out. I needed to fix that and show her she didn't need alcohol to lower her inhibitions.

Since leaving the castle, I hadn't touched a drop of alcohol and refused to scene with anyone under the influence. The risk of harm was too great.

'Sorry,' I said, failing to hide my smile.

'I doubt that,' she whispered, so low it was almost inaudible. It was no accident how her fingers caught in my hair when she pressed my head to the side. A jolt of pain rushed through me. Damn. I'd forgotten how much fun sadists could be.

'Do you go everywhere with your brother?' she asked.

'Why? Did you want to go somewhere alone with me?' Her glare made me chuckle. 'Sorry, I'll be nice.'

'Do you ever do as you're told?'

'No,' Freddy answered.

'Shut up,' I snapped.

'You're Freddy, right?' Kate said, smiling back at him.

She would smile at him? Arsehole. We were like bookends, so it was almost like having her smile at me. Almost, but not good enough.

Whether it was her unsteady voice or the guilty look on my face, Freddy finally caught on, glaring at me over the edge of his phone. 'That's right. How's it looking?'

'He'll live. Do I want to know what happened?'

'Probably not,' Freddy muttered.

I shot him a look. 'Just alcohol and bad decisions. The usual on a Saturday.'

'You don't smell like alcohol,' she mused.

'What do I smell like then?'

She smelt faintly of roses and disinfectant. The latter messed up her colours and made them more red than purple.

'Trouble,' she muttered, and I had to laugh.

'Aren't some things worth getting in trouble for?'

Kate ignored my question and continued scrubbing my skin. At an unguarded moment, her concentration slipped, and I caught her gaze. She had beautiful brown eyes, so dark I struggled to see the divide between her pupils and irises. Unlike yesterday, Kate didn't wear any makeup. Not that she needed any, but it intrigued me how someone could be confident enough to go without makeup and a bra yet seem so ashamed of her sexuality. She was such a mystery; too many battles took place behind those brown eyes. I wanted to dip into those deep wells and find what hid at the bottom. There was darkness in her, and untapped desires waited to be lured out. She was inexperienced, untamed, but that didn't deter me. I liked a challenge, even if I wasn't supposed to play with sadists anymore.

If she gave me a chance, I could show her there was no need for this shame she seemed to carry around.

I shifted my knee to the side, meeting the inside of her thigh, and nudged her legs apart. Her lips parted. The nurse's uniform failed to hide how her nipples hardened, and the corner of my mouth twitched.

Kate cleared her throat. 'You'll get a scar,' she said, swapping out the sponge.

'I'll add it to the list.'

'You strike me as someone more likely to have tattoos than scars.'

What was that supposed to mean? 'I don't have any tattoos.' I had a brand, but no woman had ever seen it. We weren't allowed to show it to anyone, but maybe it was time to stop hiding.

I tried to catch her gaze, but the grip on my hair tightened – another warning. Curious how far she'd let me take this already, I glanced at the curtain, checking no one was looking, then ran a finger up the back of her knee. Kate jolted. Her nails dug in further, and my cock thudded in response. Christ, the odds of finding someone like her at speed dating… only, I didn't think this one realised what she was – or what to do about it. Lucky for her, I knew more than most.

'Do you have a habit of fighting?' she asked.

She thought I had a temper problem? Hell no. Only if someone threatened my brother. Dad had taught me ju-jitsu and Krav Maga – skills that came in use at the castle and now at the club when customers had too much to drink.

'I don't fight. There are better ways to release tension.' My voice was low, drawing her attention, once again leaving her looking torn between launching herself at me and running away. 'It's an occupational hazard, I suppose,' I offered, feeling guilty about teasing her. It was my brother's fault; he never let me out to play anymore.

'What do you do for a living?'

'Curious kitten, aren't you?' I smiled. 'Freddy and I run a club in Kittington. That's why you can't smell any alcohol on me. I don't drink. I only deal with people who do.'

'Oh?' She fiddled with the sponge before putting it away to grab a syringe. 'What club?'

Blood rushed past my eardrums at the sight of the needle. I gripped her hand, shaking my head. 'I don't need that.'

No needles. Never again.

CHAPTER NINE

KATE

THE A&E wasn't my favourite place to work. There was plenty of adrenaline and never a dull moment, but each shift brought a unique challenge. Late shifts were the worst. The public seemed to lose all common sense once the sun dipped low.

I preferred the hospice. Less drama, fewer items to extract from random body cavities, and more time to bond with patients. A chance to offer genuine support rather than a plaster and a piece of paper. That was why I'd wanted to be a nurse, not to learn the best method to remove batteries from someone's rectum.

Then there was Jack, a walking, talking challenge like no other, with a weakness I'd never seen coming. How could someone like him fear needles?

I sighed. 'Jack, it's only a sharp scratch. I won't hurt you.'

I wanted to. If he didn't stop teasing me, I'd restrain him and leave him until the end of my shift.

He wanted to control me, and I wanted to control him. So far, I was losing. One look, and he got what he wanted.

Over the two years I'd worked in A&E, almost every shift had a rowdy, drunk or overly friendly patient, but no one had affected me like this. The rush when he looked at me, the blood on his face combined with his deep, smooth voice destabilised me. How I responded to him frightened me almost as much as giving in to my desires.

'Can we get this over with, Jack?' Freddy said. 'I don't want to spend all night here.'

'Shut up, Freddy,' Jack said.

Great. Family drama was just what I needed at work.

Freddy rose. 'What's the problem? You've had stitches loads of times—'

'I told you to shut up.' Jack rose, fists clenched by his side, but Freddy looked at him like they were having a normal conversation.

'Sit down.' I stepped in front of Jack. 'If you don't want the anaesthetic, I won't force it on you. But you need three, maybe four stitches, so sit down.'

Sometimes people refused anaesthetics, but I hadn't expected it from him.

'Just take the damn injection so we can get home,' Freddy snapped.

'I swear to god—'

'Sit down.' Having had enough of their sibling row, I put my hand on Jack's chest. 'Freddy, you're agitating my patient. I need you to step outside.'

'What? No, I'm not leaving.' He looked at Jack, then at me, shaking his head. 'No fucking way.'

'Freddy.' The snap in Jack's voice stole my breath. 'Leave.'

To my surprise, Freddy left the cubicle without saying a word. At least it wasn't just me Jack could bring to heel with that voice.

'Sit,' I said, pulling the curtain closed. 'I won't ask you again.'

Jack raked a hand through his hair as he sat back down. 'Do I look like I can't deal with pain? I'm sure I'm in excellent hands.'

'Yes, you are. Now behave yourself.'

'Or else…?' The seductive timbre in his voice made me sigh.

I leaned in to whisper, 'Else, I'll tell the doctor that you gave the wrong name to reception.'

Why I hadn't challenged him earlier or turned around and corrected the error was a mystery. It could cost me my job. Treating a patient you were involved with was another rule I'd never broken before. But thanks to his lie – whatever reason lay behind it – the patient in front of me was, on paper, Freddy, not Jack.

'If you want to trick me,' I said, attempting to break through this band of mystery surrounding him, 'you'll have to try harder. Only takes me a second to know which one is you.'

He grinned, amused with himself, no doubt. 'Even Dad struggles to tell us apart sometimes.'

'It's easy, Jack. Your brother doesn't radiate—'

'Sex?' he offered with a raised brow.

'Arrogance,' I countered, even though he was right. 'Lie down so I can fix your head, *Freddy*.'

Jack laughed but did as he was told. 'It's not what you think. He checked me in, and sometimes he forgets we're two different people.'

I glared at him. Honestly, how dumb did he think I was?

'No?'

'Try again.'

'You're cute when you're angry.' He shifted on the bed and sighed. 'Dad thinks my ADHD gets me into trouble, but it's other people's dumb, drunken tempers. If he thought Freddy could also get injured, he might listen and get us more door staff at the club.'

'Your dad doesn't seem to trust you.' I didn't believe a word of his explanation, but I wanted to find a loose brick in this wall he seemed to hide behind and see what he was really like.

'Story of my life.' He draped a hand over his head. His T-shirt lifted, revealing defined abs and fine white scars. The lines crossed his stomach in varying lengths and thicknesses. Self-harm? He didn't seem the type, but if it was one thing working the frontline had taught me, it was to never assume anything about anyone.

'That's not what you think, either,' he said.

'How would you know what I'm thinking?'

He smirked. 'I can read people well.'

'Oh yeah? What am I thinking?'

'You're wondering what I'm hiding.'

I shot him a look. 'Well done. Would you like a sticker?'

'Yes.' His deep laugh made it hard not to smile.

I cleared my throat, clinging to any kind of professionalism. 'Last chance for pain relief. This is going to hurt.'

'Some of the best moments of my life started with that statement.'

'I bet they did,' I said, ignoring his tease. 'Do you want a topical analgesic instead?'

Jack shook his head. 'I'm good.'

Before picking up the needle holder, I sterilised the area and drew a deep breath. I wished he wouldn't look at me, but his damn eyes found me no matter where I tried to hide. When they did, his deep blues darkened, and I never wanted to look away.

'Ready?' I whispered.

'Born ready.'

His mouth parted with a barely audible gasp when the needle bit into his skin. The air turned thick and loaded, and the heat from his body wrapped around me. I wanted to soak in it, to reach out and touch him and lose myself. My breaths became deeper, my ache for this man making my hands unsteady as I tugged on the thread and watched as the irises of his eyes shrank further.

Colour crept up his cheeks on the second stitch. Heat rushed to my core. I tried to focus on the needle and his cut, but my gaze was drawn to his crotch like a magnet to metal, to the bulge straining against the fabric.

A soft noise erupted at the back of my throat. Christ.

'I told you I could handle the pain.' The corner of his mouth tipped up.

'One more...'

God. I had to get him out of here before I went too far. Everything about him screamed hot sex, dominance and danger – a far too alluring combination that turned my mind to mush.

I stared at his wound, but each time I pressed the needle through his skin, he sucked in air, and those intense eyes locked on mine, pulled me in, held me captive and set me on fire.

He had refused the anaesthetic on purpose, hadn't he? To prove this to me, to tempt me. I shifted on my feet, fighting the need to rub my thighs together.

He noticed. Of course he did.

'The offer still stands, Kate,' he said in a tone so gruff I felt it on my skin. 'I'm at your disposal.'

'Behave yourself,' I said, reaching for the scissors.

I could get in so much trouble for this if anyone walked in. Knowing it only made it worse. It made me want to add another stitch he didn't need only to prolong the moment, but I had to get away before either of us went too far. The lie about his name was enough for one shift.

'Don't get it wet.' I turned to walk away before he could get off the bed. 'Your discharge papers will be at the desk.'

'Ropes.'

His voice came low as a whisper but with an edge as dark as thunder. It bit into the back of my neck and stole my breath. I didn't want to turn, but my body recognised his hunger and unspoken demand.

When my gaze found his, there was no longer anyone but Jack in my world. The noises from the busy room outside faded, and all I could hear was the rapid beating of my heart. All I could see were his eyes. And all I wanted was to feed his hunger – and mine.

'Caitlin, I want to see you again.'

So did I, but at the same time, not. He was ice cream, and I was a diabetic. Yet he was so hard to resist. The monster in me wanted to play with his, and I worried about how many scars it would leave us with.

He had given me the best damn kiss of my life. I could only imagine what it would be like to kiss him again, to feel those hands on me, to feel him in me, and dip into this darkness he promised. But what would it cost me if I did?

'I've left you speechless again.' A faint smile tugged at his mouth. 'Is that why you didn't call?'

I wanted to tell him I'd misplaced his card somewhere, but the words wouldn't come. All I could do was fight back silently. I didn't want to be dominated, but my body betrayed me around him, and it frustrated and scared me.

'Caitlin.' The demand in his voice made me suck in a breath. 'Let's discuss what's stopping you from calling me.'

'How… how do you do that?'

'Do what?'

'Don't play innocent with me. You know what I mean.'

His smile was so carnal that it made me unsteady on my feet. 'Innocence is not my style. Nor is it yours.'

'Cuts and bruises are more your specialities?'

'You're not scared of me, are you?' Those deep blues studied me with new fascination. It made me feel like a kitten that had wandered too close to a tiger's cage. 'Is that why I have to chase you?'

'I'm never scared.' But I was terrified. For so long, I'd toyed with a fantasy, confident I knew what I wanted and how it would be, and he'd turned everything upside down.

'Your body tells me something else.' He tapped a finger on his lips, and I'd never been so jealous of a finger. 'Something about me rattles your cage. I'm intrigued to find out what that is.'

'Why?' I tried to look away, but it was impossible. In his eyes writhed shadows of the most captivating sin and lust. The evidence already marked his body – a firm, powerful body I wanted pressed against mine more than I wanted my next breath. 'I doubt I'm the first woman you've tried to charm into bed.'

'I don't need to charm women.' He shifted off the bed. 'They run to me. Some even crawl.'

I suppressed the urge to sink to my knees as he approached. He even moved with confidence, so comfortable in his own skin it was hard not to admire how anyone could be so at ease with themselves.

'That's the most arrogant thing I've ever heard.'

'You're confusing confidence for arrogance.' He brushed the back of his fingers down my cheek, stirring the storm within me. 'Let's be honest with each other. I want you. You want me. You know what I can offer, and you want it. But something is holding you back. Tell me what it is.'

I did want him. But he was trouble. That he had such a profound effect on my body while being so bloody frustrating made it worse. I was torn between letting him do whatever he wanted to me and punishing him in ways I barely dared think about. If I did, he would know. He could read me better than he should.

Everything about him was familiar for reasons I couldn't understand, even his effect on my body. Familiar and different, forbidden and tempting – everything I knew I shouldn't want. Where the hell did I know him from?

'One date, Kate. I promise not to bite. Not even if you ask me to,' he added with a curl of his full lips.

'Why would I ask you to? I'm not into… that.'

My faux innocence only amused him. 'You can't hide from me. I knew what you were the first time I saw you, and I know you're new to the scene. If you want to explore this, what's stopping you?'

It was a good question and one I had no answer to.

Jack studied me like I was a riddle he had to solve to live

another day. 'Let's try a different approach. I want you to pick a safeword.'

'What?'

'One word – the right word – and everything ends. I won't chase you again.'

'You've never heard of *stop*? No? How about *fuck off*?'

'Easily misunderstood. A safeword will help you with this fear you claim not to have.' He dipped his head. 'Pick one.'

I blew out a breath. He said he'd rattled my cage, but it wasn't only my cage. He'd unsettled my entire world. What was I doing discussing safewords at work? Why had the rest of the world ceased to exist? Why did it not matter that he'd used his brother's name? Everything about him should have made me run far away.

'You know what a safeword is, right?'

I shot him a look. 'Yes. God, yes.'

I had done some research, as much as I had managed before becoming overwhelmed with shame. When Petra had realised what I was interested in, she'd wasted no time telling me about women being treated as slaves, pets, and forced to do degrading acts. It didn't appeal to me, yet here was Jack, clearly a Dominant, and he looked at me as if I was his next target and nothing would stop him from getting what he wanted.

'Those are terrible safewords.' He laughed softly. 'You'll be saying that a lot around me.'

'Arrogant arse.'

'Most Doms would spank you for insulting them.'

I sucked in a breath.

'But I've got a feeling you'd like that,' he said with a deep chuckle, 'so be a good girl and pick a safeword.'

'*Thunder*. Happy now?' I crossed my arms, wanting a barrier between us. People like him shouldn't be allowed to use terms like *good girl*. It was… irresistible. 'Why do I need one?'

'So you can have the control. Why did you choose *thunder*?'

'Because you… because that's what you are.'

'And you're fucking lightning, Caitlin. Together, we're a storm. Do you see why I'm chasing you?'

I shook my head even though I knew.

'One word and I'll stop,' he reminded me. 'But I won't harm you. I'm simply a guy who knows what he wants, and I want you, ropes. I want the fucking storm, even if it will ruin me. I crave the destruction, the sweet mix of pleasure and pain, and so do you. If you don't, I've given you the power to stop me.'

There was a silent challenge in his raised brow. He dared me to stop this, but I longed for the storm, craved the ruins and pain and every sin reflected in his eyes. Everything my family had told me I couldn't have.

'I don't want a one-night stand,' I blurted, 'and I'm never going to be anyone's slave or pet.'

His easy laugh came again. 'You're too damn powerful to be any of those things. And I'm too greedy to keep you for only one night.'

'I'll never agree to wear a collar like I'm your property.'

'Good. I have no interest in collaring anyone.'

'Who are you?' I whispered, feeling more confused than ever. 'What are you?'

'I'll show you if you dare take a chance,' he said, taking my hand. His touch rushed through me, but his eyes showed a surprising hint of longing. 'One date. We will talk. Nothing more.'

But what if I wanted more?

'How do I know you can offer me what I'm looking for?'

Jack stepped closer, so close there was no room for doubts. It had the intended effect as I struggled to stay upright, to stop myself from letting him prove he was worth the trouble – worth letting my darkness play with his.

'What if I could give you everything you've ever wanted?' He leaned down, his warm breath caressing my lips. 'Even the things you're afraid to ask for?'

Forgetting that I was at work, I bit my bottom lip, wishing he would kiss me. I hadn't known how starved I'd been all my life until the first time Jack kissed me. The thought of feeling his mouth on me again consumed me. But he didn't kiss me. Maybe he, too, knew we wouldn't be able to stop.

'How did you get this?' I asked, running a finger above his stitches. 'Tell me the truth. You said you'd be honest with me.'

He caught my hand and pressed a soft kiss to each fingertip. 'I was fighting old demons. How long have you been fighting yours?'

Demons? Did he mean my urges or my shame?

'I don't even know what I want anymore,' I admitted. 'What I am and where I fit in.'

'Ah. The crux of the problem at last.' He ran his thumb slowly over my bottom lip, tingling the sensitive flesh. 'I can help you with that.'

'How?'

'First, you need to lose this shame you carry around. It doesn't suit you.'

Lose it? How could I? It had been embedded in me since childhood – repainted on my skin as black tar every time my mother came near me.

'I'm… I'm not as strong as you.'

His smile exuded all the confidence I wished I had. 'Strength comes from being with someone you can trust never to harm you.'

Was he asking me to trust him?

'Isn't hurting people part of what you do in your world? You seem to have enough scars to—'

'I've hurt plenty of women in my life,' he said, gripping my chin to lift my gaze to his. With such a simple move, he controlled my entire world. All that mattered when he looked deep into my eyes was him – his voice, that gentle yet dominating tilt of my chin, and the heat of his body close to mine.

'That's why they come to me. But I've never *harmed* a woman. Come and see me at The Yard when you're ready to learn the difference.'

He kissed my cheek again and slipped out before what he had said made a shiver run down my spine.

Fuck. Did he say The Yard?

CHAPTER TEN

JACK

GIGGLING WOKE me the following Tuesday. Fucking *giggling*. I stretched out under the covers and blinked into my bedroom, the picture of the Manhattan skyline on the grey wall opposite coming into focus.

A squeal intruded from the room next door. Freddy's deep voice countered Lily's muffled whispering. Then came more giggling and, as expected, low, soft moans.

I groaned, wrenched my pillow out and pressed it over my head. It didn't drown out that noise, though. Nor did it muffle the unmistakable sound of a headboard banging against the wall.

'Fuck's sake.' I pressed my hands down on top of the pillow. 'Every bloody morning.'

It wasn't bad enough that Freddy lived with me, but he had to bring his goddamn happiness with him. Not that my brother didn't deserve to be happy, but did he have to rub it in my face every morning? I pulled the duvet over my head, rolled onto my side, and reached for my phone. Three days and still no message from Kate. Maybe she had lost my number, or maybe... I scrubbed my face.

The banging continued. Each knock against the wall and

bounce of picture frames reminded me of that simple fact: I had no chance of a normal life. Freddy and Lily should have moved past the morning sex routine. Not that I had much experience with long-term relationships, but when the moaning spiked on the other side of the wall, soon stretching into one continuous cry, I growled and head for the shower. But I still wasn't free of him and his normal life. I opened the shower door again and hurled the items across the room – shampoo, razor, and Lily's apricot body scrub – before scrubbing my skin hard enough to forget how different our lives were.

Water dripped onto the tiled floor as I stepped out of the shower. Not bothering with a towel, I opened the mirror cabinet. Like every morning, I glared at the array of pill packets before extracting one from each. Next came the inhalers, all three of them.

'I'm a walking, talking fucking pharmacy,' I muttered. 'No wonder I can't think straight anymore.'

Most of my medication was something I'd taken all my life – like for my asthma – but not the painkillers. Those were the hardest to accept. Pain had been something I craved and trained to appreciate, but now I took medication to prevent it.

'Fucking irony,' I mumbled.

Dad insisted I took Valium to curb my anxiety, but I loathed it. Valium combined with Ritalin was a balancing act to get my mood right. Too much of one, and I was all over the place – or ended up crashing. We'd been down that road too many times. Combining them with codeine had proven to be a terrible mistake.

I reluctantly took the Ritalin for my ADHD, chased it with Valium, and pocketed a handful of over-the-counter painkillers that would do nothing for the headache.

The banging had ceased when I left the bathroom. There was no moaning, and best of all, no fucking giggling. Instead, a whiff of roasted coffee hung in the air, and a murmur of voices came from downstairs. Back in my bedroom, I checked my phone – still nothing. I flopped back on the bed and stared at the cobwebs tangled around the spotlights. How many times did I have to chase this woman? Maybe Freddy was right; this was a terrible idea. It wasn't like I knew how to date, anyway, thanks to my father and his ridiculous restrictions on my life.

I was about to give up and join my brother downstairs when my phone vibrated on the bed – a withheld number. The urge to speak to Kate overpowered common sense as I answered it.

'I was wondering when you would call, ropes.'

'Good morning, Marquis Jack.' The familiar drawl of Juliet's voice made me sit up so fast that the room spun. 'Not even eight o'clock, and you want to play with ropes?'

Common sense would've been to hang up the phone before her words could do more damage, but it was no use. When Marquess Yulia Stepanova – or Juliet, as she preferred – called, hanging up was not an option because she outranked me, same as there had been no option not to go with her that night all those years ago.

My parents had rushed to the hospital with Freddy when a chest infection went from a minor cough to something more dangerous. Strolling through the house, I'd marvelled at this new freedom, finally away from my father's watchful eye, free to do whatever I wanted. I could have sneaked past the guards and roamed the streets alone or entered that room at the end of the hallway.

Curious about my parents' lifestyle and the people they sometimes had over, the playroom had intrigued me since I'd turned fourteen earlier that month. They kept the key in my father's study, and I was rushing down the corridor with it when a movement stilled me. Mum had home-schooled us, and Dad never let us leave the estate without one of his guards, so finding a stranger in our house stunned me, but Juliet had looked at me as if she had every right to be there.

Dressed in a maroon corset and short leather skirt, she had flaunted her voluptuous curves even then. Some years later, she'd told me that maroon was her favourite colour because its resemblance to blood reminded her of her best moments with my father.

Juliet's high cheekbones and full lips set under a sculpted nose hinted at her Russian ancestry, as did her narrowed steel-grey gaze that had cemented my feet to the floor. Her long blonde hair sat in a high plait, enhancing her exquisite features.

'Someone has left Jack home alone.' The seductive bite of her breathy voice derailed me from asking how she knew my name. 'Alone in the dark. You know what happens when the darkness takes over, do you not, *detka?*'

I shook my head.

'The Marquises come out.' The pointed heels of her knee-high boots clicked a steady beat against the hardwood floor as she approached. 'When the darkness coats the city, the Marquises want to play at the clubs. In the darkness, we also hunt our prey at the Harpyiai.'

Despite being taller and stronger than her, the urge to run away had seized me, but the black cane pressed against her right thigh warned me not to. Years after I got away from Juliet, the hissing sound such an instrument made when it came through the air still had the power to paralyse me.

'Do you want to hunt, *detka?*'

'Who are you?' I whispered.

'I am Marquess Yulia Stepanova, but you may call me *Gospozha* Juliet.'

My heart hammered. It was a Russian word my mother had spat across the room at my father during many heated arguments. Why this woman was in our house, dressed this way, and why she would want me to call her Mistress, eluded me. That she had called me *detka* – pet – should have told me to run away no matter what was in her hand, but my father had never taught me such a word or its meaning to the Harpyiai.

She glanced at the key to the playroom, still dangling from my sweaty palm. A knowing smirk tugged on her full lips. 'Your father does not allow you in that room, does he?'

I shook my head.

'Then let me show you.' When Juliet offered me her slim hand and her mouth tipped into a smile that sent tingles down my adolescent body, I couldn't understand why they would argue about her. She was the most beautiful woman I'd ever seen, and the darkness in her eyes stirred something in me. The allure of the secrets hidden behind that door had stolen my focus, and I'd failed to notice the syringe in her hand before the needle pierced my skin.

In the years I was with Juliet at the castle, I soon forgot about her beauty. She'd taken me as a replacement for my father – a pet she could tweak and distort into her ideal toy. When I had been trained as a Marquis, I was to provide her with a male heir to save her status as a high-ranking Marquess. Her phone call proved that it was a goal she still pursued.

'Tell me,' Juliet's voice teased in my ear. 'Who is *ropes*?'

I exhaled a silent curse. 'It's what I call Freddy, hoping he'll one day do me a favour and tie a noose.'

'Marquis Jack,' she elongated my name in what would've been a seductive whisper if not for the way the scars on my body burnt in response. 'You should not make poor jokes. You love your brother too much to lose him.'

Yes, I did. She knew all too well how important my brother was to me.

'What do you want, Juliet?' I refused to give her the satisfaction of addressing her as Marquess. Dad always said defiance was my worst trait. Juliet knew; she'd spent years trying to curb it.

'You have forgotten your manners,' she chided. 'I miss you, *detka*. You were always my favourite. My pride and joy.'

'Don't fucking call me that. I'm not your *pet*.' Pinching the bridge of my nose, I fought the impending headache. 'What do you want?'

'So hostile… It is almost hunting season, Marquis. Will you join the *okhota* this year?'

'No fucking way.'

I would never attend The Hunt or any of their rituals.

'Too busy pretending you are vanilla?' Juliet's sharp giggle taunted me. 'After all that training, I am to believe you are happy without an *igrushka*?'

I gritted my teeth. None of her *toys* could ever interest me again, and Juliet had no right sticking her Russian nose in my business. I certainly wouldn't be sticking anything in hers.

'Oh well,' she purred. 'Maybe we will see you at The Hunt after all. The Aurora cannot quite quench such a thirst, can it, *detka*?'

It intrigued me that she didn't know Dad had banned me from the clubs. 'You will never see me at The Hunt.'

'Never?' Juliet giggled. 'We will see. Is it not time for you to come home?'

Home? She didn't know the meaning of such a word. We hadn't come face to face in so long, but time wouldn't have touched Juliet. All those years I'd spent in her world had done nothing but enhance her beauty and feed her monster. If I closed my eyes, I could still smell the only home she'd provided for me – a cell in the basement.

'I'm not interested.'

Every ounce of her festering resentment was clear in her clipped tone. 'Send my best to your father then. I hope to see him soon. *Proshai, detka*.'

When the line went dead, I tried to remove the SIM card from the phone with trembling hands, hoping to sever her connection to my world again. But I stopped myself with a frustrated groan. This was the only number Kate had. Juliet had already taken almost everything from my life, but she was not taking this.

She had made a valid point, though. One that made me descend the staircase two steps at a time. Juliet had finally found me, and her claws would soon dig in. My father had turned my home into a modern fortress to keep me safe, but there was nowhere safe if the Harpyiai wanted you back. Juliet would keep a close eye on me now. If I broke one of their rules, they would summon me. I needed to know if Freddy had vetted Kate, but I froze on the bottom step, taking in the sight of my twin brother with his tongue so far down Lily's throat that I could almost taste it myself. When I coughed, they popped apart; Lily's round cheeks were pink, and Freddy's moist lips stretched into a grin. The hairs on my nape rose.

'Good morning, Jack.' Freddy took a seat at the kitchen island. He pulled Lily with him, settling her on the bar stool next to him. 'How's your head?'

'My head is great.' I went to the coffeemaker. 'Would you like me to find you a spare drawer, Lily?'

'Eh…' Her dark green eyes shifted between us. 'A drawer?'

I poured the coffee and leaned back against the worktop. Last year, Freddy had helped me refurbish the kitchen with black marble worktops and dark grey cabinets. The room at the back of my three-bed detached house was large enough to handle such a dark colour scheme, so it was a shame it couldn't be my home for much longer.

If Juliet had my phone number, she'd also have my address. I had to talk to Dad about moving Freddy somewhere safer. The thought appealed to me as much as calling Juliet back for another walk down a dark memory lane.

'Seeing as you're here every morning, the least I can do is offer you somewhere to store clothes.' I sniffed the coffee and took a sip. 'Maybe that way, when you walk around, I don't need to pretend that T-shirt is long enough to hide your clit piercing.'

That faint pinkness of her cheeks blossomed into full scarlet. 'I wasn't aware—' Lily laughed, twirling a lock of blonde hair. 'Sorry.'

I nodded. Not as sorry as I was. If Freddy had ever seen a picture of Juliet, he would've known better than to get into a relationship with someone who looked so much like her. Having Lily around the house was nothing but torture, even if she made my brother happy.

Freddy shot me a look as he reached for the morning paper. 'Grouchy this morning, are we?'

'No more than usual.'

'Who was on the phone?'

Nosy bastard. 'An old friend.'

His eyes narrowed. 'Who?'

'What are we doing about the anniversary on Friday?' I searched the cupboards for some cereal. 'Did you speak to Dad?'

Dad wanted The Yard's eighth anniversary to distract me from the clubs he'd made me *persona non grata* at. If he could have convinced me to become a Catholic priest or snap on a chastity belt, he would have done it. The mere thought of hosting another event at The Yard turned my stomach. Too much noise, too many people, too much of a fucking risk. I'd be on edge all night.

'Not yet.'

Strange. Either my father didn't know I'd been to the Inspiration club and the hospital, or he knew and didn't think it was worth an argument. He would soon be aware of my conversation with Juliet, so all I had to do was wait for his call.

The paper rustled as Freddy turned the pages, searching for the sports section. 'I thought you wanted to wiggle your way out of it?'

'Why?' Lily slung her arm around Freddy's shoulders. 'An anniversary would be a great hook for dragging more people through the door. Everyone loves that sort of thing.'

'Yes.' He glanced at me. 'We could do a free round of drinks at the bar? Get a band to play—'

'Make it a theme party!' Lily's tits bounced under their thin confinement as she jumped up in her seat. 'We can do a costume party or focus on a specific era. Maybe the eighties?'

'Everybody hates the eighties, Lily,' I said, dragging my eyes away from her chest. 'And what respectable adult wears a costume to a club?'

There were other clubs where a certain attire was welcome, even encouraged, but Dad had forced me to leave that life behind. The Marquises also dressed up during The Hunt. The memory made the neckline of my T-shirt feel too constricting, and bile crawled up my throat. I forced it down with another mouthful of coffee.

Maybe a theme party would work. The Aurora had those. I still owed Nate Williams – the Marquis responsible for running the Harpyiai's exclusive clubs and my old mentor – a thank-you for interrupting when he had.

Nate was my half-uncle and Theo's half-uncle – because nothing was simple about our families – and ran our clubs under Dad's instruction. Unlike the rules at the Harpyiai castle, there were safewords and limits at The Aurora. It was sheer dumb luck that Nate had walked past the room and realised the woman I was with had been unaware of my limits.

The sound of the cane coming through the air had sent me into a flashback so deep that I had no chance of getting out of it. The woman in the room had morphed into someone else, someone I hated more than anything, and I'd wanted to harm her.

Not hurt her.

Harm her as Juliet had harmed me.

I'd never willingly harmed a woman, but coming so close had scared me. Maybe it shouldn't have. Dad certainly didn't understand my reaction at first. Marquises were trained to harm, and my reluctance to do so always amused him. It made me useless in their annual hunt – the event every Marquis used as an excuse to show the true horror of their sadism. But after that incident, Dad forbade me from attending any of our clubs. No explanation. No leeway. He had even banned me from Theo's parties, cutting me off completely, like the true sadist he was.

'What do you think?' Freddy asked me. 'The nineties might work. I know of a good band we can hire.'

My hands felt clammy. I put the coffee mug down and wiped them on my jeans. 'Sure, whatever. I don't really care.'

'Why don't you call Dad and tell him you're done with the club?'

'So you can take over everything, you mean?' I snorted. 'Anything else you want from me? One of my kidneys?'

'Freddy could handle the club on his own.' Lily propped her elbows up on the worktop. 'You don't even want to be there.'

I had to give her that one.

'What I want is irrelevant. And stay out of this.'

Freddy untangled himself from Lily's arms to lean forward, his suspicions about my mood rising. 'We could ask Dad to come up from London so we can talk about this.'

Hell, no. Why would he even suggest that?

'What's the fucking point? It's not like I can work anywhere else.'

Freddy gave me a pointed look, warning me I needed to watch what I said around Lily. 'So take a break. Dad won't mind. We've got Tom trained to work behind the bar.'

I tried to focus on him and forget who had called me earlier, but my vision flickered and crackled like an 8mm film. I squeezed my eyes shut and pulled out one of those goddamn pills. It expanded in my mouth, and I stumbled to the sink and spat it out.

No more painkillers. I'd drink fucking herbal tea and meditate if that helped, but if I had to take just one more of them, I'd snap. For good this time.

I grasped the edge of the sink as my mind tipped into the past, and the memory of Juliet's sharp giggle and the unrelenting pain of her caning took over everything.

'You all right, mate?' Freddy asked. 'Perhaps you should lie down again. You don't look too good.'

I needed to find another way to cope with my triggers. If Juliet was after me again, she'd soon figure out how to bring me to my knees. What I needed was Theo. He'd helped me overcome my issues with whips, and he could do the same with canes. Perhaps I could contact him if Dad wasn't bothered to intervene in my life as usual.

'Maybe because you two woke me up again? Same as every bloody morning.'

Lily giggled. 'Sorry, Jack. We tried to keep it down.'

Bullshit.

Determined to keep Freddy from realising something was amiss, I sat opposite them on the kitchen island with a bowl of cereal. Lily nuzzled up to Freddy. I dipped the spoon, milk dribbling onto the worktop and down my chin as I forced myself to eat. When I was done with this charade of normality, an hour on the treadmill was what I needed. But I couldn't fool my brother. Most of the time we communicated without even speaking, and after he sent Lily upstairs, he gave me a knowing look.

'What's going on, Jack?'

'Did you vet Kate?'

'I've been thinking and—'

'Don't. You said you would do this!'

'You're all over the place,' he argued. 'Not taking your meds—'

'I can't do this anymore.' Pushing the cereal bowl away, I rose. 'I can't live like this. It's not... I don't have a life. Every day is the same old shit. Pills, work, more pills, sleep alone. If I get any sleep. I can't even date anyone because you're always fucking there.'

'I have to be. You know that,' he said, rising as well. 'Who called you? I need your phone. Where is it?'

'No, you don't. Leave my bloody phone alone.'

He came after me into the living room. 'I know this is hard for you, but—'

'Do you?' I swivelled to glare at him. Freddy recoiled. 'Do you really have any idea how hard it is? I'm banned from the clubs, banned from dating, and can't even leave the house on my own anymore. What's the point of getting out of bed in the morning?'

'Jack, what happened with Larissa wasn't your fault.'

I gaped. Why would he bring that up? 'Don't fucking talk to me about her.'

He'd been there when Larissa had left. I couldn't give her a normal life, be who she wanted, or even give her the children she craved. If I had a child with an outsider, they would become an illegitimate. Why would I want that? I hadn't even been able to explain my reasons to her.

Being a Marquis was a lonely existence, but – unlike my father – I craved a normal life more than anything. Larissa and I had met at the club and saw each other casually. Initially, she'd used me as a distraction after a nasty breakup, and I'd chased a dream of something solid that burst the moment reality caught up with me.

Would it ever be different with someone else?

My only chance of a long-term relationship was if I collared someone, but it would further tie me to the Harpyiai. I'd have to become a trainer and live at the castle, forcing me to leave my brother behind. Just to make my life even more complicated, protocol said I couldn't collar someone who wasn't a Marquess or a submissive approved by the Harpyiai – as if I would ever put anyone through their rituals.

'What happened at The Aurora wasn't your fault, either,'

Freddy continued, always knowing what wounds to press his thumb down on to reach through to me.

'Freddy,' I grated. 'Drop it.' Staring out into the front garden, I ran my hands through my hair to stop myself from throttling him for the words I suspected would follow.

He put a hand on my shoulder, startling me. 'Juliet was not your fault.'

I exhaled. Thank god he didn't say Mum wasn't my fault. I would've lost it. After Mum passed away, Dad knew I couldn't go through that again and always insisted I keep my brother close. Freddy protected me from myself, and I shielded my brother from those who wanted to use him against me. He took it as an invitation to intrude on every aspect of my life, and I let him. It distracted him from prying too much into the danger that had called me earlier.

Freddy squeezed my shoulder. 'Look, Dad won't approve, but take Caitlin out on a date. An actual date.'

'What?'

'Be normal for a while. Her vetting was clear. It's fine.' He lifted one shoulder in a shrug. 'I'll keep Dad from finding out for as long as I can, but you know I can't hide it forever.'

Why would he do this? When he glanced at me, wary, I rolled my eyes. My brother worried about what I'd do if this continued. He'd been after me for weeks because I'd stopped taking my Ritalin. Who could blame me when life was a constant roller-coaster?

'Am I that much of a nightmare to live with?'

He failed to hide a smile. 'No comment.'

I pulled him in for a hug. 'Sorry. I'll make it up to you by taking this damn anniversary party seriously. I'll get on with the restoration and book entertainment.' And take my goddamn medication. I owed it to my brother.

'No strippers,' he countered, pinning me with a stare he should've known was nothing but a challenge.

CHAPTER ELEVEN

KATE

'Wait.' Petra tucked her feet under her. She was on my sofa with a glass of white wine. 'Mr Complicated works with Tom?'

'I'm afraid so,' I said, nibbling on a nail.

She'd followed me home after work and shamelessly borrowed a pair of black leggings and an oversized T-shirt before suggesting wine and Chinese food. I had no appetite, though. It was Friday evening, and I still hadn't wrapped my head around it. Had Tom set up Jack to trick me? The question had been on my mind all week. With Paul's threat fresh in my mind, I'd been working double shifts to earn more money, but it had been hard to concentrate. I never found Jack's card, so I couldn't even text him to ask if Tom had anything to do with this.

'And he owns The Yard?'

'No, he said he ran it with his brother. I think his dad owns it.'

She twirled a lock of her hair. 'I wonder if his dad's kinky.'

'Petra, please.'

'He has to be. Why else would he own a club like that? Maybe the whole family is kinky.' She grabbed her mobile. 'I'll look them up.'

Owen was on the other side of my living room, pretending

not to eavesdrop on our conversation by shifting moving boxes into straight lines. He'd appeared at my front door a few hours earlier and brought a container-load of moving boxes he now stacked in neat rows along the back wall.

'Do you want a ruler or something?' I asked him. 'Why do you have so much stuff?'

Owen stepped back to study his work. As usual, he wore black jeans and an off-brand T-shirt, only this time it had so many wrinkles I wondered if Emily had deliberately mishandled his clothes.

'Seemed pointless to waste money on a storage unit, and this wall isn't being used for anything. Guess I had more things than I thought.'

'More gadgets than anyone would ever need, you mean?'

My little brother had an obsession – or hobby, as he called it – with everything electronic. It hadn't come as a surprise when he took up a career designing useless electronic gimmicks. His wife was probably glad to be rid of him and his stuff. Such a shame I was now stuck with him.

I grabbed my wine glass. Damn. Empty. 'And that's my sex wall you're blocking. Not that I can pin Jack against it now, anyway.'

Owen cringed. 'Katie, please. My ears are bleeding.'

'Go to your room, then.'

He pulled his phone out. 'Mum's asking for you again. She wants you to apologise about lunch.'

Hell, no.

'Not going to happen. I'll apologise when she stops hiding things from me.' I opened a fresh bottle and poured more wine.

'Tom's never mentioned Jack,' I said to Petra, 'but I guess he only started working there after we split. It makes no sense for them to be friends. Tom's the most vanilla person you could ever find, and Jack's—'

'Kinky as fuck?' Petra offered with a smirk. 'Look, I've never met him before, but it seems The Yard is more than a simple club.'

'What do you mean?'

She looked at me over her mobile. 'Remember that exclusive club in Essex that we couldn't get into? The Aurora?'

I shushed her, but it was too late. My brother perked up, always eager to hear about everything his big sister got herself involved in.

'Is that code for a dungeon?' He grinned. 'Mum will not approve of you going to a club like that, Katie.'

'There's no chance of me going anyway, since Paul got me banned.'

Petra winked at me. 'Won't be an issue anymore. They also own that club.'

'What?'

She showed me the club website on her mobile, and The Yard and The Aurora were indeed owned by the same private limited company, which also owned a chain of restaurants and other venues around the country.

'Electra Entertainment,' she said with a laugh. 'Funny name for a company running dozens of kinky clubs. Maybe it's a subtle hint. I'm telling you, Kate, the whole family is kinky.'

I passed her mobile back. 'Great. I'm probably banned from all of them.'

Owen laughed. 'Dad can't ban you from venues he's got nothing to do with. Are you sure you haven't been sleepwalking?'

Seriously? He thought I'd sleepwalk into a dungeon?

'If it's not Paul, who else would it be? They took one look at my ID and shipped me out the door like I was contagious. I'm telling you, Petra, it'll be the same with The Yard.'

Petra bit into a cold spring roll, chewing with her mouth open as she spoke. 'No, it won't. He asked you to come. Why are you still ignoring him?'

'I'm not ignoring. I'm considering.' Or drowning my inhibitions in a bottle of wine. Was there a difference?

'What's there to consider? You know what kind of club The Yard used to be. Even the police turned a blind eye. That should tell you everything you need to know about him...' She winked at me as she grabbed a prawn cracker. 'And the trouble he'd get you into.'

She was right. My mother had forbidden me from stepping foot in that place because of its reputation. For years, The Yard used to have dedicated nights of the week – munch parties – where kinksters from all over the region came together to sniff out new playmates.

A few years ago, Petra had asked if I wanted to go. As soon as Mum found out what we were planning, she threatened to send me to a convent. When I'd laughed at her, she started crying. It was the usual reaction my mother had to any mention of a club or event that could cause problems for our family's reputation.

Needing something to soak up all this wine, I also took a prawn cracker, but it seemed to expand in my mouth. 'They don't do those events anymore. If they did, Tom would never work there.'

Petra grinned at me over the rim of her wineglass. 'I've heard they still have strippers, and I bet even Tom likes those. If he's the only thing standing between you and Jack, I'll call him and ask if he's pulling your leg.'

'Don't you dare! As soon as Tom heard about Kamron and me, he told him to get a tetanus shot.'

Owen tipped his head back and laughed. I threw a sofa cushion at him.

'Leave your brother alone. Poor guy's already had to face the wrath of one woman this week.'

'I feel pretty shitty about it,' he said. His saddened face turned to her, seeking sympathy. When she smiled at him, he lit up like a goddamn Christmas tree. His behaviour around her puzzled me.

When he wasn't trying to irritate me or get me riled up about Jack, he kept looking at Petra, and the way he smiled didn't sit right with me.

Petra and I met on my first shift on placement. I had chosen emergency medicine, seeking that buzz of adrenaline, but Petra had specialised in mental health, finding it more fun to dig into people's minds than their broken bodies.

It had only taken her half an hour to make a sexual innuendo about the equipment I was sorting in a trolley, and she'd stuck with me since, always pushing me to embrace myself and stop listening to my parents. She was one of the few friends I had left after Tom dumped me. The rest took his side and hadn't spoken to me since.

'As you well deserve for cheating on your wife,' I said, and Petra nodded in agreement. 'If you'd been my husband, I'd be in prison, and people would be picking out a headstone for you.'

'I didn't cheat.' He raked a hand through his hair. 'I tried to tell you that—'

'What? When did you try to tell me that?'

'Right before you threw a hairbrush at me!'

'Ah, yes,' I said, picking at fluff on my leggings. 'One of the finest moments of my life.'

Petra giggled. 'You're such a sadist, Kate.'

'I told you there's a woman, and I…' Owen shifted on his feet, mumbling, 'She's funny, kind, smart, and hot, okay?'

I gaped. 'You broke up with your wife because some woman is hot?'

'She's more than that, but I haven't…' He sighed.

'It's still cheating. You men think with nothing but your dicks.'

'Says the nympho.'

I threw another cushion at him. 'Stop calling me that. You're no better than Mum.'

'Do you really think your mum's kinky?' Petra asked. I'd filled her in about the lunch and my new theories about my birth father. She hadn't been able to stop smiling since. 'Or maybe Paul is.'

'Petra,' Owen chided. 'That's my parents you're talking about. They're not kinky. Whatever's wrong with Kate, she must've got it from her dad.'

Wrong? What the hell?

'Sod off, Owen. Kink is not hereditary. Even you must have noticed how they reacted when I asked if he was like me.'

'Maybe he was.' Petra swirled the wine around in her glass. 'And he hurt your mother. Not all kinksters are nice, you know. Some are abusive, even dangerous, Kate.'

Jack was dangerous, but it appealed to me. How could my birth father be any worse? But maybe she was right. The man I remembered being with Mum had hurt her, only what if that was what she wanted? I rubbed my temples, annoyed I couldn't remember more than a few moments of my early childhood.

'She would've told me if that was why I couldn't see him. That's an excuse I could respect. I'm not interested in arseholes who boss women around as if they're a pet.'

'All I'm saying is that maybe you should back off a bit,' she said, picking up her phone when it rang. 'Speaking of men... Excuse me a moment while I deal with this guy.'

'Who?' I asked, but she simply waved me off.

When she stepped into the hallway and shut the door, Owen leaned against the kitchen island. 'Mum's not kinky, and you need to stop upsetting her.'

'Why do you keep staring at Petra?'

'I wasn't.'

'Bullshit.'

'Honestly, I wasn't.' But he couldn't look me in the eye anymore.

'Hold on.' I rose. 'Is Petra the one you like? My Petra? You can't be serious.'

Owen scurried around the kitchen island. Bless his heart. As if a block of plywood could save him.

'Shh! Please don't be angry. I swear—'

'I can't believe you. I've never gone after any of your mates.'

He shrugged. 'Most of them are younger than you, so…'

'Do you want me to hurt you?' I curled my fists.

He held up his hands, but humour glittered in his eyes. 'I've liked Petra for years, but I just haven't—'

'Does she know?'

'No, but maybe you could test the waters?'

'How? You whip out one of your electronic inventions, and I ask if it gets her wet?' I dropped back in my seat and grabbed my wine glass. 'You men are pissing me off. Why can't you just be normal? Uncomplicated?'

'Says the woman who discussed kink with a patient at work.' When I rose with a low growl, he grabbed a saucepan lid and held it as a shield. 'Thunder!'

'Fuck off. And stop eavesdropping.'

As my brother laughed, I briefly considered if I wanted to spend the rest of my life in a prison uniform. The bars appealed. So did the handcuffs and getting pinned to the floor by some burly man. But it was hard to ignore his point. It was also hard to forget how much I wanted to see Jack again, no matter how complicated he was, so I gulped down more wine instead of murdering my little brother.

Petra came back inside. 'Ah, good. You haven't killed him yet. Get dressed, Kate. We're going out. Owen, are you up for some strippers?'

I choked on my wine. 'What?'

'It's Friday evening. We're all single. You need to blow off steam.' She headed for my bedroom and was deep in my wardrobe before I could cross the threshold. 'I've just spoken to Tom, and he barely knows the guy.'

'What? You called him?'

Behind me, Owen made a low whistling sound. 'Careful, Petra. She bites.'

I shut the bedroom door in his face. 'What the hell did you do?'

Petra held up a little black dress, pouting. 'I told him I met one twin at speed dating, but he figured it out and said you'd only get involved with his boss to piss him off, so we'll ask Jack.'

'What?'

'The Yard's hosting one of their theme parties tonight. I think it's their anniversary... Anyway, I want to check out the strippers.'

'But—'

'Normally, you need to book ahead, but if Jack was serious about you coming to the club, your name would be on the list.'

'But—'

'No buts.' She threw the dress in my face. 'You look great in this one. It's elastic, tight and short. Skip the panties. Do him against a wall at the club while Owen and I dance and stick five-pound notes down ladies' underwear. We'll get a kebab after.'

I swallowed a groan. 'Can't believe you and this obsession with my sex life.'

'I just want you to be happy, and do you know how hard it is to get into The Yard? I've been dying to see the inside of that place for years.'

Had she forgotten that my mother would kill me if I went to that club? The tips of my ears pricked as I imagined the shame she would coat me in. Paul would give me that look again and rip up the cheque Tom wanted. Hell, he might even kick me out of this flat.

Sometimes I hoped my birth father would accept who I was. Or maybe he was as bad as Mum. I rubbed my forehead, torn between who they wanted me to be and who I was.

'We might not even get in. Who's saying he's added my name to the list?'

'I've faith in how much he wanted to fuck you.' She leaned against the wardrobe door as I pulled off my T-shirt. 'But you know what this means, right?'

'What?' I got my head stuck in the fabric.

'Tom's not over you.' Her chilled fingertips brushed across my skin as she yanked the T-shirt off.

'Hilarious. He'd love to see me locked up.'

'And you'd love to tie Jack to a bedpost.'

Maybe I wanted him to tie me to the bedpost.

'That makes no sense. He's trying to ruin me financially.'

'Have you ever actually spoken to him about this lawsuit?'

'No, why would I?' I wiggled into the dress and turned so she could zip it up. 'Paul's dealing with it. He says I'm not allowed to talk to Tom.'

'You're twenty-seven, not ten.'

I rolled my eyes. 'You know what my parents are like.'

Petra pulled me to the bathroom. 'Stop worrying about Tom, your mum, and everyone else. Let's do something about this face.'

An hour later, we shuffled down the crowded high street in Kittington town centre. Like most towns in the region, Tudor architecture dominated the narrow walkway and gave it a claustrophobic feeling. Maybe that was why I felt watched.

My shoulders crept up as I glanced around, certain someone was following us. That dark-clad man down the street? I squinted, certain he had been following us a while. Maybe it was Paul. No, this one was tall with blond hair, and had a ruthless expression that made me walk faster. Maybe he was there on Paul's orders. Hadn't I see him outside the hospital's staff entrance last week? The man slid into a side street, and I laughed at myself for being so on edge. This was ridiculous; I was a grown woman and shouldn't need permission to go to a club.

Across the road, the flashing blue 'The Yard' sign flickered. Thanks to its reputation and strict admissions policy that often saw people turned away at the door, police cars were already around the corner of the painted dark brick building. Their blue lights illuminated the side street, and four officers were dealing with a group of rowdy men.

My stepdad had tried to get The Yard shut down for years – throwing everything at them from health and safety violations to zoning issues. Nothing stuck. It rarely did if there was enough money involved. Sometimes I wondered why he put so much effort into removing this one club. Maybe there was a history between Jack's dad and Paul. My stepdad could hold a grudge better than anyone, and his career had been anything but straightforward.

He wasn't religious, but his beliefs about the sanctity of marriage and sex were so close that people referred to him as a closet homosexual disguised as a conservative Christian. Nothing riled him up more than being accused of being anything but normal. Whatever normal was.

'If Jack doesn't tie you up, you could always ask one of those nice officers,' Petra said. She'd borrowed the red dress I'd had on at the speed dating. Her heels thundered against the cobblestones as she pulled me across the mini-roundabout before a bus could mow us down.

'Mum would kill us if she knew where we're going,' I said to Owen as I glanced behind. That man was following us again. Who was he?

'Not me. I'm the young, innocent one being dragged into sin by my deviant sister.'

I rolled my eyes. Owen wasn't the one who risked everything if Mum found out. It might have been easier to follow such rules if she'd bothered to tell me why she had such a problem with this club and the whole lifestyle. Maybe I was wrong to pursue a Dominant; I enjoyed breaking the rules far too much to fit into a submissive role. The thought of being punished didn't discourage me. I wanted to laugh at myself. Maybe Mum was right; I wasn't wired like everyone else.

A woman on stilts tried to hand me a voucher for a nightclub nearby. Fishnet stockings hugged her slim thighs, and the outline of her shapely bottom teased under a black miniskirt. A glittering diamond piercing in her belly button almost stole the focus from her breasts which were overflowing a silver top. It made me feel somewhat better about my work outfit.

The black double doors to The Yard opened as a man slipped outside, and a low bass leaked out. The theme for that night was the eighties. I'd thought that sounded innocent enough until Petra showed me their social media page promising a Welcome to the Jungle experience, complete with strippers tied up in vines with nothing but leaves covering their nipples and sex.

As Petra chatted to Owen, two police officers tried to restrain a man urinating on the pavement. He broke loose, and the officers chased him down the street, his dick still on display. The look of utter mischief on his face made me laugh, and all thoughts about my mother's restrictions on my life were gone as I got caught up in the buzz of the town centre.

But in the corner of my eye, I noticed two more dark-clad men. They stood beneath a dull streetlight, making no effort to disguise themselves or hide the fact that they were watching everyone going into The Yard. Maybe they were from a rival club.

A mountain of a man at the door outside The Yard turned away a group of women dressed in skimpy outfits, much to their loud disappointment, and I drew a deep breath when we stepped up.

'It's by invitation or booking only,' he grumbled.

'She's on the list,' Petra countered with a smug smile. 'We're her plus one and a half.'

He put out a palm the size of my head and beckoned with his fingers. Flustered, I pulled my driving licence from my purse. He glanced at it, stabbed his stubby finger on a tablet, then looked at Petra and Owen and collected their IDs.

Nerves got the better of me as the man stepped back to speak into his radio, peering at us through dark eyes. What would I do if Jack hadn't added me to the list? What if I had to go inside by myself? God, what if Tom found out they had denied me entry?

Before those doubts festered, the man returned with our IDs and lifted the rope to let us pass.

'Finally,' Petra said, quick on her heels to get to the door.

I looked at my brother before drawing a deep breath and taking the step I hoped wouldn't destroy my whole life.

CHAPTER TWELVE

KATE

HEAT WRAPPED around me when we stepped inside, tailed by an onslaught of smells: perfume, alcohol, sweat, and even a whiff of fresh paint.

The last time we went to a club in town, we'd found ourselves cramped like sardines in a can, shouting at each other over the music and still unable to hear more than a word. The music at The Yard wasn't as loud, and the crowd was small enough to move freely into the large room and admire the decorations for the party.

A forest-green wall hugged a metal staircase decorated with vines and greenery. Black leather seats stood around the bar area. On the stage at the back of the room, a few women in corsets and feathered hats paraded around metal chairs entwined with vines, dancing in time to a song by Guns 'n Roses – 'Welcome to the Jungle.'

A lounge at the opposite end welcomed those who preferred a strong drink and casual observation of the stage. Dimmed spotlights dotting the ceiling cast blue shimmers on the glossy surfaces. Along with the beating bass, they gave the club a subtle yet distinctively sensual atmosphere.

It finally made sense why my mother had forbidden me from entering this building.

It was like coming home.

Petra clutched my hand so tightly that I had no choice but to follow when she stepped towards the stage. 'I've never seen a real stripper before,' she gushed.

'I can tell,' I said with a laugh. 'But I don't think they're strippers.'

She fanned herself. 'I don't care what you call them. They're gorgeous. Look at those legs and the outfits. I want a feather hat like that.'

It was hard not to admire their tantalising dance on the stage. Even my brother stared up at them with a sly smile. My stepdad would have been furious, but I couldn't care less about the consequences. When I turned my head towards the bar and Tom's gaze found mine, it was clear there were bigger hurdles to overcome.

Black had always suited him. It emphasised those pale green eyes and brought out the best of his sculpted cheekbones and distinctly square jaw. Black even did something to his short, chestnut hair. Now I wanted to burn every black shirt I owned.

'How the hell did you get inside?' he snapped at me.

'We're on the list,' Petra bit back.

'No, you're not.'

The back of my neck tingled. I looked around, but Tom grabbed my elbow and started pulling me towards the exit.

'Hey, don't manhandle me!'

Owen came after. 'You heard her. Get your hands off.'

'Stay out of this, Owen,' Tom said but lost his tight grip on me as I struggled.

'Tom,' I snapped, crossing my arms. 'I'm not here—'

A warm hand settled on my bare shoulder, setting my nerve endings on fire.

'What's going on?'

'The door staff has messed up, Jack. She's not welcome here.'

'Who says she's not?'

'You don't know what—'

'Put your hands on her again, and you'll be the one escorted off the premises.' Jack's clipped tone left no room for arguments. 'Get back to work, Tom.'

Jack circled me, and the outrage on my ex-boyfriend's face disappeared from view. As soon as Jack's blue hues reined me in, I lost focus on anyone else around us.

All I could feel was a deep tingling sensation in the pit of my stomach, like that long second on a roller coaster in London the year before, where the world seemed to stand still as the carriage hung on the edge of a steep drop.

That's what he made me feel.

Excitement.

Fear.

Then he smiled, crinkling the corners of his eyes, and god help me, I wanted to jump off that ledge and feel the terror of falling.

He wore dark grey jeans and one of the club's black T-shirts with *The Yard* embroidered in startling blue – a colour that only enhanced his irises.

'What a pleasant surprise. You look stunning, Kate, as always.' His lips feathered my cheek, and I inhaled deeply, desperate for his scent. Only, he smelt different. I couldn't put my finger on why, and he pulled away before I could figure it out, leaving me bereft of his heat and mystery.

'Are you okay? Did he hurt you?'

I shook my head. God, I needed to stop gawking at him. 'Sorry about that. We have… history.'

'He's her ex,' Petra said, leaning in.

Jack's brow shot up. Crap. Was this going to be a problem?

'Unfortunately.' Owen came up next to me. 'It didn't end well, as you can probably tell.'

'I knew there was a reason I didn't like him.' He kissed Petra's cheek and extended his hand to Owen. 'I'm Jack. Welcome to The Yard.'

'Owen.' He shook his hand with a grin. 'I'm Kate's brother.'

'You've brought backup, Caitlin?' Jack's eyes twinkled. 'I better be on my best behaviour, but if you ask *my* brother, that still means trouble. Can I get you guys a drink?'

Petra clapped her hands. 'A drink would be great.'

'I'm working upstairs tonight, but maybe you'd rather stay here?' He glanced at my brother, whose attention wandered to the dancers again.

Petra grasped Jack's arm. 'To be honest, I'm stoked to be here, but I thought you didn't have strippers anymore?'

'We don't. They are *burlesque dancers*. When my brother tracks me down, feel free to remind him of that distinction.' Mischief glinted in his eyes. 'Join me upstairs, Kate?'

'Sure.' I'd join him anywhere as long as he kept looking at me.

'One more question,' Petra said to Jack, nudging her head towards the bar. 'Tom makes little sense.'

'I don't disagree with that statement, but what are you referring to?'

'Come on. This club and Tom? I was telling Kate earlier about the events you used to host here, and Tom makes as much sense as a Catholic priest in a brothel. Why did you hire him? He's the most vanilla guy I know.'

'I didn't hire him.' Jack stepped out of her range to put his hand on my lower back, making my whole body flutter from his touch. 'There are many theories, and one is that Dad was hoping I'd turn vanilla if forced to work with it every day.'

'It didn't work?' I asked, hoping the forbidden lust in his eyes wasn't smoke from a distant past.

Jack's mouth twitched. 'No.'

Unable to hold back, I turned my head towards him and inhaled. God, how intoxicating.

'Caitlin,' he whispered in a low timbre. 'Are you smelling me?'

I blushed. 'What? Of course not.'

My poor attempt to mask what I'd been doing by leaning my head on his shoulder made Petra giggle.

'Subtle. Sorry, Jack. I gave her too much wine. She gets overly friendly when she's tipsy, like a dog who wants to sniff people's butts.'

I glared at her. That was not true.

Jack looked at her in askance but tucked me closer. 'I'm not wearing anything, so what do I smell like?'

I brought my nose to his neck. 'Fresh linens. Autumn leaves.' And sex. Rough, sheet-clenching sex. Someone should bottle his scent. I'd buy a pallet of it.

'I changed my bedding this morning. You should give that a sniff as well.'

The challenge in his raised brow sent a rush of heat to my cheeks, but I didn't dare break eye contact. Then his gaze dropped to my parted lips, and I shot back as if he'd burnt me.

It was the only thing I could think to do before my alcohol-weakened brain decided I should jump him in the middle of the crowd.

Petra giggled. 'Your brother's not single, is he, Jack?'

'No, I'm afraid not.' His hand returned to my lower back, gently guiding me towards the staircase as if he could do whatever he wanted with me. Not that I would stop him, anyway. 'Let me get you a drink.'

'Is it true you had munch parties here?' Petra asked, trailing behind us.

'That was years ago. Freddy won't let me host them anymore.'

Maybe he also had overbearing siblings. Mine was skulking after us, annoyed at Petra for paying him no attention, no doubt, but I ignored him. He and Petra would never work. They were too different.

There were no performers upstairs, only more of the same

wooden tables and clusters of people dotted around the room. This bar was smaller, but three free stools stood at the end.

'What can I get you?' Jack asked me, leaning against the bar as we took our seats. 'Wine? Cocktail? Something more?'

Before I could ask what *more* meant, Owen had caught his attention and ordered a beer. Jack lingered next to me until I waved my hand, needing a moment to decide and a chance to recover from his presence.

He had been right at the hospital; together, we were a storm. Even Petra had picked up on this strange chemistry between us and winked at me when he ducked behind the bar.

'You're taking him home?' she whispered.

'With Owen there? Unlikely.'

'Go home with him then,' she said, smug as a cat that had caught a canary. 'And tell me what his house looks like. I bet he has a playroom full of stuff you can test out.'

'I don't know. What if he...' I waved my hand, unable to find the words. Alcohol always had an annoying habit of suddenly creeping up on me, robbing me of words and common sense. I would go home with Jack if I didn't sober up soon.

Or would I?

Maybe he would reject me again.

No.

I needed the alcohol. It was the only way I could drown out my thoughts.

'If he, what? Come on, Kate. Don't be a wuss. It's not like you to back down from a challenge, and he's exactly what you've been looking for.'

I blew out a breath of air. It was hard to let go of those fears my mother had instilled in me. What if there was a good reason why she didn't want me in this place?

'But what if you were right earlier?'

'About what?'

'He's clearly a Dom. What if he's too dangerous?'

Her eyes swept over Jack, taking stock of his broad shoulders, slim waist, the sheer bulk of him and everything someone like him was capable of doing. Then she shrugged. 'No, I have a good feeling about him.'

I leaned in, lowering my voice to a bare whisper. 'I can't shake this feeling that I know him from somewhere, but it makes no sense.'

'How do you mean?'

'Come on, Petra. I've been forbidden from going near anyone in the scene my whole life. Why does it still feel like I've met him before? He looks… familiar.'

She wrapped an arm around me, giggling. 'Maybe it's fate?'

I snorted. Was it?

When Petra's and Owen's drinks were served, Jack rested his forearms against the bar in front of me. His gaze was soft but intense, sweeping my face as if trying to memorise every part. 'What do you think of the club?'

'Love it. And the strippers – sorry, dancers – are great.' I nibbled on my bottom lip, unsure whether I should tell him why I'd never been to the club. 'Why do you have such strict admissions criteria?'

'To keep out the troublemakers.' He winked at me. Like I was the danger. Like he didn't know the delicious tangle of fear and excitement he stirred in me with a single look. 'I'm surprised you've never been here before. Is that because of Tom?'

'No.'

He tilted his head. 'Are you sure?'

'Her dad's tried to shut you down,' Petra said. 'Kate's not allowed in here, so don't tell anyone.'

I smacked her arm. 'Shut up.'

'Do I know him?' Jack asked, his dark brows pulled together.

'Paul Howard is my stepdad. He's the local MP.'

'Ah.' Jack's laughter draped over me, soft and sleek like satin. 'Yeah, I know who he is, but don't worry. Your secret is safe with me, and as you can see, we don't sacrifice virgins or have anyone tied up in the rafters. It's just a club.'

'I don't really understand why he hates this place so much.'

Jack shrugged. 'Knowing Dad, it's probably more about him than The Yard. He's got a tendency to irritate people who don't do what he wants.' One side of his mouth quirked up, and I wondered how far the apple had fallen from that tree. 'We own a lot of clubs and businesses. It might not even be about The Yard.'

Not wanting to get onto the subject of the clubs I was banned from – and Petra would be sure to blurt that out as well – I quickly said, 'Your stitches are almost dissolved. It's healing well.'

'I had a great nurse taking care of me, and… crap, incoming,' he muttered, looking at someone behind me.

Freddy stopped next to me. He wore the same black jeans and club T-shirt as the other staff, but also had on a brown coat. His hair was damp, as if from light rain.

'Nice to see you, Kate.' Freddy kissed my cheek – taking me by surprise – before glaring at Jack. 'Strippers?'

Jack held up a hand. 'Burlesque dancers.'

'The difference is?'

'Strippers take their clothes off for the sexual gratification of greasy, middle-aged men. Burlesque dancers put on a show meant to entertain and incite laughter.' He raised a brow. 'Clearly, it didn't work on you. I'll add a clown next time.'

I bit back a grin as Freddy stared at his brother, shaking his head in disbelief. 'Your mind never ceases to amaze me. I told you to book entertainment, and this is what you came up with?'

'If you're not entertained by women dancing in enticing outfits, I think we should get a DNA test to check we're related.'

'Jack…'

'In my defence, burlesque dancers wear corsets. You know I have a soft spot for—'

'Stop.' Freddy pinched the bridge of his nose. 'I apologise on behalf of my brother, Kate. He's incorrigible.'

'I liked them,' I said, twirling a lock of my hair, 'and their corsets.'

'Yeah?' Jack leaned across the bar again.

'Kate's got a whole selection of outfits, don't you?' Petra said.

For god's sake. I pinched her. 'Shut up.'

'Do you really?' Jack teased. 'Tell me more. Actually, show, don't tell.'

Freddy sighed deeply. 'Clearly, I'm barking up the wrong tree here. In the wrong fucking forest,' he added before walking away.

Jack arched a brow. 'Methinks my brother doth protest too much.'

'Agreed.' My smile matched Jack's in a joined conspiracy. 'You can't deny the allure of a woman dressed provocatively yet hiding just enough to tease the imagination.'

The alcohol had made me brave – and louder than I intended. My cheeks heated in embarrassment, but Jack only winked at me.

'You'd like it in my imagination.'

'Get a room, you two,' Petra teased. 'Or at least get Kate a drink, Jack, so I can get her dancing.'

He drummed his fingers on the bar. 'What would you like?'

'Cocktail, please.' I pouted. 'Make me something colourful.'

'What colour would you like?'

I beckoned him closer, my lips brushing against his ear as I whispered, 'Whatever colour you see me as.'

Jack pulled back, frowning. But whatever confusion my words had given him, he soon masked with a smile and retreated to the array of bottles lined up along the mirrored back wall.

'I'm hating you a little right now,' Petra whispered. 'He's hot *and* funny. If you're not going home with him tonight, I will.'

Owen stared at her, and my heart sank. 'Dance with my brother, will you?'

'Why? Oh, you want to get rid of me?'

'No, but he needs cheering up after Emily.'

'Sure. To help Owen… It's nothing to do with you wanting us

to leave you two alone.' Petra winked at me. I shot her a pleading look, and thankfully, they took their drinks and headed down the staircase.

Jack pulled out different bottles, glancing at me every once in a while. His grip on the glass bottles made me irrationally jealous. I wanted those hands on me, his fingertips digging into my flesh. Every part of my body ached to be touched by him. It unsettled me how much I wanted him, and I looked around the room, desperate for a distraction.

Why had Mum made such a fuss about this club? There was nothing unusual about it except for a smaller crowd. Maybe it was about the owner. When I got home, I needed to research who Jack's dad was and figure out what he might have done to annoy Paul.

Jack pushed a glass towards me. 'Just the one drink for you tonight, Kate, so savour it.'

'You're restricting me?' I cocked my head to the side. Dark blue hues gathered at the bottom of the glass, fading into light purple at the rim. Did he see me as blue and purple? What did that mean?

'I'm off in an hour and would prefer if alcohol did not dull your senses.'

I swallowed the sweet drink awkwardly. 'Why? So you can see my colours better?'

'Something like that.' His smile was full of promises. 'Petra said Tom makes no sense working here. If you don't mind me saying so, he makes even less sense with you. How long were you with him?'

I looked around, grateful there was no one within earshot. His mention of my ex-boyfriend was like a cold shower.

'Two years, and as you can tell, he hates me – and maybe he should. I did something awful to him.' I scrubbed my forehead. 'Sorry, all that wine at home's getting to me.'

'Don't worry, unless you're a bunny boiler, I don't scare easily.'

'A boiled bunny would've been better than...' I pushed my hair behind my ear. 'I don't even know how to explain it.'

Jack said nothing at first, only guided me to a table in the corner, away from everyone else. Music and raucous laughter surrounded us, but he tilted his head to catch my wary gaze, creating a small space between the two of us, an intimate place in a chaotic world that had never felt like home to me.

'He was trying to drag you outside,' he said when I couldn't find the words, 'so I'm hoping he didn't put his hands on you like that when you were together. You can tell me if he did, and I'll deal with him.'

'Oh, no, nothing like that. I'm the one who—' I looked away.

Everything about what I'd done to Tom was wrong, yet it excited me beyond comprehension. The blood had focused my mind – clearing it of distractions and doubts and sharpening every sensation.

Swallowing another mouthful, I prayed for courage to hide my arousal from Jack.

He put my glass out of the way and took my hand. 'You don't have to tell me what happened, but if you don't mind, I have a theory.'

'A theory? About Tom and me?'

He couldn't possibly know what had happened and how it'd affected me.

'About what you are and why it didn't work out with Tom. I've made the same mistake.'

I snorted. 'I doubt that, but go on.'

'You're sure?' he challenged with a faint smile. 'I know I can be intense, so tell me if I'm overstepping.'

'Go on. Do your honesty thing,' I said, waving my hand. It was refreshing. He was so open-minded and carefree about everything that I felt like I could talk to him about anything.

'Okay. Here's how I see it: you're an untrained sexual sadist – possibly a sadomasochist. I haven't figured that out yet. Either way, combining you with someone like Tom is a recipe for disaster, so my theory is that one of you wanted to spice things up, and it went... wrong.'

Lost for words, I could only stare at him. My pulse thudded in my ears, and I might as well have sat naked before him. It would have been easier. He'd exposed my mind, and I fought between the need to cover it up again and the urge to invite him inside.

When he gave me a cheeky smile, I frowned. Why was he not disgusted by me? Everyone else was.

Rather than being horrified, he seemed amused. 'Don't look so surprised. How many times have I called you "ropes"? You've been dropping hints since the moment I met you. What hasn't been clear to me was how it took you this long to get into trouble, but given who your stepdad is—'

'He's nothing compared to my mother. My family thinks I'm deviant.'

'Do you think you are?'

'I don't know.'

He shook his head. 'There's nothing wrong with you, Caitlin. You only need to be trained. An untrained sadist can be dangerous, but Tom seems fine to me, so you can put away that guilty look.'

'I drew blood. It was an accident, but—'

Jack laughed softly. 'I thought so. You tried to dive in at the deep end with edge play when nobody taught you how to swim.'

'Edge play?'

'Did you know the French call an orgasm *la petite mort* – the little death? Sex and death. The forbidden pleasure. There are many variations of edge play. You seem drawn to blood play.' He ran his thumb over my knuckles. 'I realised that the moment I saw your reaction to me at the hospital.'

'How can you read me so well?'

'Because I haven't really taken my eyes off you since I met you,' he said in a low timbre, and winked. 'How's that for a line?'

I rolled my eyes. Better, but his original line had worked just as well. 'Have you done it before? Blood play?'

'It's easier to ask what I haven't done. I've been in the scene for a long time.'

Maybe Petra was right; the whole family was kinky. It made no sense; I had never been to any of their clubs, so how could he feel so familiar?

'I shouldn't have done that to Tom.'

'Not without consent, no.' He tutted. 'Naughty.'

'Maybe it's because I've no experience with rough sex—'

'Ropes.' He scooted his chair closer. 'There's a vast difference between rough sex and S&M. Anyone can rip your clothes off, pull your hair, order you around and throw you onto a bed.' Something flashed in his eyes, like an icy fire burning in the blue depths. That sharp, stinging need came with a vengeance. 'You're not talking about rough sex,' he continued, his voice dipping lower. 'That's not the itch you're trying to scratch – no pun intended,' he added with a chuckle.

'Is that why you gave me a safeword?'

'No, I gave you a safeword because I want you to feel safe around me. And I meant what I said: use it if you need to. I can be intense when I play, but I'm always careful.'

I frowned at the mystery of this man. His darkened eyes had a challenge, and my core tightened in response, yet he was fully in control, as calm as if this was a normal conversation.

'What are you?' It was the question I'd asked him at the hospital, and I was no closer to an answer.

'I'm a Dominant and a trained sadist.'

Trained? 'How did you train?'

Jack's smile didn't offer any explanations. He drummed his fingers on the table. 'That's a long story for another day.'

'I thought I wanted to be dominant, and I am around most people, except for you.'

'Yes, you respond well to me, although you keep fighting it.'

Did I?

He leaned in closer, his breath hot on my ear. 'Just so there is no confusion: dominance is not rough sex either. Dominance is trusting me with your most fragile vulnerabilities, knowing I won't break you because your happiness and well-being are my only focus.' Jack caught my earlobe between his teeth, tugging it. 'Trust always comes before submission, and submission comes willingly. It's not forced or coerced.'

Unable to speak anymore, I merely nodded.

'I'll earn your trust. Don't worry.' He smiled, running his fingertips over my cheek. 'And with the right training, you'll find your place and learn the difference between hurt and harm. If you play safe, there's nothing wrong with being a sexual sadist.'

'Are you always so…' I searched for the word.

'Forward? Yes. As I told you at the hospital, lose your shame. There's nothing you can say or do that'll ever shock me. Here. Drink your colours while I talk to my brother for a second.'

He kissed my cheek again and left me to stare at my glass.

Was this why he seemed so familiar? Because he was a sadist like me? Maybe I was so drawn to him because of his dominant nature. Or maybe it was the dangerous bite to his personality. It pulled me to him rather than made me run away.

Glancing at him and his brother, I clocked the differences between two people who were supposed to be identical. Jack's confident stance contrasted with Freddy's flickering gaze around the room. Jack's deep laugh rolled out as he tipped his head back, his obvious amusement only further souring his brother's expression.

No. If I'd met either of them before, I would've remembered, right?

A strange realisation hit me as I lifted my glass, raising the hairs on my back. My chest was tight, saliva pooling at the back of my throat, and I forced it down with another sip of his concoction, his vision of me. Did he want me purple and blue?

Bruised?

I suppressed a groan, and the sin, shame, and forbidden longings I'd fought against all my life. Was there truly no shame in sadism? My heart hammered, and I was afraid, not of him because he lacked control, but of myself and my slipping self-awareness. Did I want to take this step?

Jack came back and lifted my chin. 'Hey, what's the matter?'

'Take me somewhere,' I blurted, before those doubts could crush me again.

He looked around, tugged on my hand and led me into a dimly lit office at the back. A desk stood in the corner. Boxes rested along the wall. All I could think about was the drink he'd made me. My lips parted as I looked up at him, and the darkness in his eyes sent my arousal spinning out of control.

'Kate? What's—'

My mouth crashed to his. I didn't simply kiss him; I devoured his mouth and licked across the seam of his lips until they parted. His moan as our tongues met made my core throb with need.

He pushed me against the wall – his body pressed to mine like he had before, not even a week ago. I couldn't care less about the chill of the wall behind me or the busy club outside the door. Didn't care about being a good girl. I was lost in his touch, taste, and smell and how he claimed my body as his with each kiss.

He ran his hands up my thighs, and I wrapped one leg around his hip, giving him access. His deep chuckle vibrated against my skin as he nipped at my collarbone. 'Caitlin…' he teased in a way that made me want to tear his clothes off. 'All I did was make you a drink.'

'Shut up and kiss me.'

He kissed me again. I grabbed his hair and pulled his head back until he groaned, but when my other hand went to his groin, he took both my wrists in one of his hands and pressed them against the wall above me.

'Not here,' he said, kissing me again.

'Why not?'

'I'm at work.'

'So what?' I kissed him back, harder, more demanding.

'Your friend and brother are here, so is mine.'

'So what? I'm horny as fuck, and it's your fault. Fix it.'

Jack chuckled. 'I don't want a quickie up against a wall, ropes. I need more time with you.' But how his thumb brushed across my nipple said something else. So did the tip of his tongue running up my neck. And that sharp tug on my earlobe between his teeth? He was teasing me, testing my limits, taking control again. He'd locked my wrists above my head, exposed me to him, and was doing what he wanted with my body. I wanted to scream, push him, and make him lose his restraint.

'I'm heading home in half an hour,' he breathed against my neck. 'You're coming with me.'

I bucked my hips towards him. 'Fuck me here *and* at home.'

'No.'

I gasped as his mouth covered my nipple and sucked through the fabric of my dress. But as much as I hated the teasing, I loved the sharp pinch of my sensitive nipple caught between his hot mouth and the coarse fabric, and I arched into him, needing more.

'I love the way you look at me,' I whispered. 'When you're around, I feel it in every part of my body.'

'Can you feel this?' he growled, pressing his erection against my stomach. 'That's what you do to me. I'm so fucking hard it hurts.'

God, his deep voice. I could never explain how his voice affected me. It awoke something in me I never knew existed.

'I want you,' I breathed.

Jack moved to my other nipple; one sharp tug sent a rush of tremors down my body. 'When I get you home, I'll spend all night inside you, with my fingers, tongue, cock – there are so many rough and sweet things I want to do to you.'

'Rough? Tell me more.'

'I'm not tying you up, ropes. Not tonight.'

'Can I tie you up?'

He chuckled. 'No. No alcohol and bondage. Definitely no alcohol and edge play. Those are my rules.'

'Fuck your rules. Actually, fuck me. Now.'

'No.'

But how his fingertips dug into my skin told me he wanted me now. I wiggled my hands. His grip on my wrists loosened, and I grabbed his hand and pressed it against my sex.

He hissed out a breath. 'That's not fair.' His fingers slid between the slick folds of my cleft. 'How am I supposed to resist this?'

'You're not.'

I tried to undo the buttons on his jeans, but he caught my wrists and again pinned them above my head. I groaned in frustration.

'What do you want, ropes? This…' I moaned when he pushed two fingers inside me. He ground his fingertips against a spot that made me sink against him, and when his thumb found my clitoris, I lost myself to him again. 'Or my tongue against this swollen clit? Make your choice, Kate. I'm not fucking you against a wall. Not here.'

'Both. Give me both.' My head fell against the wall as his fingers drew tiny, slick circles. 'Give me everything.'

'Greedy. I won't spoil you. If I give you everything, you won't come back for more.'

But I would. Jack's mouth on mine and his hands on my body made me feel intoxicated. My eyelids slid shut as he continued the slow circles of his thumb over my clit. The bass of the music outside faded. The room filled with my short gasps and moans, and he seemed to know exactly what to do to bring me so close to orgasm that I gasped when he stilled his hand.

'Jack!'

'Look at me.' But he curved his fingers inside me, and my eyes slid closed with another moan. 'Ropes, look at me, or I will stop. I won't let you come.'

I did what he wanted. There was no other option – not when his voice commanded me to keep my eyes open. Jack differed from other men. His eyes spoke of desires I didn't know I had. When he touched me, I knew I would give him anything he wanted because, in his darkened gaze, I was vulnerable, exposed, yet safe and desired beyond words. He made me look into his eyes so he could own this pleasure, own me, and my body – and I gave it all to him willingly.

'Good girl.' Resuming his slow but steady rhythmic strokes of my clit, he released a soft groan. 'I want you to look at me when you come.'

We moved together, my hips against his hand, a raw, erotic syncopation searching for the same goal. Tremors started in my knees and rolled up my thighs. My breaths came shallow and fast.

But nobody had ever made me look into their eyes as I climaxed. I wasn't used to feeling so exposed, to being so open with anyone – wasn't used to anyone as intense as Jack. My old friends – doubt and shame – swirled around in my head. My family's disapproval and Tom's disgust left me on the edge, frustrated.

'Ropes.' The command in his voice was unmistakable. 'Clear your head.'

'I can't,' I whispered. My pulse thudded in my core, hard and fast, but my body refused to listen.

'You can, and you will.' He moved his fingers faster inside me, and my breath caught. When he pinched my clit, a sudden rush of pain mixing with pleasure sent me over the edge with a startled, cracked cry. The sensations danced together in a staggering climax. Groaning, Jack sank his teeth into my neck.

I struggled against his grip on my wrists, and he released me so I could fall against his chest.

'Good girl,' he whispered, kissing my swollen lips. 'I told you I'd take care of you.'

'God,' I breathed, struggling to stay upright.

'I told you that was a terrible safeword,' he said with a firm grasp around my elbow. 'And this is as vanilla as I'm willing to go.'

There was an unspoken challenge in his words. He was asking if I wanted to step into a new world – where pain and pleasure, dominance and submission came together in ways that would push my every limit. He was challenging me to accept him as he was – and to find out who I truly was.

I tightened my grip on him. 'I'm done with vanilla.'

'Good. Because the next time you don't do as I say, I will punish you.' He kissed me. 'And you'll love it and hate it – and beg for more.'

'Mr Arrogant is back.'

'Not arrogant. Confident.' The faint smile on his lips was a mystery – but I wanted nothing more than to see it every day to figure him out.

Determined to win back some power, I caught his hand, put the fingers he'd had inside me in my mouth, and sucked hard. Jack's eyes widened. He released a low growl.

'You're coming home with me. I'm not letting you leave until you struggle to walk.'

'Don't make promises you can't keep,' I said, taking his hand as he walked towards the door.

'I never do,' he said, and kissed my knuckles.

CHAPTER THIRTEEN

JACK

I SHOULD HAVE KNOWN she'd make me weak. Only an hour with her at work, and I'd already broken too many rules. That's what she did to me. She was both heaven and hell. But as much as I ached – fucking *ached* – to take her home, we were not leaving the club until I was happy she'd sobered up. I couldn't afford to make mistakes with her.

Something else also bothered me. She hadn't told me the complete story about what had happened with Tom. He'd done something to her, and she was trying to drown it with alcohol. I couldn't scene with her until I knew what it was.

'I need to help Freddy close up,' I said.

'But I thought we were leaving now?'

'We will leave soon.'

She slid her hand up my arm. I inhaled sharply. Fucking vixen. She'd be the death of me one day.

'Come on, Jack. You said we'd go, and I'm too horny to wait.'

I studied her face, those hooded eyes, the swollen lips I ached to kiss. Christ, Freddy always said I had impulse control issues, but even he would've been impressed with my resistance to bending Kate over the desk and... I drew a deep breath.

'Don't make me tell you twice.'

With a sigh, she nodded, her attempt to take control once again lost. It amused me enough to press a kiss to her forehead. Kate's desire to dominate me was no concern, only her poorly controlled sadism.

My choice was clear: run from her before she could harm me or teach her how to control those urges. There was no doubt she needed training.

The trouble an untrained sadist could get themselves into was nothing compared to the danger an untrained submissive could face in my world.

Nobody knew this better than I did.

A safeword wasn't enough. She was too eager to toe the line – and too tempting to walk away from again.

Noticing something, I tipped her head to the side with a smile. 'You have a faint bite mark on your neck.'

The vanilla thing would've been to apologise and help her cover it up. But I wasn't vanilla. Marking her skin made my heart race, and her blush only made it harder to hold back. I'd made this mistake before; this time, I wanted to be as honest about who I was as possible – no more pretending to be vanilla.

'Are you okay with this?' I asked, searching her eyes.

Could she handle me?

She nodded. I waited a moment longer, hoping she'd give a firmer confirmation, but she said nothing.

'Caitlin, please use your words.'

'It's fine.'

Fine? What the hell did that mean?

I folded my arms. 'We need to work on your communication skills. I'm not a mind reader.'

I could do many things with someone's mind – it was one of my favourite playgrounds – but Kate hid so much it was hard to get a read on her.

'You're so bossy.' She giggled – fucking *giggled*. Adorable. I wanted to take her over my knee.

'Right. I'm cutting you off alcohol.'

She laughed harder – until she realised I wasn't joking. 'You're serious?'

'Yes.'

'Who do you think you are? You can't tell me what to do.' Defiant Kate was back. I did love this side of her. It reminded me of the first time I'd told her I wanted to fuck her. She'd looked prepared to pounce on me. I wished she had.

'Do you want me to fuck you?' I asked.

'Yes.'

I bit back a grin. 'Well then. No alcohol for you.'

'But you made me a cocktail earlier?'

'I made you a mocktail. There was no alcohol in it.'

'Oh.' She giggled again, and I drew in a breath to control myself.

'No more alcohol around me, Kate. I don't want to harm you.'

'But I thought you made me a drink to… that you made the drink blue and purple to tell me you wanted me… bruised.'

What? Damn. I should've known better.

Few people understood synaesthesia. Even I struggled to deal with the fucked-up way my brain could paint the world in colours. Why Kate had purple and blue colours was a mystery. Maybe her scent or something else unique about her lit up my brain.

I searched for a way out of this. 'Yes, bruises, cuts, and welts turn me on, but that's not what I meant. If you're intoxicated, you might forget your safeword.'

And I was far too dangerous for her to forget.

She linked her hands behind my head again and smiled. 'It's fine, Jack. You can harm me.'

Hell, no. 'You don't want that. Hurt and harm are *not* the same.'

She frowned. 'Explain it to me.'

Jesus Christ. Who the hell raised this woman? I didn't want to think about what kind of relationships she'd had before, but if she'd settled for someone like Tom, I could only imagine how much vanilla she'd endured. Was this why she'd never got into trouble before? Years of only missionary? I shuddered.

Despite how vanilla Freddy had turned out, sex, pain, and everything in between was normal in our family, and sometimes it was easy to forget our way of life wasn't the norm.

'Look,' I said, tucking her hair behind her ear, 'hurt is temporary pain. It's for pleasure – mine or yours – and inflicted with consent. Harm is carelessness or abuse. True harm can put you in the hospital, Kate, or worse.'

The line between her dark brows deepened. Had she truly done no research before diving in at the deepest end of the pool? Was she that reckless?

'Did this pain excite you?' I asked, retracing the outline. 'Did it give you pleasure?'

She looked down, her voice barely a whisper. 'Yes.'

I tipped her chin. 'Okay, I can't ignore this anymore. What the hell did Tom do to you? I can only assume he's why you look so… ashamed.'

'What? No, it's not what you think. He's never hurt me. I was the one who hurt him, and his reaction was completely understandable. And maybe Mum's right. There's something wrong with me. It's the only explanation why—'

I sighed. 'Kate. Stop. You've nothing to be ashamed of.'

'You don't know that! What sort of person finds it arousing to cause someone pain? What normal person would get so turned on by the sounds he made, the rush I felt hurting him? Who would go crazy when the tiny trickle of blood mixed with sweat and…' She looked away.

I wanted to laugh. Did she realise who she was talking to?

'Go on.'

'There's nothing else to say. I took it too far, and he kicked me out. Do you know what it's like to walk to your sister's and have to explain why you've done something you can't even explain to yourself?'

My jaw clenched. 'He kicked you out?'

I wanted to ask in what state and why she had to walk to her sister's, but thankfully she only nodded. If she'd confirmed that Tom had left her vulnerable... I drew in a deep breath and tucked away thoughts of setting Tom on fire so I could focus on her.

'You didn't deserve that,' I said, cupping her face. 'All you need is to be with someone who can handle you. Come on. We should get back. We can talk about this later.'

'Jack, why aren't you afraid I'll harm you?'

The question hit me hard. Juliet had taught me the true meaning of harm only a few years after I'd first met her, when we were on the balcony outside her chambers.

'Do you know what today is, *parshivets*?' Juliet had asked, leaning against the railing with a bottle of vodka. The soft spring breeze moved the locks of her blonde hair, hanging loose over her shoulders. Sometimes when she looked at me, I wondered if she truly saw me or if she imagined I was someone else.

'Tuesday, *Gospozha*?' I asked, keeping my focus on anything but her. A thick forest lined the vast property, stretching for miles over undulating terrain. My first attempt to run away had shown me how unforgiving the forest floor was to bare feet. A month alone with Andrei had taught me never to try again.

Juliet gripped my chin. Her icy stare held mine for a second before I averted my gaze. '*Den okhoty*,' she whispered.

I frowned. Her painted nails bit into my skin, but I suppressed any reaction, depriving her in the only way I could. 'A hunt, *Gospozha*?'

'*Da.*'

'What are you hunting?'

'Prey,' she purred.

'Like foxes or deer, *Gospozha*?' I asked, unsure of what wildlife the forest was home to. Scotland wasn't known for fox hunting, but I couldn't think of other animals.

The Harpyiai grounds were surrounded by tall fencing, and guards were situated at every gate, making it impossible for most wildlife to enter the property, and for any wayward slaves to escape.

'No, *detka*. Not foxes.' Laughing, she patted my cheek. 'Tonight, our Marquises hunt the illegitimates.'

Her words made it hard to catch my breath. Had she finally made good of her threat to bring my brother to the castle? Hoping to hide my emotions, I focused on a spider crawling up the railing.

'Your father has told you nothing of our traditions, has he? It disappoints me. One day, you too will take part in The Hunt. The question is whether you will take part as prey or as a Marquis.'

'I don't want to be a Marquis, *Gospozha*.'

'You would rather be prey?'

'No. No, that's not what I meant!'

'Then you must become a Marquis as you should have been if your father had not broken our rules and bred with an impure woman. A Marquis should only breed with a Marquess. It is how we keep our families strong.'

I did know of this rule. It was what kept Juliet from touching me. As a Marquess, she would never risk trying to couple with me until I became a Marquis. Holding on to my status as an illegitimate was the only thing I had left.

She passed her bottle to me, nudging it when I didn't accept. 'Drink.'

'Why?' When she didn't answer, I took a small sip and shuddered from the burn at the back of my throat. It was moments like this when I hated my father for not preparing me for this world. Plying me with alcohol was one of her favourite games to play. It made me more receptive to whatever she planned to do with me.

'It is a true honour to be a Marquis.' Juliet looked out over the fields. 'When you are trained and branded, you will understand why it is a sin to couple with an illegitimate. It is dishonourable even for a Marquess.'

I suppressed a snort. There was nothing honourable about any of them.

I swigged another mouthful of vodka to still my racing heart as she stared into the distance. Juliet's silence frightened me most of all.

The Harpyiai castle and its vast grounds spoke of wealth and history. Dark, depraved history, but still a history Juliet loved sharing. Only months before, she had given me a tour and claimed that Marquis Pierre built the castle in 1768, and it passed to Aleksei Stepanov and Douglas Lawrence after the French nobleman ran into financial difficulties.

Our great-grandfathers brought wealth and tyranny to the remote Scottish estate and soon made friends in the worst circles. She took great pride in informing me that most of the rituals came from John Williams and Stephanos Popov, but that none of it would've been possible without my family's money – as if knowing my great-grandfather was a founding member would somehow make me more obedient.

Of course, it was all lies.

Theo had told me the truth about how the castle and its grounds had been in my family for centuries, but Juliet never liked to acknowledge how heavily the Harpyiai depended on us. The other three families would never survive without our wealth, but she had even tried to claim it was because of her my grandfather hadn't inherited the dukedom.

Juliet nudged the bottle, encouraging me to take another sip. 'We are hunters. Your father was, his father before him, and soon you will be. I know you believe Marquis Andrei's methods to be cruel, but my trainers are preparing you for The Hunt.'

After two years at the castle, I had no problem imagining what would happen if they captured the slaves. If Andrei chased you, your best option was to drop to the ground and pray.

'Do you not understand how lucky you are?' she continued. 'You are the only male illegitimate ever given the opportunity to change your status.'

'It's not an opportunity. Dad sacrificed me to save my brother.' And my mother, but I didn't dare mention her around Juliet anymore. It brought out the worst of her sadism.

'*Da.* This was decided long before you were born, so why do you keep resisting?'

I swallowed another mouthful, hoping she didn't notice the tremble in my hand.

Juliet's problem was that I didn't want to train so she could breed with me. My problem was that if I didn't, I'd remain a slave for the rest of my life. My only consolation was that I was too valuable to risk putting in The Hunt as prey.

'Would you not like to be free?' Those steel-grey eyes scanned my face as if my skin revealed secrets she hadn't been able to uncover.

'Yes.'

'Free from fear?'

'Free from you would be nice.'

A faint smile touched her lips. 'How fear and my name are synonymous in your mind pleases me.'

'It is no compliment,' I said, mimicking her Russian accent.

She slapped me. I clenched my jaw, refusing to give her a reaction as she glared. 'Do you know what your problem is, *parshivets?*'

'Yes.' It was an honest answer. *She* was my problem. Her obsession with my father and his refusal to breed with her had set her on this quest to take me instead. 'I also know what your problem is, *Gospozha*.'

Her slim brow lifted in amusement. 'Humour me.'

I swallowed another mouthful, letting the alcohol loosen my tongue as she had intended.

'You can't kill me.'

If she did, she would never get her hands on my family's wealth and power. Killing me would start a war between the families, and ultimately destroy the Harpyiai.

It was always hard to read Juliet, but the smile that flashed across her face made my heartbeat pick up. All that time with Andrei should've taught me to keep my mouth shut, and I wished I had when she reached into the pocket of her robe.

'I do not need to kill you, *detka*.' The syringe she pulled out made it impossible to draw another breath. 'I have other ways of getting what I want.'

The bottle slipped from my hand and smashed on the concrete.

The syringes Juliet used to subdue me came from Peter. Depending on his mood, the concoction could either make your skin feel on fire or leave you paralysed for hours, completely at Andrei's mercy.

Every nerve ending in my body had screamed at the slightest touch for the rest of that day. Andrei had soon come to collect me, and the last section of that memory was gone from my mind. Only fragments of it came back upon the sound of glass smashing.

My body remembered the pain, even if my mind tried to hide it from me.

Kate's hand on my cheek startled me. Her touch pulled me back, and I had never been more grateful to have left the Harpyiai than when I looked into her deep brown eyes.

'What's wrong?' she asked.

'Nothing.' I tugged her close, burying my nose in her hair to escape the emotions those memories always stirred. 'Nothing at all is wrong.'

'Your heart's racing. What were you thinking about?' Her soft voice was edged with concern.

'Nothing.'

'Jack...'

Shushing her, I slid my hands down her back and settled them on her hips, digging my fingers into the skin. With a deep exhale, I tried to shift my focus before the headache bit. As if knowing what I needed, she brought her mouth to mine but didn't kiss me, just ran her tongue along my lower lip and then took it between her teeth, biting down. The pain made heat rush through my body.

I kissed her and didn't stop until memories of the past and concerns about the future faded. How hard I'd gripped her didn't register until she moaned and leaned against me. 'Hold that thought,' I said, smiling from the disappointment on her face. 'First, we need to sober you up.'

'You're such an oxymoron, Jack.' Kate took my hand as we walked back into the club. The crowd had thinned out, yet not even Freddy's scowl was in sight. 'A bartender who disapproves of people drinking. Isn't that against the rules?'

'There are only two rules in my world: don't drink and fuck, and don't fucking touch what's mine to fuck.' I winked at her and led her to a seat at the bar.

Kate giggled. 'That's a lot of fucks in one sentence.'

I brought her a cup of coffee and a tall glass of water. 'Sober up. I need this part of you to stay with me at all times,' I added, touching her temple.

With a wicked sparkle in her eyes, she grabbed her mug. 'Yes, sir.'

A low growl escaped me. I'd make her mine – one way or another. But as I rose and saw the concern on Freddy's face across the room, goosebumps rushed over my skin. My brother always worried I would get too attached.

Someone else also caught my attention. Tom was stacking empty glasses on a tray, exchanging a few words with Petra and Owen before disappearing downstairs. How I'd remained calm while confronting Tom earlier was a fucking miracle. He needed to be put in his place.

But my plan fell through when Freddy pulled me to a halt at the bottom of the staircase.

'Jack,' he whispered in my ear. 'Care to explain where you and Kate disappeared to?'

I wanted to laugh, but it wasn't funny. He'd promised to let me have her, and now he was butting in again. I hadn't planned on doing anything with her at the club, but she'd ambushed me.

Now behind the bar, Tom had the decency to look wary about my glare. I took two seconds to mentally strangle him before answering Freddy.

'Kick my arse about it later. I need a word with Tom.'

'Stay away from Tom,' he warned. 'Tracey filled me in on what happened earlier. The last thing we need is to draw Dad's attention to the club.'

'You're not seriously asking me to let this go?'

'He's her ex. Let them sort it out between themselves.'

'He had his fucking hands on her.'

Freddy folded his arms and stared at Tom. I copied his move. Tom did everything he could to avoid looking at us. Bloody cockroach. I couldn't wait to crush him.

'It's not like you to be jealous.'

'I'm not fucking jealous.' Was I? Territorial, maybe. I wanted her. I wanted to dip him in acid. Why Freddy had a problem with either of those was beyond me.

'You're worried he'll say something to her?'

'I didn't consider that, but yeah, another reason he needs to go.' Tom knew too much about my family and me. If he was vindictive, he could unravel everything before I regained control of my life.

'Forget about him and take her home, Jack.'

'No, she needs to sober up before we leave.'

Freddy rolled his eyes. 'Fine, but let me deal with him.'

'I want him out of here. Dig through your stuff and find some shit that will stick if he won't go willingly.'

Freddy had learnt long ago to keep records on people in our lives. Little secrets. Things that could keep lips sealed. Shortcuts to help the club, and damage control when things got out of control.

Sometimes I wondered if he had a file on me as well. It was probably best not to think about it and just be grateful he was my brother.

'It's not that easy. Dad would ask questions if we fired someone who hasn't had a single warning.'

Nothing? Oh, I could find something to stick on his record, if that's what it took.

'Jack, don't,' my brother said, always the mind reader. 'Tom's only here because Dad needs him on our side. If you fire him, he won't be happy.'

We wouldn't want that. When Dad was unhappy with us, he came to visit.

'Needs him for what?'

I rarely paid attention to Freddy when he talked about Dad's business. Last I'd heard, he wanted to take over a chain of restaurants in Surrey, but what that had to do with Tom was hard to grasp.

'Dad said Tom's here because of his father's connections in the government. He needs him to expedite his recent expansion. I told you this?'

'You know I tune you out when you start speaking gibberish.'

Freddy glared. 'Thanks.'

'Welcome.' I beamed. 'Freddy,' I said as he moved to walk

away. A week earlier, I'd reached rock bottom, and once again, my brother was the one who pulled me out of it – despite the risk we both faced.

He smiled. 'Hey, you saved me from drowning once, remember? Just don't fuck this up. What do you want to do about Tom?'

'Give me five minutes alone with him and—'

'No.'

The unspoken threat in his stare stopped me. He could still change his mind about Dad. Even my brother could be pushed too far.

'Then make it clear he'll regret it if he comes near her again.' I put my hand out. 'Give me your car keys.'

'Use your own car.'

I wiggled my fingers. The guards knew Freddy was the one who always drove the Audi. They would stay behind, mistaking Freddy for me, and Dad would never find out that I'd taken a woman home.

With a sigh, Freddy passed the keys. 'You did well with the renovation.'

Praise from my brother? Maybe he was coming down with a cold.

'Disappear for the weekend, will you? Stay at Lily's. I don't want you too far away, but park my car down the street. Take the side alley.'

His hand on my arm stopped me from leaving. 'If Dad finds out we've tricked the guards again—'

'Then don't go anywhere,' I said, staring him down until he looked away.

CHAPTER FOURTEEN

KATE

JACK'S HAND rested on my lower back as we walked to his front door, spreading heat and excitement through my body.

Before we'd left the club, Petra had stilled any doubts about going home with him, assuming that I would share every detail with her the next day, but I was still nervous.

He'd said he lived in a small house on the outskirts of Kittington, but when he pulled up in front of a gate and keyed in a code, it was clear this was no ordinary residence.

A staggeringly tall fence surrounded the large brown-brick property, and red lights of cameras blinked at me from several locations. The property was tranquil, welcoming and charming, yet I couldn't help but wonder why a house in such a remote location needed so many security features. On the front step, I studied the neatly trimmed shrubs and potted plants draped in the orange glow of the outside lamp as Jack fished out his keys.

He lifted my chin, bringing my attention back to him. 'There's no need to be worried, ropes. Like the club, it's only a house, but if you want to go home—'

Before those doubts could fester in my mind, I tugged him to me and pressed my mouth to his, letting my tongue run ever so gently over his bottom lip. His body tensed, and like at the club, he froze for a moment as if processing something. Waiting for him to catch up, I trapped his lower lip and nipped it.

He only allowed me that small moment of control before his hands were around my face, tilting my head to an angle where he took what he wanted. His kiss was passionate and demanding, and a low groan vibrated deep in his throat.

How did he exercise so much control over everything? I tried to regain power by sliding my hands up his chest, but he grabbed my wrists and pinned my hands behind my back. Leaning into me, he teased my lips open before plunging in, swirling his tongue against mine until I was breathless and dazed when he pulled back.

He flashed a smile as he pushed the door open. 'Ladies first.'

'That's not fair, Jack. You can't just kiss me like that and—'

'Fair?' He laughed softly. 'Do you realise how hard it is for me to go slow?'

'So don't.' I linked my hands around his neck. 'You've flushed the alcohol from my body. Time to keep your promise.'

'What promise was that?'

The timbre in his voice suggested he knew and would have no problem keeping it. There was no doubt he would when he hoisted me off my feet and kissed me. I wrapped my legs around his waist as he gripped my backside in a possessive manner and manoeuvred us backwards inside.

White walls, an archway to a kitchen, and a few pictures on the walls briefly registered as he carried me up the stairs and into a bedroom.

It was nicely decorated with dark hardwood floors, a large sleigh bed, built-in wardrobes, and everything in shades of blue and cream. Curtains hung heavy from the bay window, and moonlight soaked the room.

I tore at his clothes, trying to lift his T-shirt over his head, desperate to feel him against me, but he pushed me against a wall and held my hands above my head.

'So impatient.' Jack pressed slow, gentle kisses against my neck in contrast to the tight grip on my wrists. 'I want to take my time with you. Feel, smell, taste all of you.'

I loved the way he was rough and gentle. I craved that feeling but also wanted to show him he was wrong. He wasn't more dominant than me.

I wiggled my fingers until he released my hands, and grabbed the hem of his T-shirt. 'Arms up, Jack. I want you naked. Now, or else…'

'We're not playing tonight, ropes.' His wet tongue dragged along the shell of my ear. 'Tonight, I will only fuck you. Hard, rough, soft, in all the ways you want me, but only fuck.'

'Why can't we play?' I ran my hands over his chest and shoulders, feeling the muscles coiled beneath. So much goddamn muscle. It would be a thrill to control something more powerful than me. 'You made me sit at the club and drink bloody coffee for an hour.'

'You'll have to settle for rough sex.'

I grabbed his hair and forced his head back. 'You know what I want.' Our open mouths almost touched, his laboured breathing matching mine. 'You know what I crave.'

'I do. Let's see if you can make it through one night with me first.'

The playful threat teased, but he put me down and sat on the edge of the bed. 'But you have my full attention. If you want to take control…' He waved his hand.

Jack was the type of man who demanded attention without ever having to ask for it. I wanted nothing more than his attention on me like this, to focus on me as I put one foot in front of the other with slow, determined sways of my hips.

He rewarded me with an alluring smile. His hands went to my hips and tugged me to him. 'The things you do to me when you look at me like that. I've never wanted a woman this badly before.'

I turned around and brushed my hair to the side. 'Unzip me.'

'In a minute.' His fingertips travelled up my bare thighs and pushed the fabric of my dress over my hips, exposing me to him. 'I'll definitely need more than one night with this body,' he said, humming his approval.

'Unzip me, Jack.'

'Shh.' He ran his hands up the back of my thighs like he had the right to touch any part of me he wanted. 'Such an impatient sub. We need to work on that.'

'I'm not a sub,' I argued.

'Oh, but you are. You just don't want to admit it.'

Bloody frustrating man. My fingers fumbled for the zip, trying to reach it, but it was too difficult, and I groaned.

'Do you want me to help you?' His fingers explored further, moving slowly up between my thighs and grazing my cleft. 'Or should I continue like this? I can feel you're wet and aching for me again.'

I grasped for the zip again. 'Stop teasing me.'

'Teasing is one of my favourite things to do, ropes. You'll learn that when you submit to me.' Jack pushed my hand out of the way. The cool metal of the zip trailed a line down my back as he pulled it down, too slow, one inch of skin at a time, as if he was unwrapping a fragile present.

'I won't submit,' I said, but that was a lie, and we both knew it. With the fabric loose around my body, I turned and took two steps back. 'You'll be the one submitting to me, Jack.'

He rested back on his elbows, a sly smile curving his lips. 'You think you can dominate me?'

I arched a brow. Oh, I would make him fall to his knees and beg. Once I figured out how he did this to me, how he could use that deep voice and a single look to turn my insides into a quivering mess, I'd get him back.

'Maybe you're used to women… how did you put it…? Crawling to you? I'm not like that.' The dress slid down my body and pooled on the floor. Lust clouded his eyes. 'See? I can leave you speechless as well.'

Jack tilted his head as if he was observing something new and fascinating. The dark glint of amusement in his eyes suggested he enjoyed this battle for control, but something else, something much more dangerous, lurked in his gaze.

It raised the hairs on the back of my neck, and an image of myself naked and bound with him looking at me like that sent my pulse racing.

'You think I do this with all women?' His tone was as dark as a bottomless well. 'Put in this much effort? Get this damn hard only from looking at them?'

No.

He and his voice were not getting to me this time. It didn't matter how hot it was and how much I wanted to see that change in him again. I was determined to show him who was in control.

'I think you know what it does to women when you…' I nibbled on my bottom lip.

'Go on.'

'When you go all dark and dangerous.'

Jack chuckled. 'You think I'm dark and dangerous?'

'I do.' And it was hot. Frightening. I simply didn't want to admit how much I enjoyed it or what it did to me. 'But it won't make me submit to you. You don't have that effect on me.'

His brow went up. Was he amused, or had I thrown down a gauntlet? I hoped it was the latter.

'If you were my sub, you'd be careful challenging me.' Everything inside me melted from his warning. With a low laugh, he observed my reaction. 'And something tells me you wouldn't mind getting punished when you step out of line.'

'Punished?' I blew out an unsteady breath. 'What would you do to me? If–if I were a sub, which I'm not,' I quickly added.

'I can get quite creative with my punishments.' He grinned, flashing white teeth. 'But we don't have that level of trust between us where I could punish you, nor are you experienced enough to know how to behave like a sub. It would be unfair of me to spank you for calling me an arse, wouldn't it?'

An image of him doing just that sent a rush of excitement and burning need through my body, making me gasp. Realising I'd given myself away, I bit on the inside of my cheeks, but it was too late.

His lips quivered. 'And that's how I know you're a sub. But you're not ready for that yet.'

'I came home with you. How much more do I need to trust you?'

'The kind of trust where you'd allow me to hurt you, yet know that I would never harm you. Do you trust me that well?' He lifted a brow, expecting an answer I wasn't sure how to give.

There was no doubt Jack was a Dominant, but he spoke of sex and pain as if he'd known it all his life. While I'd gone through life fighting a war inside myself, always pushing myself and others to find my space, he had the confidence I lacked, the answers I needed, and the calm in my chaos.

I lifted my chin, making one last feeble attempt at regaining the control he'd snapped away. 'Maybe you're not dominant enough to make me submit.'

'Is that what you think?'

'Yes.' I had him now.

He slowly stroked his chin. It was unnerving how much he could hide from me when he looked at me as if he could read every thought that went through my head.

Jack rose, and something shifted in the room. The blue in his irises shrank, chased away by a simmering storm so dark even the shadows in the corners of the room seemed as bright as lightning. Fear skittered across my skin, chased by a rush of desire so profound that I whimpered.

He snapped his fingers, cracking the air. 'Kneel.'

My knees lost strength, and I sank to the floor before him without thinking, without asking why. The command resonated with something tucked away in the back of my mind, like I had been taught to respond to a man like him in such a way.

Gone were all the doubts, all the unrest I'd struggled with for so long. I was at peace, offering him that last bit of surrender by putting my hands behind my head. My heart hammered as he surveyed me, a soft furrow forming between his dark brows.

'Hands on your thighs, ropes. Palms up.' His voice was soft, guiding, with no hint of the darkness he'd portrayed before.

He gently nudged my legs further apart and straightened my back with a firm press against my spine. I leaned into his touch, seeking assurance from his heat.

'Good girl. This is how you would submit to me.'

Shuddering, I ached for his approval, and when he tilted my head to look up at him, I couldn't breathe anymore.

His grip on my chin, demanding yet gentle, got me every time. Nobody had ever looked at me with such confidence tangled up in raw, barely constrained desire, as if it hurt him to hold back and give me this moment of calm.

I wanted him to take me, wanted him to make me his. I trusted him, but I feared his dark side, my own, and what we were together.

'What will it take for you to stop fighting yourself?' His eyes glittered in the low light as he ran his thumb slowly over my bottom lip. 'Everything about you pleases me. There's no need for this shame.'

How did he do this to me? Sitting like this was like walking through the doors to The Yard for the first time. It felt like coming home, even though it was the opposite of what I thought I'd wanted, and it confused me.

'Shh,' he soothed, as if he could see my struggle with myself. 'You overthink things, ropes. Trust me to know what you need.'

How could he when I didn't?

'But I don't want you only like this. I want all of you – to know everything about you. What makes you happy, angry, how you got this scar,' he said, running his finger across my cheek. He smiled and whatever hold he had over my mind lifted. 'And yes, I am dark and dangerous. Yes, I've been with subs before, but you are the only one I want to keep for longer than one night.'

'Why?'

He arched a brow. 'Did I give you permission to speak?'

The authoritative bite to his tone sent fear and longing coursing through my body in the most intricate dance. Soothing the reprimand, Jack tucked my hair behind my ear.

'Since you're so new to this, allow me to explain. A submissive is always respectful to their Dom. You'll only speak when given permission. I'll touch you if I want to, where I want to, and punish you if I feel it's deserved.'

His words set off a swarm of butterflies in my stomach.

He paused, and his voice took on a harder edge. 'But never lie to me. It puts us both at risk. To keep you safe, I need to uncover any secrets you're hiding from me. Do you understand?'

I nodded.

'Good. Nothing bad will happen to you while you're with me. Everything I do is for you.' His intent eyes observed me. 'Are you scared?'

My gaze flitted. Was I? I should've been, but it didn't feel like fear I wanted to run away from. It made me tingle and ache for him to touch me again.

'Answer me, ropes.'

'Yes.' I drew in a ragged breath, fighting the urge to rub my thighs together. 'I'm scared.'

He smiled. 'I know you are, but fear is a powerful aphrodisiac for both of us. Do you trust me not to harm you?'

I nodded, although I couldn't explain why. Since the first time

I'd met him, he felt familiar for reasons I still couldn't understand. Familiar and safe.

'And you remember your safeword?'

'Yes.'

He offered me his hand and pulled me to my feet. 'I don't want you on your knees tonight.'

He snaked an arm around my back and tugged me closer, pressing my naked body against the fabric of his clothes and his hard chest.

With a firm grip on my chin, he lifted my head and looked into my eyes with a hunger that seared through my veins. The corner of his mouth curled in a smile before he kissed me.

His lips were firm, taking what he wanted from me, teasing out a moan I had no strength to hold back. With a sharp nip to my lip, he coaxed my mouth open and plunged his tongue in. My hands went to his shirt, fingers clenching the fabric as he destabilised my entire world.

His laugh came with a low tease when he took my hands and interlinked our fingers. 'What do you want, ropes? Do you want me dark and dangerous or sweet and tender? I can be both.'

Did I want him like this? He exasperated me, pushed my limits, lit my entire body on fire, and we hadn't even started.

His gaze was intimate, almost too intense to hold, but like invisible restraints, it was impossible to break free from. 'Answer me, Caitlin.'

'Dark. I want you as you are now.'

If my answer pleased him, he gave nothing away. It was as if he'd already decided, and I was only now finding out.

'You won't have alcohol around me again, will you?'

I shook my head.

'Good girl. When we play together, I need you to respect my rules. They are for your safety.' Jack grabbed the hem of his T-shirt. He paused for a moment before pulling it off. 'I don't want to harm you.'

Those bulging muscles were hard to ignore, and so were the flexing of tendons and that thin trail of dark hair disappearing into the waistband of his jeans.

But what stole my focus were the white lines crossing his chest, stomach, and even shoulders, some interwoven with small white circles of scar tissue dotting his pecs.

He looked like someone had tortured him, and though it made my heart clench in sympathy, it didn't repulse me. Jack seemed to wear the scars I hid inside, drawing me further to him, but the marks on his skin were nothing compared to what hid in his eyes. I'd only seen a hint of his vulnerability at the hospital when he feared a small needle.

Now he was exposing all of himself.

Before me, a man coiled with muscles and more confidence than I could ever wish for stood with strength and authority clear in every inch of him, yet his past contained such pain that I struggled to take it all in.

'I don't want to harm you,' he repeated, and the meaning was finally clear. Someone had harmed him, and he wanted to protect me, but from whom? Himself? From the monster in him?

I wanted him to hurt me. He was my favourite kind of monster.

'What happen—' I swallowed the question I wasn't sure if I wanted the answer to and nodded. 'I understand.'

'Tonight, I want you to do what you want with me. I'm giving you the reins.'

'What? You've just shown how you are in charge, and now you want me to take control?'

His smile was so teasing yet secretive. Why would he give me this opportunity when it was so clear what our roles would be?

'Surprise me,' he whispered, his eyes crinkling.

I didn't need to be asked twice. One quick shove and Jack landed on his back on the bed. His laughter filled the room.

Aching for him and determined to see where this could take me, I went for the fastenings on his jeans.

'So much for foreplay,' he teased.

I yanked his jeans off. 'Just be glad I don't have any rope, else you'd learn the true meaning of teasing, Mr Lawrence.' My fingers locked around the lining of his boxers and pulled. His cock sprung free, every inch of it, thick and hard.

'Ouch,' I said with a small laugh.

Jack's laugh rang in my ears. 'Funnily enough, that used to be my nickname at the club.'

'Ouch?' A sharp stab of jealousy hit me. I gripped his cock with both hands and squeezed. 'Word of advice? Don't make a sadist jealous.'

'It wasn't for the reason you think,' he groaned.

Again with the mystery. I needed a lifetime with this man to figure him out.

'Stop talking. Your voice is very distracting.' Wrapping my mouth around his cock, I moaned at the taste and swirled my tongue around every ridge and hard curve.

His sharp hiss as I grazed the shaft with my teeth was a thrill, and his grip on my hair only spurred me to take him deeper.

'Enough,' he said far too soon and pulled me to him. Our mouths crashed again, tongues fighting each other for that control, both losing and winning, as we rolled over on the bed.

I pushed back and straddled him again. 'You said I was in charge.'

'You are.'

'So stop bloody backseat fucking!' His laughter did him no favours. 'Jack,' I warned, running my nails down his sides.

'If you want control, take it.' Jack bucked me forward, snaked an arm under my leg and scooted down the bed. With a tight grip around my hips, he ran his tongue up the length of my sex.

'Oh god,' I moaned. 'That's not fair.'

His chuckle vibrated against my clit. 'I never said I'd play fair.

Submission is earnt, ropes, and I intend to earn yours before morning even if I know you will submit.'

I wanted to smack him, fight him for the control again, but he flicked my clit with his tongue, and I gave in.

When he pressed his tongue inside me, my hands clawed for a grip on the sheets, and when he sucked on my clit, my mouth opened in a soundless cry.

Jack didn't play fair. He offered me control, but took it away again.

I didn't care.

Not when his hands were on me, holding my hips in place as he ran the tip of his tongue along my sex, up and down, teasing every part of me except for where I wanted his mouth.

'I'll stop if you want.' He dipped two fingers inside me, curving and stroking, finding new ways to make me moan. 'You can try again. I was enjoying you sucking my cock.'

'No,' I hissed.

His mouth was back, licking where I wanted it, teasing and rewarding until my thighs clenched and heat spread down my legs like an impending wave I couldn't escape from.

With his lips sealed around my clit, he flicked his tongue back and forth until I couldn't think or breathe and came with a sharp moan.

'Do you want only pleasure from me?' He pushed me onto my back and crawled on top of me. 'Or can you handle all of me?'

My eyelids slid shut as he kissed me. He tasted of my arousal and that intoxicating flavour that was only his. 'I want it all.'

'I think you do.' His warm hands cupped my breasts, thumbs circling but never touching my hardened nipples, and a soft moan rushed over my lips. 'Your body is telling me you want it. You want both pleasure and pain.'

'I hate how you can read me so well.'

'Are you sure you want to lie to me?' He took my nipple into his warm mouth, then pulled back and blew cold air on it. With an arch of my back, I tried to get him back, but he waited for my response.

'Fine,' I said with a huff. 'I don't hate it.'

I didn't have to tell him what I wanted or how hard or soft. He listened to every soft exhale and silent request. He sucked at my nipples, nipped, and soothed the sting with his mouth until I ached for the sweet marriage of pleasure and pain.

Growing frustrated with his slow teasing, I gripped his hair and arched my back.

'Stop teasing me.'

Jack caught my hands and pinned them above me. 'Keep it up, and I'll tie you down and tease you all night.'

I bucked my hips and groaned. 'Jack.'

He blew a steady stream of cold air on my nipple and chuckled when I gasped. 'I can't remember ever being this excited about vanilla.'

'Stop teasing. Just fuck me.'

A wicked smile curled his lips as he shifted off the bed. 'Else you'll do what?'

He opened the drawer to the bedside cabinet and tore a condom wrapper with his teeth, his raised brow a silent yet alluring temptation.

'Is this what you want?' Pinching the tip of the condom, he pulled it on, then stroked the length of his cock as he watched me.

'You know what I want.'

'Ah, but I want your words.' He tilted his head as he waited, expecting me to comply with his command again.

I smirked. Two could play this game. I drew my knees up and let them fall to the side, exposing myself to him. 'Is this what you want?'

His gaze followed every inch of the slow path of my hands down my body. My fingertips brushed through the soft hairs at the apex of my thighs. Jack's lips parted, his eyes a storm of lust and defiance, and I drowned in them. He became my entire world. All my sensations and pleasure depended on him, but I wouldn't surrender without a fight.

Teeth locked around my bottom lip, I dipped a finger inside myself, feeling the wet warmth of my arousal. 'You're punishing me for having a drink?' I asked, groaning as I replaced one finger with two. 'That's fine. If you won't fuck me, I can do it myself.'

I pulled my hand back and licked my fingers, humming my approval. 'You're missing out, Jack.'

He gripped my hands and slammed them onto the mattress over my head. A growl vibrated his lips pressed against mine. 'Stop.'

I laughed and kissed him. 'You wanted to fuck me. Are you planning on doing that soon?'

'Just be glad I went vanilla tonight.'

'Or you would've taken me over your knee?'

'Don't,' he warned, eyes so dark it was clear how close he was to the limit of his control.

'Do it,' I urged, craving the pain that would give us both plea-sure. 'Hurt me if you dare. You know you want—'

With a bruising kiss, he stole my words. His firm hand fisted in my hair as he deepened the kiss and wiped out every thought in my head. The feel of his command over my body and even how he kissed me, hard and deep, left me breathless and aching.

'You've such a mouth on you, ropes.' He nipped my bottom lip. 'One day, I'll show you why it's always a terrible idea to top a sadist from the bottom.'

'Will it get me spanked?' I teased.

Jack laughed. 'Oh yes. But I've a feeling you would enjoy that.'

Holding me in place with a steady stare, he ran his cock up and down my sex, then thrust into me, stretching, burning, filling me. I cried out, struggling against his grip on my wrists. He released my hands and pulled back to push deep into me again.

Our tongues met again as I tugged and pulled on every part of his body within reach, arched my back and followed as he manoeuvred us around.

But we rolled again, and I was on top of him. His hands gripped my hips as I rode him hard, then slowly as the doubts returned, shame following. I was losing focus, losing my body and floating away in my head. I was the sex freak everyone said I was. The nympho. I squeezed my eyes shut.

'Stop.' He shifted up and pulled me closer, so we sat face to face. His cock twitched inside me, but a stern stare pinned me. 'I won't have you ashamed.' He dropped a hand between us and rubbed circles around my clit. 'Relax and only feel.'

'I can't.'

'Don't fight yourself, ropes.'

With his fingers moving over and around my clit, he coaxed my body to relax and refocus on him. He lifted me to the tip and let me slide down, inch by inch. I moaned, supporting myself on his shoulders.

'Do you feel how hard I am?' he said on a strained groan.

'Yes,' I whimpered.

'It's because of you. You do this to me.'

Every slow thrust was sweet torture. Every circle on my clit was heaven. He was waiting for me, watching me, feeling me tightening around him. I quivered under the intensity of his gaze and the control he exercised over every slow thrust.

'Fuck me,' I pleaded. 'That's all I want.'

'Not yet. Not until you allow yourself to feel.'

I groaned in frustration. Every nerve in my body tensed under his command, heat rushing down my thighs. He murmured in my ear as we moved together, how he loved watching me fall apart, how hard he'd take me when I did, how tight I felt around his cock, how it pleased him to see my pleasure. His words drove me insane.

There was no use hiding. I dug my nails into his skin, and his groan brought me closer to the edge.

'Harder,' he demanded. 'Go as deep as you need, ropes. You can't scare me.'

I dragged my nails down his skin, up and down, as he thrust deeper, harder. Excitement rolled through me as I tested his limits. He teased me with the forbidden and allowed me to cross that line where there was no shame or fear, only pleasure and pain combined.

Arching my back, I lost myself to the sensations, to the feel of his thumb rubbing steady circles over my swollen clit, and the slow slide of his cock.

I panted, so close, too close, and a rush of vulnerability hit me again, but he tightened his grip on my hip and drove me harder onto his cock in one hard surge. The world splintered around me, and I came with a strained groan.

Jack chuckled softly, his stubble rasping against my skin as he kissed my neck, nipping softly on my skin as I breathed hard. 'Good girl.' He pushed me down onto the bed again. 'You can't hide from me. Do you understand?'

'Mhmm,' I purred, wrapping one leg around his back, needing him closer.

'Tonight, I'll make you come as many times as it takes for you to stop hiding,' he said and moved in me.

This time there were no pretensions of vanilla. He fucked me hard, relentlessly, as if it was our last hour on earth, and he could never get deep enough inside me.

This was what I'd wanted from the moment we met. His hot skin against mine, his scent flooding my senses, his large hands holding my breasts as he moved in me, angling his hips to hit that spot where he controlled every gasp, every current of pleasure spreading through my body.

Jack owned me then, and I never wanted him to let me go.

I stopped questioning who was the dominant one. That night, Jack took over my mind and body and brought me into a new world. One where there was no shame, where there was nothing wrong with me, and he was everything I needed.

But no matter how much I begged or pushed him, he refused to hurt me. There was no doubt he wanted to. It was in his dark eyes and his powerful hands as they roamed my body.

Instead, he let me hurt him.

He didn't give in, even when I hissed at him and promised never to drink again if he would give me everything. It only made him laugh and pin my wrists above my head.

The feeling of helplessness ran through me as he took control, but it only heightened every slide of his cock, and my pussy tightened, and everything tightened until I came again, harder than before, losing myself in my sharp cry and finding myself in his kiss as my body convulsed.

Jack pulled back and drove harder into me. The sound of his groan as he came was almost as erotic as the feel of him inside me, but I winced when he gently pulled out of me.

He pushed up onto his elbows to look down at me. 'Have you had enough?' The softness of his smile made my heart stutter, so at odds with how he'd controlled my body.

'Remind me never to challenge you again.'

He took my lips in a tender kiss and rubbed his nose against mine. 'What can I say? I keep my promises.'

'You're dangerous, aren't you?' I asked, brushing his hair back.

He rested his forehead against mine. 'I'm not the dangerous one, ropes. You do something to me.'

When he curled an arm around me and pulled me to him, I closed my eyes with a smile, the storm inside me calmer than ever. His chest was damp with sweat, but warm and comforting as I snuggled into him.

His heart beat a steady rhythm against my back, but my pulse raced as I considered what it would be like to submit to him. Would he always be so intense, so frustrating? What if he wanted me to do things I didn't want?

Jack nuzzled my neck and shoulder, soothing my concerns with a soft sweep of his hand down my arm. 'Don't overthink, ropes.'

'How do you do that?' I turned in his tight embrace to find him smiling at me. 'Are you a mind reader?'

'No, I don't read minds.' He gently brushed my hair over my shoulder. 'But no Dom worth his title can't read a sub. You give away subtle little signs all the time.' He kissed my neck, collarbone, and the crest of my breast. 'Changes in your pulse, breath, how you move, even how you look at me. I can see how much you struggle, and all I want is to help you.'

'You seem to keep everything hidden,' I said with a yawn.

He kissed me softly before pulling the covers over me. 'Don't fall asleep. I'm just getting us a drink.'

'Then we'll play?'

He pressed a finger to my lips and laughed softly. 'Not yet, ropes.'

Frustrating man.

Closing my eyes, I listened to his fading footsteps. His pillow smelt like him, and I tucked it closer and inhaled deeply.

As much as I wanted to stay awake, I was only faintly aware of his footfalls coming back and the soft kiss he pressed to my temple when he laid down behind me and pulled me close.

CHAPTER FIFTEEN

JACK

* * *

PAIN.

In my limbs.

On my skin.

In my fucking soul.

Raw, throbbing agony engulfed my body with each strike. Every time the cane hit, pain bit into me, until there was nowhere left to hide, until it tore apart not only my skin, but my mind.

I opened my mouth to scream, but there was no air left in my lungs, no fight left in my body – nothing left in me but pain.

* * *

WRENCHED FROM THE NIGHTMARE, the first thing I noticed when my eyes opened was Kate. With each ragged inhale, I could smell her. As I moved a hand up to wipe sweat off my forehead, I could feel the weight of her slim arm wound across my chest. Most of all, I could see her. Kate's blue and purple hues pulsated in the darkened space.

It wasn't often I paid attention to people's colours anymore, but hers had drawn me to her from the start.

Seeking something to ground me, to soothe my mind after the memory of the night of my branding, I leaned closer to inhale, first from her hair cascading over my chest, then to her shoulder pressed against me. Her scent was familiar yet new, intoxicating and overwhelming, and it flooded my senses.

I pressed a soft kiss to her arm, tasting her perfume's faint, flowery tang mixed in the most exhilarating way with sweat and her unique flavour.

Strawberries?

No.

I kissed another spot and ran my tongue over my lips. Raspberries.

'You're real, aren't you?' I whispered against her skin, catching us both off guard as she stirred.

'Jack?' She put a hand on my cheek. 'Are you okay?'

I was now. She was here, so how could I not be? I ignored the colours and focused on her smile and how it broadened when I shifted closer. The tip of her nose met mine, sending deep currents through my body, right down to my toes.

'Jack?' Her fingers brushed my damp hair away from my forehead. 'Did you have a bad dream?'

The urge to kiss her almost overwhelmed me. If I didn't, my heart wouldn't slow down. She made it race and soothed it, all in one flick of her tongue against mine. Kate was like a drug, the most dangerous intoxication ever, and I was hooked.

She shifted up onto an elbow. 'Have I left you speechless again?'

Speechless? Hell yes. How easily she had submitted earlier, even the position she chose. Everything about her stunned me. It was like she knew how to submit to a Marquis, only there was no way she would.

Her bratty behaviour made it clear she knew nothing about

my world. A submissive trained by the Harpyiai would never dare challenge a Marquis, nor would a normal submissive found in a club, but that's what I loved about her.

She wasn't like anyone I'd ever met before.

Kate struggled with her desire to be dominated, even to feel pleasure. She fought herself every step of the way until I could no longer watch her internal battle. Once she was on her knees, she had calmed and settled into her role as if she was always meant to give me this control.

If only I could understand why she'd chosen to submit in the slave position.

I had never treated a submissive as a slave since leaving the castle, yet Kate responded as if she knew what I was trained to expect. It puzzled and pleased me, drawing me to her even though I knew it would put me in danger.

Her response to fear aroused the darkest part of my mind, remnants of my training, and stirred a predatory need to possess and devour her. I wanted to inhale her fear and allow it to tease those parts of me I no longer let out to play.

Yet I couldn't stay away.

Even her eyes had destroyed me when she'd looked up at me. Dark, soft, with a look threatening to bring me to my knees. She made me feel torn between the urge to take her and the need to protect her.

Never had I allowed a woman to see my scars or brand since leaving the castle, but I wanted to share everything with her, even those things I knew I shouldn't. We weren't allowed to talk about the Harpyiai, but something about Kate made me feel connected to her somehow, like she was meant to know things about me I'd never shared with anyone else.

Before she realised how she affected me, I flopped her onto her back and kissed her until she could do nothing but moan. Her tongue tempted me again, to suck it, to fight with it as it moved around mine, but her legs went around my hips, and we rolled over again.

'I've trapped you again.' She pressed her knees tighter around my waist.

I smiled, enjoying this game she liked to play, even if it was unfamiliar to me. Being topped by a woman usually filled me with fear, but for some reason, it wasn't so bad with her. 'Now that I'm your prisoner, whatever will you do to me?'

'Anything I want,' she whispered before kissing me.

Her mouth left mine for a mere second, just enough for me to draw one sharp breath that broke into a guttural groan as her teeth dragged across my bottom lip.

Her laugh filled the air. I bucked my hips, and her teeth clamped down harder. Her attempts to take control only made me chuckle. I could overpower her if I wanted to.

Why I didn't always want to was more of a mystery.

'You'll have to try harder, Mr Lawrence.'

I smacked her butt, not to tease, not even close to gentle, as the slap against her bare skin broke the silence of the room. Kate's startled yelp soon turned into a laugh.

'You want to fight?' I growled. 'You'll lose, Kate.'

She grabbed my hands and pressed them into the mattress over my head. Those dark brown eyes looked deep into mine, and my breath caught. 'I think I'm already winning.'

She was. For some fucked-up reason, I didn't mind losing myself to her. Not when her pert nipples pressed against my chest, and not when her pussy pressed against my cock. Definitely not when she looked at me like she saw who I was and still wanted me.

'Maybe I will tease you this time,' she whispered. 'Restrain you.'

Oh, hell no. I pushed her back. Her startled scream filled the room. When her back hit the mattress again, she laughed.

'You're crazy,' I said, crawling over her. 'Crazy and a bit reckless. I should take you to a club and show you what I can do with a flogger.'

'That sounds like fun.'

Fuck, yes. But I couldn't. It wasn't allowed. I wasn't supposed to throw a woman across my bed, but she didn't understand that my fear of being restrained ran too deep to allow her to test my limits.

'What does it feel like?' she asked, curious as ever. 'Does it hurt?'

'It depends on what I want you to feel. I can make you feel anything I want,' I said, proving my point by trapping her nipple between my teeth, tugging, teasing until she cried out.

I pulled her hands over her head as I leaned in, kissing her grinning lips. 'If you don't keep it down, the neighbours might get concerned.'

Fuck the neighbours. All I cared about was her – and keeping her protected from myself. She wiggled under me, legs locked around my hips again. I wasn't falling for that trick and put my full weight on her.

'Smack me again. See how loud I can be,' she teased.

'Don't tempt me.' I meant it as a warning. She'd been pushing me all night, not realising what she was playing with. I wanted her full trust before we played.

'Do it.'

Did she want me to be rougher? Fine. I smacked her butt again. She yelped. My hand stung, and my cock ached for her, but Kate only laughed.

'That's for drinking too much wine.'

Panting, she raised her hips. 'I think I should get one per glass.'

'I don't make a habit of smacking women on the first night.'

'What a shame,' she said, bolder than she should have been, but that's what she was. She was fearless, yet inexperienced. Bold yet submissive. Perfect in every way.

I ran a hand between her legs. She was hot and slick, and those tight inner walls gripped my finger when I slid one in. 'Yet you don't seem to mind.'

'So why are you holding back?' she moaned. 'I want it as rough as you can give me. Stop underestimating me, Jack.'

I stared at her, not knowing whether to laugh, fuck her, or goddamn propose to her on the spot.

There was a flame flickering in her eyes, waiting for me to ignite her world. But there was also danger – dark, beautiful danger. It called to me.

How tempting it would be to give her what she wanted. But the risk was too high. I could lose her.

Kate had no idea what kind of monster she wanted to play with, and she was still hiding something from me. Someone had harmed her, but who?

I shook my head and refocused on her naked body. My version of vanilla would have to do. It had worked so far. The temptation to taste her, to suck her nipple and tease her with my teeth was too great.

Kate moaned and writhed under me as I moved from one nipple to the other, not stopping until her arms struggled to get free.

Shifting off the bed, I grabbed a tie from the wardrobe. It was the worst fucking bondage there was. Silk and fabrics weren't my style. I enjoyed leaving marks, little signs of my possession marking delicate flesh, but Freddy had made me clear out everything fun.

'You seem to have an issue with your hands, ropes. They get in the way.'

'I hate it when that happens.' Her grin widened as I tied her wrists together. 'I can still bite,' she warned.

Leaning close, I whispered, 'Please do.'

Kate tempted me by biting her bottom lip, and she looked like a fucking nymph. The hue around her was a deep purple now, beating in rhythm with my heart. Did she have any idea how beautiful she was?

'Are you sure you want this?' I slid off the edge of the bed to grab a condom from the bedside drawer. 'You were sore earlier. I wouldn't want to hurt you.'

Only I did, in a good way. How far would she let me take her?

With a devilish smile, she watched as I opened the wrapper. 'You can skip that. I want to feel all of you.'

Hell, no. Too much of a risk.

'You didn't answer my question.' My voice was nothing but a low growl as the veil holding back my darker urges thinned further. 'Are you sure you want this?'

'I do want you to fuck me.' She licked her lips, and my whole body longed for her. 'But not like before. I want more. I want what you promised me.'

I grabbed her by the throat, not to choke her but to kiss her and shut her up before she pushed me over the edge. Her sharp gasp sent shivers down my body.

'We have a problem, ropes.'

'We do?' She panted, desire clear in every rapid breath.

'You respond too well. Fear excites you.' My voice was deceptively soft as she feigned innocence. She had to know what she was doing to me.

'Why is this a problem?' Kate's smile was the most beautiful and frightening thing I'd ever seen, the corner of her mouth curling in a dark promise. 'Are you not up for the task?'

I tightened my grip. 'Oh, I am.'

Her lips parted with another gasp. I loved that look in her eyes, clouded with lust, yet wide and fearful. It was as intoxicating as everything else about her.

I kissed her until I forgot where I was, what I was, shoved her back onto the bed and did the only thing I knew would shut her up, crushing my mouth over her pussy. I flicked my tongue over her clit and sucked until all she couldn't string any words together.

Kate would never be a normal submissive. Even I couldn't fool myself into believing such a thing. If I'd seen her as a normal submissive and wanted to make a point, I'd have ordered her onto her knees. I'd have fucked her mouth, hard and rough.

But she scared the hell out of me. I wanted to control her, dominate her, but also kiss her, hold her, and make her feel safe. I wanted both worlds without knowing how to cope with either.

Subs loved us at the clubs because a Marquis knew how to destroy their minds and torment their bodies. It was what the Harpyiai trainers had taught us to do. They didn't create us to serve others, to love and protect.

Kate fed off my darkness, and disrupted that careful equilibrium that it had taken me years to master under Nate's careful guidance at The Aurora.

She responded better than anyone, but I wanted her to crave me in every way, sexually and emotionally. I wanted her as addicted to me as I was hooked on her, on her soft smile and her cry as she climaxed and pulsed around my fingers.

I bit the inside of her thigh and groaned, praying I could keep control. But her sharp pleas for more only made it worse. I knew all the ways to make her moan and make her writhe in pain using only my hands. She was too dangerous to be around. The rougher I was, the better she responded.

Her wispy colours were back, rising from her swollen lips as she spoke. 'Harder, Jack. I won't break.'

She might not, but I was close to breaking. I closed my eyes, drawing a deep breath.

'I want to please you,' she said, her voice breathy and submissive, her words so hard to resist.

I flipped her over and dragged her backwards as I slid off the end of the bed, and our bare feet met the cold, hardwood floor.

Bending her over the mattress with her hands trapped under her, I growled in her ear, 'Stop fucking tempting me.'

'Stop fucking holding back,' she countered with a strained groan.

'You don't know what you're playing with,' I rasped.

'So show me.' Her words came as a strained breath. She spread her legs under me, demanding more, always fucking demanding more. 'Hurt me.'

Fine. If she asked for it, who was I to argue? I didn't have to take it too far, just enough to put her back in her place, and it was so easy to slip back into that role. It calmed us both as she remained prone while I considered everything I wanted to do to her.

I ran my hand over her butt, warming the soft skin. 'You keep defying me... How should I deal with you... hand or belt?'

'Hand, no, belt.'

I bit back a smile. 'I wasn't asking for your opinion, ropes.'

She groaned, lifting her hips off the mattress. I continued warming the skin, enjoying the curves of her body as she waited.

'Jack, please.'

I wrapped my hand around her hair and tugged. 'What colour are you?'

Did we talk about colours? Did she know anything about this?

'Green if you're good,' I whispered into her ear, 'yellow if it's getting too much, red if you can't handle it. What colour are you?'

'Green.' It came as a gasp.

'Good. Eight swats are all you get tonight, four on each side. Do you want me to be gentle or rough?'

'Rough.'

I nipped at her shoulder. 'The answer is, whatever pleases you, Marquis Jack.'

'Marquis?'

'*Maa-kwhus.*' I corrected her pronunciation. It had been years since I'd last asked a woman to use my title, yet it sounded so right coming from her lips when she repeated it. Her eyes went to mine, seeking answers I couldn't give her. I waited, not offering her an explanation.

'Whatever pleases you, Marquis Jack.'

'Good girl. You still have a lot to learn, ropes.' Sliding my hand between her thighs again, I was pleased to find she was still so fucking wet, greedy for more again as she moaned.

Teasing her skin with my hand, I warmed the area, listening to her breaths. 'You have such a fine arse, ropes. Soon I will claim all of it.'

'Whatever pleases—'

The first slap caught her off guard. The second was a little harder, and she yelped. The sound stirred something dark and dangerous in me. With the next two sets of blows, she cried out, and I drew in a breath to calm myself.

'Colour, ropes?' I asked, soothing her warmed skin.

'Green,' she panted.

I stifled a chuckle. Should've gone for the belt. She could take more than I expected.

I didn't hold back on the last set. The strikes came down hard and fast. Kate cried out. The palm of my hand stung. Her strained moan when I thrust my fingers deep into her pussy teased the monster within me.

'Colour,' I asked.

'Green... no... yellow,' she breathed.

Good. I dragged the tip of my cock over her cleft, teasing, then grabbed her hips and thrust to the hilt. Maybe I could fuck some sense into her. It had worked before.

I took her as she wanted me to, hard, fast and relentlessly. Her back arched, prepared for me to push her over that edge. I moved my hips in deep, circular movements, teasing her, punishing her with each deep thrust. She grew desperate, her breath laboured pants, so I gripped her hips and thrust harder, sweat running down my back. Even when I was this rough, she still came, squeezing my cock so hard that I groaned and fell against her.

Fisting her hair, I forced her head around so I could kiss her, so I could bite her lip as my release threatened. It started in my groin and built, rushed up through every blood vessel until I could no longer hold back and came with a low groan of her name.

She'd fucking ruin me.

I wasn't supposed to play or crave the burn this much. But I wanted it. I wanted her on her knees, begging for more. I wanted to test her limits, to give her everything she asked for, and for her to be everything I'd always been told I couldn't have.

When I released her wrists, pulled her into my arms and looked into her eyes, I allowed myself a moment where it would be possible to keep her forever. To wake up every day and find her next to me, to combine the two worlds I struggled to navigate, but it wasn't possible, was it?

She would run when she realised who I was, what I had done, but when I tucked her hair behind her ear, I wondered if maybe she wouldn't. Kate was stronger, darker, and more daring than anyone I'd met.

Dad had always said my worst quality was my heart; I got attached too quickly and always to the wrong person. Maybe if I showed Kate more of who I really was, she would make that decision before my heart got involved.

'Are you okay?' I whispered.

'Mhmm,' she murmured. 'But I still want more.'

More?

She wanted more?

For fuck's sake.

'Go to sleep, Kate.'

She laughed softly and wrapped herself tighter around me. I stared at the ceiling and listened to her breaths as they deepened.

When I was sure she was asleep, I slipped out of bed and walked downstairs.

The house was quiet, the night still upon us, when I picked up my phone and dialled the number I'd promised not to call again. It went to voicemail on the first two attempts before a gruff male voice finally barked down the line.

'It's four in the fucking morning. Whoever this is—'

I tsked. 'That's no way to answer the phone, *moy droog.*'

Theo was quiet for so long that I had to check he hadn't hung up on me. It wouldn't be the first time. Over a year had passed since I'd had to cease all contact, and the only way to cope with this new normality my father had forced me into was to pretend people like Theo didn't exist. Reaching out again was both frightening and thrilling – everything hinged on his reaction.

Finally, a deep exhale came. '*Blyad...* Jack?'

'Who else would call you at four in the fucking morning, *mudak?*'

'Only fools and vagrant kinksters with an itch to scratch. Which one are you?'

'No comment.' I dragged a hand through my hair.

'How are you? Marquis Hugh still got you locked away in your tower, *printsessa?*'

'Fuck off.'

Theo's croaky laugh took me back years, and my smile widened.

'I thought about rescuing you, *moy droog,*' he said. 'Mark and I almost staged a coup when we heard you'd turned vanilla. Tell me it's not true?'

I snorted. My relationship with Larissa had been a disaster from start to finish. 'You know that'd never happen. You couldn't even beat the kink out of me.'

'I'm willing to try…'

'Of course you are. Any excuse to use your 'nines. But there's a reason I—'

A thump came from behind. I peered into the darkened living room. Was Freddy home? Sometimes he had an annoying ability to sense when I was up to something he wouldn't like.

'*Da?*' Theo prompted.

Not seeing anyone, I stared into the back garden and drew a deep breath to ask the question I hoped wouldn't start another war. 'When's your next party?'

'*Nyet,*' he replied in a clipped tone.

'No, what? You haven't got one planned?'

One thing about Theo never changed. He hosted legendary, fucking insane kink parties, the kind my father wanted me nowhere near because of the risk of illegitimates.

'*Nyet.* No more parties.'

Bullshit.

'Come on, Theo. You'd give up on parties as much as you'd turn vanilla. It's part of who you are.'

'*Da.*' He grunted. 'But you won't be coming. CBT's a hard limit for me.'

Dad was known for cock and ball torture, the threat he'd used to get me to back off from partying. He'd threatened Theo and his regular party friends when I hadn't listened.

Another thump came from somewhere inside the house. What the hell was that? The alarm system hadn't been activated. I walked into the hallway and peered up the staircase in case Kate had woken up.

'I'll keep your balls safe from Dad.'

'He's got eyes and ears everywhere, *moy droog.* My numbers are still down, thanks to him.'

'Let me worry about that.' Not hearing anything else, I walked back into the living room. 'I'll wear a mask and pretend to be French if it makes you and your balls feel safer.'

'*Nyet.* When Marquis Hugh finds out, neither of us will have balls. Go to a club if you want to play.'

I grunted. Nate was even stricter with me than Dad. As much

as I wanted to take Kate to The Aurora, he'd never let me in the doors of the Essex club. I needed Theo for a more important reason.

'I'd like to introduce you to someone.'

He laughed, but there was no mockery, only curiosity. Theo knew she had to be special for me to risk my father's wrath. 'Someone's tugged your plait, *printsessa*? Do I know her?'

'No, she's new to the scene.'

'Now I have to meet her. You'll share, I hope?'

He always asked, even if he knew I never shared. There had been a time when we'd shared subs, but that was before Mark also wanted to join in. Mark and Theo messed up too many scenes with their bickering for that to appeal anymore.

'*Nyet.* Touch her, and I'll deal with your balls myself. Will you let me in or not?'

'Maybe.' He paused. 'I am intrigued to see what playmate has tempted Marquis Jack to leave his tower, but there's one condition...'

Of course there was. I stared at the floor and hoped this phone call wouldn't turn into the worst mistake of my life. If Kate wanted an introduction to the lifestyle, this move would either make or break us. Maybe that's why I'd called him, to see if she truly could handle me. She'd met Freddy, but Theo was the one I wanted her to talk to before we went any further.

'I assume you want a scene?'

'Of course, *moy droog*. I want to show you off.'

I sighed. 'It'll be on my terms. Nothing too—'

'Jack?' Kate's voice had me spin around. She stood in the doorway to the living room, a sheet wrapped around her body.

'I have to go. Call me tomorrow,' I said to Theo in Russian before dropping my phone on the sofa. 'Sorry, did I wake you?'

'I thought I heard... Who are you talking to at this hour? Is everything okay?'

'Everything's fine.' I swooped her up and started towards the staircase. 'Except that you should be in bed sleeping.'

She flung her arms around my neck and held on. 'What language was that?'

'Russian,' I said, carrying her into my bedroom.

'I didn't know you could speak Russian.'

I put her down on the bed and crawled up to kiss her. 'I am a man of many talents, *solnyshko moyë*. Shall I demonstrate?'

CHAPTER SIXTEEN

KATE

I woke tangled up in Jack. His head lay against my shoulder, his legs wrapped around mine, and one arm rested around my waist as if he was worried I'd escape.

His soft whimper drew my attention. Another bad dream? A lock of his tousled hair drooped into his eyes, making him look so deceptively innocent as he slept.

As I reached out to brush his hair back, an exhilarating shiver ran through me before I'd even touched his skin. It was frightening how he affected me. I didn't know I was so starved of attention until he came into my life. It scared me more than the mystery of his scars and late-night conversations in Russian.

There were a thousand things I wanted to know about him – his past, scars, family, how he could afford a house like this. Everything was neat and tidy except for our clothes scattered around on the floor.

Briefly, I wondered who cleaned for him, if he did it himself, and how this would work. Dominants seemed to order submissives around like a dog; moody, emotionally stunted men who took their anger out on virginal girls looking for a father figure.

Was that what he would become if I agreed to do this? I hoped not.

'I can feel you watching me,' he murmured.

My cheeks warmed. 'I wasn't.'

'It's fine. I was watching you sleep earlier.' His eyes fluttered open, and there it was again, that pull between us, making the air thick and heavy.

Smiling, he kissed my shoulder. 'Good morning.'

'You were watching me sleep?'

'How could I resist? You're beautiful.'

Unable to hold back my smile, I shifted my attention to the picture of the Manhattan skyline behind him. But it was impossible to ignore Jack when he was awake.

He pushed up onto an elbow. 'You look so serious... Are you having second thoughts about last night?'

I scoffed. 'No.'

He ran the back of his hand slowly down my cheek. 'Something's on your mind, though... You can talk to me about anything, you know.'

'Anything?'

He challenged me with a raised brow. 'There's nothing you can't talk to me about. I told you that already.'

I mirrored his position. 'Who were you talking to in the middle of the night? You know, the whispered conversation you cut short and tried to distract me from with more wicked sex?'

'Wicked?' He chuckled as he brushed my hair over my shoulder. 'Caitlin, we must have vastly different definitions of wicked sex. All I did was lick your delicious pussy until you couldn't stop shaking.'

Memories of the night before came rushing back, of his hands on me, his mouth, the way he took control... I bit my bottom lip.

Why had it felt so natural? It should have been the opposite of what I wanted, but he had shown me a new world and all I wanted was to explore more, to please him, and let him take control of everything again. My mind, my body, my everything.

'Keep thinking those thoughts, and we'll never leave the bed,' he teased.

'You're deflecting.' I tugged the sheet tighter around me so he couldn't tell my nipples had hardened.

'It's difficult not to when you look at me like that.' His grin widened. 'I was talking to Theo last night.'

'Theo?'

'Theo Williams, my best friend.'

'That's not a Russian name.'

'He's not Russian.' He shifted further upright, making himself more comfortable. 'Next question. Let's get to the bottom of what's bothering you so early in the morning, so I can make you breakfast.'

'Are you Russian?'

'No.'

I scratched my head. 'Why would two British guys speak Russian to each other?'

'Because we trained together and had a Russian teacher. It's our thing.'

'Trained?'

'As Doms, yes.'

'Like Dom school?'

'Something like that. I want you to meet Theo.'

'Why?'

'Because I'd like to keep seeing you. Is that what you want?'

'Yes,' I said without hesitation.

'Good.' He smiled. 'I've met Petra, so it seems fair you meet one of my friends.'

'I've met your brother.'

Jack rolled his eyes. 'He doesn't count. My brother is not part of the scene.'

'Theo's also a trained sadist,' I muttered, my heartbeat

picking up. Was there someone equally intense as Jack? I could hardly imagine. Meeting one sadist had been eye-opening enough.

'You don't have to worry about Theo. He's harmless. Don't tell him I told you that, though. He'd be offended,' he added with a laugh. 'If you want, I can find someone I've played with before that you can talk to.'

'Someone you've slept with?'

'Well, subs I've scened with at clubs. It's important to do background checks in this world. I wouldn't want you to jump into something you're unprepared for. It's important to me that you feel safe around me.'

I couldn't imagine anything worse than talking to someone Jack had been intimate with. I didn't even want to think about how many women were in his past. It had to be a fair few. I'd never been with a man this in tune with my body.

Maybe it was something he had been trained to do, only I couldn't picture how that kind of training worked.

'Don't be jealous, Caitlin,' he said. 'Are you going to tell me what's bothering you?'

'Who says anything's bothering me? Maybe I'm horny?'

'You are, but that's not what's on your mind.'

He thought he could read me so well, didn't he? I pouted. Petra said I needed to be more direct, so I drew a deep breath. 'Why aren't you a moody disciplinarian?'

He raised a brow. 'Elaborate, please.'

'Isn't that what Dominants are like? You have the wealth and mysterious past down to a tee, and you can be scary as fuck—'

'Scary as fuck?' He laughed. 'Can I have that in writing? Theo would be thrilled to see it.'

I pushed at his shoulder. 'Are you saying you won't serve me with some contract full of rules and cruel punishments if I forget to use a coaster?'

He glanced at an alarm clock on the bedside table. 'It's only ten o'clock. I thought we'd have breakfast before I tied you up in the basement and whipped you bloody for waking me up.'

My mouth dropped open. He wouldn't?

'That'd teach you, wouldn't it?' His tone was serious, but the slight twitch of his lips gave him away.

'You're such an arse.'

Laughing, Jack wrapped me in his arms before I could hide under the covers. 'I'm not that kind of Dom, Caitlin. If I were, do you think I'd let you call me an arse so often?'

'I guess not.'

'Come, let's shower together, then I'll make you some food.'

'What kind of Dom are you, then?'

'The kind that wants to cook you breakfast, then eat you out for dessert.'

'Oh.' My face heated. That sounded better than any contract.

He laughed. 'You truly are adorable.'

When he swung his legs over the edge of the bed, I caught sight of his back, and a chill ran through me. I had scratched him harder than expected, but that wasn't what froze me to the spot.

About the size of my hand, the letter *H* sat between his shoulder blades, surrounded by white lines stretching up to his shoulder like wings, ready to take off and carry him somewhere. The brand was both beautiful and frightening – and a utter mystery.

Before I could ask what it was, he was on his feet. He moved around with such ease – sleek, confident strides as if he was as comfortable naked as he was with clothes on.

Not wanting him to notice how many questions swirled around in my head, I staggered after him into the bathroom. Jack bit back a smile but offered me his hand for support.

'Not a word, Jack,' I muttered.

'I'd say I was sorry, but I'm not.'

'Sadist.'

He scoffed. 'Have you seen my back? If anyone engaged in sadism last night, it was you.'

'I'm sorry,' I said, rushing through the words. He was already so scarred, and my heart twisted from the pain he must have gone through. 'I didn't mean to leave marks on—'

'Shh.' Jack put his hands around my face. 'You've done nothing wrong. I would've stopped you if I didn't want you to hurt me.'

'Are you sure?'

He gave me a stern stare. 'Kate, I can protect myself. You're not the first I've played with.'

Who had left all those scars on him? Another woman? I didn't want to imagine Jack with anyone else, but the thought of anyone hurting him made my blood boil.

'Have you ever trained anyone before?'

He pursed his lips. 'Subs, yes. Sadists, no, but I'm looking forward to it. Sadism isn't all about cuts and bruises, you know.'

'I guess not,' I said, not knowing what else it could involve.

'When's your next shift?'

'Monday. Why?'

He grabbed me a new toothbrush from the cabinet above the sink. 'Stay with me this weekend.'

'Is that an order?' If it was, it didn't match what was in his soft gaze.

Jack shook his head. 'I told you. I'm not that kind of Dom. You're more than welcome to stay here, though. I'd love it if you did,' he added, dipping his head to kiss my cheek.

'Isn't The Yard open tonight? I don't want to keep you from—'

'Freddy will take care of the club, and I've no other plans.'

Neither did I, and it was tempting to have more time to figure him out. 'I haven't got any spare clothes.'

'You won't need any,' he said, rinsing his toothbrush.

My cheeks warmed. Hoping he didn't notice, I took the toothpaste from him and focused on brushing my teeth.

Amusement danced in his eyes. 'Don't worry; I'll find you

something to wear. Lily leaves clothes all over the house. I'm sure she wouldn't mind if you borrowed something for the weekend, if that's all right with you? Or we can grab a few things from yours.'

'Who's Lily?' I asked absentmindedly. There was a small pharmacy on the shelf above me, with everything from Ritalin to anti-depressants, painkillers and inhalers. Did he take all of these? Some of them shouldn't even be combined. Or was it Freddy's? According to his file at the hospital, Freddy had ADHD and asthma.

'Freddy's girlfriend,' he said and strode out of the bathroom.

'Oh.' Checking he wasn't in sight, I studied the labels on the medication. They were all prescribed to Freddy. I'd never dated a twin before, but maybe it was normal to be so close that they still lived together.

I busied myself with brushing my teeth when Jack returned and put some clothes on top of the laundry basket. Watching him move towards me made it hard to focus on my toothbrush. His cheeky smile as he wrapped his arms around me told me he knew I'd been checking him out.

'Freddy lives with you?' I asked, closing my eyes on a soft exhale as he kissed my neck.

With his nose in my hair, he inhaled deeply. 'He does, but he's not here this weekend. Come. Let's shower.'

The shower was twice as large as mine, with glossy blue tiles and a waterfall shower head. I had no objections; it meant we could both fit, even if Jack towered over me. With the warm water and his hands on me, I could have stayed in it all day, especially when he kissed me, softly at first, then more demanding as my back met the cold tiles.

'I could get used to this,' he murmured between each kiss to my neck. 'You, in my shower, all naked, all mine.'

So could I. Desire coursed through me, but he pulled away, leaving me bereft and panting.

'Turn around.' He swirled his finger in the air. 'Let me wash your hair.'

'Why?' I asked, perplexed.

'You take care of people for a living, so let me take care of you.' He tipped my head back, letting the water soak my hair before wrapping it around his fingers to lift my chin. 'Has nobody washed your hair before? You're so tense.'

'Am I?'

'Yeah,' he murmured, massaging the shampoo into my hair. 'I need to work on getting you relaxed around me. You've got nothing to fear.'

I sighed, leaning into him as his fingers did their magic on my scalp. 'You're quite intense,' I admitted. 'And I have so many questions.'

'You can ask me anything,' he said, but all the questions I wanted to ask were about his past, and I didn't want to spoil the moment.

He rinsed my hair and lathered up his hands before washing every part of my body, coaxing my muscles to relax as he massaged my shoulders, then put soap in my hands and brought them to his chest. 'Your turn.'

I smiled, running my hands over his body, my grin widening from his soft groan as I cupped his cock, then focused on his stomach and chest. My fingertips danced over the scars, following the length of the marks until he took hold of my wrists.

'It was a long time ago, Kate. That part of my life is over.'

'Will you tell me about it?'

'One day.'

'And the brand on your back? Will you tell me about that as well?'

He kissed my forehead. 'That's nothing for you to worry about.'

'It must have hurt a lot?'

'It did, but it's something I'd rather not talk about.' He kissed my cheek, but the easy smile I expected from him at any moment was no longer there, nor did his eyes have that teasing glint. He'd shut down all emotions and retreated into a shell I couldn't get through.

Had I triggered a bad memory?

'I'm sorry. I didn't mean to—'

'Hey.' He smiled. 'Don't apologise. You've done nothing wrong. Come, I'm getting hungry.' Jack rinsed off the soap on my hands and slipped out of the shower. I followed him out, and he wrapped me in a towel and dried every inch of my body.

I wanted to respect his privacy, but I couldn't imagine why anyone would want a large brand on their body, and his reluctance to talk about it only added to my questions.

Instead of pressuring him, I lifted onto my toes and wrapped my arms around him. His heart beat fast against my chest as he pulled me closer and buried his nose in my neck. 'I'll tell you about it one day,' he said. 'But will you stay this weekend?'

I tightened my grip on him. 'Yes.'

When we walked downstairs to eat breakfast, Jack was back to his usual self, promising me pancakes and a beach trip to enjoy the sunshine. His kitchen was fresh and modern but with a dark, bold colour scheme. There was a large kitchen island in the middle of the room. French doors led to a dining room at one end and a living room at the other.

When I lived at home, Mum often hosted dinners to aid Paul's political career, so I was used to immaculate houses and expensive furnishings, but Jack's house had a homey feel to it. More earthy colour schemes and fewer frilly cushions.

I took little interest in cooking, but Jack moved around the kitchen as if he spent all day preparing food and soon had everything set up along the marble worktop, and ordered me to sit while he cooked.

Barefoot and broad-shouldered, he looked better than any breakfast. He'd put on a pair of jogging bottoms that sat low on his hips, but I only wore his The Yard T-shirt, determined to convince him I wasn't as sore as he thought. It also smelt so good. When he caught me holding it up to my nose, he grinned.

'You can cook?' I asked as he beat the batter. 'Is there anything you can't do?'

'Tax returns and knitting?' His laugh came easily. 'Yes, I love cooking. Mum was a chef, and Dad still owns several restaurants around the country, so I grew up in kitchens.'

'They work together?'

He shook his head. 'She passed when we were teenagers. They met in a restaurant in London, I believe – that's where I was born. Mum was a server then, and he stopped by to scout out the place before putting in an offer.'

'Oh. I'm sorry.' As annoying as my mother was, I couldn't imagine what it was like to lose a parent that young. 'That must have been hard for you.'

'Do you want tea or coffee? I might have apple juice—' He flung the fridge door open, and my attention went to his back. To the scars. The letter *H*. What did it mean?

'Jack…'

'No apple juice, sorry. Freddy must have drunk it all.'

'What happened to you?' I asked, feeling around the edges of this wall he was trying to hide behind. 'Your scars, that brand… You don't have to tell me everything,' I offered.

All I wanted was a little of those parts he kept hidden. It would help me understand him better.

Jack sighed but seemed more conflicted than annoyed, like he wanted to tell me but something held him back. 'Caitlin, I told you not to ask about that now. I don't want to spoil our weekend.'

'Is it why you want me to submit to you? Because of something that happened in your past?'

'Are you trying to psychoanalyse me, ropes?' His lips curled into a sensual smile. 'You think I use sex to cope with my past?'

'Don't you?'

'Do you?'

'Maybe,' I admitted, only I couldn't remember what happened to me as a child.

'Perhaps I do as well, but it's not why I want you to submit.' He left his batter alone for a moment to lean against the kitchen island in front of me. 'From the moment I met you, you've been ashamed and afraid, unable to let yourself go. As a submissive, you can give me those fears and doubts, so you can only feel.'

'Only feel?'

'Mhmm,' he whispered, kissing the corner of my mouth. 'As a sub, you hold all the power.'

'But you'll tell me about your past one day, right?'

'Yes.'

'Promise?'

He sighed. 'Trust goes both ways, you know,' he said with a strangely wary glance.

I wanted to ask him who had broken his trust, but whatever he was struggling with, he tried to mask it with a smile as he went back to cooking.

He moved so naturally, so at ease with his body. If he could teach me to be that confident and explore my sexuality, it didn't matter what was in his past. Maybe I could have a life free from this shame my mother insisted I deserved.

As Jack flipped pancakes, I told him about my mother, who did nothing but arrange charity events for my stepdad and drink tea with other posh ladies who were also married to politicians. He seemed to find it amusing to hear me talk about my family, but his brows knitted when I said I'd never met my birth father.

'Never? He wasn't interested at all?'

I lifted one shoulder in a shrug. 'Sometimes I dream about him, so I think she's lying to me about having never met him. But they must have fallen out badly because she's kept him from me all my life.'

'That's too bad. Dad and I don't get along on the best of days, but at least he's there.'

When he placed down two servings and sat next to me, I asked, 'Why do you want to go to the beach? We could have fun here.'

He chuckled as he coated his pancakes in syrup. 'You are insatiable, but we can't spend all day in bed.'

'Why not?'

'Because we're still getting to know each other.'

'Jack, I meant what I said last night. You're too gentle with me.'

'Am I now?'

I nodded, biting my bottom lip. 'It's only fair if I get to sample everything you can offer before I decide.'

He laughed. 'Fair point, but I'm trying to give you a chance to get to know me first, to learn to trust me and relax around me. Also, you can't play without knowing your limits, and as we've already established, you don't know yours.'

'Maybe I don't have any.'

His darkening eyes bored into me as he leaned closer. 'Never make that mistake in my world.'

A shiver ran through me. 'Honestly, I can't think of any, and I trust you not to go too far.'

'What if my plans included whipping? Fisting?' His voice dipped lower, taking on that dangerous edge as his hard gaze tangled itself up in my wide-eyed stare. 'Pegging? Knife play? Breath play? Bastinado?'

'I don't even know what bastinado is,' I whispered.

He smirked. 'Foot torture.'

'Hell no, leave my feet alone. I don't want to be whipped, either. The rest sounds fine. I want to try different things, and who better to show me them?'

Jack returned to his pancakes, but his intense stare rested on me. 'You want to do this?'

'Yes, I do.'

For a long moment, he studied me as I held my breath. What was going through his mind? He could read me so well, but I struggled with him. Maybe learning to hide his emotions was something he'd learnt as a Dom.

'We should talk about limits,' he said. 'What you will and won't do.'

'Like a contract?'

Jack shook his head, chuckling. 'No, Caitlin. I don't do contracts. You've already said you don't want to be a slave, so we won't have that kind of arrangement, either. But I have three non-negotiables, two of which you are already familiar with.'

Was I? My bewilderment made him smile as I tried to think what he meant. Only one thing came to mind. 'No drinking.'

'That's one.'

I bit my lip, sure I'd fail this and every test he'd put me through.

Amusement danced in his eyes. 'Would you like a hint?'

'Yes, please.'

He pulled me to my feet and slid two fingers inside me. I gasped.

'This is mine. I do not share.' His voice had dropped so low that it was almost a growl. Jack pulled his hand back and picked up his fork again as if nothing had happened. 'I believe you have one more to cover.'

Moistening my lips, I tried to regain the ability to speak. It was useless. All I wanted was those fingers back inside me.

'I don't know,' I said, sinking back into my seat.

'I also never play with canes. Do not bring them near me unless you want to see a side to me you'll never forget.'

Canes? My gaze wandered to his chest. 'Is that—'

'No more questions about my past.' He pressed a finger to my lips. His voice was stern, but the shadows in his eyes mesmerised me. Before the rejection could set in, he pressed his lips to mine, soothing those concerns. 'It's not something I talk about with anyone.'

'Maybe you should.'

His brows furrowed. Had he never spoken to anyone about his past? 'Maybe,' he said after a moment.

'Haven't you spoken about it with your exes?'

'Eh, no.' He scratched behind his ear. 'Relationships haven't really been on the cards for me.'

'Too busy playing at clubs?' I said with a scowl. Where was this jealousy coming from? 'I knew you were a player.'

'Life's just been complicated.' He ran the back of his hand down my cheek. 'But I'm hoping to change that.'

Could I trust that? Why would an experienced Dom want someone like me? 'Just don't kick me out in the middle of the night.'

His jaw clenched. 'He left you vulnerable. If your ex-boyfriend puts his hands on you again, I won't be so kind to him.'

It was hard to fight back a smile. Nothing would please me more than to see Tom put in his place. 'You'd do what, whip him? I thought you said you didn't fight.'

'I would do anything to protect someone close to me. Just tell me if he bothers you again, and I'll take care of it,' he said around a bite of pancake.

'I'd stay away from him if I were you, or he'll demand money from you as well.'

Jack stopped chewing. 'What?'

'Forget it. It's not important.' Flustered, I stared at the syrup drowning my pancakes. Why had I said anything at all?

He took my hand. 'You don't have to tell me.'

'He's pressuring me for money because I scratched him.'

Jack's brow shot up. 'I see. And how much is he asking for?'

'Two hundred thousand,' I said, dropping my face in my hands. 'Paul's footing the bill. It's not like I can afford it on my salary, but Tom refuses to back down. He claims I traumatised him and… Well, you can only imagine how that went down with my mother when she found out. They're paying him, so he doesn't reveal this to the press or her country club friends.'

'How—' He cleared his throat. 'How did this get to a court of law?'

'It never went to court. Paul's solicitor's handling it all.'

Jack pressed a fist against his mouth. Shit. What was he thinking? Had I gone too far already?

Just as I worried I might have scared him off, Jack laughed. I adored his deep, genuine laugh and how it lit up his entire face. It was hard not to smile.

'Sorry, but that's fucking hilarious. I knew he was a tosser, but for a few scratches…' He shook his head. 'I have to introduce him to Theo. He'd have great fun with him.'

'I bet he would.'

'Finish your pancakes,' he said with a smile. 'I want to go to the beach. Maybe next weekend, I'll show you there's more to this than contracts and whips.'

CHAPTER SEVENTEEN

KATE

AFTER BREAKFAST, he took me to the beach, where we walked along the sand and talked about work, annoying siblings and everything else. I learnt his birthday was on the first of December, making him exactly three months older than me. It was a funny coincidence, but Jack winked at me and said it was fate, and maybe it was. If only I could have trusted when I had been born.

None of it mattered around Jack. He was so calm, so liberating to be with, quick to smile and laugh, yet always with that dangerous edge to him that set my whole body on fire whenever he stopped and slid his hands around me. When Jack kissed me, he did it with his whole body, and there was no world around us. I lost myself to him and never wanted to be found.

Back at his house, he wanted to know what my favourite foods were and got a wicked smile when I confessed that my secret comfort food was toasted sandwiches. I soon found myself back on that bar stool in the kitchen, watching him cook.

'My second favourite indulgence is wine,' I teased.

He pointed a spatula at me. 'Don't think I won't spank you.'

'Maybe I want you to.'

His chuckle came deep and low. 'Nice try, but there's no alcohol in this house.'

'How can you work in a club and have no alcohol?' I slid off my seat to wrap my hands around his waist. 'After just an hour at work, I want to down a whole bottle.'

Jack kissed the top of my head. 'Trust me, it's tempting, but you're a nurse, so you know I can't combine Ritalin with alcohol.'

'So you have ADHD.'

'Yes, and you don't need alcohol either.'

I wasn't sure about that, but he was more tempting than any wine.

Jack wanted to find a movie to watch while we ate, but I'd spotted a chessboard on a shelf in the living room, and to my delight, he knew how to play. My mother had taught me; it was one of the few activities we ever did together, and since moving out, I'd missed having someone to play with. Tom took no interest in the game, but Jack was up for the challenge.

As he set up the pieces, I bit into my sandwich and groaned. 'You're worth keeping around just for the food. What the hell is in this?'

'Chilli, cheese, and coriander. And if you make that sound every time you eat my food, I'll cook for you anytime.'

'You'll have to. I'm one of those who can burn water,' I said with my mouth full. I could make a decent meal, but my joke was worth it just to hear Jack's laugh.

He sat across from me as confident as always with a smug smile, as if he would be better than me at chess as well, but he soon learnt. He opened too boldly, and after only five moves, his eyes widened when he realised his mistake had left him vulnerable.

'Don't you dare,' he said on a low laugh.

'It's not my fault you left your queen open like that. I have to take her.'

Jack scratched his head. 'You're full of surprises, Miss Howard.'

'Has a girl never beaten you before?' I teased.

'You've not beaten me yet.' Folding his hands, he concentrated on the board.

As he pondered his next move, I studied the photographs on the wall, wondering if the smiling dark-haired woman was his mother. With the same carefree smile as Jack, she was beautiful, but it puzzled me that there were no pictures of his dad.

Like the other rooms in the house, the living room was warm and inviting. The soft green of the patterned wallpaper nicely contrasted the white leather sofa. Tall bookcases lined one wall, a TV hung above a fireplace, and a few potted plants decorated the windowsill in the bay.

'If I let you win, can we play a different game?' I offered, biting my lip.

Jack's gaze lifted. He smirked. 'Let me win? That's not a victory worth having.'

I could've told him how to win, but he was cute when he concentrated, those dark brows drawn together as if he thought the pieces would speak to him.

He moved his bishop to save his king. 'I might consider it if you won again, but we both know that won't happen.'

I snorted. 'Bring it on, Mr Lawrence. No one's beaten me in years.'

'We'll see about that.' Jack rested back with a smile that had nothing to do with chess.

I squirmed in my seat. 'Stop looking at me like that.'

'Like what?'

'Like you want to…' I waved my hand.

His eyes darkened. 'Go on.'

'Stop talking,' I muttered. 'Your voice is distracting.'

When I'd won two games, he wanted to find a movie to watch,

and I obliged. It was nice to sit between his legs and feel the heat of his body.

Jack played with my hair as Michael Myers chased dumb women on the screen, and he chuckled every time I jumped. I hadn't realised how much I missed such trivial things about being with someone, watching a movie or sharing a meal, nor had I expected to feel comfortable with him so soon.

But he was still holding back. I wanted both versions, the soft and caring Jack who put his hands over my eyes when the movie got too scary, and the Dom who pinned my wrists above my head.

When he went to fetch us a drink, I cornered him in the kitchen and ran my hands up his chest. His sharp inhale was a delight.

'Limits established. I want to play. You've given me soft and gentle, Jack. Now I want rough, dark and dangerous. I want you as you are. That's what I'm drawn to.'

'You're drawn to fear.' He dipped his head. 'You're drawn to me because I'm dark and dangerous.'

'Is that so wrong?'

'Not if you trust me.' The curl of his mouth only emphasised what hid behind the blistering colour of his eyes. 'I've already been rough with you, yet it's not enough?'

'As rough as you can be?'

'Of course not.'

I pushed him against the kitchen counter. 'So you're holding back.'

'So are you,' he countered with a raised brow.

'I'll stop if you stop,' I challenged.

'You're so daring,' he said as he kissed me softly. I kissed him back harder, and the nature of his kiss changed, no longer tender or sweet but deep, carnal and demanding.

He inhaled deeply and groaned. 'You make me break all the rules. Come.'

'Where are you taking me?'

'Playroom. Wasn't that what you wanted?'

'What? You have a playroom?' I couldn't hide my excitement. Why the hell hadn't we visited that yesterday? There was no chance to question him. He was on a mission, and all I could do was try to keep up.

Jack brought me to a white door at the end of the hallway. He tied a black scarf around my head and blackened my world. 'Once we step inside this room, you will follow my command. Do you understand?'

'Yes.'

His voice dipped lower. 'Yes, what?'

'Yes, Marquis.'

'When you get inside, take your clothes off and kneel.'

A faint scent of flowers hung in the air, but a hint of dust tickled my nose and a rough carpet scratched against my bare feet when we entered the room. To my left came a soft humming noise, contrasted by the distant twittering of birds from my right. A window?

Jack led me a few feet inside, and as I undressed, careful not to disturb the blindfold, he put on music, filling the space with soothing piano tunes.

Goosebumps puckered my skin as I sank to my knees and waited. Jack was soon there, tutting as he tapped the inside of my knee with his hand. I shifted my legs further apart.

'Good girl,' he said and moved around the room.

Desire and anticipation coursed through my blood as I imagined what toys he would have in this room. Whips? Floggers? Ropes? Not knowing what he had planned sent my pulse racing.

As I waited, straining my ears to listen to what he was doing, Jack hummed to himself while he shifted through something – a drawer? – and placed some items on a hard surface. His footfalls were quiet and hard to hear over the music, and I startled when his hand came to rest on my head.

'Stand.'

My knees shook as I rose to my feet. 'What are you—'

'No questions, ropes.'

I drew a deep breath and focused on the warmth of his skin and the gentle way he lifted me onto a cold surface, his mouth as he kissed me, and the feel of his hands when he pulled me towards him.

'I want you on the edge of this table.' He raised my knees so they pressed against his chest. 'With your feet together and knees spread out.'

Eager to please him, I put my feet together, flopped my knees open, and then slowly closed them, feeling vulnerable and exposed to his gaze.

'Do as you're told, ropes.'

'Yes, Marquis.' He knew exactly how challenging this was for me. I could hear it in his voice and his low chuckle when he moved away. An object bounced against the floor, then seemed to trail behind him as he moved around. What was it? My skin prickled as I tried to figure out what he had planned.

The music picked up, putting me on edge with its fast beats. It made me lose track of where Jack was and what he was doing. When his warm hands found my knees, I yelped in surprise. His chuckle deepened as he pushed my legs open again.

'Stay still,' he ordered. 'Don't make me tell you again.'

I scowled at him from underneath the blindfold.

'Since you seem to struggle, I will restrain you.' He dragged a stiff, cold fabric along my knee, slipped it around the back of my thigh and pulled, keeping my right leg splayed open, my toes resting on the edge of the table. With a throaty hum, he did the same to my other leg, then put his warm hands on my knees.

'Colour, ropes.'

'Green,' I whispered, wishing he would kiss me again, touch me, fuck me. Anything.

'You look incredible. So eager, so trusting...'

'I do trust you.'

'Good. There is a bar above you. Grab it and hold on.'

I wrapped my hands around the metal. Jack brought my hands closer and tied them to the bar with something coarse. Rope? I giggled.

'First time with a rope?' he teased before kissing me. His tongue dipped in, stroking mine as the kiss intensified, but again he pulled away too soon. 'I aim to fulfil all your little fantasies.'

With my sight gone, his alluring scent and soft breaths were my entire world. He soon introduced me to other senses: the softness of his lips against my skin and the tease of his fingertips as they travelled over the curves of my breasts. My breathing deepened, but I tensed up every time his hands lifted.

'Relax,' he ordered. 'You know I won't harm you.'

'Yes, Marquis,' I whispered. What other choice did I have but to trust him?

'You overthink things. Trust me to guide you. Where do you want me to touch you?'

'Where?'

He tutted. 'Don't ask questions, ropes. Tell me where you want me to touch you.'

I dragged my bottom lip between my teeth. 'Everywhere.'

He nipped my shoulder, sending a rush down my body. 'Be more specific.' His fingertips circled my nipple. 'Do you want me to touch you here?'

'Yes,' I breathed.

His hand lifted. He waited.

'Yes, Marquis.'

Cupping one breast with his warm hand, he rolled my nipple between his fingers. 'Harder or softer?'

'Harder.'

He gave my nipple one sharp squeeze, making me gasp. A bolt of electricity shot down to my core. I wanted more, but he moved on, raking his nails slowly along my skin.

Continuing down my body with the same slow caress, he brought every inch of me alight until I relaxed more. The slight chill of the room no longer registered, nor did the tension of not knowing where his hands would be next. Every time he touched me, I came alive, leaning into his touch, and when he moved away, I was left cold and aching.

'Good girl,' he murmured. 'I want you to focus only on my voice and hands. Feel as I find which parts you want to be touched, how soft or hard you crave my touch, how it affects your heartbeat and breathing.'

His fingertips lightly grazed my clit, and my mouth parted. With slow, deep circles against my clit, and his mouth on mine, he guided my body to give it what he wanted, and drew me closer and closer to the edge, like he had done so many times the night before.

Heat spread up my thighs, and I tensed in his hold, but every time the orgasm was within reach, he slowed down. Again and again, he brought me close, only to leave me on the edge until I cried out in frustration.

'Jack,' I hissed, growing desperate.

He removed his hands again and waited.

'Please, Marquis,' I groaned.

'Patience, ropes.' His voice dipped low, like a soft, menacing whisper from a dark place. His fingertips ran down the back of my arms in slow, teasing movements until he reached my breasts. 'Oh, the things I could do with these. You have amazing breasts,' he whispered, rolling my nipples gently between his fingers.

How did he sound so calm? I ached for him, yet he was relaxed and in control as he teased my nipples, tugging, rolling, pinching... Wanting more, I pressed forward into his hands and groaned.

'You like this?' Closing his mouth over my nipple, he sucked hard. I cried out, overwhelmed by the sensation.

'Yes,' I moaned, but his mouth lifted. 'Yes, Marquis.' I arched my back, longing for his touch. 'Don't stop.'

'So greedy,' he teased, blowing cold air on my wet nipple. He took no notice of my desperation as he rolled his tongue around the taut bud in all the ways I wanted his tongue on my clit.

'I can make you come this way.' He nipped it with his teeth, and I moaned in response to the pain and pleasure. 'But I won't.'

'Please,' I pleaded. My sex throbbed, aching for release. How long was he going to torture me like this?

Jack tsked. 'You keep forgetting to address me properly. Maybe we need to make it clearer so you never forget.'

He dragged something along the table beside me and then pressed it against my arm. It was cold, like metal, with sharp edges that bit into my skin as he tilted it. I sucked in a breath. What was it?

'Pick a number between one and ten, ropes.'

A number? For what? I hoped it was something good, but it was hard to tell with Jack. My tongue darted out, moistening my lips as I hesitated.

'If you make me wait any longer, I will pick for you,' he warned.

'Three, Marquis.'

'Very well. Don't move. I wouldn't want to cut you too deep.'

My mouth fell open. 'Cut? You have a knife?'

'Is that another question?' he asked, his deep voice biting into my skin.

'N-no, Marquis,' I whispered.

'You wanted me to play hard, didn't you? This is how I play.'

Fear rushed across my skin, tailed by the most pressing desire that left me panting. He was finally letting me have what I wanted, but there was no denying the change in him. When he held the sharp edge against my throat, I gasped.

He wouldn't really hurt me, would he?

No, harm.

He wouldn't harm me.

I had to remember the difference. But damn, he could be deliciously terrifying.

The blade pressed harder against my skin. I pulled my head further back to get away.

'You're not scared of me, are you?' he said in a deceptively calm tone, his mouth close to mine. 'You can stop me with one word if you are.'

'I'm not scared of you.' But I whimpered, revealing myself.

'Have you told Petra or Owen where you are?'

'N-no.' I wished I could see him. How dark were his eyes? Was he smiling? I felt more vulnerable than ever, unable to see his intentions and truly at his mercy as he toyed with my fear.

Jack tutted. 'Nobody knows where you are... you're alone with me... restrained, exposed, allowing me to do whatever I want with you.'

His fingertips followed a trail down my breasts, over my stomach. I leaned into his touch, then arched away as he traced the same path with the knife.

Fuck.

I tugged at my bindings, but I was stuck on the table, spread out for him. My heartbeat picked up.

Jack chuckled. 'You can't get out of these. I am very good at what I do.' Again and again, he let the edge of the blade scrape along my skin, and sharp scratches mixed with soft caresses in a thrilling mix of sensations.

'You wouldn't harm me,' I breathed, losing myself to his game of pain and pleasure.

'I never said I wouldn't hurt you.'

I hardly dared inhale as the knife trailed alongside my inner thigh, so close to my aching flesh. My legs started trembling. Jack's breaths came deep and fast, revealing his own arousal from this game.

'Maybe if I carve Marquis into your skin, you'll never forget to say it.'

'N-no...'

'Is that how you should address me?'

'No, Marquis,' I said, my words choppy and fast.

Jack ran the tip of the blade up my stomach and along my neck, then followed the same path with his tongue. I leaned away from the knife and into his touch, but not knowing which would come next made it hard to breathe, hard to relax, and as he continued to tease my skin, I grew more and more desperate for the thrill of both.

The feel of his powerful body standing between my thighs, the intensity of his gaze I couldn't see but still felt on every inch of my skin as he toyed with my body. It all made it hard to breathe and think.

His mouth came close to my ear. 'What colour are you?'

I swallowed hard, releasing the word on a sharp exhale, 'Green.'

'Count,' he ordered, and I held my breath, releasing a startled gasp as the blade bit into my skin. Warmth trickled down my breast.

'One.' I shuddered as he dragged the cold metal along my skin, setting nerve endings on fire. Calming piano tunes filled the room as Jack smeared a warm drop of blood around my nipple.

'You're a very silly girl, ropes.' His deep voice came closer, his breath hot against my lips as he tugged my hair back with enough force to make me wince. 'Don't you know how dangerous it is to give a sadist free rein of your body?'

'Yes,' I squeaked, but it was what I wanted. I had dreamt of this thrill and craved it for so long.

'So silly,' he murmured, cutting the crest of my other breast.

'Two.' Biting my lip, I groaned as he dragged the blood along my other nipple.

'Your foolishness pleases me.' He ran the sharp tip of the knife across my chest. 'Bound, exposed, alone in the house with someone you barely know...' He tutted. 'Don't you know what they have trained me to do?'

I swallowed, my heart hammering. 'Jack...'

His mouth came to my ear. 'I have done things that would give you nightmares, ropes.' The sharp blade pressed against the crest of my left breast. 'And now I'm here, holding this knife over your heart, and there is nothing you can do to stop me...'

His words rose the hairs on my nape. Time seemed to stand still as he held it to my chest, waiting, testing how far I would let him take me. My strained breaths filled the air between us.

It was a game. Only a game. Right?

'You've seen the brand on my back,' he whispered in a menacing tone. 'If you knew anything about my world, you'd know who I am. I am no ordinary Dom.'

'What are you?' I whimpered, asking him the question I'd wanted an answer to since the moment I met him, since the first time the rush of fear he provoked had lit up my whole body.

He raked his teeth along my earlobe. 'I'm a Marquis, a trained sadist from the Harpyiai, the masters of sadism.'

The Harpyiai? The *H* on his back?

'We are feared and respected by anyone in the scene because of what we can do,' he continued in the same deep voice. 'You call me dark and dangerous, but you have no idea how dangerous we are.'

Jack ran the wet tip of his tongue up my neck. I tugged on the bindings, wanting to squeeze my thighs together – or run away. I wasn't sure anymore.

'We are the men your mother warned you about, the monsters under your bed, the villains in your nightmares.' He pressed his nose into my cheek and inhaled. 'And now you're mine to play with.'

My exhale came with a shudder of coiled desire.

'Colour?' he whispered in my ear.

I panted, unable to form any words. Jack waited, watching me no doubt as I struggled. My heart beat so fast I could barely hear him when he asked again.

All I could think about was that he was a master of sadism, and I was caught in his web. He was free to do whatever he wanted with me, and there was nowhere to go. The fear of him and the maddening desire he provoked sucked me into a whirlpool of sensations.

Jack's hands came around my face as he kissed me, softly at first, then harder and more demanding as he pulled me back from the edge of panic he'd left me on. He kissed me until I moaned into his mouth and met his tongue with my own.

'Colour?' he whispered again.

'O-orange.'

'Do you mean yellow?' he asked, amusement in his voice.

'Yes.'

'Have you had enough?'

'No,' I pleaded, trembling in his touch. 'I need you.'

'Shh,' he soothed. 'I've got you. You know that.'

I did, and all I wanted was him, his hands on my body, his lips on mine as he kissed me again.

Dipping two fingers inside me, he groaned. 'You are so wet. Wet and swollen. Are you aching for me, ropes?'

'Yes,' I moaned.

He removed his hand.

'Yes, Marquis!'

He kissed me again, moving his fingers in and out of me. Slow, agonising movements and I was lost to it, my body teetering on edge for so long. He curved his fingers and brought me closer to the edge, so close I hissed when he pulled away. Jack chuckled softly, then finally tugged me to him, and his cock pressed against my sex. I moaned in anticipation.

'Do you want me?' he teased.

'You know I do,' I hissed. I wanted to grab him, to lift my hips to meet him, but I couldn't move, and Jack wasn't done teasing me.

Grabbing my hips, he pushed halfway into me, then withdrew and left me aching again.

'Jack, please!'

He chuckled softly. 'You want more?'

'Yes!'

His grip on my hips tightened, and he slammed into me. I cried out and lost myself in the sensation and everything that was Jack. Nothing had ever felt as right as his body pressed against mine, his mouth on mine and our warm breaths mixing. He circled his hips, stirring my desire, then pulled out, and I wanted to kill him; I really did.

'More?'

'I will hurt you,' I grated.

Jack chuckled. 'Oh, ropes, you can't even touch me. You're at my mercy right now.'

'Please.' I tugged at my restraints and groaned in frustration, overwhelmed with need and frustrated with his teasing. Again, he pushed into me. He groaned, circling his hips over and over again, slow and deep, and I was lost. Lost in the heat, lost in the pain and pleasure, lost in myself.

Heat simmered in my core as he set up a steady pace. I wanted to straighten my legs. Longed to regain control over my impending orgasm, but it built and built. Tears sprung to my eyes. It was too intense.

I wanted to stop.

Wanted him to never stop.

The safeword sat on my tongue as Jack thrust harder, faster. It was too much. Too intense, building, spiralling, from deep within my body. It would tear me apart.

'No,' I gasped.

Panic swirled through me, but he gave no mercy as he fucked me faster, deeper, and lifted me to the peak of my orgasm. I tugged on my restraints and cried, too afraid to fall apart. But Jack wanted me to fall apart. He wanted to test all my limits – pain, pleasure and fear – and fucked me harder and faster, and the pleasure built to the point of sweet, blissful pain.

'Let go, Kate,' he growled.

His command wrenched a strained groan from my gut, and I couldn't control my body anymore. Tears streamed down my face as the orgasm pulsed through me. For a long moment, I was trapped in a silent scream as it came at me like a white fire, a crashing wave of scorching heat that ripped me apart.

'Fuck,' he growled as he found his release, but my body kept convulsing, and I floated, lost in the pleasure and feel of his hands around me.

My limbs lost all strength; his words made no sense, sounding distant and insignificant as he untied me and lifted me into his arms.

When my eyes opened, I was cradled in his lap with a fleece wrapped around me. Jack was watching me with a hint of concern in his eyes. 'Welcome back. Are you okay?'

I blinked up at him.

'Drink this.' He passed me a glass of orange juice.

My hands trembled as I took it. 'Thanks.'

His brows furrowed. 'Did I push you too far?'

'No…' As I sipped, I looked around the living room. 'How did I get here?'

'I carried you. I would've brought you upstairs for a bath, but you took a while to come back to me.' He stroked my hair. 'Had me worried for a moment.'

'What happened?'

He smiled. 'Subspace. You floated away, overwhelmed by it all. Was it too much?'

'I can handle a knife.' When his lips curled, I followed his line of sight, surprised to find no cuts on my skin. No blood, either. Only thin red lines, as if someone had scratched me. Jack's playful shrug only added to my confusion. 'But I felt the cuts? And the blood on my skin?'

'You felt what I wanted you to feel.'

'You tricked me?'

He tapped a finger against my temple. 'The mind is a wonderful thing, Caitlin. One of my favourite playgrounds.'

I gaped at him.

'Welcome to my world.' He kissed my forehead. 'Are you running away yet?'

Why would I run away from him? I searched his eyes, surprised at his wary tone. 'No, Jack. I'm not going anywhere.'

His arms tightened around me. 'This is the kind of Dom I am, ropes. No contracts, whips, or cruel punishments. I like playing with people's heads instead of relying on toys or tools. I find what excites you, what scares you, and will push your limits, but I've always got you.'

I put the glass on the table and sat astride him. Jack's eyes widened as I put my hands around his face and leaned closer, losing myself in the depths of his dark blues. 'And this is how I want you.'

A smile spread across his face. 'You're reckless, ropes. Few people dare play with a Marquis outside a club.'

'I'm not like most people,' I whispered, kissing the corner of his mouth. 'You don't scare me.'

'I do.' He twisted his hands in my hair to tug my head back. 'It's what draws you to me, knowing I will ignite that fear you crave and that you still hold all the power to stop me with just one word.' He kissed my neck and inhaled, as if savouring my scent. 'And you know I will. I'll always protect you, even from myself.'

I did. He was dangerous, capable of doing things I barely dared imagine, but his dark edge brought my body and soul alive, and so did his soft side as he pulled me down onto the sofa and held me close, wrapping the blanket around me.

'No contracts? No calling you Marquis in public and asking for permission before I can speak?'

Jack laughed. 'No, Caitlin. If we had a Master/slave relationship, I'd have to punish you every time you called me an arse or rolled your eyes at me.'

I snorted. 'Good luck with that.'

His laugh deepened. 'Your butt would've been nice and pink now if I was that kind of Dom.'

Not wanting him to see how much the tease of such a punishment intrigued me, I put my arm around his broad chest and listened to the steady beat of his heart.

Maybe he wouldn't change and could be everything I'd ever wanted. I loved his dark side, but I enjoyed being independent and voicing my opinion.

I smirked. 'I'm making that one of my non-negotiables. If you're an arse, I may call you on it, and you can't punish me.'

Jack's deep laugh filled the room. 'Disrespecting your Dom is always a bad idea.'

'It seems a fair trade for all the alcohol I'll give up.'

'You don't need alcohol.'

Maybe I didn't. After his demonstration earlier, I could see why it would be a terrible idea to mix alcohol with mind games.

'It's my body.'

'Is it?' He gave me one of his darkened stares that sent shivers down my spine. 'You're mine now. I'm responsible for your well-being. I wouldn't be happy if you put yourself at risk, like standing alone outside a club in Kittington whilst under the influence.'

'Why do you despise alcohol so much?'

'Why do you not?'

'Don't answer a question with a question.'

His smile was wry but bittersweet. 'Do you know how much crime is committed because of alcohol? It can make you do things you wouldn't normally do. I like to stay in control of my mind, and for those I'm with to be in control of theirs. It's very important to me.'

I brushed a lock of his hair back from his forehead. 'When were you not in control?'

He looked surprised, open and bare for a second and it wasn't a confident Dominant looking back at me anymore. It was someone who'd once been deeply wounded. Then he shut it down and smiled.

'No alcohol when you're with me, and you can call me an arse when we're alone.' He gave me a stern stare. 'Not when we're around other Doms. Deal?'

I pursed my lips. 'Else you'll punish me?'

'I've got a feeling you'd like another spanking.' His brow arched in a silent challenge, mischief lurking in the depths of his deep blues.

'I would not,' I tried, but Jack laughed, and I pushed at his chest. 'You're such an arse.'

'Oh, well.' He tipped my chin to kiss me. 'I'm your arse now, so be a good girl.'

'Do you even have a playroom?'

'No, ropes. I don't.' He smiled as he tucked my hair behind my ear. 'I don't need one.'

'Where did you learn to do that? To play with people's heads?'

'That's a story for another day.' He strained to reach the remote on the coffee table. 'Do you want to watch another movie? If you're hungry, I'll cook you something.'

I pushed up onto my elbow. 'Is the Harpynai where you trained?'

'The Harpyiai, yes.' He flicked on the TV, scrolling through the movies. 'What do you want to watch?'

The dip in his voice warned me he was putting his wall back up, but learning when to stop picking at people's boundaries had never been my strength.

'I've never heard of it before.'

'There aren't many of us, but we can be found in clubs.' He cast me a stern glance, making it clear he wanted me to drop the subject. 'Something tells me you've never been to one, though.'

I wiggled my fingers to get the remote, a small struggle to regain some dominance. When he handed it over, his smirk told me he knew what I was doing. 'No, I've never been to a club.'

He didn't need to know that the few times I'd tried to visit a dungeon, I'd found my name was barred from entry, thanks to my stepdad. But maybe he could get me inside. I was curious to learn more about all of this, especially his past, but baby steps seemed the only way to peel back all his layers. When I got home, I had to look up the Harpyiai on the internet.

'Maybe we can go to one?' I started another horror movie; more hopeless dumb women running from a masked killer. 'One that doesn't only have imaginary playrooms.'

Jack laughed. 'We'll go to one of Theo's parties. It seems a fair trade for how many horror movies you're making me watch.'

'Next weekend?' It was only a matter of time before my mother realised I was seeing him and tried to stop it. I wanted to experience as much as possible before I ended up homeless and bankrupt, to savour every stolen moment with someone like Jack before my family ruined it.

'Hopefully,' Jack said, kissing the top of my head.

CHAPTER EIGHTEEN

JACK

* * *

Blood.

It was everywhere.

In my hair.

On my skin.

The Hunt had left its mark on me.

I could taste the blood, smell its coppery tinge intermingled with the sharp tang of my urine.

The pool of dark red on the floor scared me, and having no strength left to fight terrified me.

But nothing petrified me more than the curl of Andrei's mouth when he lifted a glowing brand from the fireplace and came towards me. The moment the sizzling hot metal pressed into my skin, I screamed.

* * *

I JERKED AWAKE, my heart beating so hard that the edges of my vision jittered. Rubbing a fist against my chest, I tried to catch my breath. The skin on my back tingled, the pain never forgotten. I could never run from it because I carried it with me, body and soul.

Juliet had once said our training had to be tough because the Marquises were special. To create something truly spectacular, you had to break it apart. In my case, the pieces didn't go back together again as they should have.

My father had the same brand, but as far as I knew, nightmares never plagued him. He'd never had an issue talking about the night of his branding, but I refused to talk to anyone about mine.

After Kate's probing questions, the nightmare shouldn't have come as a surprise. I'd tried to share as much as I could, but every time she dug deeper, I struggled to stay present. If she'd touched me unexpectedly, I could've had a flashback, and she didn't need to see me like that.

Hell, maybe my father was right. Relationships weren't for a Marquis. How could I explain my years as a slave, or my training, without scaring her away? That I had been declared dead? What if she reported it as a crime? I shuddered.

I shouldn't have told her what the *H* stood for. If Dad ever found out, he'd be furious. At clubs, we were simply referred to as the Marquises, and everyone assumed they trained us at The Aurora, our largest club. Everything else about the Harpyiai had to stay a secret, even our brand, only I was tired of keeping secrets.

Kate was fast asleep, with one arm draped across my stomach. The moonlight dimly illuminated the bedroom, revealing her every line, plane and curve. I turned onto my side to brush a lock of her hair away from her face.

She'd fallen asleep on the sofa earlier, midway through our movie marathon, no doubt worn out, and I'd carried her upstairs.

I had watched her sleep for hours, not quite understanding why she hadn't run yet. She knew more about me than any woman I'd been with. I tucked my pillow closer. A flutter of hope for a better future, one with her, stirred in the pit of my stomach, but I was afraid to let that feeling take root.

It had been easy to hide my past from Larissa. After she'd once felt the scars on my chest, she'd been horrified and never questioned why I always kept my T-shirt on. Marquises were expected to wear our uniform around subs and slaves. Kate was the first woman I'd let see all of me, and it puzzled me why she'd looked at me like I was a victim.

I wanted to tuck her closer, but a thump downstairs made me freeze. A clattering followed, like something rolling across the floor.

I swung my legs over the edge of the bed. The alarm was silent. No one should have been in the house. Yet another thump came.

Was Freddy home? I grabbed my phone and peered into the darkened hallway. His bedroom was empty, the bed neatly made as usual. Below his window, the driveway showed no sign of a second car.

Maybe I was imagining things. Sometimes my nightmares stuck with me for a while after I woke. But as I crossed the hallway to climb back into bed, the creak of a door opening came from downstairs.

For the first time, I wished I'd listened to Freddy when he wanted to keep a gun in the house. When Dad had bought this place eight years ago, he'd insisted on a remote location and high fences. Since then, we'd added alarms to every window and exterior door.

There was no way anyone would get into the house without triggering a sensor, yet, as I stood on the landing and looked down the stairwell, it was clear someone – or something – was inside.

I retreated into Freddy's room and dialled his number. He answered on the second ring, his voice groggy. 'Fuck's sake, Jack—'

'Get back here. Someone's in the house,' I whispered and hung up.

Lily lived a few miles away, on the outskirts of Kittington. It should only take him ten minutes to get here. My brother was no good in a fight, but two was always better than one, and I wouldn't take any chances with Kate. The best move would've been to call in the guards no doubt lurking near my house as usual, but it would draw Dad's attention as well.

While I waited, I checked the spare bedroom and main bathroom, then Kate again. She was still asleep, safe and unaware of what was happening downstairs. I stood there for a while, watching her sleep as I counted the minutes in my head until my brother would arrive. Who it could be? A burglar? Unlikely. It was someone clever enough to get past the alarm system. Whoever it was, they would have to get through me to get upstairs, so I went to the bottom step of the staircase. The fridge in the kitchen hummed. Whispers came from the back of the house, and the hairs on my nape rose.

Not burglars. If it was, they were dumb and easy to take down.

Headlights from a car brushed across the frosted glass of the front door, and soon Freddy's footfalls crunched on the gravel. I disarmed the front door, and he slipped through the gap.

'Who is it?' He looked me up and down and snorted. 'You're going to fight them naked?'

I put my finger to my lips and indicated for him to stay at the bottom of the staircase while I checked the house.

The kitchen lay dark and deserted, as did the dining room behind. In the living room, an overenthusiastic guy on TV wanted to sell me jewellery. After carrying Kate upstairs, I'd switched everything off and checked all the doors like every night. The back of my neck prickled, my suspicions rising that this was no burglar and that there was a reason why this person had managed to sneak past the guards.

When I got back to the kitchen, Freddy was grabbing a knife from a drawer.

'Keep that away from my balls,' I whispered. 'And I told you to stay by the staircase.'

'But what if they came that way?'

I glared at him. 'Exactly.'

As we moved into the hallway, another thump came from the back of the house. I looked at Freddy. They had to be in the garage. He swallowed noisily and gestured for me to go first. I rolled my eyes. My brother was many things, but brave was not one of them.

The door to the garage was ajar and creaked as I nudged it open. A cold draft brushed over my skin as I stepped inside and flipped the light switch. The overhead lights flickered as they illuminated the space.

After Freddy moved in, we'd split the garage in half. I had my treadmill and weights at the back, and he had his workbenches with an array of tools at the opposite end. In the middle of the room was the wooden table Kate had sat on yesterday, the straps still hanging loose from the table legs. Now on this table, a pale, furless cat lounged, casually licking its paw. The golden *H* dangling from its red collar made the room spin before my eyes, and I steadied myself on the door.

'What the hell is that?' Freddy blurted.

'Oh, fuck,' I growled. 'Freddy, you idiot!'

'What?' He scrunched up his face. 'Why is that cat naked?'

Juliet adored her Sphynx cats almost as much as she loved toying with me. But now, I'd made a mistake, and this was no longer a game. Juliet hadn't called me by accident. She was not only aware that I was seeing Kate, but she also knew something about her I should've found out.

The Harpyiai only sent a Sphynx cat to a Marquis who had been caught coupling with an illegitimate.

My pulse thudded in my throat as I glared at the cat, hoping it would disappear and that all of this was nothing but a nightmare.

How the hell could Kate be an illegitimate? Why hadn't Freddy found this link when he vetted her?

'I thought you were allergic to cats,' Freddy said as I shut the garage door.

My brother failed to realise the significance of it. He also failed to notice my struggle to keep myself upright. Juliet sent Sphynx cats because they were – as Freddy had said – naked. Like the slaves at the castle.

She'd once told me it was her little joke to a Marquis caught breaking such a rule, a warning that their illegitimate plaything would become a naked pet.

'The back door is open.' Freddy moved to close it. 'Maybe it's the neighbour's cat.'

'Call Dad,' I groaned.

It was only a matter of time before he found out, and if I was to have any chance to take control of this situation, I needed to make my decision tonight.

A Marquis caught coupling with an illegitimate had to send someone to The Hunt as prey. I had two illegitimates in my life now: Kate, sleeping upstairs, and my brother, who gaped at me, shocked by those words he never thought would come from me.

'You want me to call Dad?'

'Now! Do it.'

'Jesus, mate. Don't bite my head off.' He edged around the table, waving the knife around as he tried to get his phone out of his pocket. 'It's just a freaking cat.'

'Give me that.' I grabbed the steak knife and tossed it onto the workbench. 'You are, as always, a hazard in a fight.'

The ugly, hairless creature stared at me with its pale blue eyes. I couldn't understand how this had happened. Who was Kate's father?

'Dad,' Freddy said, 'umm, sorry to call so early, but… Yes, he's fine, but there's an ugly, naked cat here and—' Frowning, he stared at his phone. 'He hung up.'

Of course he did. When a Sphynx cat showed up at your house, you dropped everything. I wanted to blame my brother for this mistake, but it wasn't all his fault. I had taken too many risks, and now The Hunt awaited.

Four years after Juliet had taken me, she brought me to the tower to observe the annual hunt. It was a cold June evening, and she'd dressed up for the occasion. Despite my hatred of her, it was hard not to admire the deep purple Victorian corset dress hugging her curves.

'Tell me, *parshivets*,' Juliet said, staring out the window. 'What has your dear father told you about The Hunt?'

I shifted my weight on the cold stone floor. 'Nothing, *Gospozha*. You know this already.'

She tutted. 'Your father has failed you in so many ways. One day you, too, will become a Marquis. It is a great honour.'

I didn't see any of it as an honour, but the last time I'd said that out loud, she hadn't fed me for a week, so I settled for a silent glare.

'Come, *detka*.' She snapped her fingers and beckoned me closer to the window. 'Tell me what you see.'

I didn't want to look, but she gripped the back of my neck. On the pristine lawn below, eight women knelt in a line, their hands behind their heads in the slave position she still forced me to assume.

The floodlights dotted around the castle's exterior walls lit up their bare skin. The women stared at the ground as Andrei paced the grass in front of them. With so many slaves under his command, he was in his element. Peter – Theo's father – was also on the lawn, offering a chalice to each female slave. I didn't want to think about what was in the drink, but knowing him, it wouldn't be good.

'Do you see the armorial painted on their backs?' Juliet asked.

'We have marked the Marquesses in the same manner. I wish it were unnecessary, but with such close bloodlines, we must avoid any unfortunate couplings between family members. A Marquis needs an heir, not a burden. Although we have means to take care of such issues, of course.'

Theo had told me about the almost incestuous traditions of the Marquises. The slaves were sent out into the forest after the Marquesses – the breeders. Only the danger of The Hunt meant there were hardly any Marquesses left to breed with, leading to more illegitimates, and more prey for The Hunt.

Juliet patted my cheek, startling me. 'Those who make it through the night are brought to the dungeon so their Marquis can play with them. Those who do not...' She smirked. 'As Darwin said, it is a survival of the fittest.'

'The Hunt is only for breeding, *Gospozha?*' I asked, staring at my bare feet.

'*Nyet.* We also use The Hunt to cull slaves.'

My stomach dropped. Theo had once compared the tradition with fox hunting, but I had hoped it wasn't true. Would she send me out there?

Giggling, she patted my arm. 'Not to worry, *parshivets.* We have not yet given up hope. You will become a Marquis and only then can you be bred.'

I suppressed a glare.

'Soon, we will let these loose, and the Marquises will take chase. Some want to capture a Marquess and breed, some want to play with an illegitimate, and some... Well, they have their own reasons for what they do during The Hunt. There are no rules. No consequences. It is quite a thrill. You will see how special The Hunt is when you take part.'

She tried to catch my gaze. 'One day, I will break through to you. Or do you wish to remain a slave forever?'

'*Nyet, Gospozha.*'

Nor did I want to become a Marquis, even if it was my only

option to rise from my status as a slave. I didn't want to breed, either – especially not with her.

'I thought so.'

'I don't want to be a Marquis, *Gospozha*.'

She sighed. 'So you say, *parshivets*, but perhaps today's special guest will help cure your continued insubordination, *da?*'

'Guest, *Gospozha?*'

'When a Marquis breeds outside the approved bloodlines, they must make a sacrifice. You know this. It is why you are here. With twins, the firstborn male will train as a Marquis to restore their father's honour. But if such an illegitimate does not fall in line, we must ask for a second sacrifice.'

My heartbeat picked up. '*Gospozha*, don't hurt my brother!'

She had never told me this before; the only reason I was stuck with her was to spare my brother and mother.

Juliet's laugh echoed in the tower. '*Detka*, I adore your brother. Such an innocent boy. He can take your place if you wish, since you are so...' Her voice dropped to a soft growl. 'Resistant to our trainers.'

'I will make no such swap.' I folded my arms so she couldn't see the tremors in my hands.

'As you wish.' She gripped the back of my neck and shoved me closer to the window. 'Tonight will be a good lesson in what happens if you keep this up.'

Juliet picked up a flashlight and flickered it. Below, Andrei crooked his finger at someone out of view. Sweat trickled down my bare back as I waited, silently praying it wasn't Freddy. My brother wasn't strong enough to survive any of their rituals.

'There she is,' Juliet said in her silky voice as a woman approached Andrei.

She? I stepped closer to the glass, my heart hammering. There was something familiar about her long, dark hair and how she moved. But it couldn't be. My breath caught when Andrei gripped my mother's arm and swivelled her around to face the tower.

'No,' I gasped.

'*Da, parshivets,*' Juliet purred, patting my shoulder.

I shook her hand off. How dare she touch me? How fucking dare Andrei touch my mother? I clenched my fists. I wanted to scream. Wanted to destroy all of them. Wanted to offer myself to The Hunt if it would save my mother. Tears trickled down my cheeks, and I swiped them away, hoping Juliet didn't notice.

'*Detka.* Seventeen years ago, I stood on that lawn. Your father was mine; instead, he bred with your mother. It is not something I will forget.'

'*Gospozha*, I won't cause you any more trouble.' Rushing through the words, I looked into her eyes for the first time in years. 'Please. Dad already gave you me. Why do you need my mother? She hasn't done anything! Put me in The Hunt. I will restore my father's honour as a prey.'

My panicked words only made her smile. 'Your father has chosen the prey he will sacrifice to The Hunt. There is nothing we can do. Next year it will be your dear brother.'

That day had changed so many things. It forced me to train as a Marquis to prevent them from taking Freddy, but my mother didn't survive The Hunt. Unable to cope with my guilt, I never spoke of Mum again. Unable to forgive my father, I only spoke to him if I had to.

Having seen the consequences of my father's mistake, I had always been so careful. I had no children and thought I had avoided getting involved with an illegitimate because Freddy's insistent vetting should have made sure.

The Sphynx cat proved me wrong.

'You all right?' Freddy looked between me and the disgusting feline on the table.

I was far from all right, but Freddy didn't need to know yet. I wanted to talk to Dad first. As Head Marquis, he might know who Kate's birth father was and if there was another way out of this.

I switched off the lights. 'Come on. I don't want to look at it anymore.'

'Don't we have to feed it, get some cat litter or something?' he asked, following me back into the kitchen.

I dragged an unsteady hand over my face, struggling with the swirling panic. Feeding one of Juliet's pets was not at the top of my list of priorities.

'Coffee?' I asked, wishing I had something stronger in the house to calm me down. A bottle of whisky would have gone down well now.

'Do you think it's Juliet?'

'Of course it is. Don't be stupid.'

'Why would she give you a cat?'

Freddy leaned against the kitchen island as I grabbed mugs from the cupboard. His stare prickled the back of my neck, but he could wait. The fucking cat could wait as well. I had to figure out what to do about Kate.

It would take Dad hours to get here from London, and she had to be gone before he arrived. If she wasn't, he would insist I send her to The Hunt.

'You played chess with Kate?' Freddy moved the pieces around on the kitchen island.

We had. She was full of surprises, but her chess talent was more welcome than learning she was an illegitimate.

I draped a hand over my face and laughed softly. 'For fuck's sake.'

'What's so funny?'

'Nothing.' There truly wasn't, but Dad would be here soon to tell me how much I'd fucked up. 'What time's sunrise?'

'I don't know? In an hour?'

'I'll take Kate to the beach to watch the sunrise. You can wait here for Dad, and I'll join you after I've dropped her off at—'

The front door opened, and before either of us could react, Dad stood in the doorway.

Oh, hell. I bit down on my tongue to stop myself from screaming in his face. Mum used to say we were spitting images of our father. Maybe it was true, but Dad was taller, broader, and over the years, it had become clear that he was only capable of a few facial expressions.

Offering no form of greeting, he met my glare without a hint of emotion. Behind him, two blond brutes appeared. The guards scanned the room, pausing briefly to stare at me before disappearing to do their usual check of the rooms.

The reflection from the spotlights above highlighted Dad's ever-receding hairline. Like his guards, he wore black dress trousers and a crisp black shirt, so similar to the Marquis uniform it made my skin crawl. Only a slight twitch at the corner of his mouth hinted at amusement with my lack of clothing.

'You're dating,' Dad stated in his usual too-calm tone.

'I am.' I leaned against the kitchen counter. If my balls offended him, maybe he shouldn't have lurked nearby. Dad was never where you thought he would be. 'And I'd appreciate it if your guards didn't wake her up. Freddy and I have already checked the house. The cat's in the garage.'

Next to me, Freddy did his best to make himself invisible. I ignored him, more worried about what Dad would do with Kate. Illegitimate females were at the bottom of the food chain at the Harpyiai. I didn't even want to imagine what thoughts were going through my father's head now that such a woman had put his family in danger.

'Frederick told me the anniversary party was a success.' As always, Dad spoke about Freddy as if he wasn't present. 'Although he expressed dissatisfaction with the strippers you booked.'

I scowled. He wanted to talk about The Yard? 'Burlesque dancers, Dad. Not strippers.'

The faintest of smiles crossed his face. 'You have always had an uncanny ability to reinterpret simple instructions.'

What was I supposed to say? That I was sorry for having a bit of fun? Fuck that.

'Look, as pleasant as it is to catch up, I didn't ask you to come here to discuss the club.'

One brute – Jonas, if I remembered right – reappeared in the doorway and whispered something in my father's ear before retreating into the hallway. I sipped my coffee, refusing to give Dad the satisfaction of knowing his sudden arrival worried me.

'Jonas says she's still asleep.'

'Good.'

'Frederick, would you excuse us for a moment?'

My brother moved forward, but I put a hand out. Since leaving the castle, I'd never spoken to Dad in private for more than a few minutes. If Freddy stayed, we both had to watch what we said. A flicker of annoyance crossed Dad's features before he looked into the darkened living room.

'Early yesterday morning, the sensor on your backdoor was disabled. Since neither of you contacted me about a fault with the system, I presume this is news to you?'

He knew it was disabled and didn't tell me? Did Freddy know? No, my brother looked as surprised by this news as me.

'I saw no one then or now,' I said. 'The cat wasn't there when I went to bed earlier. That's all I know.'

'There's also the phone call you received earlier in the week. Would you like to tell me who it was from?'

I put the mug down and folded my arms. 'Something tells me you already know.'

'I do.' He turned to look at me. 'And now you're dating Caitlin Howard.'

For god's sake. The house wasn't soundproof. Cursing my father to hell and back, I shut the kitchen door, ignoring the two men standing guard at the bottom of the staircase.

'Dad, you can't keep me locked up forever. The cameras, my phone, Freddy, the clubs – the fucking pills.'

'Your restrictions are to help you. So is your medication.'

He called it restrictions; I called it control. Dad knew how valuable I was to the Harpyiai and to Juliet. Keeping me from her was my father's favourite little game to play. I'd given up on privacy years ago. Because of him, I had none.

'I wouldn't need any of it if you hadn't sent me there,' I gritted out.

'You are a Marquis, son. Your life will never be normal, nor will mine. You knew this day could come when you left with Theodore Williams. When you started hitting the clubs, I warned you again about the risk of illegitimates and the lengths Juliet will go to.' He took a seat at the kitchen island, his gaze wandering down my front. 'Do I need to increase your clothing allowance?'

'Can we discuss what's in my garage and how the hell this happened?'

'Your brother tells me you still struggle with some triggers, but you're managing better. I'm glad.'

I gritted my teeth. If he skirted around my questions one more time, I would lose it.

'Sorry,' Freddy muttered, 'but what does the cat mean?'

'It means I have to sacrifice an illegitimate to The Hunt because you fucked up Kate's background check.' I regretted my sharp tone when he blanched. Freddy was aware of his status as an illegitimate, but he didn't need to worry. I would never let them have my brother.

Dad ran two fingers along his forehead, one of the few indications he ever gave when he was stressed. 'Frederick, when you conducted checks on Caitlin Howard, what did you find?'

'I swear there was nothing linking her to the Harpyiai.' Freddy's unsteady voice revealed his fear of what consequences this would have. 'My only concern was that her stepdad is the MP who's tried to shut down the club.'

'And her birth father?' Dad asked. 'What could you find out about him?'

Freddy shook his head. 'His name's not listed anywhere. I assumed it was a one-night stand. We've come across those before.'

What? For Christ's sake. He should have known better. When I was banned from The Aurora, Dad insisted that Freddy do the checks, claiming I was too reckless and impulsive. If I'd known my brother would take such risks, I would've done it myself. Fuck. I should've demanded Nate did my checks, not just Theo and Mark's.

Nate vetted everyone who entered our clubs and would never have cleared Kate if she hadn't had a father on her birth certificate. There was usually an innocent explanation, but Freddy should've done further checks on her mother.

When the Marquises at the castle coupled with outsiders, it was always at one of our clubs to avoid breaching protocol. Those records were used to find the illegitimates so they could be taken to the castle, but clearly Freddy never bothered checking if Kate's mother had any links to our clubs and now there was a damn cat in my garage.

'Hmm.' Dad stroked his chin. 'Regardless, you have been caught coupling with an illegitimate, Jack. The rules are clear. You must send an illegitimate to The Hunt. Jonas can make the arrangements to take her to Scotland.'

Coupling.

Trust the Harpyiai to use such a fancy word for fucking. That was all I had done. I'd fucked a woman who happened to be an illegitimate. Now Juliet had a way of pressuring me into giving her an heir.

The risk of The Hunt scared me, but I was tired of living under this threat. I wanted a life no matter how short it would be. Unlike what my father thought, I knew the rules and there was another option. I could sacrifice myself and buy time.

I folded my arms. 'No.'

'No?'

'You heard me.'

Dad rose, a move no doubt meant to intimidate me. 'They'll come for you if you don't send her.'

'So let them fucking come!'

'You don't mean that. You have only taken part in The Hunt as a Marquis, not prey. This is why I told you to stay away from other clubs. You're too reckless.'

'This would never have happened if you hadn't banned me from the clubs I want to go to.'

He dipped his head. 'You were told to stay at The Yard.'

Fuck him. If he thought for a minute that I'd hand over Kate, he was insane. She might be an illegitimate, but so was I. Our fathers were Marquises; as always, it was up to the children to pay for those mistakes. But I refused to pass this mistake on to someone else as my father had.

'I'd rather face Juliet myself.'

'Son, you can't—'

I raised a hand. 'Enough. If you're worried, get your men to babysit until The Hunt is over. It's not like you haven't got the resources.'

My father took a step forward. Freddy retreated into the corner of the worktops. 'I am not interested in a war. My resources can also make your life significantly less comfortable if you put Frederick at risk.'

I laughed. 'You think you can scare me? I spent almost five years with Andrei. What the hell do you think you can do to me that I haven't already survived?'

His lips twitched. Oh, he thought this was amusing, did he? Fucking sadist.

'You're Head Marquis, Dad. Don't even try to pretend you can't influence what happens now.'

'Yulia is Head Marquess.'

'The Head Marquis outranks the Head Marquess.'

He sighed. 'I have to follow protocol, which is why I'm asking you if you're sure about this decision. We have already lost your mother, Jack.'

As always, he had to pick at that wound. I swallowed down the guilt his words provoked. Dad hadn't seen Mum's mangled body when they dragged her back from the forest. If he had, maybe he'd understand why I had no choice.

Dad pinned me with an icy stare. 'We have been over this before. You cannot go to any club you want because you let your feelings get in the way. How you've involved yourself with an illegitimate is beyond my comprehension. You've put both of you at risk.'

'I didn't find anything.' Freddy shrank further into his corner.

'You knew Jack was taking her home, Frederick. I know you swapped cars again.'

I placed myself in front of my brother. 'It's not his fault. I don't even think Kate knows her father is a Marquis.'

Dad huffed. 'Of course she doesn't. Not even the Head Marquess knew about Caitlin.'

'Whose is she? How the hell did someone keep her hidden for this long?'

He came closer, so close I could smell sour cigarettes on his breath. It puzzled me; he'd given up smoking before we were born. 'Are you willing to send her?'

'No, and I'm not sending my brother. This is my mistake.'

Dad put a hand on my shoulder. 'I know Yulia gave you the option to swap with Frederick, and you didn't. You've always had a good heart.'

I shook him off. How dare he share that information with Freddy? He already carried too much guilt. I didn't even need to look at my brother to sense his shock.

'Don't upset him,' I gritted out in Russian.

'Then let me talk to you alone.'

'You made me an illegitimate—'

Dad gave me a pointed look. 'I made you a Marquis.'

'As an illegitimate, I can sacrifice myself.'

'This is not what I wanted for you.'

'Well, you should've fucking thought about that before you had me!'

'You cannot disobey a direct order, and I'm—' When I laughed in disbelief at his arrogance to try and pull rank on me, his features hardened.

'I know protocol as well as you do, Dad. This is my decision.'

Freddy's eyes darted between us, confusion furrowing his brows. He had never learnt Russian. There was no need.

'Leave my brother out of this,' I said in an icy tone. 'Do not upset him again.'

Dad folded his arms. Every inch of his darkness stood out like the sharp edge of a sword as he glared at me.

'I will go,' I said in English, hoping my voice revealed no hint of fear of going back to the castle. My father would use it to talk me out of this. 'No one else. Nothing you say will change my mind. I've survived The Hunt before. I can do it again. It will buy us time to figure out what to do.'

Dad sighed. 'It's your decision. Not one I would have made, though.'

My father thought I was foolish. Weak. A true Marquis was honoured to train and willing to sacrifice anyone to The Hunt. He would know. He'd sent me and then my mother. It was why I refused to have children. This madness would end with me.

'It's in June, isn't it?' Freddy asked, his voice barely a whisper.

'Yes. Believe it or not, Jack, I was young once. I know how you feel.'

'I do find it hard to believe you have feelings, yes,' I said drily.

Dad's narrowed gaze wandered down my front. My nape prickled as he no doubt assessed whether he wanted to add another scar to my body. My glare dared him to try it.

'So, we have a few weeks,' Freddy continued behind my back. 'If Jack wants to go—'

'What I want and have to do are two very different things! I will go because we both know you would never make it. She's not even up for discussion. As always, Dad, you know how to twist my arm.'

The corner of Dad's mouth twitched. 'I think your brother is trying to say that since you've already made this mistake, your restrictions are no longer needed. Perhaps you will think more rationally come August.'

'What happens in August?' Freddy asked.

'The collaring ceremony.' I clenched my fists, fighting the urge to breach protocol further by flooring my father. 'I'll have no choice but to collar her, or she'll become a slave.'

She would lose everything if I didn't collar her, but I would commit myself to take on the responsibility I'd run away from all those years ago, to become my father's successor. With a collared submissive, I'd also become a trainer and be pressured to have children so even more people could get wrapped up in this world.

'Will you inform Juliet of my decision?' I asked, hating every word out of my mouth.

'I will.'

I tried to swallow past the lump forming in my throat. 'What do I tell Kate?'

Dad tucked his hands in his pockets. 'There's no need to worry about that until after The Hunt.'

'I can't just not tell her!'

'If she runs or threatens to expose the Harpyiai, they'll take her, Jack.' Dad's eyes narrowed. 'You assumed responsibility for her well-being when you made her your sub. Do not put everyone at risk by sharing information she doesn't need at this point. You have until August to prepare her for the ceremony, if that's your decision.'

Collaring wasn't what I wanted. I'd have to live at the castle and leave my brother behind. Dad should have known that was impossible for me.

The thought of no longer having Freddy in my life broke my heart. The threat of Kate dying like my mother had made it impossible to breathe. When I looked at my father, tears pricked my eyes.

'Son, if you collar someone, the Head Marquess can no longer breed with you.' He smiled faintly. 'Perhaps it's the best—'

I left the kitchen, passed the brutes that followed Dad everywhere because he wouldn't face Juliet, and slipped back into my bedroom. Kate was still asleep, unaware of how my entire world had crashed. I crawled into bed next to her, squeezed my eyes shut and bit back all those emotions. Fear constricted my throat, and I gasped as the urge to scream threatened.

CHAPTER NINETEEN

JACK

How did we end up here?

I'd never wanted Kate caught up in my world. I didn't even want to be in it. As an illegitimate child of a Marquis, no one wanted her body except to torment and destroy it. Everything I adored about Kate – her bratty behaviour and daring nature – would be ruined at the castle if she became a slave.

An hour had passed since Dad and Freddy left, yet I still struggled to control my anger. It was hard to breathe, to look at her, and even harder to stay away. I wanted her, hated what she represented, and loathed myself for wanting her still.

I was sinking.

The hope of a life away from the Harpyiai faded with each strained breath as my mind swirled with memories of the castle: the long walk to the lower levels, the cries and howls, and the whistling of the cane. It pressed down on me and built in my chest as a silent scream.

Honour was everything to the Marquises. Some would rather die than be dishonoured. Peter Williams was one of those. All that time I'd trained under him, he'd been nothing but proud of what he did to the slaves. He trained them to become perfect toys for the Marquises – obedient masochists whose minds were twisted to believe it was a privilege to serve us.

A week after my mother died, he'd summoned me for my first training session as a Marquis. I'd found him standing in front of one of the barred cells watching a young woman eating something out of a bowl.

Like Theo, Peter's dark copper hair curled around his ears, though the scruff on his chin was as dark as his Marquis uniform: leather trousers, a pressed shirt with the sleeves rolled up, and a thick, studded belt. It made it hard to spot him in the corridors of the lower level.

His smile worried me that morning. I'd stopped a few feet away, but Peter crooked his finger until I stood before him. As always, he smelled of something musty and stale, a sickening maroon cloud, but it was nothing compared to the stench of vomit and sweat from the young woman in the cell.

Every rational thought had told me not to look, but curiosity was my weakness. Now an adult, I'd spent over four years of my life in the castle and had missed out on all those teenage years when I should've been chasing girls. I hadn't seen a female except for Juliet in so long that my eyes were drawn to the wretch in the cell.

She stuck a trembling hand into the ceramic bowl and held up a twitching cockroach for Peter's approval. At his nod, she brought it to her mouth. I looked away, pretending I couldn't hear the muffled crunching noises as she chewed, gagged, and chewed again until I finally heard her strained swallow.

'Open,' Peter demanded. 'Good. Keep it down this time, or we will be here all day.' He turned to me, dismissing her. 'I am surprised you are still here with all limbs intact. Marquis Andrei has the wildest of fantasies about you, little one.'

Peter always called slaves *little one*. Like Dad, Peter was so tall even I had to crane my neck to look at his face, but there was no need for his nickname, or his threat about Andrei. The Russian trainer had shared every one of his fantasies with me, and nothing his sick mind could come up with surprised me anymore.

It was Andrei's fault I still wasn't allowed clothes. He'd said it would make me feel subordinate to the other Marquises-in-training, a fitting reminder that I was still an illegitimate and Juliet's favourite toy, but the chill of the castle's lower levels only raised goosebumps on my bare skin.

'Look at me,' Peter demanded.

I refused to. He had been the one to drag my mother's broken body back to the castle. No one would confirm who had killed her, but only the thought of my brother kept me from hurling myself at him.

'I will make you eat worse things than cockroaches if you keep disobeying me.'

I shifted my gaze upwards. The grey of his irises was pale as ice, and the hardness of his stare made me feel two feet tall.

'Better. I cannot train someone I cannot read.' He folded his arms, emphasising his heavy bulk. 'Has Marquis Andrei actually ripped out your tongue, or is this silent treatment the next level of your infamous insubordination?'

I chewed on the inside of my cheek. The only words I wanted to say to him would get me whipped.

'I see.' He pulled a pair of scissors from his back pocket. 'Open wide.'

I recoiled. What?

'Come on. The illegitimate is still hungry.'

She scrambled back. I also wanted to run away, but it would only make it worse. Instead, I tried to shut down every emotion Peter wanted to tease out of me: shock, fear, raw grief intermingled with rage – they all threatened to pull me under.

Peter raised a brow. 'No? Ah, but what is the purpose of a tongue if you refuse to use it? Cunnilingus training does not start until next month, so you have time to grow it back,' he added with a throaty laugh.

I glared at him. Fucking sadist.

'The Head Marquess tells me not even Marquis Andrei can get you to speak anymore.' He tipped my chin with the cold blades. The lines around his eyes deepened as he stared into mine. 'But I know you are still in there. All I need is to find a way in. There is a way to turn even this bratty illegitimate into a true Marquis.'

It would never happen. I refused to give him the only thing I could deny him: my words. Peter loved playing with words. He sucked them up, twisted them around, and whispered them back at you in a way that made you wish you were deaf. Nothing he said could be trusted.

The tip of the scissors dug into my skin, and my heartbeat picked up. 'It will be a joy to twist your mind, little one,' he whispered.

That's what he would do to me, turn me into someone like him. I looked away, fighting the urge to throw myself at the scissors and end all of this.

'Eyes,' he snapped, and I stared at the ice in his gaze. 'Better. Do not make me fantasise about you as well. I have little patience with brats, as Theodore should have told you.'

He had. Theo feared his father as much as I did.

Peter drew a sigh. 'I will give you one last chance to speak, else I am happy to let Marquis Ivan reintroduce you to the fine art of sodomy. You will not be able to sit for a fortnight, but what the hell do I care?'

My stomach dropped. The chill in his eyes was a stark warning.

'What do you want, Marquis Peter?' My voice dropped to a growl with his name.

'All your secrets, little one,' he purred.

'Fuck you. You're as evil as Marquis Andrei.'

He rolled his eyes. 'Oh, please. I am much worse.'

'It's not a compliment,' I shouted, frustrated and tired of all of this.

Peter sighed. 'You are still upset about The Hunt? Your mother… Aye, a fine woman.' His words made my blood boil. There was no hint of remorse in him. No doubt aware of my growing rage, he handed me the scissors. 'If revenge is what it takes, then do your best, little one.'

Seriously, how dumb did he think I was?

The corner of his thin lips lifted in mocking amusement. 'Go on. I know you want to. I can see it in those baby blues you try to hide.'

I did want to. The sharp points of those scissors would make the most satisfying sound when they went into his eyes. Maybe I could crack that ice. But I was no fool.

Peter tutted. 'Your father would have been—'

I ripped the scissors from his hand and swung at him. His forearm came up, blocking my attempt to thrust them through his heart. Before I could react, he threw me face-first to the floor. His knee pressed so hard into my back that I screamed.

'A pathetic attempt, little one,' he growled in my ear. 'By the time I'm done with you, you too will have learnt to do terrible things, and do them well.'

His heavy weight lifted. I sucked in mouthfuls of dust and air, coughed, and sucked in more. Tears streamed down my cheeks, and I hated myself, despised him, and loathed my father more than ever.

'Get up.'

'Fuck you!'

He grabbed my hands and yanked my arms above my head. White, searing pain erupted in my shoulders. My sharp scream filled the air.

'Are you done?' He lowered my arms slightly, leaving me panting on the cold, dusty floor.

No.

'Yes!'

'Get up.' He dropped my arms. My hands slammed into the floor, making me yelp. 'I have things to do other than deal with you.'

I rolled onto my side, groaning. 'I don't want to be a Marquis.'

'Why not?'

'Because sadists are monsters,' I spat the words at him.

He chuckled. 'You think I am a monster?'

'Yes.'

'You are wrong to remove my humanity. I am as human as you.'

'Then you're insane!'

Peter's laugh deepened, echoing off the bare walls. 'Aye, that would comfort you, would it not? But I am not insane, and is that not the most terrifying thought of all? How I know right from wrong and can still evoke this fear in you?' He leaned in, inhaling. 'And your fear is so intoxicating.'

I scrambled to my feet, hating him with every inch of my being. Dust, spit, and tears covered my face. I wiped it with the back of my hand. I would kill him. One day, I would destroy him.

The corner of Peter's mouth twitched. 'Good. I have got you to look at me, speak to me, and want to harm me. Maybe there is hope for this brat. Come. I have something special for you.'

His boots kicked up dust as he started down a narrow corridor. The scissors were still on the floor, and I stepped toward them.

'Touch them, and I will dislocate your shoulders,' he warned, without looking back.

I growled. I was so tired of fighting, of being stuck in this castle, but there was no option but to follow him.

A large, scuffed wooden table stood in the centre of the dimly lit room he led me into. The rear wall behind sported a disturbing selection of paraphernalia – whips, knives, ropes, tongs, and a large metal box with spikes I didn't even want to look at. In the corner, a young woman perched in a large bird-cage, staring at us through gaps in long, dirty-blond locks of hair.

I stepped back, bumping into the door. 'Who's that?'

Peter waved his hand. 'One of our illegitimates.'

'What's her name?'

'Name?' He laughed. 'I do not bother with names, and you should not, either. Using an illegitimate's given name is a breach of protocol.'

He opened the cage and held his hand out. She took it and clambered out to kneel in the slave position, arms behind her head, pert breasts arched forward.

'How may I please you, Marquis?' she asked.

Peter hummed softly. 'Aye, I tried to pick a good one.' He lifted her chin and directed her attention to me. 'Today, I want you to please our new Marquis-in-training.'

'Yes, Marquis,' she said, turning those pale blue eyes on me.

'How many do you have?' I whispered, fighting the building panic. I didn't want to look at her breasts, legs, or that patch of dark hair between her thighs, but it was hard not to when she smiled at me, and it only made me feel worse.

'Slaves?' Peter looked surprised at the question. 'I have not done a stock check in a while, but there is enough to see you through your training. This is my gift to you. Your *igrushka*.'

I gaped at him. 'I don't want a toy!'

The slave looked taken aback by my rejection and cast her eyes downwards.

Peter's deep sigh spoke of his exasperation with my defiance. 'So tell me what you want, little one.'

'I want to go home!'

'This is your home. Try again.'

I clenched my fists. 'I want to kill you.'

He chuckled. 'Killing is so… final. I would rather talk about how you want to torture me. I can work with that.'

'So you can make me do it to her? I don't think so.'

Stroking her hair, Peter tutted. 'Your temper... it makes you stupid. Stupid is what will get you killed in this castle.'

'You can't kill me. My father would never allow it.'

'True, but I can make you wish I would.' His mouth curled into a crooked smile. 'Marquess Juliet only needs one part of you functional, and it is time to train that.'

My breathing grew ragged. The instruments on the wall dominated my attention; pliers, wires, gags, and things I struggled to look at. The woman kneeling by his feet didn't even have a name. It bothered me, and how it might not bother me for much longer horrified me.

'Your training has two sides, little one. Pain and pleasure. So far, you have only experienced one of these.' As he continued to stroke her hair, she leaned against his thigh. 'How long has it been since you have touched a woman?'

I looked away, not wanting him to realise that I had never been with a woman, but his dark chuckle soon came.

'Aye, you have much to learn.' His hand slipped to her slim shoulders. 'Your training is the only opportunity you have to play with illegitimates I have not brought upstairs yet. Once you enter the grand hall, a high-ranking Marquis must be present when you play with our trained slaves. I hope you are not shy.'

'I know the rules. You cannot force a Marquis-in-training to —' My tongue wouldn't even say the word.

Peter chuckled. 'Do what, little one? Don't be coy.'

'You know what I mean.' I clenched my fists. 'You can't make me.'

'True,' he mused. 'But you will want to couple with her. Trust me. Meanwhile, you have a choice to make. You can abide by your training, show me I am not wasting my time, or you can spend the rest of your life pretending you are not a sadist.'

I shook my head. 'I'm not a sadist.'

'So I should walk you over to Marquis Ivan?'

'What? No.'

'Perhaps your twin would be easier to train.'

'No!'

He put his large hand on her head, slid it down to fist her hair, and yanked her head back. The woman let out a sharp gasp. I froze when a smile spread across her face. Peter was watching my reaction, finding what would entice me to take that step. He tugged harder, and her deep groan filled the air. A thrill ran through me. My breathing deepened and slowed as hers quickened.

'Marquis—'

'What is it?' He pulled her hair tighter around his fingers and brought her to her feet. She let out a choked groan, and fuck if that sound didn't stir something in me, something primal and dark as blood rushed to my dick.

'Nothing.' I tried to look anywhere but at the woman.

Peter's gaze shifted to my groin. He smirked. 'I train our slaves as masochists. Every tug on her hair, every strike against her skin, anything your mind can think of will give her pleasure. I picked her, but she has been looking forward to this for days, little one. Do you truly want to deny her?'

The woman smiled provocatively. But how did I know if it was genuine?

I swallowed hard. 'And if I refuse?'

'Would you like me to cull your *igrushka*?'

'No!'

Slaves who didn't perform as desired – whether in response to pain or pleasure – could be culled in the annual hunt. She knew it. I knew it. Nobody would care if he marked her for culling. She was an illegitimate. We were free to do whatever we wanted to them. He could – and had – done whatever he wanted to me.

'Females are incredible creatures, little one. Their bodies can cope with the most excruciating pain imaginable.' He slid a hand between her legs, and she moaned. Peter's darkened eyes found mine. 'They are also capable of intense pleasure, and combining the two takes the finest of skills.'

Another moan came from the slave when Peter pushed his fingers into her. She was wet. I could hear, smell, and almost taste it in the air. I tried to look away, but her moans deepened as he thrust his fingers into her harder, faster, and I was drawn to how her back arched, wanting more.

'Touch her,' he ordered. 'Now.'

A groan vibrated in my chest as my hand found her hip. Her skin was warm, so soft, so tempting. I swallowed hard, grew harder, and squeezed her skin until the last of my restraints faded away.

He knew. I could see it in his eyes as he pulled his hand back and licked his fingers. He'd found my weakness. Found a way through to me.

'Your turn.'

Anger coursed through me – at him, her, and everything that'd happened. I looked down at her, lost in the thrill of her, lost in her slick heat as I slid my fingers into her. Fuck. I didn't want to be this person. It was her fault. His fault. All my fault.

For the next two years, I trained with that slave. Peter thought I would give in and fuck her after a week. When I hadn't, he saw it as a challenge.

Refusing to take that step was my only control over my training, not that it made it any easier. Peter became increasingly inventive and cruel in his teaching methods, but I never took that last step.

Never found out her name, either.

I didn't want to go back. This time, I might not survive. But how many times had I seen what happened to the illegitimates? Peter always turned them into perfect slaves, even if it broke them, and when I looked at Kate sleeping in my bed, I had to close my eyes to not see her the same way. I fought my fear of going back with anger, letting it consume me until there was no space for other emotions.

I had to get away from Kate before it was too late and get myself under control before I did something I would regret. After a weekend with no medication to take the edge off, I was going under, and I grasped for the door handle to put some space between us.

'Jack?' Her soft voice rolled over me. It was the light in my darkness. The pleasure in my pain. Her breathy voice was temptation incarnate.

'Are you all right?'

I turned around slowly, leaving my emotions open for her to see. Even illuminated only by the pale dusk, the change in her was palpable. Her eyes widened and those lips parted as she sensed my darkness and hunger. She was so beautiful.

I drew an unsteady breath. Her scent teased my nostrils and enticed the hunger. It had always done something to me – she'd always done something to me. But it was worse than ever. Now I was losing control.

There was nothing left in me. Nothing but memories, rage, and hunger.

'Jack,' she whispered, all breathy and submissive, a voice that went straight to my groin.

When she rose off the bed, the sight of her thickened my blood. Naked, vulnerable, so easy to destroy. I'd once told her I'd never harmed a woman. She'd never asked me what I'd had to do to an illegitimate – to the ones who didn't count – and here was another free pass.

In our world, I was her worst nightmare – and she didn't even know it.

Yet she was my biggest weakness.

Her dark hair swished over those small shoulders, and her round hips swayed as she came closer, fearless as always. Her skin begged for teeth to sink into, and her slim waist demanded squeezing hands. The sight of her tormented my soul. It pushed my feelings for her aside and replaced the void with something else – some untapped urge that made me suck in a breath.

She still came closer.

My hands trembled. This was all her fault. As I glared at her, I didn't see Kate, someone who I'd do anything to protect – even from myself. I saw a mistake that could cost me my life. My brother's life.

I took a step towards her.

Kate whimpered.

Stop me.

Use your safeword.

I took another step. Her mouth opened with a soft gasp.

Say it.

Fucking say it, Kate.

One more step brought us so close that the heat of her body wrapped around me. Her sharp breath tickled my skin, and the sweet smell of her arousal enticed me.

Kate stared up at me as my chest heaved with barely restrained emotions. Her naked body and the fear and lust in her eyes only made it worse. My darkness turned her on, and her fear turned me on. We were perfect for each other – and so dangerous together.

She was all I wanted, and all I needed to stay away from.

Our eyes were locked in a silent battle of lust and sin, fear and anger – one I lost when I closed my eyes and gave in to the darkness.

'Leave.' My whispered plea broke the silence.

But I knew she wouldn't. She craved the fear. It flicked a switch in her, making her stupid and careless around me. Had she no idea what I could do to her? No, she didn't even know who she was.

'Leave,' I warned her again, my voice raspy but cold. 'If you don't, nothing will be for your pleasure.'

She shook her head – quick, fast movements, sleek dark hair dancing over those bare shoulders.

'You want me…' She lifted her chin. 'But you'll have to catch me first.'

I tipped my head back and laughed. The edges of my vision shook with the movement. 'You want to play, ropes?' My voice dipped low. 'Let's play a game you'll never forget.'

Before I had a chance to prepare, she bolted. Adrenaline coursed through me as I followed. She made it to the staircase. I grasped for her smooth skin, almost had her, her heat a whisper beneath my fingertips – but she was quicker.

Our feet pounded on the staircase. Kate's hair bounced as she ran down the hallway. I reached for her again, but she turned and disappeared into the kitchen.

Her bare feet slapped against the tiles. Mine followed, gaining on her. The widening of her eyes as she looked back excited me, but it was too late for her to run now. She'd taunted me, and there was nowhere to hide. If only she'd stop fucking running, I would give her everything she'd asked me for. I would show her who I truly was.

Her feet came down hard and fast as she darted around the furniture in the dining room, always just out of my reach.

'Fuck,' I pressed out in frustration as I chased her into the living room. She slipped back into the kitchen before I got to the hallway. A low growl rumbled in my chest.

Kate made it to the kitchen island. The world around her was a jittery blur as I came to a halt. Her hair was wild. Her face was flushed. Each strained breath lifted her chest and drew my attention to her breasts.

I smirked. 'Have you given up, *igrushka?*'

CHAPTER TWENTY

KATE

Igrushka.

His word brought back memories of dark rooms and muffled sobs. Memories of my childhood that my mother always claimed were only my imagination.

There had always been something familiar about Jack, his words, and even how he moved. He reached into the darkest corners of my mind and soul and exposed what I'd hidden even from myself.

Now Jack eyed me like a predator would study his prey. Maybe that was how he saw me. The scars on his body told a different story. They made him a victim, but of what?

Who was he?

What had happened to him?

His barely contained emotions were palpable, assailing me with every strained breath, every twitch of his hands. The grey morning light cast a dull glow in his dark hair, framing those clouded blue eyes. Eyes that studied me in that way he often did; the shadows inside him stood out from every feature, every grind of his strong jaw, and changed his voice to a low growl.

'Don't run from me, ropes. You only make it worse.'

I never knew the power of fear, but that was before I'd met him. Before he'd stirred this in me. Now it was one of my most desired emotions. It made me a slave to him, hooked its claws in me, and refused to let go.

He'd never been darker, more dangerous – and I'd never wanted him more. My body responded to him as if we were meant to play this game. Standing on the other side of the kitchen island, I sucked in as much air as my lungs could take.

I hadn't meant to run for this long, hadn't meant to run at all, but something in his voice had told me to.

'Are you with me?' His low voice came as a whisper, but with an edge as sharp as a knife.

'Are you?'

His full lips curled into a smile. 'Almost, *radost moya*.'

His gaze wandered down my body and set it alight even from across the kitchen island. A shiver rolled across my skin like the tease of an exhale. Sucking in a breath, I pressed my thighs together.

What would he do to me? What did I want him to do? The uncertainty was almost worse than the anticipation of who would make the first move.

I could stop him. One word was all it took.

He could order me to my knees. He had the same power to end this game as I did.

'Do you like running from me, ropes?'

I raised my chin. 'Do you enjoy chasing me?'

'We *are* playing.'

I smirked.

Jack flicked his gaze around. He picked up his phone from the kitchen worktop. Soon 'In The Hall of The Mountain King' played on the surround system in the living room.

He drew a deep breath, like he was calming himself down. 'Ready, ropes?'

'Born ready, Marquis Jack.'

His eyes widened, but he couldn't hide from me. I knew this was him in his role. It had been obvious from the start that Jack was no ordinary Dom, but I didn't want ordinary. I wanted him as he was now – dark, dangerous, and so fucking hot as he took a determined step to the left.

A smile tugged at my lips as I stepped to the right. As Edvard Grieg's dramatic notes streamed from the speakers, we slowly circled the kitchen island.

Jack tutted. 'What am I going to do with you, ropes?'

'You'll never catch me. I'm faster and stronger than you think.'

He lunged for me. I sprinted around the corner of the kitchen island. Shaking his head, Jack started stalking the same path.

'You are dangerous, ropes. The thrill of fear makes you do things you shouldn't.'

I moved around the bar stools. 'I'm not the trained master of sadism.'

Jack's grin brought back memories of the game we'd played yesterday, and I shuddered in delight. The danger of playing with him wasn't lost on me. It was why I did it.

La petite mort – the little death.

It was our game.

'I'm well-trained, yes.' Heat flared in the dark glow of his eyes. 'But don't think that makes me less dangerous, especially around you. You are my greatest temptation.'

As the music built, our feet also moved quicker and quicker. Jack's eyes grew darker and darker until there was no blue left in them. I raced around the corner of the kitchen island, panting, aching. Did I want him to catch me? Or did I want him to keep chasing?

'What are you going to do to me?' My words came out chopped and fast as I jumped around the corner, narrowly avoiding his hand.

Stalking towards me, he smirked. 'Oh, ropes. There is no end to what I want to do to you.'

He changed direction, and I broke away, running into the dining room. He followed, quick and hard footsteps right on my tail as I ran to the living room and into the hallway. I turned again, sprinting into the kitchen. His sharp curses came from behind, and I laughed, a throaty croak that echoed through the house.

He scared the hell out of me, but that was the point. Knowing what he could do to me, yet having the power to stop him, was such a thrill. It was what I'd craved for so long.

I raced across the kitchen tiles and back into the dining room. As the song built to a crescendo again, I froze.

Where did he go?

I flicked my head around. The fast music matched my heart rate as I stepped across the room.

Where the hell did he go?

Was he in the living room? I tiptoed into the hallway. Not seeing him or hearing his breathing was worse than having him behind me. My pulse pounded against my eardrums. The scent of my sweat intermingled with the smell of him lingering in the air. It tugged on my longing for him, made me want to give in and call out, but then footfalls pounded against the floor behind me.

I bolted forward, tripping over the edge of a carpet. A breathy shriek escaped me. I scrambled back up and pressed on.

His hands clamped onto my hips. I yelped as he lifted me off my feet and pushed me over the arm of the sofa. His thighs pressed into the back of mine as he crushed me into the cushions.

'Stop running.' His deep growl vibrated against my skin. 'You don't know what it does to me.'

Panting, I closed my eyes as his full weight pressed onto me. 'Tell me.'

He pinned my arms against my lower back. 'It makes me want

to fuck your mind, fuck your body,' he rasped. 'It makes me want to fuck you until you feel both violated and cherished, and then fuck you again until you know you are mine and will never fucking run from me again.'

I wasn't sure what scared me more – his words, or how much I wanted him. How much I needed him. More than he needed his release. The edge of the sofa bit into my thighs, and his cock lay thick and hard against me.

He twisted his fingers into my hair and tugged. Warm, sharp pain rolled through me. 'You are mine, ropes. Mine.'

'Yes, Marquis.' The title spilt from my throat as a deep plea.

He tore loose a cable from the side of the sofa and twined it around my wrists, immobilising my hands at the base of my spine.

'Mine.' He nudged my legs apart and thrust into me. I cried out – an equal mix of sweet pain and pleasure. His deep growl of relief at the end of our game flooded my skin with goosebumps. I pushed my hips back, wanting more, but he stilled.

'Ropes.' He groaned the name as if it hurt him to speak. 'Colour?'

'Green,' I breathed. 'Fucking green.'

'You're so dangerous…' Jack's breaths came hard and fast as his hand slid to my throat. I held my breath. He kept his hand there for a long moment, possessively, not tight enough to constrict my airway, but its presence made me whimper.

'Shh,' he soothed. 'I would destroy anyone who dares harm you, even myself.'

He pushed upright, grasped my hips and thrust into me, hard, deep, again and again, driving the demon out himself, stirring the hunger in me.

My body responded to him in ways that scared me more than that look in his eyes. Every stroke added to the pleasure. Every rush of his breath on my skin as he leaned forward drove me insane. His fingers found my nipple and rolled the hardened peak until I begged for more. Jack always knew how to tweak my body to respond as he wanted. An intense heat rolled up my thighs, and my mouth opened with a low moan.

'Not yet,' he growled and stilled in me.

I groaned in frustration. 'Jack!'

He smacked my backside, the sound echoing in the room. I yelped in surprise, but the stinging warning only pushed me closer to the edge.

'Please, Marquis Jack,' I begged with a whimper.

'Not yet,' he repeated, nipping at my shoulder, tiny bites of sweet pain that did me no favours.

'Why are you punishing me?' My words came on a rushed exhale.

'Look at me.' His harsh command turned my head. Those eyes were so black, it stole my breath. 'You are the one punishing me, ropes.'

'It sure doesn't fucking feel like it!'

His mouth curled into a devious grin. 'But you are. You force me to break all my rules, so you will come only when I want you to.'

'Fuck you!' I ground my hips into his. Two could play this game.

He smacked my butt harder than before, and I whimpered again. My pussy clenched him tighter.

His chuckle was dark and low. 'Don't top from the bottom, ropes. You are mine to do with as I please.'

I suppressed the urge to glare, but he knew anyway. I could see it in his smirk, feel it as he moved in me again, slowly, too slowly to give me what I needed.

'Good girl.' His hands ran down my back and over the curves of my hips. 'You have no idea what I'm willing to do for you.'

I wished he'd stop teasing me. But Jack ignored my silent

glare and how I pushed back into him, trying to increase the pressure of his slow thrusts.

'Have I told you what you do to me?' His fingertips trailed a path to my sex. He pinched my clit between his thumb and finger, humming his approval as I groaned. 'You make me forget who I am. Who I should be. You take me to the edge of what I can handle, ropes.'

'So do you, Marquis Jack.'

'My edge is more dangerous.'

I couldn't argue with that. I only wished he'd push me over the edge in a whole different way.

'Spread your legs wider,' he ordered, and I obliged willingly.

Jack released my hands and brought one between my legs. My fingertips slid across the hot, silky skin of his cock as he pushed in and out of me in slow, agonising movements.

'Do you feel that?'

'Yes, Marquis Jack.'

Where was he going with this?

His hand was back in my hair, twisting, pulling a sharp cry from my lips. 'Do you know how many women I've fucked without a condom?'

'No, Marquis Jack,' I hissed. The mere thought of Jack with anyone else infuriated me.

'Only you. That's what you do to me, ropes.'

Gripping my hair tighter, he moved faster, harder, in tune with the building crescendo of the music. He was relentless in how he fucked me, continually changing angles, leaving me nowhere to hide, as if he wanted me to fall apart. As if he dared me to come close only so he could stop me.

'Marquis Jack,' I moaned, warning him for reasons unknown to me. I wanted to come. I needed to.

'I know,' he bit out. 'Not yet.'

He flicked my nipples. I hissed out a moan. His hips moved in deep circles, teasing me, punishing me with each sharp thrust. It was right there. I was so fucking close. So close. White spots danced behind my eyelids. My breath lodged in my throat as I fought a losing battle.

I pressed back, meeting his every thrust with my hips as he built me higher, and higher. But he needed to test me more. Punish me more. He tilted my hips and rammed his cock in even deeper. The depth and angle stole my breath, stole my mind.

Something made him darker, more tormented than ever before. I was lost in it, lost in him. He dug his fingers into my hip as he increased speed.

A desperate plea escaped my lips, and I couldn't hold out anymore. Not when he did this to me.

Then he stilled, and I let out a groan of frustration. 'Jack!'

'Marquis Jack, little sub,' he said with a low chuckle.

'Stop holding back.'

'You want to know what I like doing to subs?' His warm breath rushed over my skin as he whispered the words in my ear. With a rough tug on my hair, he drew a sharp gasp from my lips. 'They come to me to fulfil their fantasy of being completely at my mercy. I will truly do whatever I want with them. Find what they're afraid to admit they want and push their limits.'

Something spurred to life inside me, a frightening yet exhilarating tingling pleasure at the thought of being completely under Jack's command for a full scene, the idea of all my struggles absolutely useless sending a rush of desire through me.

'What kind of fantasies?' I breathed.

He tightened his hold on my hair. 'Is that another question?'

'No, Marquis Jack,' I gasped, my scalp stinging.

'Maybe you're right; I'm too soft on you.' He nipped at my shoulder, tiny bites that didn't help my burning need. 'I've never been a soft Dom, yet you…' He chuckled darkly. 'Around you, I'm fucking torn between taking you hard on the floor to teach you a lesson, and doing whatever it takes just to see you smile.'

'Maybe it would make me smile if you did that.' The words demanded to come out no matter how shameful they were.

His large hand slid around my throat. 'What makes you think I should take this risk?'

The possessive nature of which his hand rested against my jugular both terrified and excited me. 'Because I want you to push my limits,' I whispered. 'That's why I chose you.'

'It's my job to keep you safe.' His grip tightened ever so slightly around my throat. 'To take you to the edge of what you can handle without harming you.'

I groaned in frustration. 'Stop holding back!' A startled croak escaped me when he withdrew and pushed into me so hard, I felt every hard inch of his cock.

'I'm going to fuck you hard and fast now.' A low groan rumbled in his throat. 'Tap my arm if you want to safeword.' Using his other hand, he brushed my hair out of my face. 'Do not look away. Am I clear?'

Nodding, I stared at him wide-eyed, my cheek pressed into the sofa cushions.

'Don't fucking nod, ropes. Give me your words,' he growled.

'Y-yes, Marquis Jack.'

Adrenaline surged within me as he started to move, fast and deep. Fuck, he felt so good. Why was he so goddamn good at this? I had no chance of resisting him, the intensity of his dark gaze so mesmerising, I couldn't have looked away even if I wanted to. He was so dark, so dangerous, his expression terrifying in so many ways.

His hand came back around my throat, pressing into my jugular, his tight grip bound to leave marks. Still, he continued fucking me. Hard. Fast.

He was going to make me regret daring him.

A vicious heat started building in my chest as he robbed me of air. I tried to push away from him, but he flattened me to the sofa with his heavy weight. Panic loomed. Every thrust brought me closer to my climax, but knowing how long Jack could go before finding his release and how tightly he squeezed my throat left me gasping, and gasping, scratching at his hand, arm, but still, he didn't stop.

The edges of my vision flickered. Pulling at his fingers, I tried to loosen his grip. But he was too strong.

His groan rushed over my skin as he slammed into me, but when his mouth crushed to mine, I bit hard into his bottom lip until the taste of blood hit my tongue.

Jack growled. 'Little brat. You'll regret that.' He gripped my hair and forced my head back, exposing more of my throat to his strong hand as he pulled me flush to his body. My vision started to blur. The pressure mounted.

'Stop,' I croaked.

'If you truly mean that, you know what to do.'

I scratched at his hand, digging my nails in. 'Stop.'

But I didn't want him to stop. I wanted to feel this fear, to lose myself in his darkness, and know that he would do whatever he wanted with me.

He slammed harder into me, splintering my vision.

He terrified me.

He could kill me.

Yet I was coming. Arching my back, I let out a strangled cry as my body truly fell apart. His hand slipped from my throat as the convulsions ripped through me. I sucked in air and let out a scream so loud, it sounded like it came from someone else.

Tears sprung from my eyes for the second time that weekend.

He took me to the point of exhilarating pain and pleasure, an overwhelming wave of fire ripping me apart until I floated, lost in his dangerous game.

I never wanted to be apart from him. I wanted him to be mine and to belong to him. To fulfil every one of his desires, no matter how dark or dangerous. There was no one safer than Jack because he was always watching me, even when his gaze was so menacing it rose every hair on my body.

He tugged me closer with his last slow, hard thrusts. 'Fuck's sake, Kate,' he groaned as my pussy pulsated around him, milking every drop of his release.

I lost all strength and fell against the cushions. Jack pulled me with him onto the soft carpet on the floor, settling me on top of him, safe in his arms as he wrapped them around me. His heart pounded beneath my ear, picking up speed rather than slowing down as we recovered.

'Are you okay?' he murmured. His breaths came as a harsh, deep wheeze, and I lifted my head when he coughed.

'Are you?'

He coughed again. 'I think you were right, ropes.' The strained emotions in his voice caught me off guard. 'I should've run from you. Maybe you will ruin me.'

'What's wrong?'

He kissed my cheek before shifting upright to grab an inhaler on the coffee table. As he used it, he looked at me as though he knew a dark, dangerous secret he could never share. Closing his eyes, he shook his head. 'I shouldn't have done that. You're on the pill, right?'

'Eh, no.' When his eyes widened, I laughed. 'I have an implant. Jesus, Jack. I've been with you for days. You'd know if I was on the pill.'

'Don't scare me like that.'

'Well, next time you decide to chase me around the house, maybe you should be better prepared. What the hell was riding you, anyway?' But he wouldn't tell me. It was clear by how he fiddled with his inhaler, avoiding my gaze. His features shuttered as he helped me stand, and I felt him pulling away, hiding from me again. Brick by brick, he set up a wall between us.

'I can't tell you.'

'Can't?'

He folded his arms. 'Won't. I won't tell you.'

'Why not?'

'Because I can't.'

'Jack.' I put a hand on his chest, feeling the rapid beat of his heart. 'Tell me.'

'I thought you'd use your safeword earlier.'

'I didn't feel the need to.'

Jack stared at me as if I'd sprouted two heads. 'If you knew what I was thinking, what I could've... Caitlin, I'm the most fucked-up person there is. That safeword is there for a reason.'

'Well, you're *my* fucked-up person, and I'll use my safeword when I feel like it.'

A myriad of emotions crossed his face as he stepped back. Disbelief? Amusement? Shock?

'What?' I propped my hands on my hips. 'You've ruined normal sex for me, so I'm afraid you're stuck with me now. Get used to it, Mr Lawrence. It's time for you to work on your communication skills and tell me what the hell is going on.'

His mouth split into a grin. 'I've ruined normal sex? Tell me more.'

'Don't you dare.' I held up a hand as he came closer. 'Don't try to sex your way out of this.'

'Are you sure?' Snaking an arm around me, he tugged me closer. 'You fall apart so easily on my tongue.'

I lifted my chin. 'Use your skilled tongue for words, Jack.'

'I can't tell you,' he said, his voice dropping to that low tone. 'Don't ask me again.'

'Mr Dark and Mysterious is back.'

'Look, as much as I'd like to—'

The front door slammed shut, and we both turned.

'Jack?' Footfalls fast approached.

Oh hell.

Jack tucked me behind him just as Freddy appeared in the doorway.

'Jesus Christ,' Freddy said. 'Well, that explains why you're not answering your phone.'

Jack chuckled. 'Morning, Freddy.'

'The hell is this music? What have you been up to?' Freddy turned off the stereo. 'You know what? I don't want to know. At least you're still… umm, morning, Kate.'

'Morning,' I squeaked, peeking around Jack's arm. Freddy ran a hand through his hair, looking at everything in the room except us.

'I need some coffee.' He muttered something under his breath and disappeared from view.

'Sorry about that,' Jack said. 'There's a bit of a family emergency happening at the moment.'

'That's what's going on?' I smacked his arm. 'You could've told me that! Is it serious?'

'Still figuring it out.' He caught my hand and kissed the back of it. 'I'll have to take you home soon to deal with it. Do you mind?'

'Oh.' The disappointment leaked into my voice. 'Of course, that's fine.'

'Don't, Kate. I wish I didn't have to deal with this.' He sighed. 'Truly, I do.'

'It's fine. I need to see what my brother has done to my flat, anyway.'

'Owen's staying with you?'

'Unfortunately, he lives with me now. It's temporary.'

'I say that about Freddy living here, but he seems to forget we're not still attached to the same placenta.' He rolled his eyes in a way only a sibling could.

'Maybe I can see you next weekend instead?'

'Count on it.' He winked. 'Come on. Let's have a bath, then grab some food before I take you home. A nice brunch at a pub sounds like a good end to the weekend.'

It sounded like the most vanilla ending to a wild weekend. I couldn't help but smile.

He pulled a blanket from the sofa and wrapped it around me, and I followed him into the hallway. Freddy glared at me from a bar stool by the kitchen island. What was his problem?

'What about your brother?' I whispered.

'He can wait.'

While Jack ran the corner bath in his en suite, I gathered my clothes off the floor and glanced at my mobile for the first time since early Friday evening. Seven missed calls from my mother, another two from Petra and even one from Owen. Countless messages urged me to call my mother.

I'd almost forgotten these people existed. Guess it was time to get back to normal life. Hopefully, Mum hadn't heard about my visit to The Yard.

'Your bath is ready, milady.' Jack stood in the doorway.

I left my phone – and no doubt my own impending family emergency – on the bed, and let him guide me to the warm, soapy water. Jack slid in behind me, and I truly was in heaven. Despite my objections that I could care for myself, he poured water over my hair and started massaging shampoo into my scalp. He was such a mystery. So caring, yet hid so much beneath those gentle touches.

He was everything I'd ever wanted, and at that moment, I felt more at home than I ever had. But he surprised me again when he tipped my head to the side to examine my neck.

'No marks.'

There wasn't? I ran my fingertips over my throat. 'It doesn't matter if you did. I don't mind.' Wearing his marks sent a thrill through me, no matter how much trouble it would get me into if my mother ever found out what I'd been up to.

'For some reason, I don't want to,' he said in a low murmur.

When the seconds ticked past and he didn't elaborate, I put my hand on his cheek. What was he struggling with? But he only smiled and resumed washing my hair.

'You will tell me one day, right?' I asked, wanting him to know that it wouldn't scare me away no matter what he hid from me. Nothing could. His eyes hid a world of pain, and I wanted nothing more than to lose myself in them.

His fingers stilled. 'Tell you what?'

'All your secrets.'

It was another gauntlet thrown down. I wanted him dark, but with a darkness I could understand and cherish. There was nowhere for me to hide from him; he had seen all of my secrets the moment we met. I needed him to be as afraid of losing me as I had been of him coating me in the ocean of shame he'd pulled me out of.

He was quiet for a long moment before his hands started massaging my scalp again. 'Will you give me six weeks?'

'Six weeks?'

'I will tell you everything you want to know about me then.'

I shifted around. 'What happens in six weeks?'

Jack didn't answer. Instead, he kissed me, slow and deep, like it was the only way he could breathe. His hands came around my nape, and he held on to me as if he couldn't stand any space between us.

I wanted to pull him closer to me, run my hands through his dark hair, but the emotions he poured into that kiss were too overwhelming, too raw and exposed; I was afraid of finding out the reason for this change.

It felt too much like goodbye.

He pressed his lips to my neck, clavicle, and the base of my throat. 'I didn't mark you.'

His words confused me. 'I wanted it as well.'

He shook his head softly, like he couldn't understand why he had held back. The pained look in his eyes stilled my breath. His hands moved down my back, a slow, gentle caress of my skin as if he was memorising every inch of me.

My heart kept missing beats as he spoke to me in silence,

pouring everything he couldn't tell me into those slow seconds when there was no world around us.

Something had shifted between us. It was no longer about sex, boundaries, or play. There was longing in his eyes, a deep desire hidden in their depths. It matched the tender kiss he gave me as he leaned down. His lips only brushed mine, but it seemed to last an hour, maybe more, yet it was all too short when he pulled away.

'Let me rinse your hair. You're getting shampoo in your eyes.' His easy smile came, but his unsteady voice revealed the truth.

'What is it?' I whispered, brushing his wet hair back.

He caught my hand and pressed it to his lips, keeping it close to his mouth as if it was the last time he would kiss it. 'It's nothing, ropes. Sometimes I forget, that's all.'

'Forget what?'

'Nothing.'

Despite the warmth of the water, a chill rushed through me. 'I will see you again, won't I?'

'Caitlin.' He put his hands around my face. 'If you understood the things I would do to see you again, you'd never ask such a question.'

'What happens in six weeks?'

'Just a family matter, and maybe I need to be sure you won't leave. Believe it or not, ropes, most women run long before six weeks.'

I scoffed. 'Can't imagine why.'

'Hey.' He flicked water at me. 'Be nice.'

'It wasn't a dig.' I wiped the water from my eyes. 'But maybe you shouldn't tell me everything about yourself.'

'No?'

I rested back against his chest and pulled his arms around me, so he had no way to hide. 'We'd have to get married if you confessed how many dead bodies you've buried, else they could compel me to testify in court. You know how easily I fold if someone puts the fear of god in me.'

Jack's laugh vibrated against my back. That sound made me happy. 'I've never killed anyone, so don't worry. I won't let anyone else play with your fear.'

I wanted to ask if he'd ever come close to killing someone, but maybe it was best not to know. Maybe I should've been more worried about why none of these things about Jack bothered me.

CHAPTER TWENTY-ONE

JACK

Six weeks?

What the hell was I doing?

Dad was wrong; I had to explain what was happening, who she was, where I was going, but I couldn't bring myself to do it. What if she ran and put herself in danger? Her stepdad was an MP. What if she told him? Jesus, the trouble this could cause.

'You're fidgety today,' Kate said when we ate brunch at the pub, noticing how I was twirling my fork between my fingers.

'Sorry.' I put my fork down. 'Forgot to take my Ritalin before we left.' I hadn't taken my medication since Friday, and my body refused to stay still. Hopefully, Freddy had some in the car; otherwise, he'd rip into me when I got home.

While she ate her pasta and chatted about work and patients she'd dealt with recently, I poked at my fried eggs.

When she pushed her plate away, I took a deep breath and blurted, 'Kate, I need to tell you something.'

She smiled, and I couldn't get those words out. What if she put herself at risk? Christ. I'd never appreciated how difficult it must have been for Dad to shield us from this for so long. I'd had fourteen years with my mother before I was taken. Would it have been easier if I'd known?

I tried to smile. 'Just wanted to say this weekend's been amazing. You continue to surprise me.' In more ways than she knew. I drummed my fingers on the table.

That was the fool I was, validating her trust in me as I dug myself deeper into this mess.

'It's been an eventful weekend,' she said, watching me through her lashes. 'Unforgettable.'

'Hopefully, one of many to come.'

Kate gave me one of her soft smiles. How could I tell her that her freedom was gone if she didn't commit to me for life? That she might never see her family or friends again? Jesus, how did I get myself into this mess?

She was destined to be prey, and I was trained as a hunter. Those were the roles we'd played earlier. She had thought it was only a scene, but it wasn't. It made me feel sick to my stomach to think about her running for her life through the forest.

She stared out the window on the drive to her flat, and I wondered what she was thinking. She'd been quiet since we left the pub. Had she picked up on my mood? It was becoming increasingly difficult to pretend everything was fine.

'You all right?' I asked.

She crossed her legs. 'Were you abused?'

I stared at her as if she'd slapped me. It would've been better if she had.

Abused?

Hell.

'What do you mean?'

'Your training. Your scars. Every time I ask about it, you seem different, detached, like I've triggered you.'

The compassion in her eyes ripped my armour off. Tightening my grip on the steering wheel, I stared ahead at the road. What was I supposed to say? Abused? No, I was trained.

'You don't have to answer. It's easy to recognise trauma. I see the effects of it at work all the time, but I wish you would talk to me about it.'

Seen the effects? What the hell did that mean? 'I've shared more with you than anyone else,' I said, more defensively than I wanted.

Her voice softened. 'I just want to know what happened to you. Maybe I can help.'

'You don't want to know these things about me.'

Parts of me had died in that castle, and in my darkest moments, those memories ruined everything. If she gave me a chance, I would show her I could still be everything she wanted, even if she was an illegitimate and I was a Marquis. I'd deal with my damn triggers if that's what it took to keep her safe and happy.

If it hadn't been inappropriate, I would have laughed, not only because of the absurdity of it all but because I was clueless about why or how it had got this complicated this fast.

'I need to know,' she insisted, annoyance leaking into her voice.

'No, you don't,' I said, sterner than intended.

Nate had always insisted that although a Dom needed to know about any triggers a sub could have, no sub ever needed to know about a Dom's troubled past. Trying to elicit sympathy from a sub distorted everything.

My argument had been that it wouldn't be an issue since we weren't allowed to talk about our training, anyway.

It was different with Kate. She was no longer an ordinary sub, but the damage was already done, and I needed more time to figure out how to fix this mistake before she lost everything.

Scaring her with details about what went on at the castle wouldn't help her. How could I convince her to go to the collaring ceremony if I told her how we were trained?

Kate folded her arms. 'So questions only work one way with

you? You want me to be open and honest with you, but you won't share a thing?'

'No, there's a time and place for questions.'

'What's wrong with now?'

I scrubbed my face when we joined a queue on the main road. 'Look, my past made me who I am today,' I tried, offering her a middle ground rather than the impossible she was asking for. 'It brought me to you, to this moment, and for that, I'm grateful. I'll share it with you one day, but not now.'

Her eyes narrowed, and I waited for it.

The end.

The final word from her.

The nail in the fucking coffin.

All she gave me was silence – pin-dropping, apocalyptic silence that raised the hairs on my arms. I imagined her to be the type of woman who yelled when she was pissed off – given how she was in bed – so whatever line I'd crossed this time had to be the threshold into hell.

'I will tell you when I can,' I offered.

She scoffed. 'You need a safeword.'

What the hell?

'You know what a safeword is, right?'

My jaw clenched. She was trying to top me from the bottom again. I wanted to take her over my knee, but she'd done well bringing this up in a car.

'Yes, I'm familiar with the term,' I said drily.

The car behind me honked, startling me. I glared in the rear-view mirror as I pushed on the accelerator.

'You're like a porcupine, Jack. Full of sharp points. Choose a safeword, so I know—'

I chuckled. 'A porcupine?'

She was adorable. Terrifying but adorable.

'I'm serious.'

'Fine. Porcupine will be my safeword.' I smiled. 'If it makes you feel better, we'll both have one.'

She ran her hand down my arm, pausing before brushing her fingertips over the scratches she'd left on my hand. When her wary gaze found mine, I gave her a reassuring smile. 'I need you safe as well, Jack.'

'You don't have to worry about me. You're the one I need safe.'

'When you're fighting your demons?'

'Caitlin…' I didn't like that look in her eyes. It made me feel naked and vulnerable, something I hadn't felt in so long, not since I was a slave. I never wanted her to feel like this.

'Use your words,' she prompted.

I glared at her. 'Stop.'

'You can do better than that.'

Her smirk was hard to interpret. Was she goading me? I drew a deep breath, releasing it on a low growl. She'd be the death of me one day. What the hell was going on with her? She'd always been bratty, but this was different.

'As you pointed out, you're stronger, bigger and better trained. It's fun to play with you, but I want to know why you looked at me like I was your worst enemy.'

Shit.

Too close for comfort.

We stopped at a red light and I kissed her cheek. 'I'd never harm you.'

'It felt like you weren't yourself.'

My stomach dropped. 'When?'

The chase? She'd challenged me before running. She'd laughed. Encouraged me. I had given her every option to stop, even put on music to ground myself and had never taken my eyes off her face.

Had I gone too far already? Scared her off? She didn't have a mark on her except for those light scratches on her chest. It still puzzled me why I didn't want to leave any marks on her.

'When you called me something in Russian.' There was no hint of fear in her voice, only curiosity. 'What does it mean?'

'*Radost moya?*' I hoped she had heard nothing else. 'It means *my joy.*'

'No, that's not it.'

'*Igrushka?*' It had slipped out, and I would've done anything to take it back. 'It means *toy*, like a playmate,' I said, opting for something close to the truth.

She propped up an elbow on the door. 'Yes, I've heard it before.'

'You have? When?'

Was her father Russian? Her brown eyes didn't fit with any of the families. The Harpyiai had a problem with too-close family relations; most of us had blue or grey eyes, and only a few had green. I needed to ask Freddy for her file when I got home. He would have pictures of her mother.

'Sometimes I have these dreams,' she whispered, staring out the window. 'Only I think they're memories. It's hard to explain, but there's a man in our house and Mum's crying.'

In the house? Jesus. Why would her mother invite a Marquis home? Was this how Freddy hadn't found the link? When I'd asked her about Tom at the club, it had seemed clear he had done something to her, but maybe it wasn't Tom.

I reached over to take her hand, squeezing it gently. 'Kate, you don't have to talk about it. Forget I asked.'

'There was a man,' she continued, her brows drawn together as if she was trying to look into the past. 'They were in the living room, but I only made it to the middle of the staircase. There was a noise, like a whistling sound, then a loud crack and Mum cried so much it scared me.' Kate pulled in her bottom lip, dragging it between her teeth. 'I don't remember what he looked like, only a voice.'

'And he called you *igrushka?*'

'One of them did.'

'There was more than one?' I tried to keep the horror out of my voice. Ivan had been Head Marquis back then; it shouldn't have surprised me, but it chilled me to the bone.

She drew a deep breath and shook off whatever memory she'd visited. 'But it makes no sense if it means toy. Are you sure that's all it can mean?'

I didn't know how to answer her. How she had responded to me, the slave position she'd assumed, even her fear response – had someone trained her? Why the hell would they do that, and why would her mother allow it to happen?

I hoped she wasn't Ivan's daughter. That made no sense. Ivan died years ago and would never have kept an illegitimate hidden. Two of his daughters were slaves at the castle when I was training. No, the only Russian she could belong to was Andrei. He was gay, but maybe I was wrong about that. It made no sense for him to keep an illegitimate hidden, either.

The last time I saw Andrei had been on the day of The Hunt. I had one more night at the castle before I could leave for good. All I had to do was survive the night.

Seven Marquises had been gathered in the grand hall when Andrei walked in, a Delrin cane in his hand. Theo stood to my right, staring straight ahead, but perspiration dotted his face as he tried to ignore the Russian. Mark was to my left and met my gaze only for a second.

Peter sat in one of the maroon armchairs by the fireplace, content to observe the final preparations after he'd made us drink one of his special concoctions. Theo claimed the drugs his father had put into the vodka made the room tilt to the side whenever he turned his head. But they had no effect on me.

Ivan sat next to Peter, whispering to Arthur, who had been brought downstairs in his wheelchair. Behind them, ten castle guards lined the wall.

Running the tip of my tongue over the grooves in my teeth, I tried to rid myself of the taste of alcohol, despising it as much as the trainers who plied us with it.

The open fire in the grand marble fireplace crackled, shooting sparks onto the stone floor, but I still shivered. Dressed in only our leather trousers, we were restless and eager to finish this. Juliet had made the slaves strut around in front of us all morning, knowing too well they had deprived us for a week. During The Culling, we were forced to touch and never be touched. It was a special kind of torture when our bodies were conditioned to find release as often as possible. Enough testosterone was trapped in the room to make even the twenty-foot ceiling feel suffocating.

The quick pace of Andrei's riding boots hitting the rough stone floor matched the rapid beat of my pulse. His long blond hair bounced on his shoulders as he came toward us. Although he was only five foot five, Andrei was the kind of man whose eyes you avoided, but looking down was no longer an option. A Marquis did not avert his gaze, and this was our last test.

Andrei's irises were forest-green, like the woods we'd be sent into, and they soon rested on me. The corner of his thin lips lifted in a crooked smirk as he stared up at me.

'You're the last person I thought would make it this far, Marquis Jack.' My title – the one I'd sacrificed so much for and was only hours away from earning – moved across his lips like a hiss. Arsehole. I couldn't wait to get away from him.

Always eager to taunt me, he pressed the tip of the cane into my cheek. Part of our preparation involved letting Andrei loose on us with his whip to flood our bodies with adrenaline, but that should've been over. What was the purpose of the cane? I was already jittery and struggling to contain my anger. Sweat trickled down my chest and blended with the coat of arms painted on my skin.

'I'm glad I could surprise you, Marquis Andrei.' Sarcasm dripped from my voice.

He flicked his wrist, and the cane bit into my cheek, but my flinch only widened his smile. 'A true sadist can control the mind better than any body. You still have much to learn.'

'One day, I hope to show you what I feel about your teaching.'

Andrei's croaked chuckle came low, yet sharp. 'How arrogant of you to think I care about your feelings.'

He turned on his heels, and my shoulders dipped, grateful he was moving on, but he swung around and whacked the cane across my face. Blood poured from my nose and into my hand as I tried to catch it.

Andrei stalked closer as I glared at him. He didn't need to remind me not to bleed on his floor. I knew his rules all too well – and the consequences of breaking them.

At times like this, I couldn't help but wonder what my father had been like as a trainer. It was impossible to marry the image of the loving father that had raised us with the monsters he'd stuck me with at the castle.

Not once had he ever laid a hand on us. How could he be so different from Andrei, who used every opportunity to mark my skin?

Juliet had told me Dad would be arriving after The Hunt, eager to see his son now that his honour had been restored. If my father thought even for a minute that I would go anywhere near him after he'd allowed these people to keep me for five years, he had lost his mind. I wouldn't breed with the damn Head Marquess, either.

Tapping the cane against his boot, Andrei waited for me to make a mistake as blood trickled down my chin. After a long moment, the bleeding slowed down enough for me to wipe my hand across my chest, smearing blood across the Lawrence family crest.

Nice try, arsehole.

'I have longed to see the blood of a Lawrence. You should clean that off before Marquess Juliet breeds with you.' He looked down my body, pausing at my groin. 'You might be the only

Marquis who can give her an heir, but she won't accept soiled goods'

Early the next morning, I had returned to the castle with a captured slave, and the last time I saw Andrei was when he'd left me shackled to the floor in the grand hall after my branding.

Soon I would have to face him again and survive The Hunt. Eight years wouldn't have made him any kinder, and I clenched the steering wheel harder at the thought of having to go back to the castle.

Kate put her hand on my arm, startling me. 'You're doing it again, slipping away.'

'I'm here, *moye solnyshko.*'

I tried to smile in a way to reassure her, but images of Kate perched in one of the large birdcages slid into my mind and I rubbed at my chest, struggling to draw a full breath.

'Again with the Russian... Is it something I'm doing wrong? You said I push you to the limit, but you won't tell me what those limits are.'

'You're not doing anything wrong.' I stopped at a red light. 'Kate, it's got nothing to do with you.'

'But you said I was punishing you, and I forced you to break your rules. What did you mean?'

Whatever was wrong with my mood, I needed to snap out of it. Now.

'Something made you forget to use a condom,' she continued, 'which is fine, but I want to know what's going through your mind.'

For god's sake. I looked for somewhere to pull over and turned into a supermarket car park.

I took her hand. 'Caitlin, I am not a normal Dom. I'm a Marquis. When we play, we play hard. You want me as dark as I can get, and there's an inherent risk when you push me so hard and refuse to back down.'

'I do want you dark.' She lifted her chin in the way she often did, challenging me. 'It's what draws me to you.'

'That's why you're dangerous to me.' I ran the back of my fingers down her cheek. 'But I am sorry. I didn't intend to take it that far. And I should've asked for your permission before fucking you bare. It won't happen again. I promise.'

'Something triggered you?'

I looked out the window. 'I expected you to safeword.'

'That's not an answer, Jack.'

'For fuck's sake. Yes, I was triggered.'

'Because of your training?' She put a hand on my cheek. 'What was it like?'

'Kate…'

'Tell me,' she insisted.

'You really want to know? It was like having your head held under water every damn day, but nobody would let you fucking die. I don't like to talk about it. Whenever I do, I can't connect with myself, let alone anyone else, so—' I drew a deep breath. 'I don't talk to anyone about it, okay? It's not just you.'

To my complete surprise, she leaned forward and kissed me, soothing my temper and shattering my last defences. She left me open and raw, and when she smiled, I'd never been more terrified of anyone in my life.

I slid my hand around her nape and pressed my lips to hers. 'Stop asking questions.'

'Can I ask one more? Not about your past.'

'Go on.' I sighed.

'Why did you get so freaked out about the condom? I told you to go without one.'

How the hell did I explain the impossible?

'I have to be careful with condoms because I don't want kids.'

She scratched her head. 'Why don't you just get a vasectomy if that's… Oh, your needle phobia?'

That was the least of my problems. It was also against protocol, and Dad would never allow it, no matter how many times I insisted I didn't want kids.

Her gaze went to my chest, and I tensed, waiting for all those questions I had to turn down. She would no doubt make me tell her anyway – it was hard to resist her dark eyes – but rather than probe further, she only nodded. It baffled me.

I kissed her forehead, lingering for a moment to inhale her scent. It calmed me.

'You still need to let me in more.'

'I promise I'll try.'

My phone rang, and Theo's name popped up on the display.

Fucking great. Another person who knew how to get under my skin.

I glanced at her. Although maybe his timing was perfect. His name had caught her attention.

'Is that the same Theo you spoke to the other night?' she asked, curiosity lighting up her eyes.

'Yes. Do you want to speak to him?'

'What? Now?' She looked around as if we were about to break the law.

'You wanted to be let in…' I pressed the button on the steering wheel. 'Theo, you're slow to respond, as always.'

'Sorry. There was a woman and—' He laughed. Knowing Theo, drugs and more than one woman had been involved. He struggled as much as I did. Maybe more. I couldn't even imagine what it was like to have Peter as a father. Mine was bad enough.

I propped my elbow on the steering wheel. 'You're on speakerphone, so spare me the details. Say hello to Kate.'

'Well, hello there, Kate.' The silky smoothness of his deep voice wasn't lost on me.

'Um, hi.' Flushing, she glanced at me, and I bit back a grin.

'What are you doing with that arsehole?' he continued, bold as always. 'You should come and see me. I'll show you a proper good time.'

'Behave, Theo.' I rolled my eyes at Kate.

'Jack's more than enough for me,' she countered, giving me a coy smile.

He laughed. 'I bet he is. Jack, what we discussed last time—'

'She's an illegitimate,' I said to Theo in Russian.

Kate's eyes snapped to mine. I smiled innocently.

'*Blyad*,' Theo said on an exhale. 'How?'

How did I get myself involved with an illegitimate? Fuck if I knew.

'We should meet up,' I said, glancing at a couple pushing a shopping trolley past the car.

'Yes, I think we have to. I have a party on Saturday, and I'd love to meet you, Kate.'

'Are you free?' I asked her.

'What kind of party?'

Theo chuckled. 'The kind where you put on something nice, and I take it off with my teeth.'

Kate snorted. 'I doubt Jack would approve.'

'I would not, *durak*.'

Despite my slip earlier, Kate was no toy. Theo also knew better than to touch another Dom's submissive, and he'd never risk getting too close to an illegitimate. Like me, he stayed away from the Harpyiai by keeping out of trouble and avoiding his father.

'Jack's promised me a scene I think you'd like to see, Kate.'

'You play at these parties?'

'We do.' And I wanted to show her something I hadn't done in years. She'd responded so well yesterday. The thought of taking it further made my jeans uncomfortably tight.

'*Malyshka*, we do everything at my parties,' Theo teased.

An image of Kate on a St Andrew's cross slid into my mind – bound and at my mercy. When she looked at me, no doubt aware of the change in my breathing, I ran a finger up the side of her neck.

'I hope you don't plan on playing with someone else,' she warned me.

'No, I won't touch anyone but you that way.' I cupped the back of her head to kiss her.

Theo laughed. 'Jack, please. You're making me nauseous.'

'Shut up, *mudak*.' I winked at Kate. 'You can call him that any time you want.'

Theo grunted.

'*Mudak*,' she repeated, testing the insult no illegitimate would dare say to a Marquis. Her mischievous smile heated my body. 'I think I get the gist of what that means.'

'I'll call you back, Theo,' I said, and hung up.

'He reminds me of you,' she murmured, looking at me through her lashes. 'What do I actually wear?'

'Whatever you want.' I tilted her head and nipped at her soft neck.

'Maybe I can ask Theo questions,' she whispered, her pulse beating faster against my lips.

'About me?' I ran the tip of my nose along the outline of her ear. 'Go ahead. That's why I want you to meet him.'

Theo wouldn't over-share. We all knew what was at risk if we told anyone too much about the Harpyiai. I only wanted her to meet him so she could get a better feel for who I was. Theo was easy-going, great with numbers and people – one reason Dad had let him run one of our clubs in Brighton for years – but Theo hadn't been the same since his sister, Stephanie, died during The Hunt some years previously.

I slid my hand into Kate's hair and tugged her head back to kiss her. Her soft moan against my lips was nothing but torture. We were in public, and I had to pull back, but she tasted so damn good.

'I've spent half the weekend inside you and still can't get enough,' I groaned. 'You do something to me.'

'Something bad?' she whispered, lust heating those dark eyes.

'You make me weak. I'm not sure how I feel about that.'

'It's not my fault you're insatiable.'

'Don't blame this all on me. You are just as bad.' I propped my left arm on the centre console, slid my right hand up her thigh, and slipped under the fabric of her dress.

She gasped. 'Jack, there are people nearby.'

'They can't see a thing. Just pretend we're having a normal conversation.' Raising a brow, I challenged her willingness to follow my orders. 'Spread your legs, ropes.'

Her cheeks coloured, but after a glance around the car park, she opened her legs wider.

'Good girl,' I murmured, running my fingers down her cleft, teasing the sensitive flesh. 'Do you like the idea of other people watching?'

There were so many things I still wanted to learn about her. Theo's parties were wild, but I could work around it if she didn't want to be watched.

'No,' she whispered, staring at a man rolling his trolley towards our car.

I lifted my hand. Waited.

'No, Marquis.'

'Good girl.' I slid a finger inside her. 'Yet you're wet, ropes. Are you sure it doesn't excite you?'

'I'm sure, Mar—' She gasped as I replaced one digit with two and rubbed that spot certain to make her surrender. Her hand came up to grasp my shirt, but I grabbed it with my free hand, interlinked our fingers, and pressed it to my lips. If she touched me, we would get arrested for public indecency.

'You know how to stop me,' I whispered, drawing circles on her clit with my thumb. 'You're always in control, *radost moya*.'

But she didn't stop me, only squeezed my hand as I worked her body, bringing her closer and closer to the edge, her hips rocking against my hand – then I pulled my hand away and left her hanging.

'Jack!' She gaped at me.

I brought my fingers to her lips. 'Taste yourself.'

Fury, lust, defiance and other delicious emotions flashed in her eyes, but she took my fingers into her hot mouth and sucked. I suppressed a groan. She might as well have had my cock in her mouth. Her gaze narrowed.

Oh, I knew she wanted to hurt me, and it was tempting to let her.

'Good girl.' I shifted the car into gear. 'I'll take you home.'

'What? You can't just do that and then drop me off at home!'

'Yes, I can.'

She squirmed in her seat. 'That's just mean.'

This was mean? She would truly never make it through a day at the castle.

'I warned you, Kate. Don't top me from the bottom.' But as I adjusted my trousers, I wondered who the hell I was punishing.

When we parked outside her flat, I walked around the car to open her door and suppressed a laugh at her murderous glare. 'Don't sulk, Caitlin. I'll see you next weekend.'

'That's six days from now.' Her heels clicked rapidly on the pavement. 'You better make it up to me.'

On the steps outside her door, I pulled her to a halt. 'Would you like me to take care of it sooner?'

'You want to come inside?'

No, I'd lose too much time. My brother was upset, and I had to get back to him. 'I might be able to see you midweek.'

'Oh?' Her gaze dropped to my mouth. 'I work days from Wednesday. Do you want to come over for dinner?'

'Wednesday sounds good, but I have a caveat.' I leaned down, looking into the dark depths of her eyes. It was time to start training her if we were ever going to have a chance at saving her life. 'Don't come until you're with me again.'

'You're joking?'

'Wait, and I'll reward you. Defy me, and I'll punish you again.'

Would she take the challenge? It seemed so when she glared at me again. I kissed the corner of her mouth. 'Text me later. Be good, ropes.'

She scowled as she went inside, but a faint smile played on her face as she shut the door. When I got back to my car, a black BMW parked at the end of her road caught my attention. The guards at the Harpyiai used such cars, and I froze before recognising the blond brute in the driver's seat as Jonas, one of Dad's guards.

Leaning against my car, I called Dad. 'Why is Jonas outside Kate's?'

'A simple hello wouldn't kill you,' he admonished.

I rolled my eyes. 'Just answer my question.'

'We have to keep illegitimates under guard, Jack. You know that.'

I got back in the car, turned the ignition on, then off again. 'You told them I'm going, right?'

'Yes.'

'So why isn't a castle guard watching her?'

'Because I didn't think you would want Yulia's guards near her, but she is aware of your intention to train and collar Caitlin.' His deep sigh came down the phone. 'Go home, Jack. Your brother needs you. Caitlin's safe with my guards.'

I clenched my jaw. 'Freddy wouldn't be upset if you hadn't said that to him.'

'Jack—'

Before he could say anything else, I ended the call. I drummed my fingers on the steering wheel as I debated whether to take Kate back to mine, but I couldn't keep her with me at all times. If I did, she'd want to know why.

'Fuck's sake.'

I called Theo as soon as I got back on the road. As much as I loved my brother, Theo was the only one I could talk to about these things.

'I don't know what the hell went wrong,' I said as a greeting. 'I met her at bloody speed dating, mate.'

He barked a laugh. 'Speed dating? Is that what vanilla does to the brain?'

'Shut up.' I pushed on the accelerator to overtake some arsehole doing twenty in a forty zone. 'How are you doing?'

'Fine. You're going then?'

'Don't have much choice, do I?'

'You do, but I understand.' He sighed. 'You okay?'

I slowed for a red light, tried to swallow past the lump in my throat as I waited for it to turn green, then blew out a heavy sigh. 'I don't know. Trying not to – you know.'

'Lose it?'

Turning onto the dual carriageway, I gripped the wheel tighter. 'Yeah.'

'What did your dad say?'

I snorted. 'What do you think?'

Theo made a small laugh. 'Bet he wasn't happy you sacrificed yourself. That's what you've done, isn't it?'

'Of course.'

'Do you think he'll join The Hunt this year? He wouldn't want to lose you.' His voice held an unspoken concern, but he held back, knowing how difficult this would be for me.

'Dad would never put his own life at risk,' I said with a scoff. 'And someone has to stay with Freddy.'

'True.' He clicked his tongue. 'So, what's she like?'

How could I describe Kate? 'She's... fuck, I don't know. Fearless, challenging, inexperienced, yet darker than anyone I've met. She pushes my buttons. All of them at once,' I added with a strained laugh.

'She's got in your head.'

'What? I've only known her for a couple of weeks.'

'Romeo and Juliet only knew each other for three days,' he teased.

'Hilarious, Theo.'

'You know it's true. I can hear it in your voice.'

I told him about the weekend – how it had gone from perfect to a nightmare, how she kept pushing me and asking for information I couldn't give. 'And to top it off, she suggested that I should have a safeword.'

He tutted. 'I know it's been a while since you played, but do I need to point out the obvious? You're in a drop.'

'What?'

'Or you've fallen for her, and that's why you're being soft on her.'

The wind on the bridge nudged the car, and I gripped the steering wheel with both hands. Fuck. Was I in a drop? It could explain why I had lost control of my emotions.

'I might have been earlier, but—'

'Do you have feelings for her?'

'Get out of my head, Theo,' I snapped, ignoring his chuckle. It was none of his business. 'I need you to cane me.'

His laugh deepened. 'I'm sure it would be easier to turn around and get her to blow you.'

'I wasn't talking about Kate.' Taking the exit to get off the dual carriageway, I tried to find the right words. 'Juliet will test my limits, and I need help with my triggers. You know we use canes in The Culling, and I can't risk falling apart.'

'*Blyad*, you're serious?'

'You're the only one I can trust to do this.'

'I was also the one who found you after—'

'Don't.' Feeling nauseous, I turned up the air con. 'Can you come up tonight? I'd come to you, but I have things to deal with at home.'

Theo sighed. 'Freddy?'

'Yeah. Do you mind?'

Asking him to drop everything and drive two hours to deal with my triggers wasn't an easy favour to ask, but he understood why I couldn't afford to ignore this anymore. The Hunt was in three weeks, which meant I only had a fortnight to prepare for The Culling.

'If you come down on Saturday. I need to meet this little troublemaker before you leave.'

'Deal.' I ended the call and shook my head at the absurdity of what I was about to do.

CHAPTER TWENTY-TWO

JACK

FREDDY WAS SITTING at the kitchen island when I got home. Passenger played on the surround system. I tossed the car keys on the worktop and sighed. He stared at me as I poured coffee and sat opposite him. His gaze dropped to my hands, to the scratches Kate had left on my fingers, and his lips flattened.

After a long minute of tense silence, he dug out a pack of chocolate chip cookies from a drawer. It was always a bad sign when my brother started comfort eating. If he played sad music and ate chocolate cookies, it was as bad as it got.

'I have to do this,' I said, unable to take the depressing music – or munching – anymore.

'I know.' He brushed off his T-shirt, obsessing over the smallest crumbs, and turned off the music.

Did he?

'You never told me we could've swapped places.'

'Why would I?'

His guilt was bottomless already. I wouldn't have been left alone if he hadn't needed to go to the hospital. He wouldn't have been ill if he hadn't almost drowned at the lake. If he'd been born first... My brother had tormented himself with such nonsense since I'd been taken. If he'd known that we could've swapped places, he would've offered and walked into a trap. Without him, I'd have no reason to fight back.

'I would never have swapped places with you, so put away that guilty face.'

He wiped his hands. 'You're coming back.'

'Of course I am. Who would annoy you every day if I don't?'

He rolled his eyes. I sipped more coffee and looked around, wondering what would happen to all of this if I didn't come back. My brother could have a normal life. There was some comfort in that.

'Do you need anything?' Freddy asked. 'I'm not sure how you would prepare yourself.'

'The sacrifice of three virgins should do it,' I deadpanned.

His mouth dropped open. I laughed. God, it felt good to laugh at my brother again. His withering stare amused me, as always. After twenty-eight years, he should've known better.

'You're such an arsehole, Jack.'

I shrugged. My sense of humour kept me on the right side of insanity. Why change something that worked?

He dragged a hand through his hair. 'You won't go in as a Marquis, so what if it goes wrong? What if you have to kill someone?'

That's what he was worried about?

'It's a basic survival instinct, Freddy,' I said, lifting one shoulder in faux nonchalance to soothe his concerns. 'Anyone who claims they wouldn't kill to stay alive is lying.'

'Would you kill me?'

Jesus. The things that went through his head.

'You're my brother. I'd kill *for* you.'

He looked into the dining room. 'When you've done The Hunt, you can come home, right?'

Probably not, but there was no need to worry my brother.

'Yes.'

Juliet needed a male heir before she turned forty-three the following year. There was no doubt she'd try to force my hand, and I shuddered at the thought of the breeding ceremony. My libido would never recover, and giving up a child to the Harpyiai would destroy me. It was unlikely she could even have a child at her age, but rationality had never been a factor in her plans.

Freddy collected a black box from the utility room and placed it on the kitchen island as carefully as if it were an armed bomb. It might as well have been.

Printed on the lid was the golden Harpyiai crest I'd never wanted to see again – a harpy holding a coiled whip. Beneath it was the Lawrence family crest – a blue shield featuring the Bridlype castle, from the Scottish region where my great-grandfather had been born.

'Dad left it for you.'

Of course he fucking did. I dropped my head in my hands.

'Can I open it?' Freddy asked. 'I had a sneak peek, sorry.'

I waved my hand. It contained, as expected, a maroon collar studded with black pearls. A teardrop ruby hung from a small black ring at the front, ensnared by silver thorns. Underneath the collar was a silver necklace with the harpy bird claw pendant, a sapphire ring, and the keys to the collar.

'It's yours, isn't it?' Freddy asked, turning the collar over to examine the lock at the back.

I nodded. A Marquis received three gifts upon graduation, besides the brand. A collar to show my ownership and protection of a submissive, a necklace to be worn when a collar was not appropriate attire, and a ring a Marquis only wore if he had collared someone.

I never imagined I'd use any of these items. I hadn't even seen them in years and had put them to the back of my mind with everything else from those days. That my father had brought them to me the night before meant that he knew my decision. As always, Dad was one step ahead of me.

'The ring is for her as well?'

'No, it's for me.' I picked it up, feeling the weight of the ring, and of making such a decision.

'At least the blue matches your eyes.'

I scoffed. 'Juliet explained it once. She said rubies and sapphires come from the same mineral. The sapphire in my ring signifies transformative energy, and the ruby in the collar is the epitome of sexuality, love and passion.'

'Epitome?' He laughed, catching me by surprise again. My brother rarely laughed anymore. 'You said it in a Russian accent.'

'*Blyad.*'

Freddy held his hand out, and I passed him the ring. 'Do I want to know how much these stones are worth?'

'Probably not.' I couldn't help but smirk. As a slave, I'd stolen Peter's ring and hidden it. He had almost turned the castle upside down looking for it, but as far as I knew, he'd never found it. 'But it's not my decision, anyway. She has to offer me her submission.'

'Do you want her to?'

I picked up the collar and tried to picture it on Kate. Having a collared submissive was a huge undertaking. I would be fully responsible for her well-being, and if she submitted to me, it was for life. In the eyes of the Harpyiai, death was the only way out.

She'd made it clear she didn't want to be a slave or pet. A Harpyiai-collared submissive was expected to be trained to a standard close to a slave. No, I had no interest in a Master/slave relationship. Hell, I'd only had one relationship before her, and it had been based on lies. I wasn't ready for this.

'No, I don't,' I said, putting it back in the box.

'So why would Dad leave this here?'

'Because he's an arsehole?' And something wasn't right about all of this. 'Get all the family files. I'll grab the whiteboard from the garage.'

He followed me into the hallway. 'Why?'

'I need to make a family tree.'

'Why?'

'So I can send out fucking Christmas cards. Jesus, Freddy.' I opened the garage door, grateful to see no sign of the cat. Dad must have taken it with him. 'I need to figure out who Kate's dad is.'

It took us until early evening to compile the family tree and narrow our options. As Coyotes played on the stereo, Freddy ate pretzels on the floor beneath the whiteboard propped up on the sofa. I sat opposite, not liking what I saw on the board.

'It has to be Ivan, Andrei, Peter, Nathan or Arthur,' Freddy said, grabbing another handful.

'It won't be Arthur. Peter castrated him in the late eighties. Nate is gay and so is Andrei.'

There was the possibility that Andrei had still fathered a child, but it was unlikely. Nate had never been with a woman, and he would've told Dad about her.

'Andrei's gay? You're sure?'

I stared at him. 'Really? You're going to make me explain how I know?'

He paled. 'Sorry. So, Ivan or Peter? It must be Peter. Why else would she have Peterson as a middle name?'

'What?' I shuffled through the papers to find her birth certificate. 'It's not on here.'

'Deed polls,' he said around a mouthful of pretzels.

'She wasn't married? Or it's a relative's name?'

'Not that I could find.'

My jaw clenched. And my brother didn't think it was worth mentioning that she'd legally changed her name? He'd told me her vetting was fine. It was anything but *fine*.

Goddammit. I dragged a hand through my hair. Peter wouldn't be stupid enough to give her his name. Would he?

'Do you think Dad knows?'

It would have surprised me if he didn't. Dad hadn't been to the castle in decades, but as Head Marquis, he still kept an eye on everything and controlled most of the guards. The only benefit of being his son was that he would know when I would be taken and could warn me.

'Let's find out.' I grabbed my phone and smiled when I saw a message from Kate. *Wednesday cannot come soon enough.*

I quickly texted back, *Be good, Caitlin. I'll know if you haven't.*

At least she was safe. It made it a little easier to breathe as I called Dad to ask if the person I loathed most of all was her father.

'Twice in one day,' Dad answered as a greeting. 'What can I do for you this time?'

'Is she Peter's?'

Freddy shoved more pretzels into his mouth. I rolled my eyes at him.

'I believe so, yes.'

'Fuck.'

There had to be an explanation why Peter had kept Kate hidden, why he'd given her the Peterson name as if he was taunting someone. He had collared Nikita over a year before Kate was born. If this was true, he was done as a trainer, as head of the Williams family – dishonoured for life.

I dug my nails into my palm, struggling to connect with myself. 'Do you know what he's up to? What are you up to?'

'Do you want to share what you're up to with Theodore? Three phone calls in a week.'

I fell back onto the sofa. Of course, he knew. 'I'm preparing myself.'

'Playing is not preparing.'

'We deal with things differently, Dad. Are you going to answer my questions?'

'I don't know what Peter is up to. I'm making arrangements to keep your sub safe.'

'Will Jonas stay with her the whole time?'

'Yes.'

It should have reassured me, but I couldn't rid myself of this sickening feeling that I was missing something. 'Should we move her and Freddy somewhere safer? Just in case Juliet—'

'Caitlin cannot find out who her father is. When it's time for the castle guards to collect you, I'll move them to a safer location. Did you get the box?'

'You know how I feel about—'

'Jack, you got yourself into this mess. We have an opportunity to stop Yulia for good. She can't breed with you if you have a collared submissive. The collar will also protect Caitlin. I suggest you train her so she's ready for the ceremony in August.'

He hung up, and I stared at my phone. 'Arsehole.'

He wanted me to train her as a Harpyiai submissive, but it was a monumental task to achieve in such a short period of time, given how bratty and inexperienced Kate was.

'What did he say?' Freddy's phone pinged with a message from the security system. 'Someone's at the gate. Christ, why's Dad here?'

I rose. 'It's Theo. Let him in.'

'What?' He shifted off the floor. 'Why is he here?'

'Because I can't go to fucking therapy to deal with my triggers, so I have to face them head-on.'

Freddy gaped. 'You're going to let him cane you?'

I went to the front door and leaned against the door frame as Theo extracted his long legs from a blue Audi and hoisted a black bag from the backseat. The sight of the bag and what it contained made me shiver.

I hadn't seen Theo in over a year, but it made no difference when he grinned, revealing those dimples that distracted from the too-familiar grey shade of his irises. As always, his dark copper hair curled around his ears. If he was Kate's half-brother, they looked nothing alike. Except for his dimples, he was a carbon copy of Peter.

'Jack.' He ducked his head to enter the house. 'You look like shit. Vanilla has aged you ten years.'

'Well, you look more like your dad than ever, so we're even.' I pulled him in for a hug, grateful he always made a point of wearing anything but black. In blue jeans and a grey long-sleeved jumper, he bore no resemblance to a Marquis. 'Thanks for doing this.'

He patted my back, winding me. 'My pleasure, I think. Ah, Freddy. Nice to see you again.'

Freddy glared at Theo as he walked past, then disappeared upstairs.

Theo chuckled. 'I'll try not to take offence.'

'Ignore him,' I said, leading the way to the garage. 'Let's do one round of this first, and then we need to talk.'

CHAPTER TWENTY-THREE

KATE

I HADN'T EVEN SHUT the front door before Petra shouted, 'Caitlin, you're home!'

A quick assessment of the situation brought a firm end to a wonderful weekend. Petra was on the sofa drinking a glass of my Pinot, and Owen was in the kitchen tucking into my favourite ice cream.

For god's sake.

I dropped my purse and keys on the radiator shelf by the front door and slipped my heels off. 'Hello, people who do not live here. Are you enjoying yourselves?'

'I do live here now, and Mum's looking for you.' Chocolate brownie ice cream muffled Owen's words. 'She's already called me three times today.'

I pointed at him. 'You better replace that. And don't even think about getting me the cheap knock-off brand.'

Petra dragged her feet off my coffee table. 'Have you been with Jack all weekend?'

'Where else would I have been?'

'You dirty cow.' She raised her glass of wine. 'To new pastures conquered.'

I snorted. 'How much wine have you had?' And where was my glass? Oh, yeah. Jack and his damn rule about alcohol. But I wouldn't see him until Wednesday, so that bastard wouldn't leave me both frustrated and sober. It was one of the two.

I grabbed the bottle of Pinot and chugged down a mouthful. 'God, I've missed you, my sweet, sweet crushed grapes.'

Petra pulled me onto the sofa. 'You don't look—' She grabbed my wrist. 'Marked.'

'Marked?'

'No ligature marks, no finger marks around your neck.' She tutted. 'I thought he was kinky?'

'He is.' I pulled my hand back. I probably had a slight bruise somewhere. Certain parts of me felt well used.

'So, what did you get up to?' She settled back onto the cushions, eager for details as always. 'I want to hear all about it.'

From the kitchen came Owen's muffled groan. 'I don't want to hear any of it.'

'I'm not sharing.' I downed another mouthful. 'Why are you here, Petra?'

'Oh.' She giggled. 'Your brother was worried. And your mum. Everyone seemed to think some big bad wolf had kidnapped you.'

Big bad wolf? I scoffed. 'Unfortunately not, but thank you for the concern. Owen, you can tell Mum I'm fine.'

'Maybe you should tell her yourself.' He came to sit on the edge of the sofa, scraping the bottom of the ice-cream tub. 'She got into one of her moods when she realised you were probably with a guy.'

'I can't be arsed to deal with Mum right now, Owen,' I said, nursing my wine. 'All I want is to watch some TV and finish this bottle before bed.'

'I'll help you.' Petra took the bottle and poured herself another glass. 'Bet you've used up all your energy.'

Seriously? 'You're not getting a rundown of everything we got up to.'

'Thank god,' Owen muttered, but Petra looked offended.

'Why not? You always share.'

'Not this time.' How on earth did I explain what we had done that morning? Petra would think I was insane.

'At least tell me he's good in the sack?'

What could I say? Everything about him was amazing, everything I'd ever dared dream of. A smile spread across my face.

'Oh yes, someone had a very good weekend. I don't think I've seen you this smug in years. It's quite' – she made a face – 'disgusting, to be honest.'

'You're just jealous.'

'I am. You're wearing the same dress as Friday, and yet you're glowing. Please stop.'

But I couldn't stop smiling, not even when she put on a movie – a romantic drama with steamy scenes she probably hoped would get me to open up. But I wanted to keep those memories to myself.

I missed him and the many ways he looked into my eyes. Tender as he brushed my hair back and kissed me – like I was the only person in the world for him. Hungry and carnal when he pushed into me – as if he wanted to enter my soul. Vulnerable and open when he ran out of places to hide.

I felt bad about pushing him so hard earlier, but I only wanted to understand him. Why wouldn't he let me in? Whatever had happened to him in the past wouldn't deter me. I wanted the parts of him he wouldn't share with anyone else, no matter how dark they were.

Petra stayed for a while, then gave up trying to extract dirty details from me and went home, leaving me with the threat that she would be after me at work the next day. Maybe she knew Jack was different; this wasn't simply another one-night stand.

As the evening drew in, I changed into pyjamas, and Owen and I were on the sofa watching crime documentaries when the doorbell rang.

'Expecting anyone?' he asked.

Jack? No, he had his family emergency to deal with.

I shook my head. 'Did Petra forget something?'

The spring in Owen's step was hard to miss, but I choked on my next mouthful of wine when he opened the door. Mum rushed into my flat, a blur of purple and black as the fabric of her long dress struggled to keep up with her pace.

'I was this close to phoning the police, young lady,' she said, her voice breaking.

'Why?'

Paul came after her, hands clamped by his side. He wore dress trousers and a pale blue cotton shirt that strained over his stomach, but the creases in the fabric suggested he'd worn them for at least two days.

'Nobody has seen or heard from you since Friday,' he spat out. 'Do you have any idea how worried your mother has been?'

'Worried? I'm a grown woman.'

'A grown woman who can't even answer her phone?'

'Sod off, Paul.'

'Caitlin!' Mum clutched her imaginary pearls, and it took every ounce of restraint not to roll my eyes.

I rose and held up my hands to soothe my mother's concerns. Even her hair struggled to stay in place as she fidgeted. 'I'm fine, Mum. You can go home.'

'Where have you been? Why didn't you call? Who were you with?' Her words tripped over each other.

I thought about telling her the truth, but why would I? She would get hysterical and demand I stop seeing Jack. It was none of her business who I dated, but my mother would never approve. Jack was everything I wanted, and everything she had tried to keep me from my whole life.

'I was with Tom.' The lie slipped out so easily that it felt like the truth even to me, and when obvious relief rushed over my mother's face, I swallowed away the guilt. 'We had some things to talk about. I'm sorry you were worried, but I was planning on calling you tomorrow to explain.'

Paul's narrowed gaze stayed on me. My stepdad had always been indifferent towards me, but now he looked concerned.

It was unnatural.

Unsettling.

'You've been with Tom?' he asked, testing my lie. 'All weekend?'

'We talked, had some Chinese and wine, you know – one thing led to another and—' I shrugged.

Did he buy it? It seemed so when he rolled his eyes and looked away, disgusted with me, as always.

Mum put her chilled hands around my face. 'Did you go to The Yard? Your brother said you took him there.'

That's what this is about? I tried to catch Owen's ever-elusive gaze, but he'd retreated into the kitchen and stared at the worktop as if it contained all the world's secrets. I would bloody kill him. Slowly, painfully.

'Caitlin,' my mother urged. 'Did you go to the club?'

For god's sake. 'Yes, I went to The Yard, but you know Tom works there and—'

'Tell me you didn't get involved with one of the Lawrence twins.'

I shifted out of her reach. 'Mum, you're being ridiculous. I went to see Tom.'

'Oh, thank god.' My mother started sobbing. 'We cannot have our family associated with the Lawrences.'

What the hell was wrong with her? 'Mum, it's a club. Not the mafia. I'm sure the Lawrences are fine.' Paul's gaze snapped to mine, and I quickly added, 'Whoever they are.'

'They're not.' My mother wiped at her mascara-stained eyes. 'I don't want you anywhere near them.'

I splayed my hands. 'Why not? What have they done to you?'

'You know what they do at that club,' my mother wailed. 'The strippers and parties… This could ruin our lives, Paul's career, our reputation.'

For the love of god. 'Don't cry, Mum. Honestly, all I did was settle things with Tom. You've always said I should apologise to him and end things on a better note. Maybe now he'll drop the lawsuit.'

'Did you talk to him about it?' Paul asked, and the obvious relief on his face when I shook my head confused me.

'I was so worried.' Mum dabbed her eyes with a handkerchief. God, she was always so emotional. 'You have no consideration for anyone but yourself, do you? All you care about is yourself and your—' She grimaced.

'My what?' I crossed my arms. 'This better not be another lecture about my sex life.'

'The worst thoughts went through my mind,' my mother sobbed. 'I thought everything I've worked so hard for would be ruined because of you and your urges.'

I closed my eyes and tried to suppress the suffocating feelings as they gripped me again. The shame of that last night with Tom, the look of disappointment on my mother's face, Owen's laugh, Paul's silent glare as he sat me down at the kitchen table for a birds-and-the-bees talk no one should have to endure.

My mother ran the handkerchief under her eyes, smearing mascara and blue eye shadow. 'Hannah would never put us through this. Why can't you be—'

'Because I'm not bloody Hannah!' The shock on Mum's face didn't deter me. 'I'm sorry you were worried about me, but you're overstepping. I'm an adult, and who I spend time with is my business.'

Paul's icy glare found mine. 'If you want to be treated like an adult, you need to act like one. We've paid for your education, this flat, even sorted the incident with Tom, but still you defy your mother by going to that club.'

'Oh, fuck off, Paul!'

A sickening silence settled over the room. The rapid beat of my pulse pounded against my eardrum, counting down the seconds until my stepdad made good on his threats to cut me off completely if I didn't apologise.

But this time, I wouldn't.

'Caitlin.' Paul pointed at me, his hand shaking. 'I will not tolerate—'

'Is this about my real father?' My question left him gaping. It always did. Even as a small child, I'd known the power of that question. It could end most arguments with my stepdad.

'We are not discussing him,' Paul spat out. 'And you will not visit that club again. I forbid it.'

Forbid it? What was I, five?

'Why? Was he also involved with the Lawrences?'

Paul scoffed. 'Don't be ridiculous. You are not allowed to go there. I cannot afford to pay for any more of your mistakes.'

'Fine,' I said, having had enough of this ridiculous conversation. 'Tom and I have said our last words to each other, anyway. There is no reason I ever need to go there again.'

'Oh, thank you, sweetie.' My mother exhaled. 'I knew you would understand.'

I didn't, but I wanted them to get the hell out of my flat, so I nodded and pretended I would go back to being a good girl, exactly how my mother wanted me. Never tempt my urges, never ask questions about my father, and do nothing to disgrace the Howard family name.

'Come, Rachel.' Paul made a beeline for the front door. My mother lingered for a moment before following him. The look on her face left me with a mountain of guilt.

I should have apologised; I always did. It was how she got me to do what she wanted, but I was tired of pretending to be someone I was not.

When the door clicked shut behind them, Owen grinned. 'So, should I ask Tom how his weekend was?'

'What the hell is wrong with those two?' I dropped onto the sofa and clutched my trembling hands. 'I would've got into less trouble for manslaughter.'

'You know how Mum feels about anything that could be considered… deviant.'

I messaged Jack to say Wednesday couldn't come soon enough, then picked up the bottle of wine again, intent on drowning my guilt, but it was empty.

'Dammit.'

'Maybe it's a sign you've had enough.'

'Or maybe it's because someone's helped themselves to whatever they want. The same someone who should've kept his mouth shut about The Yard.'

'I'm sorry, okay? She seemed to already know that we'd been there, so I thought maybe you'd told her.' He splayed his hands. 'You know how hard it is to understand her when she's hysterical.'

'Why the hell would I tell her that?'

'Maybe one of Hannah's friends saw you again?'

'I don't remember seeing anyone I knew.' I grabbed my glass again. Maybe Paul had sent that dark-clad man to follow me? No, that made no sense. He would've stopped me from going inside. 'You owe me at least two bottles of wine for this.'

He sighed. 'I'll go to the shop. We need milk, anyway.'

'Don't forget ice cream.' I tucked my feet under me. 'I want a big tub, since you've put me through Paul's infamous wrath.'

'Dad's not that bad.' He grabbed his phone and wallet off the table. 'You know he'd never kick you out of this flat.'

'Only because you're still staying here.'

When he grinned, I threw a sofa cushion at him, missed, and he ducked out the front door before I could throw another one. Bloody bastard. I pulled a blanket off the back of the sofa and grabbed the remote, determined to find something to lift my mood, but as I was scrolling through programmes, a knock came at the door.

Oh, great. Someone else wanted to tell me off? Had Paul come back to make good on his threats?

I flung the door open. 'What do you want?'

A man dressed in leather trousers and a black dress shirt stood on the other side, so tall I had to crane my neck to find his weather-beaten face, and when I did, those grey irises stole my breath.

The outside lamp illuminated his dark copper curls as he cocked his head to the side. His eyes were so cold, it was like staring into nothingness. He made me feel small and insignificant, like an ant he couldn't wait to crush beneath those black boots.

I took a step back, but he grabbed my arm. His fierce grip combined with those steely eyes blew dust off a memory tucked away at the back of my mind. I had met him before. Fear crawled over my skin, leaving goosebumps.

Before I could snap out of it, he'd pulled a syringe from his pocket. My mouth opened. I wanted to scream, but my lungs craved air I couldn't inhale as a smile curled the corner of his thin lips.

'Hello, little one.'

* * *

To Be Continued...

THE STORY CONTINUES in Thrill of Surrender. If you can take the time to leave an honest review of this book on Amazon or Goodreads, it would be much appreciated!

Sign up for my newsletter to receive extracts of later volumes in this series before they are released, backstory to the characters, family trees, and so much more.

ABOUT THE AUTHOR

Dina Hawthorn is a dark romance writer with a keen interest in psychology, tea-drinking, and long walks in the countryside.

She lives in Suffolk, England, and is often found writing dark, gritty stories with a ginger cat on her lap.

Connect with her on social media and sign up for her newsletter to receive a FREE copy of the prequel novella, Forbidden Thrills.

ALSO BY DINA HAWTHORN

The Harpies:

Forbidden Thrills (prequel)

Thrill of Fear (Book one)

Thrill of Surrender (Book two)

Thrill of Pursuit (Book three)

Thrill of Capture (Book four)

Printed in Great Britain
by Amazon

34349480R00185